A
SECRET
WOMAN

Also by Rose Solari

Difficult Weather
Orpheus in the Park
(poetry)

Looking for Guenevere
(drama)

A
SECRET
WOMAN

a novel

ROSE SOLARI

Sections of this book appeared, in an earlier version, in *Enhanced Gravity: More Fiction by Washington Area Women*, edited by Richard Peabody, Paycock Press, 2006.

A Secret Woman is published by Alan Squire Publishing in association with Santa Fe Writers Project, Chris Andrews Publications Ltd, and Left Coast Writers.

Library of Congress Cataloging-in-Publication Data
Solari, Rose.
A secret woman : a novel / Rose Solari.
p. cm.
ISBN 978-0-9826251-9-4
1. Women artists–Fiction. 2. Mothers and daughters–Fiction.
3. Family secrets–Fiction. I. Title.
PS3569.O497S43 2012
813'.54–dc23

2011050373

ISBN: 978-0-98-262519-4

Cover art and jacket design by Randy Stanard, Dewitt Designs, www.dewittdesigns.com.
Author photo by James J. Patterson.
All other photos by Chris Andrews.
Copy editing and interior design by Nita Congress.
Printing consultation by Steven Waxman.
Printed by RR Donnelley.

This book is a work of fiction. Names, characters, and incidents are either products of the author's imagination or are used fictitiously. Any resemblance to actual events or persons, living or dead, is entirely coincidental.

Table of Contents

For James J. Patterson and

Verlyn Flieger

Nel mezzo del camin di nostra vita

mi ritrovai per una selva oscura

ché la diritta via era smaritta.

—*Dante*, The Inferno

PART I

The Painted Box, 2005

1

In the middle of my thirty-seventh year, I found myself driving, lost, on a single-lane dirt road canopied by trees, many miles from home. The sheet of directions I'd been mailed lay crumpled on the seat beside me. I'd followed them carefully, but had not seen the driveway they mentioned, nor the sign I'd been told to look for. Now it was getting dark, I was late for my appointment, and my destination, wherever it was, seemed to be sinking quickly into the shadowed farmland as I passed. In the manner of all anxious travelers, I asked myself questions. How long is this road? When can I turn around? And—in my case, a very important question—what am I doing here, anyway?

I was on my way to a Catholic monastery somewhere in the Maryland countryside, more than an hour from where I live. Other than for my mother's funeral, I had not been inside a house of worship in nearly twenty years. My parents sent all three of their children to Catholic primary schools, but their devotion to the church had fallen off by the time I was ten or so. We all graduated from public high schools, got accustomed to skipping Mass on

Sunday. If asked, my father calls himself an agnostic now. My mother later returned to the church, but I assumed it was her illness, her fear of dying badly, with the old resentments still on her soul, that drove her back to the priests and prayers and sacraments in the last years of her life. It was because of that, because of her, that I'd gotten lost.

The first phone call I'd received in my new home was from a young man who introduced himself as Brother Paul. He said he was an assistant to Father Thomas, the priest who had been my mother's last confessor.

It was an Indian summer day, late September, and the movers had just left. I was sitting on the floor, surrounded by boxes, drinking the last of a bottle of water.

"This is kind of a bad time," I said. "I'm in the middle of something here."

My voice echoed in the room around me. My new home.

"I'll make this quick, then."

Thomas, he told me, had died. Going through his things, they'd discovered a box of books and papers that had belonged to my mother.

"Papers. You mean, letters?"

"Not really," he said. "More like, well, a research project."

I felt the old resentments creep up my throat.

"Brother—Brother…" I began.

"Paul."

"Well, Paul, I should tell you. My brother is the executor of my mother's will. She picked him, you see. So legally, I think that what you might want to do is call him—"

"I appreciate your telling me that. I do. But your mother was very clear. She wanted Thomas to look through the box, see if he thought anything was of value.

To publish, maybe. I don't really know. But then—and she was very clear about this—the box was to go to you. To Louise."

"He told you this?"

"No, I was there. In the room when she told him what to do."

My head began to ache. I switched the phone to my left hand, rubbed the right one across my forehead, which was damp and tight.

"You knew my mother," I said.

"Not well, no. She came out here to Fellowship House a few times, on retreat, for services, but her work was with Tom. He took me with him once, toward the end, to visit her. We went to her house, in—oh, where was it?— where she lived with—with her husband..."

"Kenny."

"Yes. Close to the university..."

"College Park."

"Right. Anyway, she said—very clearly, she said— 'Give this to Louise. My youngest. The artist.'"

There was a triple knock on the door, and then it flew open.

"I got pepperoni, I couldn't resist. And two bottles, a red and a white, so we—oh, sorry."

Lynda was there, holding a carry-out pizza box, a brown bag under her arm. She mouthed, *Jason?* I shook my head, held up a finger.

"That is you, right? The artist?"

"Yes. Yes, that is me."

Into the silence, he began to speak of practicalities: the monastery was about a ninety-minute drive from the city, he had use of a car two days a week, sometimes more, and he could bring me the box one of those days, unless he was called for other chores. Or if I preferred, I could come out there and pick it up myself.

"You have been to Fellowship House before?"

"No."

"Well, you might like to see it. Many people, many different kinds of people, have found something good here."

I don't know how much that moved me. But I couldn't think of any other way to get him off the phone. And though I had worked hard for years to erase any curiosity I might have had about my mother's strange interior life, it was hard not to be just a little curious about what was in that box.

And she had called me an artist. That was important too.

I said I'd come and get it. The drive, at least, would be nice. I didn't get out of the city much anymore, since I'd left Jason.

It was that line of thinking that brought me to the middle of nowhere, on a chilly Thursday evening, the leaves already disengaging from the trees, wheeling sadly to earth. It would be cold soon. I have always hated winter. On a road marked "Private: No Trespassing," I turned around, heading back to where I'd come from. It's pointless, I thought. I will never find the place. I remembered an inn I'd passed, closer to the highway; it had looked friendly, the diners inside silhouetted by what seemed, through the windows, to be firelight. I decided to stop and treat myself to the dinner I'd skipped, have some wine. I'd call the young monk from the restaurant, apologize, ask him to mail me my mother's things.

Which I would then give to Dylan. He always loved solving my mother's problems. What had I been thinking, to get involved in one of her messes again?

Just as I thought this, my headlights picked up a small sign on the left, white letters on dark wood, pitched on a post low to the ground. Fellowship House. The Brothers and Sisters of Saint Benedict. Catholic Retreat and Study Center. Established 1983.

Now you've done it, I thought, almost angry with myself for having seen the marker. Now I had no choice but to go through with it. And so, tucking away the anticipation of that almost-dinner, I turned onto the dark and rutted road that led to the monastery.

✖

A THERAPIST FRIEND TOLD ME that it is a common reaction to grief to want to make big changes in other parts of one's life—divorce, a job change, a move. Therapeutic wisdom says that such hasty, grief-driven acts should be discouraged. I didn't know that then, but I doubt it would have slowed me down. I behaved badly in the months after my mother's death, and hurt people who deserved much better treatment than I was, just then, capable of giving them.

But the blame is all mine.

It wasn't my mother's dwindling body on the metal bed that made me chafe at the sound of Jason's voice, describing how this or that producer had at last seen his vision, acknowledged his genius, increased his budget or his credit. It was not standing over my mother's body in the casket without Jason beside me that made me realize I would never marry him. And I cannot blame my mother for the afternoon Jason returned, two days early, from a shoot in New Zealand to find me in our bed and T.J. in our kitchen, wearing Jason's bathrobe and nothing else, making us Bloody Marys for our hangovers.

Nor was it the sound of my mother's cough—which I still hear in my dreams, which I think I will always hear—that made me decide I could not sit through one more discussion at A Woman's Place about how forward-thinking or politically sensitive the art we were showing really was. It was not my mother's fault that I turned against my best and oldest friend, Natalie, with whom I'd founded the Place seven years before.

"Grief can make it hard to deal with the everyday," she said one tense afternoon, after I'd lashed out at some hapless intern for typos in a fundraising letter. She wanted to understand; she wanted to see me through it.

But that wasn't what I wanted. I was fed up with everything all at once and I wanted *out*—out of my wedding plans, out of my job, out of the life I had so carefully, intentionally built. Nothing felt right anymore. Nothing fit. I was always vaguely, rumblingly angry, and almost always close to screaming, or to tears.

Jason caught me with T.J. the same week that I told Nat I was leaving A Woman's Place.

As if sent by the gods to aid my escape, a little money came my way. I won a small grant I'd applied for months before; I sold almost everything in my last show at the Place. It meant I was able to move out of Jason's Old Town condominium, which I'd never much liked anyway, into a more modest place of my own, just on the D.C. border in Takoma Park. It meant I could set up a new life, and fast.

Meanwhile, Jason and I had the typical hideous, rasping arguments. It hurt me less than it should have because, on any objective level, I deserved it. Besides, the last thing I wanted to hear was that he forgave me; forgiveness would mean he'd want to try again. So I remained sullen and self-righteous and ready to bring up at any time how neglected I'd felt, what with his constant traveling for work and our insufficient sex life. It was cruel, I know, but it was the price I paid to keep him angry while I got out the door.

Natalie was harder. Hurting her felt terrible, and only my determination to abandon everything familiar, everything I had been doing up until now, kept me firm. I was in a state of frantic, almost visionary selfishness that stemmed, in part, from an equally frantic exhaustion.

The last time I'd had no obligations besides my art, I'd been on a fellowship, my last year of graduate school. Since then I'd taught, worked for various galleries, been in juried shows, and had solo shows, always trying to climb higher on that near-invisible ladder, trying to get the work out, get it seen, get it noticed. And of course, for most of that time, Nat and I had been running the Place. It made me tired just to think of how busy I'd been. It was time to stop, to devote myself to nothing but my painting. That alone was worth setting fire to any number of sacred places.

This had, I am sure, nothing to do with my mother, with the sight of her once lively and oh, so human body withered down to what looked like wood made ready to burn to ash. She'd treated her body carelessly for so many years, and then, all at once, it fought back. But it was not any foolish desire to run from the memory of that that drove me forward. Her last days were and would be with me always.

But what I'd earned and owned as well was the exhilaration that comes from doing something drastic and irrevocable and destructive, something all of one's own making. That was the reward for all the hurt I'd caused and felt. It seemed to me that I'd done something most people long to do, but can't. I had looked around and, unhappy with what I saw, swept my life clean and started over.

❈

THERE WAS ONLY A LITTLE light left as my car began to climb the slowly rising driveway to the monastery. Orange reflectors, irregularly spaced, outlined the curving gravel road, furrowed with tire tracks, lined with trees and bushes. The temperature dropped, and I felt the night close in around me, so many more stars out here than where I lived, the silence different, fuller. And then the road opened up onto a flat parking lot, and at the top of a rise the buildings of Fellowship House were scattered across the grass.

I got out of the car, my high-heeled boots slippery on the gravel. In front of me was a white two-story farmhouse. To my left and right, stretching out into the fields, were long low buildings that looked, in the dark, like barns. There seemed to be other buildings, or at least, other humped shapes scattered on the mountain. Above the front door of the house, a light flicked on, rinsing the path a greenish-white. The door opened.

"Louise," a voice said. "Louise Terry?"

His pants were black, his shirt was white, his smile blinked on and off. His voice, from the doorway, was soft and high. It was Brother Paul, smiling, waiting for me.

"Louise Terry."

"Yes. That's me."

He was slight, narrow-shouldered as a choirboy, with curly hair and thick glasses.

"Oh, I am relieved," he said. "I thought you might have had a problem."

He shook my hand, then took it in both of his and held it still.

"I'm sorry to be so late. I missed the turn."

"People do that."

"I can imagine."

"Poor signage, I think they call it."

"Yes."

"Well, then. I am Brother Paul Carter, of the Brothers and Sisters of Saint Benedict. Welcome to Fellowship House."

His eyes, through the glasses, were warm, though it was impossible to tell their true color. Gray, perhaps, but not quite, and not quite blue. His hand hovered in the air behind my back as he ushered me into the house.

"Welcome," he said again.

Inside, the uneven floorboards of the hallway were covered with a strip of worn carpet. On the left, a set of double doors opened onto a big room where men of various ages were arranging folding tables and stacks of plastic chairs.

Paul gestured toward them.

"Things are a little hectic right now. We've got a fathers-and-sons retreat starting tomorrow, and it's a full house, so there's a lot to do."

"A full house."

"Not a bed left. In either dormitory. And here we are."

He stopped short—I almost ran into him—and opened a door on the right, tapping the light switch, and making soft apologies about how messy things were. But I didn't see the mess, didn't see anything at all, except the wide, battered desk that sat in the middle of the room, and more particularly, the box on top of it.

A wooden chest with a hinged lid, about two feet long. Most likely made to hold children's toys, probably some time in the 1950s. The wood had been painted over with a blue background, and over that, many tangled, leafy branches that blossomed into creamy white flowers— gardenias, lilies-of-the-valley, calla lilies. It had taken hours—the sanding, the gessoing, then the mixing and laying in of that blue, intended to have the warmth and shimmer of a late spring sky, and then the veined leaves, the tiny blue-white bells and waxy, yellow-white blossoms.

I knew because I had painted it myself. I'd found the old chest in a secondhand store and turned it into a gift for my mother one Christmas. That was the year before she ran away from us for the first time.

Brother Paul came to stand beside me.

"I take it that you have seen that before."

"Yes, of course. I made it. I mean, not the box itself but I—I painted it. For my mother."

"Ah, I should have guessed. The artist, yes. Well then, perhaps it is not so bad a thing, to see it again."

I ran my fingers over the lid. The finish had held up remarkably well. There was a chip on one corner, where a gardenia blossom had lost the tip of a petal, and a scuff ran low along one side. I would paint more gradations of color, more subtleties, into those flowers now, more shades of green in their leaves. But the sky was beautiful. Overall, it was, as he said, not so bad to see it again.

"So, what's inside?"

"That I do not know."

He was behind his desk now, and bending over a little sideboard that held an electric teakettle, mugs, and spoons.

"Please, sit down. Would you like some tea?"

I took the chair across from him.

"Yes, please." I said. "But I don't understand. You don't know…"

His face was in shadow as he busied himself with pouring. He held up a bowl.

"Sugar?"

"A little."

He put in two big spoonfuls and would have gone on if I had not stopped him, then put three in his own cup.

"A sweet tooth," I said.

"Yes," he replied. "But I believe it to be one of the lesser vices. Anyway," he went on, handing the mug across the big, battered desk to me and taking his seat behind it, "I don't know much about what is in that box. Only what I gathered from things Tom said. But he was your mother's confessor, you know. There was much that he could not tell me."

He sipped his tea, looked at me over it.

"But I do know that he had a high opinion of your mother, very high. He admired her. He thought she had a special gift."

"Gift?"

"Tom believed that your mother had a kind of talent—not unlike your gift for painting, now that I think about it—a sort of natural talent for the religious life. He thought that, under different circumstances, she might have taken vows herself."

"Become a *nun?* My mother?"

"That surprises you?"

"Well, yes, I guess surprise would be one word."

I stopped myself from saying more. I was used to being flip about my mother. It was a way of trying to make her behavior—her various kinds of infidelity to my father, her outright lies to all of us, the uncertain ground we always walked on when she was with us, the fierce terror of her first flight, the awful predictability of her second—somehow less painful, less confusing than it was. But it was hard to be flip with Brother Paul.

"Well, I'm sure you know of your mother's interest in hagiography."

"Hagio...?"

"The lives of the saints."

"Oh, yes. Of course." I remembered the pile of books next to her bed, at the end.

"Well, Tom shared her interest. Particularly in the medieval mystics. They read and studied together, they kept notes. Tom encouraged her, I think, to write things down. Not just facts, but her reactions to them. He wanted her to write a series of meditations on some of her favorite medieval mystics. Perhaps turn them into a book."

A book. My mother.

"Well," I said, "that is news to me."

"Tom said she was secretive about it. Lack of confidence."

"Or just her habit. She was a very secretive woman, my mother."

"You are very angry with her, aren't you, Louise?"

An image of my mother as she was toward the end suddenly filled my mind. The bed cranked up to reduce pressure on her chest. The little prongs of the oxygen tube in her nostrils. It deflated me. It always did.

"Not now, no," I said. "I mean, not *at* her exactly. Or not as much, anyway. Not after—everything."

"Everything?"

"It was so ugly, at the end. Whatever she did, she didn't deserve that. To go like that. It was too harsh."

"Too harsh."

"For what she'd done. Too harsh a punishment."

"So you believe your mother was punished, in the manner of her death, for her life?"

"I don't know—I think, sometimes—well, maybe."

"By whom?"

The question was so outside of what I might have expected that I had nothing to say. Paul lifted his right hand in the air, palm up, as if to catch my answer. I tried hard to think.

Then there were footsteps outside the door, and a sharp knock.

"Brother? Brother Paul?"

"Just a moment, Anthony."

"I'm sorry Brother, but it's Father Damian, he says he's been waiting half an hour already and there're some changes. Tomorrow's program. He says he has to see you right away."

"All right, Anthony. Two more minutes."

"Yes, Brother."

Sounds of quick retreating footsteps. I got up and moved toward the desk again, and Paul rose, too.

"I should get going," I said.

"Louise, I do wish we had more time."

"Please," I said, "it's my fault, for being late. I'll just take the box and get out of your way."

"I'll have Anthony carry it for you."

"Oh, I can do it."

I tried to lift it from the desk, faltered.

Brother Paul opened his door, called out for Anthony. Then he took both of my hands in his. It was the first time he had touched me since we'd shaken hands at the front door, and at first I was startled by it. I'd come to think of him as disembodied, somehow. But then my hands warmed in his.

"There is so much that we might talk about, Louise. I hope you will come back and see me again."

"Yes," I said. "I would like that. Maybe after I have a chance to look at what—at what I've got."

"Yes," he said. "Mondays are good visiting days. The house is quiet then."

He looked at the box, still holding onto both of my hands.

"I don't know you, Louise. And I barely knew your mother. But it seems to me that the girl who painted that"—he nodded toward the box—"must have loved her mother very much to go to all that trouble to make something so very beautiful for her."

Anthony arrived, and Paul asked him to carry the box to my car.

"Come back in daylight, if you can," Paul said. "We can go for a walk together."

As I pulled out of the parking lot, he waved and called to me from beneath the porch light.

"God bless you, Louise Terry. Get home safely."

But I'd already decided that I wasn't going home just yet.

❈

IT WAS THURSDAY NIGHT, A big bar night, and T.J.'s Landing was packed when I walked in. From the door I could see Lynda behind the bar that ran the length of the whole back wall, the bright yellow-white spikes of her hair reflected in the mirrors behind her, with row after row of clean glass shelves holding their shiny bottles. As I made my way between the crowded tables, a couple of people called out, waved.

Lynda is one of those small-boned, lively women who always look a little like girls. In the spring, the music club where she'd been tending bar in Virginia had shut down. She found a new gig right away, at a bar not too far from my new apartment, in the hip new part of downtown Silver Spring.

"The crowd is a little more straight than what I'm used to," she said. "But the owner's not an asshole, which is getting harder to find these days. And he's gonna let me bring in some bands on the weekends, see how they do."

I went to the Landing her first week behind the bar, and there was T.J.

It was T.J. I was hoping to see now, though I tried not to scan the room for him. If he was there, he would find me. And if he took me aside, asked if he might come over after he'd finished closing the restaurant for the night, it was better not to be too conspicuous. His girlfriend, Elizabeth, was in law school in Chicago, but she had friends in D.C.

That night, there was a vibrating cluster of young men in business suits at one end of the bar. They were talking very animatedly about something, and one or two of them were trying hard to flirt with Lynda. But she was moving too fast—every bar stool filled, and every table, too, the two waitresses moving back and forth between them. Usually, on a night this busy, T.J. would be backing her up.

"Louie! Hey, girl! Get yourself on over here!"

Heads turned as Lynda called out to me. I was glad I was dressed up. If T.J. was here, he must have heard her call my name. I smiled back at a few familiar faces as I made my way to the bar. None of them were his.

"Looking *good*. Check out the boots. Yo, Rob, why don't you let the lady have a seat for a little while?

Lynda held up a bottle of merlot, and when I nodded, poured me a glass. I slid onto the stool that the amiable Rob gave up for me. After she set my drink down, she leaned across the bar, grabbing my hand in that funny little upraised hippie handshake you hardly ever see anymore.

"Good to see you, girl."

"You, too."

"You get your errand done?"

"Oh, yeah."

"Everything OK? The priest was cool?"

"Actually, really cool. You'd like him."

"Oh, I think it's only you ex-Catholic girls who do that whole priest fantasy thing. But I'm glad you're all right."

A new group gathered at the other end of the bar. She made her way toward them, running a clean towel across the surface of the bar as she went, barely pausing to lift glasses and ashtrays. Her bartending rule was to never do just one thing at a time, and she made it like a dance. Natalie and I both missed her performing days, but Lynda was firm about that all being in the past. I just don't have it, she'd told us, whenever we brought it up. Not the talent for performing, but the ability to keep going through the uncertainty. I'm sick of living from audition to audition. I want a more regular life.

"Can you hang for a while, Louie?"

She was in front of me again.

"Teej'll be back soon and then I can take a little break."

"Where is he?'"

She leaned into me across the bar.

"Elizabeth called, right as we were getting slammed. I said, he needs to call you *back*, we're in the *weeds*. She does this whiney, *oh*, it's so important, *oh* it'll only take a minute. I've heard it a million times. So I'm like, Teej, I am begging you, do *not* take this call. He said, I just need ten minutes. I said, try to make it five. And that was nearly twenty minutes ago and I've buzzed the office twice now and he's not picking up. I want to *kill* him."

"That doesn't sound like him," I said.

"I know, I don't know what's going on. Anyway, *please* don't tell him I told you, it would just piss him off."

"No problem."

"Lynda, help! We're dying of thirst over here."

"I'm on my way, boys. Hang in there."

"And *that* clown," she said, before turning away, "he works for some bank, keeps trying to impress me by talking about in*vest*ments. Says he wants to give me financial advice. I said, is that how we're doing it now? Whatever happened to 'Want to come back to my place? I've got some Peruvian sinsemilla, and I'll play you a tape of my band.'"

"These are complicated times we live in."

"And I am a simple Maryland girl."

A moment before he put his hand on my shoulder I felt him there, in a flush that ran through my whole body. Then T.J. was leaning on the bar next to me, his hand on the small of my back, his eyes on mine.

"Louise. Good to see you."

He kissed my cheek once, lightly. He does that to lots of his female customers. It was OK.

"Good to see you. And I think Lynda will be glad as well."

"Yeah, I had...to take a call." He looked away, then back at me, and his eyes were hopeful. For the first time all day, I relaxed a little.

"Anyway, I'm gonna go give her some relief. Stick around, OK?"

"OK."

LATE THAT NIGHT, AFTER HE followed me home, T.J. carried my mother's box inside. He didn't ask what was in it, but he praised how I'd painted it, the way people who don't really know much about art praise things like that—lavishly, and without any specifics. He set it on the shelf next to my drawing table. I poured us both glasses of whiskey, but he only took a little sip before setting it down and pulling me close to him. His eyes still looked cloudy, like they had in the club, and when he kissed me his lips were tight and rough. Between kisses, he whispered questions to me.

"So you're all settled into your new place?"

"Getting there."

"Do you like it?"

"Love it."

"It's not like your old place."

"Which wasn't really mine, anyway."

"You don't miss it? That swank house?"

"Not at all."

"You're sure?"

"I'm sure. Why do you ask?"

"No reason."

He ran his fingers down my back and over my hips. Some men touch you as if you're made of glass, but T.J. knows how to handle a woman's body. My body, anyway. I never had to tell him a thing.

"You know, it's funny," he said. "I had a feeling all night that I was going to see you. And then you came in."

"Were you glad?"

"Are you kidding?"

He always showered after work, said he needed to wash the club and its smell off of him before we made love. I went to the bedroom and got out of my clothes. I lit some candles, put one of T.J.'s favorite jazz CDs on the stereo, Miles Davis, *In a Silent Way.*

I rely on music to help me keep my memories in place. No matter what happens years from now, I know I will remember how T.J. made love to me when I hear that music.

Naked, I got under the covers.

Then he was at the foot of the bed, a towel wrapped around him. He turned out the lights and gathered me into his arms.

We had been lovers for nearly four months. We both knew it was only a temporary thing. We kept telling ourselves, each other, how little it meant. Or maybe that's not quite right—we'd tell each other that this means something, yes, but not in the run of daily life. It means something, but outside of time. We can open the door and slip through it for a while and what we do on the other side doesn't count, not if we keep it secret.

One day, when I was ready, I'd have a real boyfriend again. He'd be some kind of artist, ambitious, like me, like the men I really fall for. And one day T.J. would marry a traditional sort of girl, Elizabeth or someone like her, who would quit her job and raise their children. But in the meantime, this would do. This would more than do.

Lovers have made these bargains since the beginning of time. It is a more honest agreement than, say, my parents' marriage.

2

It was a cruel kind of poetic justice that my last day at A Woman's Place coincided with the opening of the Barbie installation.

Created by an artist who went by the single name Sahara, it involved heaps of sand against the walls, on which 101 Barbie dolls—the number was significant, I forget why—were arranged in various costumes and tableaux. Extra outfits were also tossed on the sand, pants and shirts and dresses and stretchy tubelike outfits and tiny plastic shoes. Visitors to the gallery were invited to rearrange the dolls, or dress them in different clothes, or even to act out a play with them. The artist's statement of intent, which hung on the wall by the door, said that in doing so, participants would "rewrite the old Barbie scripts."

On the other walls, above the sand piles, were enormous color digital prints in which Sahara had photoshopped the dolls. There was Barbie pregnant, Barbie fat, Barbie flat chested; there was a series of Barbies superimposed on the great sculptures of the Renaissance, such as Michelangelo's *Madonna of the Stairs* and Bernini's

Saint Theresa; there were Barbies turned into Eleanor Roosevelt, Amelia Earhart, and Hillary Clinton. I
thought the idea outdated and underdeveloped, but I was
alone in the collective on this. And though I suggested
that their enthusiasm for Sahara's work had more to do
with her life story than any talent she might have—an
abusive childhood, suicide attempts, a turn in a psychi-
atric hospital, which was where she began to make her
"art"—my fighting spirit was in low supply in the weeks
when we were reviewing slides for the season's exhibits.
My mother's cancer took its last bad turn during those
same weeks. My energy was elsewhere.

I arrived at the opening reception later than I should
have. Angela, my least favorite member of A Woman's
Place, was at the door greeting guests. Sahara was her
protégée. I heard the words "primitive" and "visionary"
being tossed around, and wanted to turn and go home.
Instead, I slid past her and headed for the bar.

"Well, there she is at last. The mystery woman herself."

I turned, and there he was—Tim Gould, the *Post*'s
junior arts critic, author of a popular new blog, DCArts,
and unreliable advocate of A Woman's Place.

"Hello, Tim. What are you drinking?"

"Beer, thanks. So, I got the press release. You're
really leaving?"

"Looks that way."

"I can't believe it. I mean, this is your baby, this gallery."

"Actually, Tim, a gallery is nothing like a baby. And
anyway, it's not mine. It's a collective. Natalie and I
started it, but the whole purpose of a collective is that no
one person runs it."

"Come on. That's just PR talk. We all know who makes the big decisions."

His hair was short and stuck straight up. His suit was thrift-store hip. Behind his round wire-rimmed glasses, his eyes gleamed up at me with mischief. I am five foot eight without the heels I almost always wear. Standing next to Tim reminded me of why it was so much fun to be able to look down on certain men.

"Really, Tim? And who is *we?*"

"Well, I was just talking to Angela, and she seemed to think that you pretty much ran the ship. Until now, anyway."

He gestured around the room.

"I mean, this scarcely looks like Louise Terry's sort of thing. Remember what you said on that Hirshhorn panel about computer-generated art? Clicking and dragging is not drawing and painting?"

"My reputation as a Luddite is well established, Tim."

He leaned in closer.

"I mean, frankly, Louise, I can't believe you even like this installation."

"Well, that would just prove that I don't run the ship, as you put it. Now, if you don't mind..."

"Just one more thing. Where will Louise Terry be showing next?"

"I don't know, Tim. For now, I'm just painting. I got that Mid-Atlantic grant, you know."

"But you must have some idea of where you'd like to show next? Some gallery you're talking to?"

"Nope, not a clue," I said. "And now Tim, you must excuse me. I need to find Natalie."

"Of course. It must be an emotional night for you both. I'd like to get some quotes later about that. Meanwhile, I'll go talk to the artist."

He wiggled his eyebrows at me. I restrained the temptation to hurl my wineglass at his back.

"Louie!"

"Nat!"

She wrapped her arms around me, gave me a real hug. The heavy jewelry she wore clinked and jangled. I often teased her that, like a cat with bells on its collar, she could be heard approaching. Her long, messy black hair tangled with my long, curly hair, currently dyed a Titian red with gold highlights. We looked great together, posed back to back in the Place's PR photos.

She held me by the shoulders and looked at me.

"How are you, girl?"

"Good, good. How about you? Is Janice coming?"

"Oh, no. That relationship didn't quite go, well, anywhere."

"I'm sorry, Nat."

"Well, I'm OK with it. But what really feels funny, Louie, is knowing that when we open the doors tomorrow, you won't be here."

"It feels funny to me, too, Nat. Believe me. But it's time."

"I'm sure you're right. I'm sure I'm just being selfish."

"You're the least selfish person in the world, Natalie Anderson. And the wisest. And the best."

There were tears in her eyes as she let go of me.

"Lunch next week, then? As usual?"

"Of course."

I tried to mingle, but without the spur of networking for A Woman's Place, I felt a bit lost. No point in chatting up grant officers for projects I wouldn't be working on, or approaching possible collectors about sales. Sahara's installation wasn't really buyable, and anyway, even Tim Gould could tell I didn't care for it. I waited until the crowd seemed to reach its peak size, and then I just slipped out. No goodbyes, no toasts, no fuss. This was the way I thought I wanted it.

Driving home from Mount Pleasant and my old life, I took the long way in order to pass the bright storefront of a particular uptown Connecticut Avenue gallery. In the window was a huge Venetian landscape, gorgeously lit; in the upstairs office, a single light burned. I'd gotten in the habit lately of driving past the place, as if exerting some kind of sympathetic magic on it. For I had lied to Tim Gould. I did have a new landing pad in mind, a gallery owner who had already seen and admired my work and wanted to see more: Dana Reilly, of the trendy and very much for-profit Reilly Gallery. It was with her that I hoped to have my next show.

✳

FOR A FEW DAYS, UNPACKING boxes and setting up my new studio provided a welcome diversion from actually exploring my mother's box. When I lived with Jason, I rented a studio downtown near the Place. Now, I was renting a shabby one-bedroom apartment that had the advantage of a great northwest light. I turned the big combined living and dining areas into my studio. I was all in one place, and all alone. At last.

I also felt the need to include my brother and sister in the matter of the mysterious box. Whatever remnants of my mother's chaotic life resided there, I was uneasy about facing them alone. But when I called Katherine's number in San Francisco, her partner, David, told me she was on a month-long silent retreat at a Zen monastery in Oregon. My sister, the eldest, is a Buddhist and a psychotherapist, which means that she spends her life studying things that are immensely difficult and mostly irresolvable.

David began to tell me about a labyrinthine system for leaving messages at the monastery—"Of course, Louise," he said, in a slow, weighty voice that he intended, I'm sure, to indicate enlightenment, but in fact made him sound like he'd learned to speak English by listening to Public Radio, "it ought to be...a real emergency"—but I told him it wasn't urgent. He wished me peace and we hung up. David has always gotten on my nerves.

After a couple of tries, I finally reached Dylan on a Friday night. He was in a swaggering mood, having just come from some kind of business dinner that involved, clearly, many drinks. I could hear the sounds of the household behind him, Jennifer's voice, soft and high, talking to Maggie, my niece, and the sound of the little girl's shoes clapping the hardwood floor. I love my brother, and it was good to hear him rattling away, so pleased with himself and his life. There are times, however, when I wish that he had a little of Katherine's sensitivity.

When I told him about the box, there was a long silence. Then he became all business.

"Well, there's really no chance that there'll be any surprises in there, from the estate's point of view. Go through the whole thing first for any legal or bank documents. Send those to me right away. You don't even need to read them."

He paused, sighed. As the executor of my mother's will, Dylan had presided over the little she'd left us— about forty thousand dollars each, after taxes. But you'd think he had been entrusted with the federal budget. In the weeks after we'd read the will, my sister and I were flooded with emails from Dylan outlining different investment strategies, the result of hours of conversation with his broker friends, and more hours doing research in print or on the web. It was touching, but troubling, too. The intensity with which he threw himself into this task of helping his sisters, neither of whom has, as he does, the interest in or the knack for accruing wealth, was born of genuine love. But the obsessive way he went about it made me think he might be having some kind of breakdown.

Katherine said it was part of his way of grieving for our mother. "It will pass," she said, and she turned out to be right. After a few weeks, the flow of financial information slowed to a trickle and then stopped. He began to talk and write of other things. Katherine donated her inheritance to a Buddhist study center, and Jennifer talked Dylan into spending his on some new living room furniture.

I put mine in the bank, and left it there. It was my reserve, in case my faith in the marketability of my new work turned out to be premature.

"Dylan," I said, "I don't think this has anything to do with money."

"What is it, then? Something about the church, you said?"

"Research, that's what Brother Paul told me. About saints. He said—he said that Mom wanted to write a book."

I paused. When he didn't respond, I said, "Dylan, did you hear me? Don't you think that's strange?"

"What?"

"That Mom was working on a book before she died and none of us knew anything about it?"

"She always had some kind of hobby, Louie. Ceramics, psychology, whatever. You know how she is—I mean, was." He stopped, went on. "And besides, she was a freak for those old saint stories. They were like, I don't know, graphic novels to her. Superheroes for Christ, or something."

"Yeah, but to be working on a book, a religious book…I mean, that's more serious, don't you think?"

There was no point in trying to explain it. Maybe, as I felt sure he was about to tell me, I was making too big a deal out of this.

"You always make such a big deal out of things, Louie. I don't get it. I mean, what do you think is in there, anyway? A couple of snoozer books about church history? Who cares? Maybe she talked to Kenny about it—or maybe Kath."

"I tried to call her."

"Don't bother. She's out treading softly upon the earth somewhere. Aligning her cha-chas."

"*Chakras.*" I enjoyed a guilty thrill when he made fun of Katherine, but still felt obliged to correct him. "The word is chakras. You have seven."

"Maybe *you* do," he said. "Yeah, I called out there the other day, talked to Mr. Sincere."

Dylan likes to make up nicknames for people, and reserves the particularly sarcastic ones for men involved with his sisters. He used to call Jason "Film Boy."

"I told him we need to start thinking about the Christmas holidays."

"Dylan, it's October."

"Never too early to start making plans," he said. "And I think we need to do something really special for this Christmas. After, you know."

He and Katherine and I had spent last Christmas at our mother's bedside, in Kenny's house. I never got used to thinking of it as her house, too.

"We need to see Dad," Dylan was saying, "and god knows I don't want to go to Florida. I was thinking that Jen and I should have everybody up here."

Massachusetts in December. I shuddered.

"Kind of a long way for Katherine to come," I said. "And pricey."

"I got a guy who can set you all up with a sweet deal. The firm's travel agent. He owes me big time."

"And it's a lot on Jen."

"Shit, we can get it catered, she won't have to do a thing. I'm more worried about trying to get the old man to come up here that time of year. He's like you about the fucking weather. Anyway," he sighed, "I'll talk to him, see what's up. But he'll probably suggest that we all go down there."

"Dylan," I said, very seriously.

"What, baby?"

"One thing we must avoid at all costs is Carrie's cooking."

"Don't worry, Louie," he said. "I would never let you down like that. No more boiled ham casserole for this *hombre*."

"Boiled ham and canned cream-of-mushroom soup casserole."

"And that scary pink Jell-O thing, what's it called?"

"Wacky Cake," I said.

"Shit, if I can avoid that, I'll fly all of you up here myself."

"But that's so expensive, Dyl."

"I had a good year, Louie," he said. "I can afford it. And like I said, we need it."

"Yeah," I said. "Something positive. Something fun."

"Exactly," Dylan said. "We need to have some fun."

I hung up the phone and went directly to work. I had been painting a layered ground on a rectangular canvas, one of several I'd stretched, roughly the dimensions of giant playing cards. *The Seven Deadly Sins*, my last series, were that size, and now I was moving on to the corresponding virtues. I had thought I was starting on Felicity, but the idea now seemed too predictable. The medieval imagery I'd been using, inspired by work in the Musée de Cluny that I'd seen on a trip to Paris the year before my mother died, had suddenly worn itself out.

You've become too tied to working in sequence, I told myself. *Remember what Dana Reilly said. Don't be afraid to be uncomfortable, to try something new.* I was pacing through the apartment, out of the studio to the kitchen, then down the hall to the bedroom, then back to the studio again, until without realizing it I was standing next to the box.

I lifted the lid.

It stuck a little and I had to use both hands. It had been stored somewhere too damp, that was certain; flakes of stuck paint fell from the inside lip as I pushed the lid back on its hinge. The smell that rose up to me was complex—the bitter residue of oak, the sweetness of the cedar blocks that had been tucked in the corners to fight the moisture, the particulate must of old paper and old books, the almost human smell of leather, and finally, the two scents that were always and so my mother, cigarette smoke and Shalimar.

The contents of the box were surprisingly orderly. I had expected some kind of mess, a jumble of papers and books. Instead, an accordion file, about two inches thick, took up one of the short walls; I saw a fringe of typed pages peeking out of the strained binding string. There were also two neat piles of books—mostly old, hardbound in leather or cloth—and as I flipped through a couple of them I saw they were heavily underlined. On top was a spiral-bound notebook.

Research, Brother Paul had said. About saints.

Inside I found my mother's name in her big, loopy hand, and, tucked into the front cover, an old floppy disk and two photos. One of the photos was of her alone on the side of a hill somewhere. The grass sloped up behind her, there was wind in her hair, she was laughing. The second was of Mom in the same spot with two other women. On her right was her Aunt Angie, a formidable figure from my youth, dressed elegantly, as always, and with her usual self-important, self-satisfied expression. On her left was a woman I had never seen, her hair scraped back into a knot or ponytail, her face small and calm. On the next page, I found what looked like a journal entry. Was it right for me to read it?

She must have wanted me to read it. *The youngest. The artist.* So I did.

January 20, 1987

It is like the time before the time before.

Angie says write it down it will help you but how?

When I am like this. When I am in one of my moods. She wants to see proof that I am working to get hold of myself. She believes in will and discipline and she loves me. She does not want me to be weak.

John does not want, does not, does not know

January 23

It is not the weather. Yes winter makes me sad but that is not it, not all of it — sad is one thing. This is something else.

That woman Katherine took me to hear at the Buddhist place when she was here last summer said that love has to be a choice. Every day. Or it isn't love. I wish she came home more often. She steadies us all I think. Like Dylan makes us laugh. Like Louise makes us see.

January 27

The doctor says that physical exercise is an old cure for melancholy. So today I went for a walk.

A sort of womens shop has opened about three blocks from here. They sell books and T-shirts with sayings on them and incense and posters with women singers and writers and clunky silver jewelry. Its the sort of place Katherine would love. The sort of place that people I knew back then went to in the '60s.

The owner came over and introduced herself. Eleanor something and she was very nice. We talked for a little while. She is older than me — but I can't tell how old. Her hair is dyed red, badly dyed and I could see gray underneath and thought it is time for her to get her roots done. She has a kind face. Her eyes are young and old. At the same time.

February 5

I walked back up to Eleanors tonight after dinner. She invited me to join something called a womens circle. They get together at the shop on Sundays after it closes and drink tea and have discussions about politics and art and life.

I said I don't know much about any of those things.

She said neither do any of us thats why we talk about them.

I said my daughter is a Buddhist and you sound like her. I said I might come by one Sunday.

Should I bring anything, I asked her, meaning food.

Most of us bring our journals, she said. Sometimes we read from them.

A month ago I might not have known what she meant. But now I could look at her and say of course my journal.

February 14

Valentines Day. Every year since I came back it has been the same — dinner at Ruths Chris for my surf and turf with lobster tails and chocolate mousse and it is always good and the host never forgets to tell me how beautiful I am.

The children are all gone — that is one thing. I would not be leaving them not really. K is 22 and D will be 20 in May. K always understands everything and D loves me. L will be in college soon. She will be furious, but she always is anyway at me. I am not forgiven, not by her. What difference then. What difference do I make really?

Feb. 27

Last night I got up my nerve and asked Eleanor for a reading list to get ready for the womens circle and she laughed and said I should make my own. I said I would tell her something that no one else had the courage to tell her if she would give me the names of three books she thought I should read.

You are a flirt she said but all right then tell me.

You're too old I said to be dying your own hair. I'm guessing you don't time it the way you should. But you'd look so much prettier if you put yourself in the hands of a professional.

For a minute she looked at me so funny and I thought I had really hurt her feelings. But then she let out a big whoop and gave me a hug.

Venus she said I knew it. I said it when you walked through my front door. Somebody get her a clamshell.

Then she walked through her store grabbing books off the shelf
— you need this and this and this she said. There were a whole
lot more then three when she was done. I have in a pile right now
a book called "When God Was a Woman," and a couple of books
by a woman who goes by one name Starhawk, and a couple more
very serious ones by a woman psychologist Carl used to talk about,
Marian Woodman.

Nothing about gardening she said and nothing about menopause.
Though these days the two seem to go hand in hand. I asked her if she
gardened and she said her apartment was where plants come to die.

Oh and one called "Gynecology" and one called "The Second Sex."
And a womens encyclopedia of myths and gods. She would not let me
pay for them, she insisted that I take them all and she kissed me on
each cheek after she bagged them up. There were only a few women
there but they all saw and heard her.

I was in such a good mood when I got home last night I could
hardly wait to jump into those books. But then John said I shouldn't
be accepting things for free that people always want something in
return. I think he was talking about Carl. But then I thought to myself
here you go again just like with John or Angie or Carl you are asking
someone to solve your problems to make you a life but it is all wrong.
Angie is right. You have to decide for yourself.

My self. My self.

March 3

She has a way of making me blush and I do not like it though I like
her. She makes me feel sometimes like a kid. Sometimes I want to say
look Eleanor I'm an adult I'm a mother. Don't talk to me like I'm a
child.

She called and said she hadn't seen me in a while how about
dinner. Her treat. It was as if she knew I was feeling down. John
didn't like me just saying that I was going out. He likes me to plan
ahead. That is one of the things we do not agree about. One of the
things.

Maybe I should not have told Eleanor all the things I did. But it is hard not to talk about what has happened to you and what is happening. I miss that about Carl more than I miss his body or his laugh. He was never afraid of me. I could talk about anything drink anything do anything with him. There wasn't anything he hadn't seen already in his job. I remember the afternoon he looked at me and said Margaret your problem is that you are much more normal than you think you are.

He did help me. He knew things about me about how the mind works and he understood me. He explained me to myself in ways that nobody ever had. I don't care what Angie or Eleanor say about ethics. He was not my shrink. He never asked for anything I didn't want to give him. Yes I know that therapists have rules to follow. But people are human, too.

Eleanor says she thinks that Carl should be sued. She says he took advantage of me he abused me. She has had a lot of lovers men and women and a couple of husbands and it is clear to me that she has money though I'm not sure how or from where.

Eleanor said You sound like a woman who does not want to be married to anyone, period. Maybe she is right. And I promised her I would come to the next circle.

March 10

It must have been right to come back I must have done the right thing. But not when he looks at me like he did tonight. There is something terrible about the love of a man who has forgiven you for something he will never forget.

I thought of walking up to Eleanor's store and getting out from under his eyes. But I thought no I will take it. I can take it. Let him look at me.

March 14

I went to the womens circle last night and felt so stupid. I must read more I must learn more things.

March 28

I want to think I can make my life the way I want it and not hurt anybody else. But I make bad starts and scare my family and then they are afraid to trust me.

The world feels so small. It makes you want to break loose break things.

April 7

Angie says her life began when she was in her forties.

She says you have to decide what you want in this life and then take it take it.

It is as if they're all giving me permission to go.

April 14

Last night after dinner I walked up to Eleanors. I told myself that I would just drop by and that I would not stay for very long. But there were only five of us so anyone leaving would stand out. I did not want to be rude.

These women only talk about things that matter to them a lot. They are very intense very ready to argue. They love to argue with each other. Sometimes one of them will tell a story or make a point and they all listen so close so seriously. It is an honor to be listened to like that.

But it makes you wonder if you've got anything to say that deserves that much attention. They have all read the same books and heard the same music and visited the same countries. Maybe because they have all been to college.

But I am not going to start feeling sorry for myself now. It was an interesting experience.

When I got there, one woman was reading aloud from a book called "Goddesses of Old Greece." She is young and skinny and very tense. Her name is Kayla. The idea behind the book is that there used to be religions based around goddesses, and that men took those religions apart and replaced them with their own. Eleanor lent me her copy. It has very strange beautiful pictures of statues of goddesses in it.

Kayla was very excited and very angry. She said that she felt centuries and centuries of anger over what had been done to women. One of the other women — older closer to Eleanor's age, from Canada and very nice I liked her, her name is Deborah — said it was good, that Kayla could use that anger to do some good. Kayla said she was too angry to do good. She wanted to tear things down break things up.

Then a woman named Libby who I disliked for some reason as soon as I saw her started arguing with Kayla. She said the problem wasn't who we worship male or female but that we need to worship at all. She said that as long as people believe the answers lie outside of themselves in the hands of a god or goddess, they're lost. She started talking about a book called "The Fountainhead." I have never read it but it made Eleanor snort through both nostrils.

Eleanor said that people have needed to worship as long as they've been around. Kayla said she'd already set up an altar to one of the goddesses pictured in the book. Deborah said that she has an altar in her home with lots of different goddesses. Libby called her an equal opportunity worshipper and then Eleanor said that if Libby had an altar to worship at, it would have a big sculpture of a human brain on it and the word reason carved on a plaque over it. I thought Libby would get angry but she laughed and said that Eleanors altar just had the word sex written on it, and Eleanor blushed a little and said she might be right.

Then Deborah smiled and asked what I would put on mine.

Everyone looked at me. I hadn't said a word since I had been introduced. I said I had never thought about it. And Eleanor leaned back in her chair and said Well why not think about it now?

So I did. And I remember it, I remember almost every word of what I told them —

Well, first, the Virgin Mary. When I was a girl, I prayed to her. She had a kind face. She did not punish. I wanted my mother to be like that. I wanted. Well so many things.

And then I got married and then I found out how hard that was. Harder for me I think than for other women and I don't know why. I tried. I tried. So then I guess I took the lady off the altar and put an idea in her place. A word; passion. And a new man. But that did not work either.

So now I have come back to my former life and I am trying once again to be a wife and mother. But there is nothing on my altar right now.

It sounded so bleak to me as I said it that I thought they'd all think I was insane. But they started clapping. Libby said I was in the perfect place, now all I had to do was throw away the altar. Kayla said smashing it to bits would be even better. Deborah said she liked the idea of a blank space an empty altar. Libby said it was very Zen which would make K happy.

Then Eleanor said she envied me. I asked why.

You're in a state of potentiality she said. Don't you see? When all the gods and goddesses have been swept away anything is possible.

That was the last entry.

I put the journal down, poured myself a shot of single malt, Macallan, and drank it fast. The burn in my throat made my eyes water, and I closed them. As soon as I did, there they were, projected like a movie on the insides of my eyelids: my mother and her old lover, Carl Brun.

I saw them laughing together at some neighborhood cookout, soon after the Bruns moved in, his arm ever so briefly draped across her shoulders, while behind me someone murmured about his Swiss wife, her money, his reliance on it. I saw the wife, Teresa, who I thought I had forgotten, tall and muscled, with a mean straight mouth and judging eyes. I heard her saying how coarse and provincial Washington, D.C., was compared to Zurich—where were we then? An evening, a party at our house,

maybe? Dylan and Katherine both were there—and Carl
breaking in, too loudly, reminding her that he was an
American man and appreciated a little coarseness. They
were a handsome couple, tall, fair haired, with year-
round tans—they skied, they snorkeled, they scuba dived
in exotic locales—and for nearly a year the whole neighborhood was in love with them, her hard glamour, his
softer charm.

He had the purring voice of a really good therapist,
and hazel eyes with enviable eyelashes, and despite the
demands of his Jungian training seemed to also know
everything worth knowing about film, about music, about
art. To the girl I was then—I was just beginning my sophomore year of high school when the Bruns fell like gods
from the sky into our humble suburban neighborhood—
he seemed an ideal adult man, cultured, sophisticated,
with work that was a vocation, not a job, just as painting
was a vocation for me. Whenever I saw him, no matter
how many adults were around, he always took time to
speak to me alone, to ask about my painting, my college
plans, my goals, my dreams. He took me seriously, and
the serious girl I was loved him for it.

Did I say love? No, that is too strong a word. But the
truth is that I had a crush on Carl Brun, the sort of sear-
ing anxious crush that a teenage girl can get on an adult
man whose very being seems to open doors to the self she
wants to be. And while I did not think, not really, that
this crush was returned, I did think he had some special regard for me. Sometimes at parties he'd slip me a
rum and Coke, and once, when we were briefly alone in
somebody's kitchen, he lifted my hand to his mouth and
kissed it, saying that I was growing into a very beautiful
woman.

I had no experience, then, of the sort of man who makes a game of seducing women. There were a couple of heartbreakers in my high school, but they were easy to spot. Carl Brun was a new experience for me, and it never occurred to me that our gentle flirtations were not a new experience for him. And then, just as the summer between sophomore and junior year was starting, Carl Brun ran away with my mother.

Of course I was angry—furious at her for all the obvious reasons. She'd betrayed my father. She'd lied and plotted and connived. But I had also always thought she knew how I felt about Carl. Now, reading her journal, it seemed to me that she had no idea of that at all; she'd just been desperate and lonely and in need of help. Angie and Dad had tried to help, but couldn't. Carl seemed as if he could. And I knew how she felt, because I'd thought him a kind of answer for me, as well. We'd both been fooled.

Suddenly, I was mixing paint on the palette in shades of gray, and digging for a bag of mica that could give the paint the shimmer of stone. In another spot, I mixed a red the color of my mother's hair. I turned the rectangular canvas horizontal on the easel, and began to sketch out the shape of an empty altar, and the shape of my mother kneeling—no, standing—beside it.

3

I opened my eyes and saw that the sky, through the window shades, was just beginning to lighten. T.J.'s jeans were still where he'd tossed them the night before at the foot of the bed, his boots leaning against my closet door. Then he walked into the bedroom in his boxers, wiping his face on a towel.

"Got a delivery to meet. Half an hour. Didn't want to wake you."

"That's all right."

"A kiss?"

"Sure."

He sat beside me on the bed, pulled me into his arms. He kissed my forehead, my cheeks, my mouth. There was a small, sharp shriek from the floor below. A pause, and then another shriek, and then a torrent of crying began.

"They've got a new grandbaby visiting," I said. "Try to ignore it."

He kissed me and laughed.

"That's OK. Baby sounds don't bother me."

"That makes one of us."

"That's 'cause you're so sensitive. My artist," he said, and kissed me again.

Below us, we heard a woman's hushing voice and the baby's cries subsiding. It occurred to me that I had never heard T.J. call me *his*, not even in this light-hearted way.

"Hey," he said, "I figure, we've all got to deal with it sooner or later. No use making a fuss."

"Deal with what?"

"Babies crying in the wee morning hours. Diapers to change in the middle of the night. It's gonna happen— even to people like us."

"Like us?"

"You know. The ones who play around for a while. Who take their time about settling down. We still want the same stuff everybody else does."

I felt my body stiffen. He drew back, looked at me carefully.

"What's that *look* mean?"

"I was just wondering what it is that we're all supposed to want."

"A home. A partner. Family. Kids. That's what we're all looking for, right?"

"Not me," I said. "That's not what I'm looking for, not at all."

He pulled away then, and got up to put on his jeans.

"Well, OK," he said. "Maybe *looking* is the wrong word. A woman like you doesn't have to go looking. I know that."

He zipped up his jeans, reached for the sweater he'd thrown over the back of my chair.

"I mean, one day, some guy who's been circling for who knows how long is gonna make his move. Say, 'Come on, girl, let's go make some babies.'"

"Oh, please. That's about the least appealing invitation I've ever heard." We probably should have dropped the subject. But his conviction, this business of us all wanting the same things, angered me.

"I don't want," I said, "to make anybody's babies. I've got art to make."

"Some people," he said cautiously, "do both. Have both. A career, and kids." He pulled his sweater over his head. "I mean, didn't Picasso have children?"

"If he did, I'm sure it was the mother who did all the work."

"But what if things—what if your life—was different? What if you married—I'm just thinking out loud now—say, a guy who made some dough. And who stayed in one place for his work. Not like your ex. And he hired somebody. You know, a nanny. To take care of the kids while you painted."

"No good. I mean, that's not enough. I want my whole life, for me. A steady guy, sure. I'd like to do that again. To have a partner."

"But no kids," he said.

"No."

"So you've never—you would never even consider it."

"I have considered it," I said, "and I've decided against it."

"Can I ask why?"

"It's just not for me, motherhood. It would make me miserable. I'm sure of it."

"Wow," he said. "I've never known a woman who felt that way before."

I was angry now and sick of talking. It had been years since I'd had to defend my decision not to become a mother to anybody. Most of my artist friends understood, didn't even comment. Natalie had always felt the same way. Besides, it made no sense to me that T.J. should get so worked up about the subject.

This must have something to do with Elizabeth, I thought. Maybe she's pushing the baby talk. It can't have anything to do with me.

I stretched, looked toward the window.

"I need to get some more sleep," I said.

I walked him to the door, like I always did, and he kissed me goodbye. The irritation I'd felt vanished, and it occurred to me that it would be hard to stay mad at T.J. for very long about anything. He was just too simple, too straightforward a guy. And then I shook it all off, and went back to bed for a few more hours of sleep.

But later, in the studio, the conversation came back to me and made me angry all over again. I had thought T.J. was more enlightened than that. To think that every woman in the world longed to have a child—how narrow-minded, how shortsighted, how very male. And he subscribed to the old dollar theory: if you just had the right man with the right amount of money, you'd say yes. Even Dylan, who can be a bit of a Neanderthal when it comes to women, was too smart for that.

But then, it was very clear in our family that whatever having children did for a woman it certainly did not guarantee happiness, or even contentment. I knew that without reading my mother's journal. No wonder Dylan was the only one of the three of us to have a child.

❈

DANA ASKED ME TO DROP off a copy of my CV and some slides of the past year's work at the gallery. When I got there, a large abstract work now filled the front window. I remembered that there was an opening that night. Gerry Heller, an abstract artist from Santa Fe whom Dana had been courting, was having his first Reilly Gallery show. Daniel Orton, Dana's assistant, spotted me through the glass, set down the stepladder he was carrying, and let me in.

"Things are crazy here, Louise."

"I've just got some stuff to drop off for Dana."

"Give it to me. But I can tell you, she won't get to it until Thursday at the earliest."

"She seems very excited about Heller."

"You're telling me. We've had him underfoot for days. Always oversees his own installations. Not so much as a nail goes in the wall without his OK."

He looked across the room.

"Christ, the caterers are due any minute. Those boys need to finish whatever it is they're doing and get out of the way. Later."

And off he went, up the stairs to Dana's office. I turned around to see what boys he might be talking about.

He was crouched with his back to me, his head turned toward the neck of his guitar, so what I saw was a profile, long nose, strong brow, strong chin, a winged cheekbone. He reminded me of a hawk I'd seen once perched on a rock over Great Falls, pausing before he swooped down over the water. He had that same sense of great power in repose. His hair was thick and straight and very long, gathered into a ponytail at the nape of his neck. His lips were full, and as he tuned his guitar, he bit the lower one from time to time—a kind of card-player's tell, revealing the youth beneath the assured exterior.

As I crossed the gallery floor behind him, he stood up, as if in response to me, but didn't turn around. He and the others put down their instruments and huddled, talking quietly. And then Dana was sweeping down the stairs, Daniel behind her.

"Vincent! Darling!"

"Aunt Dana," he said, accepting her hug. She leaned back, theatrically, and took his face into her hands.

"Why, you're a man, sweetheart," she purred. "What happened to the baby I remember?"

For just a second, he caught my eye over her shoulder, and I swear there was a look of complicity in his gaze, as though he and I shared a secret that the others were not in on.

"I grew up, I guess," he said, smiling, and the others laughed.

"Oh, Louise, you haven't met. This is Vincent Volpe, my honorary nephew, who will be providing our music tonight. And Vincent, this is Louise Terry, a marvelous young painter I've just discovered. I predict that in five years you'll both be famous."

Vincent put out his hand to me and had just begun to say something when someone banged loudly on the gallery door.

"The caterers!" Dana exclaimed. "OK everyone, shoo!"

As I made my way out, I pulled on Daniel's sleeve.

"What's his story?" I asked. "The guitarist."

"Oh, young Vincent. Sweet, isn't he? His family and Dana's go back forever. She says people have been calling him a genius since he could walk, practically. He went to Berklee."

"And what's the name of the band?"

"Oh, something clever—what is it? Something to do with science. Oh, right, Einstein. They're called Einstein's Pillow."

I HADN'T PLANNED ON ATTENDING the Heller opening. The painting I had started of my mother had turned into a diptych and I had the sense of a different kind of series developing, something new. But when I got home all I could think of was Vincent Volpe, his profile, his hair, his smile. So I got out my sketchbook and drew his face, that brow, those slanted lips. A few hours later, dressed in sapphire blue silk and black velvet shoes, I was back at Reilly Gallery.

When I arrived, the musicians were nowhere to be seen. The big front room, however, was packed. As I made my way through it, I was greeted by one person, then another. It seemed Dana had been saying flattering things about my work. I had, for just a moment, a flooding, satisfying sense of well-being. My new work was going well. And I was here, in a room full of successful, well-fed, well-dressed people, in a dress that was my first splurge after the grant came through. So what if the only guy I was seeing had primitive ideas about motherhood as well as a real girlfriend? Who cared that Dana and I had no firm commitment to each other yet? Sure, I had taken some big risks, and burned some bridges. But all around me was evidence of how well I was doing in my new life.

Suddenly, I spied Tim Gould, angling his way through the crowd toward me, pulling someone by the hand. He introduced his date, Brittany, as a painter, then dove right in.

"So," he said, "it's going to be Reilly Gallery, huh?"

"I don't know what you mean."

"What a wonderful space," Brittany broke in. "And look—isn't that Senator Walters?"

"Yes," I said. "Dana advises him on his collection."

"No wonder you've kept it a secret," Tim went on. "Louise Terry. Going for the big bucks."

"Whatever I'm doing has nothing to do with money, Tim. I can tell you that much."

"What *are* you doing these days?"

"New stuff. New...sequences."

"Subject matter?"

"I never talk about work in progress, Tim, you know that."

"Well, I'm just surprised. To find you *here*," he gestured around the room, "which, you gotta admit, is a far cry from A Woman's Place."

"I guess you could say I'm expanding my horizons."

"But what happened to...let's see, what was it?" Tim scratched his goatee theatrically. "'Giving voices to those who have been silenced,' am I right? 'Unearthing the buried stories of women's lives'—I thought that was your thing, your agenda."

He was quoting from our old fundraising brochure for A Woman's Place, from our mission statement. Remembering how many hours it had taken to hammer that document out, to reach consensus on every phrase, every word, I had a sudden urge to slap him. Instead, I smiled.

"Well," I said, "it was time for a change. People do change, you know."

"Yeah," he said, "they do. But not that much. And not that fast."

His seriousness surprised me. Then, from across the room, I heard Dana's sing-song voice calling me.

"Sorry, Tim. If you'll excuse me."

"Nice to meet you," Brittany said, tugging him away.

"Lou-Lou darling." Dana was waving red-tipped fingers at me. "Come here, would you dear?"

Tim looked at her, then back to me, and raised a brow.

"Lou-Lou *dar*ling?" he said. His voice was soft and mocking.

"Shut up, Tim," I said, very quietly, and walked away. But not before I saw him raise his free hand, point the finger of an imaginary gun at me, as kids do, and cock the barrel.

Dana introduced me to one wealthy collector, then another. She had a skillful way of steering the conversation toward prizes and grants I'd won without making me seem pushy or arrogant. She tossed in a few hints about when I might have my first show with her, and the annoyance I'd felt at Tim dissolved in her bright, glamorous presence. A crowd pulled us apart, and I looked around, briefly at sea. Then I heard a sound—beautiful, familiar—and turned to see where it was coming from.

It was Vincent. Standing alone amid the rest of the band's propped instruments, he was playing the first bars of Pachelbel's *Canon in D Major*. His hands pulled the notes up and out of the guitar while he pressed forward and back on a pedal with his right foot, his whole body rocking gently forward and back with every sustain, every rise and fall. Sometimes he'd look down at his feet, so that all I could see of his face was a slice of forehead and the sculpted lids of his eyes. Then he'd raise his face to the sky, eyes closed, and shake his head a little, as if to clear his mind before beginning the next phrase. It seemed to me that he was pulling the sound up out of the floor, out of the ground, and through his body, and I felt the music run through my body, too. The sound was mournful and exultant, the tone very clear and very full. Around him the talking quieted, then stopped. The room went still for him.

Then the bass player came out and joined him. He used a bow on his stand-up bass as if he were playing a cello, and the sound reverberated in the big room. Posed halfway up the stairs to Dana's office, holding forth, Gerry Heller had stopped talking to listen to the music. Even Dana, who now had Senator Walters by the arm, was silent.

Then the keyboard player joined them, then the drummer. The sound they made together was old and new, original and familiar. It was, in its way, absolutely perfect.

The music dropped, then swelled again, then glided to its close. People clapped with more enthusiasm than is usual at such things. The keyboard player leaned into his mike, mouth open, but Vincent made a small, slicing gesture with his hand, and he sat back. It was startling and a little cruel. Talk started up again, a little, here and there around the room. The band moved quickly into the next composition, one I didn't recognize.

But I recognized the feeling I was having well enough. It had happened before, though not for a long time. I remembered the night I'd met Jason, at a D.C. Film Festival screening in the early '90s, and how his documentary on threatened wildlife in the Grand Canyon made all the other films on the program seem sloppy, half finished. I remembered his handsome serious face during the discussion after, and how his passion for his art lived in his eyes. How could I help but fall for that?

Then Dana was beside me.

"A nice little routine they have, huh? Coming out one by one. Very dramatic."

"Yes, yes. They're very good," I said.

"And what a relief, let me tell you. Connie hasn't had an easy time with that one."

"Connie?"

"My old pal Constantine Volpe, honey. You've met him. He's over there, drooling on Desiree. His wife must not be here tonight."

She shook her head.

"But then, I always say, nobody can hurt you like your own. And if the kid's got a gift like that, what can you do? Forget law school. You've got to let him use it."

She leaned back, narrowed her eyes. It was business time.

"How is the new work coming?"

"Good, very good. Big canvases, lots of imagery. I'm loading them up."

"I'd like to come by sometime soon."

"Of course."

"You're good, Lou-Lou. I knew I was right about you. I've got big plans—"

She broke off. I saw her look across the room, where Gerry Heller was holding forth.

"Later, darling," she said, moving away from me. "Later."

When the band took a break, I saw them slip outside as they had before, and followed them. Out in the garden, the air was cool and it felt good after the heat of the bodies crushed into the gallery. In a corner, by a grouping of Frederick Lane sculptures, I spotted Vincent standing, talking to the rest of them.

"Remember," I heard him say as I got closer, "you have to take it seriously. Play it straight. Don't accent it, like you're making a joke."

"But it *is* a joke," said the keyboard player. "Shit. You've got a piece of the *Nutcracker* in there. How will they get it if we don't show them?"

"If they get it, Jay, they get it. But you don't have to underline it."

"I don't know if anyone's gonna get it," the bass player said.

"I'm not sure *I* get it," the drummer said.

"Look, it doesn't matter," Vincent said. "Just play it straight."

A little cluster of people came up to the keyboard player, and he broke away to talk to them. The drummer and bass player drifted off toward the bar. I saw a very young, very pretty woman start to make her way toward Vincent. I stepped up.

"Excuse me," I said. "I'm Louise Terry."

"Of course," he said. "We met this afternoon. Just before Aunt Dana sent us all packing."

I laughed.

"Well, I just wanted to tell you that your music is wonderful. That was a beautiful set."

"Thanks. Glad you liked it."

That was all. The younger girl was hovering. I tried again.

"Do you have a CD out? I'd like to buy one."

"Not yet. Soon. I'm still mixing it."

"You're producing it yourself?"

"Sort of, yeah. I mean, we have this engineer, but he's clueless, really."

He stopped himself.

"I mean, not clueless, that's not cool, it's just—you know. I know what I hear. I know what I want."

For an instant, something about him, his seriousness, his young voice, reminded me of Brother Paul.

"Well, I would think that would be the easy part..."

"You'd think so, right?" His voice warmed in agreement, and his hands moved emphatically in the air. "But no. I mean, sometimes I think nobody, or hardly anybody, knows what they really want. It's why almost everything on the radio or the Internet is just crap, you know? I mean, do you ever hear anything you could actually call music?"

He moved a little closer. My head just reached his shoulder. If I leaned into him, if he held me, it would feel just right.

"I wouldn't know," I said. "I listen to jazz, mostly. Miles. Coltrane. That's what I paint to."

"Well, Louise," he said, "maybe one day you'll paint to some of my music."

The other girl drifted away. I was trying to think of something to say in return when I felt an avuncular hand on my shoulder.

"So, Louise Tully. You remember me, I hope? Connie Volpe? We were on the Mayor's awards panel last year."

"Of course. So good to see you. By the way, it's Terry. Louise Terry."

"Ah, yes." Dr. Volpe leaned in to kiss my cheek. "And you've met my son."

Vincent's face, which had been so warm while we talked, went blank.

"Hello, Father."

"The outfit sounds good tonight, son. Very good."

"Thank you, sir."

"Your stepmother will be sorry she missed it. She wasn't feeling well, sends her regards."

Vincent was silent. It was as if his father's presence had turned him into one of the patio's stone sculptures.

Dr. Volpe turned to me.

"So what do you think of my son, eh? Quite the talent."

"I was just telling him," I said, "how much I enjoyed that set. It opened so beautifully."

I tried to catch Vincent's eye, but he was looking at the ground.

"Hit 'em with a bang, that's what I always say. Of course, not that I have any musical talent. No, not me. He gets that from his mother's side. No, my only thought— my only worry, son, frankly, is the name. I'm just not sure about that name."

Vincent looked up. I wondered how his father could have missed the irritation in his face. Or perhaps, I thought, he was used to having his son look at him like that and had ceased to notice.

"The name."

"Yes. I mean, Einstein's Bed—"

"Einstein's *Pillow*," Vincent said.

"Pillow, yes, of course. The point is, son, I'm not sure anybody will get it."

"I don't know what's so hard to get," Vincent said impatiently. "It's Einstein's Pillow. As in, the pillow belonging to Albert Einstein." He looked at his father, shrugged.

"Well, I don't know. Louise, you tell me—what do you think of it?"

"I think it's a great name. Einstein's Pillow. The place where Albert Einstein dreams. The place where he rests that magnificent brain of his. The place where he kisses his wife. Everything. I think it's a wonderful name."

I felt Vincent's eyes on me while I was talking. When I turned back to him, he was smiling.

"Well, you should get this little girl to write your ad copy. That was terrific. Anyway, I have to go say hello to some people. Good to see you, Louise. Vincent, we'll talk tomorrow."

Then we were alone again.

"Sorry about that."

"What?"

"My father. He called you a little girl."

"Oh," I said, "he didn't mean anything by it. Guys his generation, they forget the rules sometimes."

"That's no excuse. People cut him too much slack. I should have said something."

He stubbed the toe of his boot into the ground, like a kid who had lost a ball game. I tried to think of a different subject, something to get us back to where we'd been before, but then the keyboard player was there, pointing to his watch. Time for the second set.

"Nice meeting you," Vincent said. "I'm glad you like the music. There's more, you know, original stuff in the second set. My stuff. If you're interested."

"Oh, I am."

I assumed that I'd have plenty of chances to talk to him later as the evening was winding down. But by the time their next set started, the reception had shifted from a decorous art event to a lively, well-liquored party. No one was paying much attention to the band anymore. I heard only fragments of melodies, most I didn't recognize, and I wanted to stop and sit down and listen but there was too much going on, too many people in the way, for me to hear.

They broke the equipment down fast, and had carried most of it outside before I could get away from a lawyer who was trying to impress me with his admiration for Frida Kahlo. I reached the gallery door just in time to see Vincent and the keyboard player climb into a Jeep on the other side of the street and drive away.

After that, I stayed long enough for politeness's sake. Outside, a chilly wind was blowing, with the taste of snow to come. As I walked to my car, a familiar self-scolding kicked in. I should have stayed home, working. Instead I was here, keyed up, let down, alone, after an almost-conversation with a man who, despite his great beauty and obvious talent, was far too young for me. Georgia O'Keefe didn't waste her time at parties when there was work to be done. Stupid, stupid.

As I put the key in the car door, fuming at myself, a Jeep skidded to a stop next to mine. Vincent slipped out of the driver's seat and came bounding toward me.

"Hey, Louise," he said. "It's me. You said you liked it, so I thought, well, maybe you'd be…interested in this."

He handed me a flyer for a performance by Einstein's Pillow, a concert at the Stillmore Arts Center. A photo of the band showed all four of them looking very sleek and serious.

"We've got the whole night," he said. "We can do a lot more stuff than we could here. I think—I think you might like it."

"I'm sure I would," I said. "I'll try to make it. And thanks for bringing this by."

"No problem. I meant to give it to you, you know, earlier, but Jay was all freaked out about getting home early."

"Why? Does he turn into a pumpkin at midnight?"

He hesitated—he almost didn't get it—but then he broke out in a real laugh, deep and genuine. I wanted to make him do that again.

"His significant other kind of wishes that he did. I mean, turn into a pumpkin. He's been out a couple of nights this week past, like, three. Shawna was pretty twirled up about it."

He shook his head and said, with a fatalistic sigh, "Now he's trying to be good. Whatever. It can't last."

"It sounds like you don't have much faith in your friend."

"Jay's way talented. But he's got some very bad habits."

I thought of how he'd cut his best friend off at the mike earlier. And then, for some reason, I thought of Natalie.

"Collaborating can be hard," I said.

"It's cool," Vincent said. "It can be cool, anyway. As long as you have one person with final say. *Yes* or *no. This is the sound* or *this is not the sound.* A band leader, in the real sense."

"And that's you."

"Of course." He looked surprised that I would even need to say it.

It was getting colder. I wondered if we were just going to stand there like that beside our cars until we froze. The date on the flyer was more than two weeks away. It seemed a long time to wait before seeing him again, and even then, it wasn't a date. For all I knew, he was handing out flyers to women all over the city. Younger women, most likely.

And I had been hoping he'd ask for my phone number—after all, he'd come back to the gallery to give me the flyer himself. He could have mailed it. He must have wanted to see me, at least a little.

"It's still going on, you know. The party," I tried. "We could go back in, if you'd like a drink or something."

"Nah, that's cool," he said. "Anyway, I don't drink."

"You don't drink."

"Not alcohol."

"Not at all? No wine, no beer—nothing?"

"That's right."

I remembered seeing the rest of the band carrying drinks from the bar, not once but several times over the night.

"But the other guys," I began.

"Hey, as long as they can play, I don't care what they do," he said. "Me, I can pass. I've been drunk before, you know. A couple of times, when I was younger. I know what it's like. I don't need to do that now."

I tried to imagine what "younger" was for him. I thought of how much alcohol I'd put away in just the past few days. I tried to remember the last time I'd had sex with a man without having a few drinks first.

"Well," I said, going for my keys one more time, "I'll be seeing you then."

"At Stillmore?"

"I'll try."

"Please try," he said. "It would make everything great. It would make things just perfect. If you were there."

He smiled, tilting his head as if to say, *I know you want me and you know I want you.*

What happened then was very strange. As he walked away, Vincent's body seemed to shimmer, then dissolve into the air. Beneath or beyond it was something, no, someone else. A shorter man than Vincent, lighter haired, carrying some kind of small pack on his back. His bare feet were dirty. He smelled. There were leaves and clumps of mud in his hair. He looked one way then another before stepping out into the street.

I blinked, shook my head against the sight. I opened them just as Vincent swung his Jeep out into the street and disappeared into the blue-black night. I looked down at his face on the flyer, then back at the empty street. What was happening to me?

❆

WHEN THE PAINTING OF MY mother beside her empty altar was nearly done, I had started another, working from the photo of her on the hill with the other two women, Angie and the stranger. In the painting, they were no longer side by side with her but in the background, farther up the slope. I began to work into the unrelieved green of the grass, casting stones here and there. Still, there was something missing. I remembered that the box also had some books on medieval religious art and architecture, and though I had leafed though a few of them, I wasn't sure what, if anything, of importance lay in the print on those dull pages. But some of the images, drawings or photos of ruins, had been appealing. I wanted to see those again.

I opened the box again and began pulling out the old leather-bound books, one by one. I don't know what I was looking for, I only know that with each one I touched, I thought *no*, and then *no*, again, and laid each one aside. And then my hand found a thin book bound in blue leather, and began to tingle, as if I had touched the hand of someone I wanted, someone I loved.

4

he pages inside it were manuscript size and looked, from the deep impressions of each letter, to have been typed on a manual typewriter. There was no title page, no author's name.

Oxford, 1179

The boy can smell it before he sees its source—the stomach-twisting, sweet-sour smell of rotting flesh. He leans into his little horse for comfort. The horse, too, was a mistake, he sees that now. Sneaking out of his uncle's stables, he had thought only of speed and stealth, and the little hobby was light and quiet and knew him. When he joined up with the pair of older players who for nearly two moons were his performing and traveling companions, the horse again seemed right. People mistook Benedict for the son of the smaller, fairer man, and this aroused sympathy as well as enthusiasm for their music. The animal was right for a son, but for a man on his own? He is aware of how ridiculous he must look.

It was for the music's sake that he had first run away. It has been with him always, this gift, this curse. Tunes come to him as easily as leaves come to the trees; he keeps time evenly, and never has to count. When the two goliards had come to Evesham, he saw in them the skills he needed, and the life he lacked. They knew a handful of old ballads, but their strength and fame lay in the making of songs to suit whatever town they were in. They gathered gossip during the day in the streets and taverns, and gave it back to the townspeople at night in songs and jokes. They invited him to play one after-noon and that was that. The following night he snuck off to join them.

At first it was good. He was learning, he was making his music. This was what he wanted. But with the beginning of the warm weather, the two older men had begun to quarrel. First, it was something about a woman, then about a song, and then about money, until the thread of reason was lost. Two nights running they had let their quarrel seep into the show, exchang-ing words on the tiny stage between songs, then coming to blows. The crowd, full of eruptions of its own, had scarcely noticed it, or cheered it on, or thought it a part of the act. But Benedict saw the blade in the bigger man's hand and smelled danger, as he had in his uncle's house.

Last night while they slept, he took his share of the food, saddled his horse with the velvet touch he had learned, too, in his uncle's house, and slipped off again.

Hungry and aching, sores on his legs from the little horse, he distracts himself from his body and from the smell, stronger now, by humming bits of various tunes. In his bag, he carries three pipes, a drum, a wooden bowl strung with catgut, and a dozen other carved things that with his breath and fingers can be coaxed into music. Even now, he is tempted to stop, tie up the horse, take out his pipe, and see one song through. He knows this is his fault, his worst habit. Always, he will choose the tune over time or food or circumstance. He daydreams, his aunt used to say, like a rich man's son.

But Benedict cannot help his nature. He lives only for the music.

As he rounds the field, he sees the source of the rotten smell. Beneath a flapping mound of cloth, a pair of legs or what used to be legs emerge, gnawed at, nearer to meat than man. A few feet away, against the trunk of an oak, another rotting body is slumped. A crow picks at strings of flesh. Flies swarm the slices where the black blood shines and hardens.

Benedict's heart jerks up and down inside his chest. He wills himself not to be faint or sick. He chucks his horse hard in the side with his heels, and as he rides, he does not allow himself to look back.

Those wounds are old, he thinks. The murderer must already be far from here. All I have to do is get to town. In Oxford, there will be a fair, and people to hear my music, and food, and maybe a bed. All I have to do is get to town.

* * *

As BENEDICT TRIES TO CALM his racing heart, another solitary traveler is riding from the west toward the same town.

Brother Martin of Glastonbury Abbey is as comfortable in worldly things as Benedict is not. Wealthy by birth, he has risen to power, next in line only to his abbot, Robert; when he travels, he does so easily and well, staying at one comfortable abbey guesthouse, then another. He is a large man, with powerful hands and strong, thick-muscled arms and legs. His palfrey, an elegant animal, is as different as can be from the hobby carrying Benedict into town.

Martin is traveling from the abbey in York, where he was once a novice, back to Glastonbury, stopping off to visit another religious house in Oxford. This morning, he left the two young brothers he is traveling with at the guesthouse of a small monastery just outside of town. They are well meaning, but Martin is tired of their talk, and has, at any rate, no desire for an audience while he completes his task in Oxford.

He has always loved the company of the young. But that is one more thing that has changed with Brother William's death.

Grief, he thinks, is like a heavy cape, cut narrow, constricting the body, muffling the breath. Grief is muddy water one must swim through. Grief is a weight in the stomach, a hollowness in the heart, a dullness in the head. Grief creates its own separate, nighttime world. He wonders if he will ever return to the daylight, to the world where there are texts to study and arguments to have, students to teach and causes to advance.

Perhaps, he thinks, we live half in this world, and half in the other with our dead until we die, too. Perhaps it is the weight of those we have lost that pulls us, finally and entirely, to the other side. He does not know if this view of things is a comfort. He wishes, more than anything, that he had William here to talk with him about it.

Lost in his heart, he makes his way toward Dove Abbey, where he must tell the prioress that her protector and friend in York is dead.

* * *

SOMETIMES SHE THINKS HER BODY IS a cage of bones that will surely break from the beating of her heart's wings. For ten days, she has lain in the infirmary, besieged, awake and asleep, with nightmares. She has visions of a burning earth plagued with demons, a foul place where the good are wracked with suffering, while the evil swoop in the sky like crows, malevolent and sleek, pecking at the innocent, laughing at their pain.

Mother Elizabeth or Sister Christina are by her side always. They hold her hand. They want to know just what it is she sees. She is grateful for their presence, like a thread to tie her back to the world, to this life, for she sometimes thinks that she might slip over altogether into the world of visions. But when they ask her what she sees, it is hard to find words. They do not want to hear her say, *you cannot imagine it.* But when she can talk at all, that is what she wants to say.

She groans.

Mother Elizabeth wipes her forehead.

"Rest, child. Try to sleep."

Christina, on her knees, scrubs the bloody rags from another girl's courses in a bucket of soapy water. Margaret is not the only sister in her care. There are two others whose monthly bleeding seems to never stop, and another whose fever only last night began to break. But you would never know from the abbess's words or actions that there is anyone else for whom Christina must mix herbs and crush medicinal flowers, anyone else whose pain or recovery matter. Since the girl came to them, it is only Margaret, always Margaret.

"Christina," she says. "I must go now. Keep watch, and when she wakes, send for me."

Elizabeth stands aside while Christina pulls the infirmary door open for her. As the abbess walks out into the afternoon light, her foot catches on something. Around the door, the sisters have left offerings for Margaret's health and soul, little bundles of sweet grass and lavender, tiny dolls made of straw and marigolds, candles, medals. The sort of thing that could make a girl too proud, and others jealous. She shakes the trinkets off her shoe, turns back to the half-open door.

"Christina, come clean this up."

Christina hurries outside with her pail and broom.

In the beginning, Margaret had seemed a gift to the abbey. Once the grime and worse of her former life had been washed away, she was revealed to be a plain, serious girl, solemn, slow to smile. She was wary, she did not try to charm with smiles or obedient eyes. But she also did not chatter or steal food or try to turn one girl against another. If she was, at first, almost too given to silence, Elizabeth thought it must be the result of what horrors the child had seen.

The tale of the dead mother, almost certainly a lie, told by the wretched, filthy aunt. There must have been some grace present at Margaret's conception that marked her for a different life. She must have always been the Lord's Child.

Just as Elizabeth had come to think this way, Margaret had changed. Agatha caught her more than once in the refectory, gulping at a pitcher of milk until it seemed she would drown herself. Christina had found her twice by the south well, scrubbing her own flesh until it broke and bled. Feverish, she cried out so often in her dreams that she had to be moved to the infirmary in order to let the other girls sleep. When she woke, she babbled nonsense, clutched at any hand. Now, Elizabeth had given orders for her never to be left alone.

She knew she should appeal to the bishop for help, or at least ask William for counsel. But she did not want to write of what was happening—there was no messenger she could trust—and she was not sure what she would say. Even if an escort could be found, she could not leave the abbey now. And so she put off her deciding and her acting, day to day.

I will take from you even that which you hold dearest. Was that the Lord's lesson?

She was near her quarters now, and began to think of the treat she might allow herself tonight. On William's last visit, he had given her a bottle of liqueur, sweet with a bitter aftertaste, the color of spring grass. They had shared small cups of it— "It is to be savored," he told her, "take it slowly"—the night before he returned to York. They had talked until the sky began to lighten, and the hours had passed like seconds. If she allowed herself to miss anyone, it would be him, now. But drinking the gift he gave her sometimes made him feel more near.

She hears a flurry of girls' voices, excited, coming from the west side of the grounds. It is the kind of show of temperament that she must correct and she is torn, knowing that it is her duty to attend the matter, but longing now for her room, for that drink. But before she can make up her mind, Sister Agatha is at her side.

A monk at the gate asks to be admitted. His name is Martin. He comes from York.

William. Elizabeth feels the thud of presentiment in her heart, a knot in her throat. She knows without knowing what it is the man has come to tell her, and as she moves toward the gate—her stride so long that Agatha, two decades her junior, cannot keep up—the younger women blush and bless themselves and fall back to their tasks, embarrassed by her naked worry and pain.

She has not seen Martin since he was brought here as a boy, on a visit with his teacher. He still has the plump smooth face that she remembers. He has gone on to great things.

He steps toward her, drops to one knee at her feet, kisses the ring that William gave her. The seal of her abbey. A dove in the center of a cross.

"May the Lord be with you, madam."

His eyes confirm what she already knows.

"He is gone."

"Yes. How did you…"

"I knew. I knew."

"He said you could speak without words. But I did not know how far your sight extended."

"He always made of me more than I was."

"That was the gift he gave. To all of us."

Later, Martin sits with the abbess in her quarters, talking of William. On the table between them, a girl has placed some dried apples, a hard loaf of bread, and a pitcher of watered, vinegary wine. He thinks of the good wine, the sausages and puddings of the abbot's guest table at Glastonbury, and is ashamed. William had warned him of being too attached to the things of this world. He had been right; it seems he had been right in everything.

"Tell me," the abbess says, "how did it come? His death." Her voice shakes a little, then smooths. "I saw him just after the turn of the year. He was not ill, not then."

"No one could have foreseen it. He was in the garden, talking to Thomas, when it happened. A sudden pain, he said, sharp and repeating, in his side. We were able to bring him to his bed, but he never walked again."

"You were there."

"It was by chance. I had gone to York for, oh, various things. I was beside him when he fell."

As I should have been, she thinks.

"How was he? After?"

"Clear as the light. He was teaching until the end, calling his boys around him."

"He was a good man."

"He was the best man that I have ever known."

There is a pause. She feels outbid. Martin speaks again.

"The support of York for Dove Abbey will continue. He was clear on that. He spoke of you at the end."

"He spoke of me."

"Yes. He said that you had been, for many years, his dearest friend. And that he missed you, lady."

Elizabeth looks down at her folded arms.

"As I miss him."

They sit awhile in silence. It is getting dark outside, and the room is cooling fast. Martin rises and goes to stand by the casement in the last light, where he can see a slice of the abbey grounds. The abbess's quarters overlook the cloister; at its entrance, two young women are on their knees, scrubbing the stone steps, their faces uncomplaining, even joyful. Despite the rule of silence, he is sure that he could just hear, on the air, the sound of one of them humming. Her voice is high, not strong, but very sweet.

"William said you had made something beautiful here, madam. It is true."

He has thought to lighten her mood with the compliment, but it only seems to darken her.

"It is nowhere near my imagining. We ran out of stone before the Lady Chapel was half done. The men ran off. The cloister flooded this spring, and Christina complains to me constantly about the floors, the damp, her needs for the infirmary. We are always running to catch up to where we ought to be."

And I am no longer young, she thinks. *I want to rest.*

Instead she adds, "With William gone, I do not know who will help me."

"You might ask the archbishop for help, lady."

"The archbishop could stitch together a warm cloak from the letters I have sent him."

Martin turns from the window, looks at her. "Perhaps I might write to him."

"You think he will be more inclined to hear your voice than mine?"

"I am sure your own words are far more beautiful, madam. But the archbishop is my father's cousin."

Outbid, again. How this man, unthinking, could diminish her. How it galls that she could not afford to refuse his help.

"It would be a great kindness to us if you would write to him, then. About the chapel. And the floors."

"And all the rest. I have business in town today," he says, "but if you will allow me, I will return this evening. We will make a list of your needs, and I will send it to him."

"And he will respond?"

"If he does not, I will call on him myself."

"You are too kind."

"It is as William would have wanted it. And it will be an honor to serve you, Mother, and your abbey."

She feels a sudden generous impulse, the reverse of how she had felt toward him the moment before. She reaches for his hand.

"William would have been proud of you," she says.

"That is all I have to live for, now."

* * *

INSIDE THE CITY, THE NARROW streets are packed full of carts and bodies, all jostling along in loud concurrence. Listening, Benedict learns that he was right; the horse fair begins tomorrow. His hopes rise, then fall. Yes, the buyers and sellers would want entertainment, but surely there are players who have already staked out their favorite spots, as well as their beds. Finding a place to play, or a place to sleep, would not be easy now.

The crowd thickens. He dismounts, and leads his horse through the swarm of bodies. He feels a hand slip down his leg toward his purse; he swats it away, only to feel another skimming over his belt, looking for buttons or clasps, something of value. Someone bumps him from behind, and he turns to see a leering face that sticks out its tongue at him before disappearing into the jumble of the crowd.

A narrow alley on his left shows a bit of light at the end, blue sky, brown grass. There are far fewer bodies down that street, and he turns onto it, taking one deep breath, then another.

Martin, meanwhile, is walking south, toward the center of town. In the days since William's death he has found that his grief is of the mobile kind; it longs to move, to walk. If he holds still for too long, his mind begins to feed on itself, to torment him. And so he has excused himself from the abbess on the pretext of having other business in the town. He would see her again at the evening meal. He would do whatever he could to help her. But he could not bear the closeness of her abbey walls for long. The whole of it made Glastonbury Abbey look as big as London.

How do they manage it, he wonders, being held in a cage so tiny? How do they not go mad? But then, women had the gift of contentment. Would that he had it, now.

All around him the street is humming with life and merriment, but none of it reaches him. He has, by nature, a lively interest in the affairs of men, and William had taught him to know that interest as holy. It was, he said, an outgrowth of Christ's dictum to love others as we do ourselves. William could talk with anyone, listen to anyone, as could his pupil. But it seems that, without his teacher, Martin has changed in that way, too. The merchants he passes call out to him, offering beer, bacon, and cider, as well as stories of the horses for sale the next day. Once, he would have laughed with them, bargained, told stories of his own. But now it is all too much, the smell of the streets a stench, the scent of cooking fowl and pigs oppressive, sickening.

William had been weakening for some time. He should have found reasons to see him. He should have gone without being asked. Instead, he had chosen to stay in Glastonbury, promote his own causes. More than two years had passed without their seeing each other. William had never complained of neglect and there were, as always, many young brothers who were devoted to him. Martin had consoled himself that his teacher was well cared for, and gone on.

What a fool I am, he thinks. I am not half of what he was, and yet I had ambitions.

Meanwhile, Benedict reaches the end of the alley, and sees before him, past the brown expanse of land and a stand of elms, the rush of the river in the sunlight. The air is cooler here, and he feels his body, which has for hours gripped itself close and tight, relax a little. He thinks of the dried beef and bread in his bag, the wineskin he filled in the night. He decides that it is time to rest, to eat.

He ties his horse to one of the trees, brings him a pail of river water, two fistfuls of hay. Then he carries his lunch to the riverbank and sits on a flat low stone to eat. He cautions himself to save, and at first cuts only a sliver of meat, measures out only a small portion of the bread. But hunger intervenes, and soon he is eating heartily and taking comforting swallows of wine.

As Benedict tucks away the rest of his food, he remembers the tune that had begun to come to him this morning. He reaches into his satchel and takes out a half-circle of wood, strung with bells, with a wide notch cut into its center, and a long pipe with several holes of different widths. He walks back toward the bank again and tosses the bell-ring on the ground, then slides the toe of his right boot through the notch. He taps his foot, counts out three, six, twelve. He raises the pipe to his lips.

Martin, walking quickly with his head tilted down, ignoring the press of eyes around him—the merchants, the drunks, the beggars—hears the first notes without knowing that he hears them. It is not until Benedict has completed the whole of the melody's first cycle that Martin recognizes what he hears as music and moves toward it. He turns east, moving closer to the sound over rough stones, long ignored, that wind between two shabby inns where students stay. He has friends here, he remembers, but does not stop. What he is hearing is too beautiful to relinquish. He must find its source.

He steps out onto the grass and sees, near the riverbank, a boy, fair-haired and narrowly built, playing a pipe. His foot moves up and down, carrying, Martin now sees, a ring of bells. It seems that the boy is conjuring bright spirits out of the ground with his gentle taps, pulling them up and through his body, turning them, with a breath, into music.

Martin moves closer, very slowly, as if he were moving toward a wild, unsuspecting animal. He does not want the boy to see him, for if he does, he might stop playing. It has become essential to Martin that the boy keep playing.

The sound of Benedict's pipe and bells have not relieved him of his grief, but rather, made a space beside it for something else to speak. He is still aching, but there is part of him that has been lightened, too. There is room inside the human heart to love such beauty, even in the face of death. And what the boy is making is very beautiful.

Suddenly, two other boys stumble onto the grass, disrupting the scene. Benedict is facing away from them, his back to the slanting sun, and in any case is blocked by the grove of trees and so does not see them. But Martin does, and knows, even before the two make hushing sounds at each other and begin to move, too quietly, toward Benedict's horse, that they have no good in mind. He picks up his pace.

Just then, Benedict halts, slips on a note, then takes the pipe away from his lips to shake the spittle out. As he does so, he hears the rustling and turns around.

The boys are at the animal fast, struggling to untie it while Benedict scrambles toward them, dropping his pipe. The bigger boy turns and throws him to the ground.

"So the lady has a pipe, eh? She makes a song?"

Benedict begins to rise. The boy kicks him in the side, once, twice.

And then Martin is there.

"And what do you think to do here, lads?"

The two boys look up at the big man with the frightening voice, and both want to run. The smaller one makes to, but Martin catches him by the back of the neck and holds him, close and wriggling, while the other, the leader, sneers an answer.

"Our job, you know. Finding stolen horses."

Benedict was now at Martin's side.

"Sir," he begins.

"No apologies now, my boy. The music called you away. You are forgiven."

Benedict looks at him with confused eyes. Martin tries to urge him, with a look, to go along.

"We will talk later. For now, the bishop will want a word with these two, who have tried to steal the property of Our Lord and His Church."

The thieves look from Martin to Benedict, taking in the wealth of the former's clothes. Benedict was no better off than themselves, and two against one should always win. But they had not meant to steal a rich priest's horse. Though they are not sure that God exists, they still do not want to anger Him.

But the bigger one decides to play for larger stakes.

"Your bishop might want us rather than this lady," he says, gesturing to Benedict. "Nothing between those legs, I reckon, save for—"

Before he can finish, Martin swings his heavy, ringed right hand out fast, striking the boy flat across the face, knocking him to the ground.

There is a sound of something shattering into wetness, and the boy falls onto the grass, rolling, clutching his nose. Benedict jumps back as if he himself has been hit, opens his mouth, then closes it. The younger one, still in Martin's grasp, looks down at his friend for guidance and whimpers.

The monk tosses him to the ground like a sack of bad apples, delivers one fierce kick that sends the boy sprawling. He scrambles to his feet and runs.

"And you," Martin says, advancing on the other one, "I will teach you the difference between men and women."

The blood is boiling in his brain. The vicious thing cowering on the ground, blood spurting between his fingers, must be beyond Christ's love. What matter could it be if he kicked and beat it, showed it how he had felt when the music had been snatched away?

The boy looks up, his eyes pleading, all insolence gone.

Then Benedict is between them.

"Sir! No," he says, tugging on Martin's upraised arm. "Please, no!"

Martin looks at him as if from far away.

"What, boy?"

"If you do not stop, you will kill him."

It is the boy, the one with the pipe, who has spoken. But it sounded for all the world like William's voice.

Martin steps back, loses his footing a little, and reels, returning now, dizzy and overwhelmed, to where he is. Benedict holds onto his arm. The thief, still on the ground, holds his shattered nose together, breathing through his mouth. Benedict wonders why he does not run.

"Go," Martin says then, looking down.

The thief hesitates, shaking.

"Go *now*," Martin says, more loudly. And at that, the boy feels around with one hand for the ground beneath him, and, still protecting his nose with the other, half-scrabbles and half-crawls across the grass and away from the river.

Martin looks out across the grass to where Benedict had been standing when he played. He breathes in and out, once, twice.

"You dropped your pipe," he says.

"I have many pipes but only one horse," Benedict replies. "I am in your debt, sir."

"Oh, you might have fought them," Martin says.

"Two against one?"

"The younger was weak and stupid, too. The other—well, you see what I made of him."

"But I am not you, sir."

"Nor am I you. If I were, I might make of those simple tools," and here he gestures to Benedict's abandoned instruments, "the heaven that you make."

Benedict looks at him. The murderous fellow of a moment before was now replaced by this large, kind man. He does not know which to believe. He believes in both of them.

"Would you like to hear more, sir?" he asks. "I was just beginning, really."

"Well, then, if you would like an audience, I will stay and hear the middle. And the end."

As soon as the words are said, the boy is off across the grass, running to retrieve his instruments while Martin watches.

* * *

SOMETIME LATER, THE TWO MAKE their way, with Benedict leading his horse, north and east toward Dove Abbey. It has been agreed that Benedict's music, so soothing to Martin, might also have a good effect on the abbess, who after all is suffering from the same blow. Tomorrow, they say, they will most likely part ways, Brother Martin off to Glastonbury with his boys, Benedict off to who knew where.

Martin has just begun to describe the comfort and compan-
ionship that might be available to Benedict should he choose to
proceed to Glastonbury, too. It is a good town. The monks are
kind, the abbey rich. But such a thing, if it were to happen, must
seem to be the boy's idea.

Martin cannot say, *you are too soft for the road.* He cannot
say, *on your own for a night and a day and look what might
have happened.* He does not want to insult Benedict, the source
of the music.

Tonight, it will be enough to share his discovery with the
abbess. Tonight, after supper, Benedict will play for them.

As they approach the abbey, the grounds are as still as a
breath held in. Martin imagines the sisters inside, praying over
their chores. Benedict, who knows nothing of abbeys, is thinking of where he might go tomorrow. He likes the priest who,
after all, has saved his horse, which is near to saving his life. He
wonders if he might travel along with him for a few more days.
His attempt at self-sufficiency has so far not gone well.

The two men and the horse stop at the abbey gate. The sky
is a rich blue, pitted with stars. Martin reaches for the brass bell
that will summon Sister Agatha.

"Look," says Benedict. Martin's hand stops.

On the other side of the gate, a few yards away, a creature,
no, a girl, is moving, seemingly busy about some task. Martin
would guess that she is no more than ten or eleven years old, her
body still straight as a boy's in its thin shift. She must be cold,
he thinks, but the girl does not look cold at all. Her face is red.
She is murmuring something rapidly to herself as she moves,
bending and straightening again.

She is arranging, he sees now, a pile of stones to make some
shape. They must be, he thinks, the stones intended for the
unfinished Lady Chapel.

Her voice is louder now. Martin can make out just a few
words.

"She is," Benedict begins.

"Shhh," says Martin.

"Safe," says the girl. Then more muttering; then, "Only this
corner, this is Her corner."

Then, "Cannot get me. Cannot. In the Mother's arms."

"What is she doing?" Martin whispers, not expecting an answer. But Benedict's voice comes back to him, firm and low.

"Making refuge," he says.

Martin wants to ask him what he means, but now the girl's voice is louder, her movements more frantic.

"Must hurry, hurry," she says. "They are coming. Coming."

She settles down on the ground in the middle of what looked to Martin to be a somewhat irregular, elongated circle of stones. Sitting, she draws her knees in tight to her chest, places the last stone beneath her feet and holds herself tight.

"Safe now. Safe," she says, and, sighing a long sigh, buries her head in her arms.

"She is," Benedict tries again, but again, Martin motions him to be silent, gesturing toward the infirmary door which now swings open, and out of which the abbess and Sister Christina emerge.

"I told you," the abbess is saying, in a low, harsh voice that would hurt more, Benedict thinks, than his uncle's switch, "not to let her out of your sight. Not for one moment. No. And what did you do?"

"She was asleep," Christina says. "There were others to tend to. I thought she would sleep for a long time. She always does, you know, after—"

"Always? No, not always. She is not sleeping now, is she?"

"No, but she might—"

"She might be what? She might be where? A sick girl, wandering, alone. Your sister."

"Please, I was only—oh! Oh, look!"

Christina points to the silent figure huddled inside the circle of stones. Mother Elizabeth follows her gaze, and then is across the grass and at Margaret's side.

"My dear," she says, crouching low to wrap her arms around the girl. "My angel, angel child. I am here. I am here."

The girl accepts the embrace, allows herself to be folded, like a cloth doll, into the abbess's arms. Christina stands back a little, watching, before turning and disappearing into the abbey grounds.

The abbess helps the girl to her feet and as she does, she sees, over Margaret's shoulder, Martin and Benedict standing on the other side of the gate watching her.

She opens her mouth as if to speak, but then the girl heaves and sighs, forward and back, and the lady must struggle to hold onto her. Martin steps forward, as if to reach across the gate to help her.

"I will send Agatha to let you in," she says, not looking at Benedict, then turns and makes her way off across the grass with her charge.

Martin shakes his head, folding his hands behind his back.

"What," he says, "in the name of God our Father was that?"

"I know her," Benedict says.

"The abbess?"

"No, not her. The girl."

Martin looks at him.

"You know that child?"

"Yes. We were born in the same town."

"When did you see her last?"

"A long time now. Since spring, anyway. Maybe winter. I went off, like I said."

He had not told Martin of stealing his uncle's horse, but most of the rest.

"What do you know of her?"

"Her father died a long time ago. My aunt told me that, anyway. She said he was a bad man, but Margaret—Margaret was always good."

He pauses, looks down, goes on.

"She did not have an easy life."

Martin turns and looks at the circle of stones the girl has made.

"What was not easy?" he asked.

"They never cared what they did to her. They blamed her for everything. Sick pigs. A blight. A stillborn child."

"Blamed her?" Martin asks. The stones remind him of something; he has seen something of their shape, that pattern, somewhere before. Right now, he is trying very hard to remember just what and where that was. But he also knows that he should be listening to the boy.

"For everything," Benedict says again. "It was so easy. Every time something went wrong. 'There she goes,' they would whisper, 'giving us the evil eye. There she goes, throwing her curses over us. The witch's daughter.'"

5

In the daylight, I found the entrance to Fellowship House with no trouble. After a few days with my mother's books and papers, I needed some input from an expert in religious matters. So I'd taken Brother Paul up on his offer of a hike.

When I pulled into the parking lot at Fellowship House, the spaces were nearly all taken. I followed the flow of traffic down the front hall and turned left into the big room where they'd been setting out rows of folding chairs when I was there before. Now the chairs were pushed up against the walls, and everyone was milling around a long table in the center of the room filled with platters of doughnuts and muffins and big coffee urns. I remembered Brother Paul's sweet tooth.

Maybe this is what really religious people do, I thought; they sublimate their baser urges, give them over to sugar. Looking around, I saw no sign of Brother Paul.

All around me people were greeting each other, embracing. It was hard to tell who might be a monk or priest or nun from who might not—everyone seemed to be dressed plainly in navy blue or black, and nearly everyone had a cross or crucifix around his or her neck. My jeans were quite a bit more snug than anyone else's trousers, and only a few of the women wore any makeup at all. I'm not shy, but I felt awkward and out of place in this fresh-faced bunch.

I turned to leave the room, deciding to look for Paul in his office. But just inside the door, a gray-haired lady in a baggy blue suit stepped up to me, and put her hand on my arm, as if we were old friends.

"If I were you I'd grab some breakfast now, my dear," she said. "There's no telling how fast these scavengers will exhaust the provisions."

"Excuse me?"

She pointed to the people massed around the food tables.

"You'd think they never saw doughnuts before," she sighed. "Well, at least it'll keep them awake through Father Lewis's talk. Goodness knows, they'll need fortification for that."

I laughed. She looked like somebody's spinster aunt, with her chubby face, short sensible hair, and rubber-soled shoes, but her eyes were mischievous and much younger in spirit than her wrinkles suggested.

"Nice to meet you," I said, and put out my hand. "I'm Louise Terry."

"And I'm Kathy Morgan," she said. Instead of shaking hands, she took mine in both of hers and held it there, as Brother Paul had.

"Sister Kathy Morgan. Glad to have you to Fellowship House. Are you here for the hospice volunteers meeting?"

"Actually, Brother Paul invited me. We're supposed to go hiking."

She patted me on the shoulder.

"You'll find him outside, my dear. I gave him a little chore to do. He's in the back garden."

She gave me directions for navigating to the kitchen door, and soon I was outside again, on a flagstone patio lined with statues of Christ, the Blessed Mother, and various saints. In front of each there was a clay candleholder, and as I stepped outside, Brother Paul was crouched in front of one of them, cleaning it with a rag. Then he put a new candle in, and stood up to move onto the next. Then he saw me.

"Louise. So good to see you again."

"You, too."

I had forgotten how beautiful his smile was. As I stepped closer, he held out his dirty hands.

"I can't touch, I am filthy. But let me finish my task and we will talk. Just one more to go."

Paul upended the candle bowl, and bits of leaves and sticks tumbled out. He wiped the inside of the holder, righted it, and cleaned the outside.

"Sister Kathy had hoped I would have this done earlier. But to her everlasting displeasure I am not, nor have I ever been, a morning person."

"I just met Sister Kathy. She was great."

"Ah, yes. She has her volunteers meeting."

He dropped a new candle into the holder and stood up, brushing off his hands with the rag.

"And since I managed to alienate her old professor last night, she thought perhaps it would be best to get me out of the way."

"Her old professor?"

"Father Lewis. He's her hero."

"But she said—"

I looked at Paul. His face showed no sign that he was joking.

"What did she say?" he asked.

"Oh, never mind," I said. "You mean, you're being punished?"

"In a sense, perhaps. But now it is done. I'll go wash my hands, and then we'll go for a walk."

He returned with a backpack slung over his shoulders, and led me down a path to the edge of the grounds of Fellowship House, and then into the woods.

I had brought along with me the manuscript of the musician and the monk, hoping Paul might help me make sense of it, and of other things. But talking was not possible, at least on our way up the hill. He set out at so brisk a pace that our brief exchanges—about the foliage, which really was gorgeous, so many variations and gradations of gold to red to brown—soon gave way to a stream of observations and remarks from only him. I had to conserve all my breath just to keep up. Each time I adjusted to his pace, he quickened it a little, so that by the time we reached the crest of the mountain next to the one on whose side the buildings of Fellowship House were set, sweat dotted my face, pooled in the curve of my back, the insides of my thighs.

Paul seemed oblivious to my discomfort, continuing to point out all the while the various features of the mountain—owls' nests, the remains of a nineteenth-century one-room schoolhouse, mountain pines. His knowledge of the place might have impressed me more had I been able to concentrate on what he was saying. But I was distracted by my body—my calves ached, my jeans chafed, and I could feel a blister beginning on one heel.

The top of the mountain was scattered with pink and white boulders. Paul was explaining what kind of rock it was—quartzite, typical of the Piedmont region—when I collapsed onto one of the biggest boulders.

"If I had known," I said, "that I was coming out here for aerobics, I might have brought some water."

"Oh, I am sorry, Louise. I've been thoughtless. Here."

He lowered his backpack onto another boulder, unzipped it, pulled out two water bottles, and handed one to me.

"They were nearly frozen when we left. It should still be cold."

I downed nearly a third of it before I stopped to thank him.

"That's delicious," I gulped.

"It's been in my pack all this time. You should have said something. All you had to do was ask."

I splashed some water onto my hand, ran it over my face and neck. I'd long ago forgone any notion of keeping my makeup intact. He reached into the pack again, tossed me a paper napkin.

"Your shoes misled me, I suppose," he said. "Vasque, aren't they? A good brand. I took you for an experienced hiker."

"These? They were a gift from my old—from my ex. My ex-fiancé. He was always dragging me to obscure places where he was shooting. I needed tough shoes."

"To shoot? As in hunting?"

"As in film. He's a cinematographer. He makes documentaries about endangered places."

"Well, that sounds interesting."

"It was. I mean, is. I mean, he's very good. He's won all kinds of awards."

It was a reflex I couldn't seem to shake. By the time we broke up, I could barely stand to be in the same room with Jason. But whenever his name came up, I still couldn't stop myself from telling people how good he was at what he did.

"That sounds like quite an achievement," Paul said.

"Yes."

"If you don't mind my asking—how long ago was it? When you separated, I mean."

"Let's see, it must have been—well, a little over four months ago."

"I am sorry, Louise," he said, so tenderly that I thought, for one horrified moment, that I might cry. For a guy I didn't love or want anymore, and I'd hurt so badly.

"Don't be," I said, quickly. "I've made a lot of changes lately. In my life. But I wanted it that way. And besides, that's not what I came here to talk about."

I thought he'd ask me one of his gentle questions, but instead he began rooting around in his pack again. He pulled out foil-wrapped packages, a paper bag spilling with pale yellow apples, and more napkins.

"I brought lunch," he said. "A couple of different kinds of sandwiches. And these apples. And some chocolate, for after."

"Sweets."

"Of course. Fruit doesn't count, you know. It's too good for you."

He slid up onto the rock next to mine, spread out the picnic. The sandwiches were thick, some with chicken salad and lettuce, some with cheese and tomatoes. I realized how hungry I was.

"Thank you," I said. "For thinking of this."

All around us, there were those small sounds—of wind, of falling leaves, of the last of the insects humming their way around and over us—that blended into something bigger, as if the mountain itself were breathing beneath us. My shoulders loosened. My legs didn't ache anymore.

"So," he said, "what did you want to talk about, Louise?"

I told him about the journal, the bound manuscript about the monk and the musician and the nuns. And I told him, too, about the reading I'd been doing since we last met, following Mom's underlinings in some of the scholarly books in the box. Nearly all of them referred to a twelfth-century nun, a Saint Margaret.

"Near as I can tell," I said, "She might not even have really existed. One scholar says it's all apocryphal. Another says she really existed, and had these extraordinary visions, and even quotes some of her writings. Stuff about a lady coming to her, and climbing a hill. It didn't make much sense to me, and evidently the source text is in a library in England somewhere, and in Latin, which I can't read. And there's a floppy disk, too. The old kind."

I had found it tucked in the back of the bound manuscript.

"No one I know has a computer like that anymore, I don't even know if they exist. And I keep wondering, what did she expect me to do with all of this? What's it *for?*"

"Is it possible to accept that she wanted you to have it, without knowing why?"

"I don't know. I don't know."

"Well, one thing I do know," he said. "If you want that floppy disk read, we can probably do it right here. One thing we have no shortage of is ancient computer equipment. Sister Kathy, like Tom before her, uses everything until it collapses or bursts into flame."

"How did you come to be *here*, anyway?" I asked, meaning, in the priesthood.

"I met Thomas at a conference in Nicaragua. I was working in Brazil then, in Salvador."

This was a surprise. With his pale skin and even, uninflected voice, Paul looked to me like he'd been born for temperate weather. But then, there was the way he'd climbed that mountain.

"What did you do there?"

"There was a small community there, a group of good theologians. Committed to the care of our parishioners' lives as well as their souls. It was work, real and honest work, of the kind that few of my brethren seem interested in these days. But then, you didn't come here to be bored by a lecture on liberation theology."

"I couldn't be bored by it. I don't even know what it is."

"It's actually very simple. Liberation theology is based on the premise that when Christ said, 'Whatsoever you do to the least of my brethren, that you do unto me,' He meant it. In other words, pray with and for them, yes. But feed the hungry. Shelter the homeless."

"Well, that sounds completely reasonable."

"Ah, but you are not a bishop. The higher one climbs, the less clear some things might seem—especially the plight of certain people who live, shall we say, very close to the ground."

He shook his head.

"I had begun to despair, to feel distant, estranged from my own order, my own beliefs. Thomas said he thought I should come here after he'd known me for—well, not even an hour. He said, 'You are too angry. This will cool you. This will instruct you.' Meaning this sky," Paul said, gesturing up and then down in the open air. "This ground."

"And was he right?"

"I am still in the cooling process, I guess you could say. But yes, I am learning. I will have to learn faster, now that he is gone."

"You must miss him."

"I miss him every minute," he said, "of every single day. As you must miss her."

"Funny you say that." All of a sudden, out of nowhere, I was angry. Not at him, but at her.

"I'm through missing her. I did all my missing years ago, when she was alive. That's all we ever did, was miss her."

I stopped, then started again.

"She said I always hated her for leaving. But it's not that. OK, so everybody's human, they make mistakes, I *know*. But she left and came back and left again and even while she was with us you could always tell she had one foot out the door. *No*, she didn't belong with us. *No*, she didn't want to be there. But instead of just admitting it and moving on, she kept bouncing back and forth like— like a goddamn Ping-Pong ball. 'Oh, I need to be away for a while,' and then, 'Oh, John, I want to come back now,' and then, 'Oh, I was wrong, I've got to go.' Like the only thing that mattered was *her* feelings, what *she* wanted."

I could feel my voice starting to rise and I made myself stop, take a deep breath, before going on.

"Did you know that she actually tried to get back together with Dad one more time? Angie died over there, you know, in France, and Mom and the writer had broken up, and I guess she just had nowhere else to go. After all that. After all that, she still expected him to take her back again. And you know, I think he would have done it. I'm glad about Carrie for that, anyway. If Dad hadn't already proposed to her, I think he might have done it."

"He sounds like a good man, your father."

"When I was a kid, I thought he was the greatest man in the world. He was the one who taught me how to draw. And paint. But oh, she worked him over. She could get him to put up with anything. And I remember thinking, you know, when I was like thirteen, *I will never let any-body do this to me. I don't give a shit what people call love.* My father loved my mother and it destroyed him, it destroyed him. It wasted years of his life and did him no fucking good. I said to myself, screw love. I'm going to be a painter. Screw love."

I realized I was crying, very softly. The tears were slow and easy. I didn't sob. It did not hurt. I hadn't cried like that since the evening of my mother's funeral, when Dylan and I sat on the porch outside Kenny's house crying silently, continually, occasionally taking each other's hand or patting each other's shoulder, for what felt like hours.

Brother Paul didn't pat my shoulder or hold my hand. But he did hand me some paper napkins from his pack, and waited, and he let me cry and did not say a word, only looked at me in that tender, serious way he had until my tears began to subside. I blew my nose, wiped my face.

"Jesus, I'm sorry. About the language and everything. And the weeping."

"Please stop apologizing, Louise. I have heard people swear before. And seen them cry. These are all things that friends share with each other."

"Friends. Is that what we are?"

"Of course! We have been called into friendship by the deaths of those we loved. Thomas and Margaret. They gave us this gift."

"I hadn't thought about it like that," I said. "But it makes sense."

I wiped my eyes again. I had stopped crying completely now.

"'Called into friendship.' I like that."

"I do, too," he said. "So please, no more apologies."

"It's a deal," I said.

"Good, good." He was looking away, toward where the sun was beginning to move slowly toward the earth.

Before I could say anything he was rummaging around in his pack again.

"I almost forgot," he said. "Dessert."

He pulled out two thick dark chocolate bars, and handed one to me. We sat and ate in contented silence. I thought that priests took vows of poverty, but this was expensive stuff, creamy and bitter and very sweet, with a foreign name.

"Brother," I asked between bites, "what do you think it means when people have visions?"

"Ah, mysticism is not my strong point. But I think we all from time to time have something like visions. We feel something, see something that hints at a world beyond this one. I would think, though I'm guessing now, that artistic inspiration is something like that."

"It can be. A lot of times, it's just work—thinking through a composition, mixing colors. And then sometimes, it just all comes together. You're flying. It's happening."

"Funny. I wouldn't have guessed it. But your vocation is not unlike mine, Louise."

"Except for the source. The source of artistic inspiration can be anything. But if you're a Catholic, the spirit comes from God, right?"

"You speak as though you were never Catholic."

"Well, I haven't practiced since I was, oh, I don't know, thirteen or fourteen. It was Mom who took it...seriously."

"Well then, I would say that in any case, inspiration comes from the divine. Meaning, for me, God, and for you whatever you conceive as your sustenance and your source. Whatever is eternal. Remember, Louise, someone else would give you a far different interpretation. A psychoanalyst might speak of the collective unconscious. Or a wise Greek might speak of the old gods. I can only speak as who I am. A man. A Catholic monk. And your friend."

We gathered the remains of our feast, and Paul tucked them into his pack. We headed down the mountain, sharing the last bottle of water as we went. At the door to my car, he invited me to come back again, perhaps for another hike. Then he did something that I still shiver to remember. He reached out, and with the thumb of his right hand, rubbed a small cross into my forehead. The he took my head in his hands, and kissed the spot where his thumb had been. As his lips touched my skin I felt my forehead grow warm beneath them and then that warmth spread, like a disturbance in a pond, through my body.

"For the paintings," he said.

When I got home, I looked in the mirror and saw that I was, indeed, flushed, and that my eyes were over-bright. I looked, in fact, like someone who had just fallen in love. Or perhaps not quite. It was more, I think, that I saw a reflection of Brother Paul in my eyes. I did not believe in his God, but I could believe in the man I'd met, and in his goodness. Maybe some of it might even rub off on me.

Called into friendship. Of course.

✳

"So, I take it you've got some good news to share with me, Louie?"

Natalie and I were sitting on the floor of my studio, picking at the Middle Eastern feast she'd brought in her backpack—hummus, tabouli, baba ghanoush, flatbread, and wine.

"Why do you say that?"

"I saw Tim Gould a few days ago, and he said you're going to sign with Reilly Gallery. Congratulations, Louie."

"I have not been signed to Reilly Gallery. Jesus, Tim Gould—is there some reason we've let that little fucker live?"

"Overall, he likes us," Nat said calmly. "Likes the Place, I mean. And your work, and mine. You two just have issues."

"We do not have issues. Other than that he's an asshole. And no, I am not signed to Reilly Gallery. Dana is interested. That's all."

"Well, that is good news."

"Maybe. Perhaps."

"Louise, listen to me. You don't have to be so secretive about it. I assumed you were looking for another place to show as soon as you told me you were leaving the Place."

"I know. I just...well, well, we weren't getting along too well right then. I could tell you were angry with me."

"Angry? No. But worried, Louie. Because *you* seemed so angry. All the time. Over things that just...just shouldn't have mattered to you so much."

"Look, if you're talking about the Barbie installation, I still think it's...well, shit."

"I know. But that's what the collective was for. That's why we founded the Place that way. So that no one person's taste or opinions could drive the shows. So that we'd be inclusive."

I opened my mouth, but she went on.

"You did believe in that, Louie. When we started."

"I did. But I don't think I do now. It's just too...*messy*."

She sighed, shaking her head at the floor. But when she looked up again and met my eyes, she was smiling.

"Look, I get it. You did what you needed to do and that's fine. And I'm so glad we talked about this at last. Which reminds me—don't forget about England."

"England?"

"We should know about Atlantic Exchange just after the first of the year. So get those frequent flyer miles out, girl. We might be hitting the road again."

Just before I'd left A Woman's Place, we'd submitted a proposal to be part of a big spring multimedia festival called Atlantic Exchange. Artists from the U.S. and Britain would be exhibiting and performing their work in each other's countries. In our case, it meant that A Woman's Place and a Covent Garden women's arts collective called Mina's would show works by each other's members.

"England."

"London, to be precise. Though if we do get it, we should wander around a little. I mean, why not?"

"I was thinking I might do a little research over there," I said, then stopped myself. I didn't want to talk about the new paintings. It wasn't time, not yet.

"I see you've turned your paintings around."

"It's not personal, Nat. It's just too soon."

"Hey, I know. In progress. Maybe next time we get together, you can show me something. And I'll bring some slides of my new pieces. Anyway, I've got to go. I love you."

Out into the cool night she went, still beautiful, still strong, going gray now at her widow's peak, the weight she'd gained in the past few years suiting her somehow, making her grand. I'd felt her unstated forgiveness, reminded myself that I owed her something. And she'd left behind a beautiful gift, bought on some Greek island—a pair of dangling silver and turquoise earrings, hammered, etched with a double coil. A labyrinth, she said, an ancient pagan symbol of women's mysteries, of the path that leads to death, then to rebirth.

⌖

THE DAY BEFORE THE CONCERT, a notice appeared in the *Post*'s Sunday Arts section in a column called "Picks of the Week."

The struggling contemporary music series at Stillmore Arts Center should get a big boost tomorrow with the appearance of the quirky jazz ensemble Einstein's Pillow. Potomac-born guitar prodigy Vincent Volpe returns from stints at the Berklee College of Music and with NYC's ultra-hip, now-defunct Tea for Five in a new lineup. He's got an ace rhythm section, with session pros Phil Wexler on bass and Brian Gleason on drums; meanwhile, Volpe and his keyboardist

from Tea for Five, Jay Stanapolis, weave their sometimes excessive but always interesting sound. The
two halves of the band are still getting to know each
other, but Volpe, at twenty-three, already runs a tight
ship. The show starts at 8:00 p.m.; admission is a bar-
gain at $5.

My first thought, though it was more professional
instinct than anything, was that this was a terrific write-
up and that I was happy for Vincent.

My second thought was that the difference between
thirty-six and twenty-three was thirteen years.

The evening of the show, everything went wrong. I
ran two pairs of pantyhose. The dress I'd bought seemed
sleek and sophisticated in the store mirror, but now made
me look old enough to be Vincent's mother. A desperate
plunge into the closet revealed that I'd forgotten to have
the zipper repaired on my best black skirt. My new dressy
clothes looked too stiff and fussy, and all my old clothes
looked like they belonged to somebody else.

At that realization, the phone rang. It was Lynda,
who I had asked to meet me at Stillmore. The night cook
and the host at the Landing had both called in sick, and
the backup bartender was out of town. T.J. had to run the
kitchen, and was begging her to stay and work the front
of the house.

"I acted all pissed, like I had a hot date, you know?
Told him I wasn't going to let his bar get in the way of
my *sex* life. But, girl, it's gonna be *bad* if I don't stay. You
know he's desperate—cheap as the boy is, he offered me
double time."

We agreed that I'd call her tomorrow and tell her all
about it.

I put down the phone and looked outside. It had started to snow.

At least that simplified the clothing problem. I put on black jeans, chunky, rubber-soled boots, and an indigo cashmere sweater, snug and low cut. Like all the women on my mother's side of the family, I am well endowed, so the neckline and the way it looked on me cheered me up, a little. But the drive to Stillmore was wheel-clenching. The snow was coming down harder now, and the temperature was dropping. The roads were icing up fast. Everyone was either going too fast or creeping along far below the speed limit, hitting their brakes every twenty feet.

It occurred to me that if the concert was canceled, I had no idea of how to get in touch with Vincent—no phone number, no idea where he lived. Dana could put me in touch with his father, of course, but what reason could I give Dr. Volpe for wanting to reach his son, his very young son?

When I pulled into the parking lot, there were only half a dozen cars there. Inside, the first thing I saw was a sign saying that all events and programs had been canceled for the evening due to weather.

I walked up to the box office window. A plump middle-aged woman was behind it, with a volunteer badge and bright smile.

"Do you need a refund, dear?" she said.

"No, I need to see—I need to speak with one of the musicians. He's expecting me."

"They're in the concert hall," she said, pointing. "You can go right in. By the way, would you like to be on our mailing list? You'll receive notice—"

"I already am," I said. "Thank you."

The door to the concert hall creaked when I opened it. On stage, the bass player and drummer were packing up, winding cords, slipping mikes into cases. Jay was standing in the center aisle talking to two young women. One was thin and black haired, the other shorter, a little plump, and blonde. It occurred to me that one of them might be here for Vincent. My stomach tightened. They were both pretty, and very young.

I walked down the aisle slowly, looking left and right. No Vincent. As I got closer, I could hear what sounded like an argument.

"I cannot be*lieve*," the dark-haired one said, "what I am *hear*ing."

"Look, baby, it's not like I can control the guy," Jay said.

"I'm not asking you to control anybody. But Deb and I came all the way *out* here—"

"It's cool," the blonde said. "Really. It's OK."

"It is totally *not* OK," the dark one said, "for this to be happening. You need to find Vincent, whatever he's doing, and *tell* him—"

But I never did hear what Jay was supposed to tell him, because just then, the bass player spotted me.

"Sorry, the show's been canceled," he said.

Everyone was looking at me now. There was still no Vincent, though I could see his guitar perched on its stand at the back of the stage.

"Hey, I remember you," he went on. "You were at that gallery where we played last week."

"Reilly Gallery," I said. "Yes."

"Sorry to disappoint. But we're gonna reschedule. If you're interested, Jay can add you to the mailing list."

But Jay had gone back to whispered consultation with the dark-haired girl. I saw him lay a hand on her arm, watched her jerk it away. Her friend had stepped away from them a little and was fidgeting with her purse like a woman who needed a cigarette.

The bass player looked at me and smiled.

"So, you like music?" he ventured.

Just as I opened my mouth to ask if Vincent had left, I heard the big door creak again. I turned around.

He was wearing a winter jacket. There was snow on it, and on his gloves and in his hair. "Vee," Jay said, "where have you been, man?"

"You see the coat? Where do you think I've been? Outside."

I had been about to step forward, say his name, but he sounded so angry the words stopped in my throat. *You don't belong here,* I thought. *You are a foolish woman. Go home.*

And then Vincent looked up and saw me.

"Louise," he said. "You made it."

He came toward me, pulling his gloves off and stuffing them in his pockets, shaking the snow back out of his hair. I felt my blood beating in my ears.

"I was looking for you," he said. "In the parking lot."

"I came to find you," I said.

He was in front of me. Before I knew what I was doing, my arms were around his neck, and his were around my back, my waist. He lifted me off the ground and spun me once, twice, like an ingenue in a 1950s movie.

I am not the sort of girl men can easily lift and toss around. But in his arms, I felt as light as air. When he set me down, I had to hang onto his shoulders for a moment

to regain my footing. Behind him, I saw the blonde bite
her lip and turn away.

"You can stick around, right?"

"Stick around?"

"I was thinking we could, you, know, hang out a little.
Maybe go have something to eat, or something."

"I'd love to," I said. "But the weather."

"I can drive," he said. "The Jeep goes through anything."

The two girls, pulling on their coats, made a loud,
sighing exit.

"I think your friends had other plans for you," I said.

"That is a whole lot of nothing. Their deal, not mine."

We both looked back then to the stage, where Jay
was stacking the monitors. He shot Vincent a meaningful
look.

"I'll tell you all about it later, if you want," Vincent
said. "Right now I've got to pack up. Can you wait for
me?"

"Sure," I said. "I'll go powder my nose."

"Meet me in the front hall in ten minutes?"

"Perfect."

"Perfect."

He turned to go, then turned back.

"Oh, by the way—Louise. Do you like cocoa?"

"What?"

"You know, hot cocoa. Do you like it?"

"Well, sure. I mean, who doesn't?"

"Great. I know a guy who makes the world's best
cocoa. When I'm done here, we'll go get some, OK?"

Cocoa, I thought. *Hmm.* I envisioned some grimy
diner that reeked of bacon, with shriveling pies in a glass
safe, the kind of place that young guys think is romantic

when it's really just seedy. What I wanted right then more than anything was a good, stiff drink, but it seemed that if I was going to spend time with Vincent, I was going to have to learn to do without.

"That sounds wonderful," I said.

✖

HE WAS A GOOD, CAREFUL driver, and steered the Jeep skidlessly through the snowy night. I'd expected it to be messy inside, but Vincent's car was spotless, and the leather seats gave off a sweet exhalation as we settled into them.

Without my asking, he told me about the young women in the hall. The dark-haired one was, as I'd thought, Jay's girlfriend, Shawna. The blonde was her best friend, Deb.

"I made the mistake of being nice to Deb at Jay's birthday party," he said. "I'm afraid she got the wrong idea. And Shawna's been selling it hard. She'd love it if she could have an extra spy to keep her posted on what Jay's up to."

"She sounds a little insecure. Shawna, that is," I said, cautiously.

"You could say that. Anyway, it's their deal, not mine."

Vincent shifted gears, slowing down to a near stop, turning to look at me.

"So that's the story. A whole lot of nothing. I just wanted you to know so you wouldn't think—bad thoughts."

"Bad thoughts?"

"You know, that I was messing with you, or something."

He sped up again, turned his eyes back to the road.

"So," I said, trying to sound casual, "where's this cocoa place, anyway?"

He turned left down a long driveway. At the end of it, I could see the outline of an enormous, awkwardly sprawling house. Closer in, I could see a much smaller building, framed by tall trees.

Vincent pointed to that one.

"Right there," he said. "Best cocoa in the world."

"It looks like somebody's house," I said.

"It was my grandmother's," he said. "Now it's mine."

Well, that was fast, I thought. The first time we're alone together, and already you take me to your place. It seemed pretty obvious that if the storm kept up, I'd have to sleep at Vincent's. But if he was aware of the implications of what he was doing, he didn't show it.

"This was her house when I was growing up. I spent more time in it than I did at my dad's. Every minute that I could, really. Anyway, he—my father—was her firstborn, and I am his. So when she died, she left it to me."

"When was that?"

"Last year."

"I'm sorry," I said.

"Thanks. It was rough at first, real rough. But I'm OK, now. She died in her sleep—the only way to go, I think—and she had a good long run. Everybody loved her."

Even beneath its covering of snow, I could see that it was a beautiful house, two stories of white-painted brick, with big windows and a clay-tiled roof. I tried to imagine what it might have been like to be his age and own a home, especially one like this, and felt a sudden, unexpected kick of jealousy. Great talent, maybe even genius;

obvious wealth; incredible beauty. Was there any way in which Vincent wasn't blessed?

"It's lovely," I said.

"Yeah," he said. "So was she."

He pulled into the driveway and shut off the car.

"And the famous cocoa man?"

He smiled.

"That's me."

While he unloaded his gear into the basement, I had a chance to a look around the first floor of his house. Just past the little vestibule, a central stairwell led to the second floor. The dining room and kitchen were to the left; on the right, there was a big living room, with what looked like a study just off of it, with a desk, computer, and book-lined walls. The living room had a glass-screened fireplace and a baby grand piano, with an acoustic guitar next to it on a stand. Everything on the first floor was so neatly arranged and so clean that it gave the impression of hardly being lived in. I wondered how recently he had returned to Maryland, and from where. New York City, where his old band was from? Or someplace else?

When he was back inside, we didn't say much at first, both suddenly shy. He settled me into an armchair by the fireplace, then lit a fire, then went off to the kitchen to make cocoa. Before he disappeared, he slipped a disk into the CD player, saying, "See what you think of this."

There were tall windows on either side of the fireplace, and through them I watched the heavy, falling snow as I listened. It was a solo guitar, acoustic. I sank back into the warm chair, with its wide, padded arms, its nubbly sky-blue silk upholstery, and felt the various tensions falling away into the stream of the music and the warm firelight. The muscles in my neck and shoulders relaxed; I kicked off my boots and wiggled my toes. I realized with some surprise how long it had been since I had let myself relax. My body hummed with the hum of the strings; I felt the music massage me, loosen me.

My eyes were nearly closed when something I saw, or thought I saw, inside the fire opened them wide. I sat up, staring. Behind the cut-glass fireplace screen, the burning pile of logs seemed to have taken on another shape, one that was familiar and yet not. I saw two parallel rows of arched stone walls, finely carved, curving in toward each other. A church, I thought, and a very old one. I blinked and blinked again, trying to focus, but it shimmered and flickered in the red and gold tongues of flame, solid and then transparent, first here, then not. One moment I was sure I had invented it; then I rubbed my eyes, and, opening them again, saw the building as clear as the chair I rested my body in, as real as the floor beneath my feet.

Just then Vincent was beside me, carrying a tray with two mugs and a plate of cookies. He handed me a mug. I took a sip.

"Want to know the secret ingredient?" he asked.

"Well, there's cinnamon, I guess," I said, looking back at the fire. Was the building there or not?

"Sure. What else?"

It was still there, I was certain of it.

Vincent was looking at me expectantly.

"Can you give me a hint?" I tried.

"That's kind of cheating but, well, let's see. OK—it grows on trees."

Trees, I thought. I could see trees now, running along one side of the church. Yes, it was a church. I could see the cross on its roof, and in the air behind it, in the background, I saw, too, an outline of what looked like a small mountain or a hill.

"Well?" Vincent said.

"OK, I give up. What's in this, anyway?"

"Coconut," he said, triumphantly. "It's coconut milk. Really something, isn't it?"

He settled himself into the chair next to mine, picked up a cookie, and took a big bite. I looked back at the fire, and all I saw were flames and logs, the charred kindling beneath. You are overtired, I told myself, and way too worked up about this boy. No wonder you're seeing things.

I bit into a cookie. In the firelight, Vincent nodded at me approvingly.

"This," he said, "is my idea of a perfect night."

"I was wondering," I began. "I mean, the snow..."

"Is fantastic," he finished.

"Well, yes. But your show getting canceled—you don't seem upset about that at all."

"No point in getting upset about it."

"But all your work," I went on. "You must have been looking forward to it. You must have been excited about it."

"I'll be a lot more excited when the CD is out. Besides, this lineup is kind of temporary. Jay and me, we've got something going. But Brian and Phil, they're session guys, really. They were here, they were available, and I can pay them. But it's all just another gig to them. I'm looking to do better."

He sat forward in his chair, his face warming as he talked.

"Players like that, they fill their roles. They're never going to surprise you. They're craftspeople, you know? Very good craftspeople. And that's fine for now, anyway.

But I want a band—I want Einstein's Pillow to be a band of all creators. All artists."

The music ended. I gestured toward the CD player.

"That was beautiful."

"Some new stuff. Works in progress."

"They sounded pretty finished to me. That first piece was just gorgeous."

"Some people think that's a problem," he said. "Jay says whenever I pick up an acoustic, it gets too pretty."

"Isn't that a contradiction in terms? Like saying a diamond is too big?"

He laughed, then looked at me slyly.

"I've been hearing some good things about *your* work, you know."

"Hearing things? From who?"

"Aunt Dana. She calls you a rising star."

I had a sudden flash of Dana then, as if she were looking over my shoulder at this boy who called her "aunt," watching me drink his cocoa. What would she think if she knew where I was tonight?

As if he heard my thought, Vincent stood up, and put his hands out, and I let him pull me to my feet.

"By the way," he said, slipping his arms around me, "I just want to know. Am I stepping on anybody's toes here? By having you with me tonight?"

T.J.'s face flashed through my mind. As if he, with his steady girlfriend, had any right to care where I was or what I was doing.

"I *was* involved with somebody—I was living with him, in fact—but we broke up months ago."

"So it's OK, then."

"What's OK?"

"For me to do this."

Then, like someone about to dive into cool water, he took a breath, closed his eyes, and leaned down to kiss me.

It was a gentle kiss, tentative, his lips very light on mine. I thought I felt him tremble a little, and wondered if he might be scared. *Go slow*, I told myself, though it was the last thing I wanted to do. He kissed me again, a little harder, and now his mouth opened and his tongue slid into mine. He tasted sweet, like cocoa. He ran his hands gently up and down my back, and I pressed closer to him, feeling the length of his body against mine. Even through our clothes, I could feel how muscular he was, despite his slenderness, and had a moment of panic. His body was a young man's body, and I was no longer a young woman. If we undressed—when we undressed—would he be disappointed?

I pushed the thought away. I pressed my lips to his neck, to that tender spot just below his ear, and he groaned. I felt his heartbeat quicken and the warmth of his breath on my skin.

He whispered, "Will you sleep with me tonight, Louise?"

"Yes. *Yes.*"

He led me upstairs to a small, pretty bedroom that looked like it hadn't been slept in by anyone for a long time. We undressed, awkwardly. He offered me an oversized T-shirt to wear as a nightgown, and pulled on the bottoms to a pair of flannel pajamas. Beneath the blankets and quilts, we kissed a little, talked a little, kissed some more.

But then a strange thing happened. Vincent made it clear, with his body, that he had no intention of going any further. When I pressed against him, feeling for him, he pulled ever so gently away. When I tried to shift so that my breasts fell into his hands, he moved them.

Finally, I sat up, looked at him.

"I feel like—I feel like I'm missing something here."

"What do you mean?"

"It's just that when you asked me to stay, I thought—I just thought—"

He rolled over on his back and looked up at me, folding his arms under his head. His hair splashed like dark water across the pillow. In the moonlight echoing off the snow outside the window, his eyes were calm and serious.

"What did you think?"

"Well, obviously, I thought you wanted to make love to me."

"Oh, I do, Louise. I do."

He lifted his hand to my left cheek, stroked it slowly, gently, up and down with his fingertips. My body tingled, infuriatingly, at his touch.

"Then why not—"

"Why not *now*, right?"

"Yes. Exactly."

"Because I think it's so much better to go slow. I want to know you, Louise Terry. I want to know your smell. I want to know what it's like to kiss you all kinds of ways."

He took my right hand then and kissed it, and then the inside of my wrist, and all along the inside of my forearm, soft, gentle kisses as he pulled me down back into his arms. And still the kisses continued, falling like rain on my hair, my forehead, my cheeks, my closed eyes.

"I want to know what you like and how you sleep. I want to dream in your arms. I want to stay in this place, for a little while, anyway. And then—well, imagine how sweet it will be. When we first make love."

His words stirred me in precisely the direction he had decided not to go.

"But isn't it difficult?"

"Of course. Most good things are."

I had no answer to that, though his tone made me bristle a little. Then I thought, how sweet, really, how innocent, even old-fashioned. So we'll go slow. Then we fell asleep, my hands in his hair, his arms tight around my waist.

✳

THE WEATHER CHANGES QUICKLY AND unpredictably in Maryland. The morning after the snowstorm, the sky was bright with yellow-white sunlight, the temperature was almost warm. Vincent drove me back to my car at Stillmore through streets slick with running water.

It was earlier than I'd hoped. He woke before me and was playing his acoustic, his face serious and distant, while I went off to shower and dress. I had time for a cup of coffee, but no breakfast, though a quick scan of his kitchen revealed little that might be turned into a meal.

In the parking lot, he scribbled my phone number into a small brown notebook, kissed me once, twice, distractedly. Then he was gone.

I sat in my car for a little while, staring at the melting piles of snow all around me before driving away, feeling suddenly melancholy. Vincent had explained so sweetly why he didn't want to make love to me the night before. Surely he was interested. Surely what had felt like indifference this morning was simply his desire to get back to his music. I had felt like that about painting on who knew how many occasions. But I knew, too, that had we spent the night at my apartment, I would have been warmer, kinder, more thoughtful to him when we awoke than he had been to me.

Steering home through the cold winter light, I thought of Christmas, and the fact that it is inevitably followed by New Year's Eve. This year, for the first time in more years than I could remember, I had no plans as yet for that night, no man with whom I was sure to spend it. Vincent, so lovely and serious, did not seem likely to indulge in the typical festivities, and champagne was clearly out. My mood sank further.

When I got home, the light on my phone was blinking. My brother, having seen a weather report, called to make sure that I was all right, and my father and sister had called too. Katherine said she hoped the snow was beautiful. Dad said he hoped I was safe and had food in the house and wasn't doing anything foolish, like driving. T.J. had left three messages, each time saying some suggestive thing about wanting to get snowed in with me. Lynda had called to ask how the concert was and if there were any updates about the guitarist.

The last message was the most surprising. At first I thought I had never heard the man's voice before; then I realized that I did know it, though the memory was old and brief. Some time that afternoon—perhaps while I'd been sitting in my car at Stillmore watching the snow melt—Lawrence Ware had called. In his beautiful, theatrical voice, he said that he had just heard of my mother's death and that he was terribly sorry. He said that she had been a wonderful, a truly astonishing woman. He said that he remembered my siblings and me very well, and that he extended his condolences to all of us.

Then he said that there was something—"a small matter," as he put it—that he wanted to discuss with me. I wrote down his number on a pad by the phone.

The gesture reminded me of Vincent writing my own number down, and I wondered how soon I might hear from him. For despite the odd, sweet chastity of our night together, he'd said nothing when we parted to indicate any particular urgency about seeing me again.

Then I remembered the fire he'd built for us and the building I'd seen burning inside of it. I opened my sketchbook and drew everything I could remember of the burning building, the trees surrounding it, the stones, the flames.

INTERLUDE 1

London and Oxford, 1996

The light in London is nothing like the light at home. In Maryland, the blue sky is shot with gold on September afternoons, and slants into your eyes. Here, gray-blue clouds shed a quieter, silvery light. It feels kinder, somehow, which makes Margaret feel kinder toward herself. She does not feel guilty this morning about the family she has left behind again.

She finishes her tea, pays her receipt at the bake-shop counter, then carries her things outside. Despite the cost, she thinks it best to hail a cab to Paddington Station, where she will take the train to Oxford. The map confounds her, and she's none too sure of the tube. Yesterday, she'd gotten lost trying to find Harrods and had walked in circles, her feet aching, until the sort of grim and anxious mood settled over her that she has been trying to avoid. Hard to control, these moods, and yet they must surely be normal, after all she has been through, after all she has decided, then redecided, then undone.

Her doctor's solution is in her purse, but Margaret has yet to swallow one of the yellow tablets. There have been various diagnoses—depression, bipolar disorder, OCD—and various solutions, always in the form of a pill. She carries the little orange plastic bottle with her in her purse like a sad talisman. Serotonin reuptake inhibitors. John wishes she would take them. Wished, she corrects herself—when they were still a couple, John wished that she would take them.

There is a bookstore on the corner, and she decides to stop and pick up a volume to read on the train. As she reaches the shop door, a man pushes it open from inside, holding it for her while she manages her bulky suitcase and shoulder bag. He has a stack of two or three cloth-bound books under an arm covered in beige linen. She sees only bits of him—white shirt and charcoal trousers, thick dark hair—as she hurries past, struggling with the weight of her things. He reaches out one hand as if to help her, to catch whatever she is about to drop. But she steps past him with a quick "Thank you," ducking her way over and through the threshold.

The store's dusty window displays give no hint of the chaos and pleasure that lie inside. It's an orgy of books—volumes stashed in every conceivable space, on top of radiators and windowsills, books piled sideways and jammed into shelves on top of other upright books, or stacked on the floor in precarious towers. Margaret wants to dive in and wander the aisles with no plan, no shape to her attack. But her itinerary leaves her too little time to work that way.

She threads her way between piles of books to the register, where a pleasant-faced woman, quite round in the middle, is barely visible between two stacks. She pauses in her task of penciling prices to offer Margaret a printed map of the store. Yes, the works on medieval

British history would be on the next floor. Yes, she can set her bag behind the register while she looks.

"Do watch your step, madam," the woman says. "Those stairs are tricky." And she nods at Margaret's narrow-toed high heels.

Outside the shop window, the man who held the door for her stands beneath the awning for a moment, watching her set down her unwieldy bag, shake back her hair, and survey the map. Aside from her accent—he has only heard two words—there is a kind of shiny newness to her clothes, her eyes, that makes him sure she is American. Her face is earnest and pretty, intelligent and a little sad, and he creates, briefly, a backstory for her: a lecturer, he thinks, from some university in the States, where she teaches undergraduates about Modern Poetry, perhaps, or the American Novel.

Probably a feminist something-or-other, despite the makeup. Probably divorced. He chuckles, admires her legs. His stomach rumbles a distraction.

Lawrence Ware looks at his watch and decides to take a table at the restaurant across the alley from the bookshop, order a coffee, a biscotti. It is several hours before he must drive home and he is in no great hurry to get there anyway. He has never recovered from his love affair with London, and still loves it better than any other city. For now, he will sit unencumbered at a table by the street. He will thumb through his acquisitions and sip his coffee. And perhaps, when the woman emerges from the shop, he will get another glimpse of her, add a scene or two to her story. There is plenty of time to get to Oxford.

If the waiter recognizes him, he gives no sign of it. Lawrence winces, remembering a different time.

When *The Fallacy of Pleasure* was running, strangers pointed at him on the street and whispered; Michael Billington, in the *Guardian*, said British theater had found the next Joe Orton in Lawrence Ware. And then—well, this and that had not worked out. Some of it had been, admittedly, his fault. That film deal, for example—all the things he missed. But still, it seemed to him that fame and fate were too unfair. For a brief time, London had loved him. Then suddenly all the talk was of Tom Stoppard and some American named Mamet. Though the city was still the center of his affection, London seemed to have moved on.

He should have used his time in the sun more wisely. He should have found a way to hold onto his luck.

But these are useless, self-tormenting thoughts, as Claire would remind him if she were here, if she were not performing in what Ware grudgingly thinks of as some kind of hippie cabaret in Edinburgh. Claire is always good at bucking him up. Besides, she would say, it is not as if he has no plans, nothing in progress. He has enormous plans—a plan so ambitious, so ingenious, really, that it will silence all his critics, including himself. Most of all, himself.

That is part of what these books are for. And with that thought, he takes a volume from the top of the pile, shoves the rest to the other side of the table. From his pocket he takes a pen and a small notebook, spiral bound, unlined, sets them next to the book, and begins to read.

As he does so, turning away from the text from time to time to make a note, the rain begins to fall softly outside. It is slow at first, even kind; it would feel warm if he were out in it, it would caress him. But he is not even aware that he hears it, so subtle is the sound. And when

American accents. He guesses she is from the West ast, perhaps northern California.

He turns a page, pretending to be deep in thought hile he watches her read the menu. Her face, from the de, serious, purposeful, as it had been when she read he bookstore map. She closes the menu, reaches into her ag, and takes out a thin book. He sees that it is Helen Waddell's *Peter Abelard*.

"Ah, Waddell," he murmurs, as if to himself. "Yes, yes. The true lover."

As if he were directing her, she turns her head, cocks it a little at him.

"Pardon me?"

He raises his eyes to hers.

"Yes?"

"Did you say something—to me?"

"Why, no, I don't think—oh, I do apologize. You see, I have a terrible habit of talking to myself when I am working."

He gestures to his notebook, shrugs.

"I do apologize."

"Oh, that's all right. No problem."

Carlo is there. She orders tea and chocolate cake, then opens her book.

"Excuse me, madam?"

She looks up again, sees that he is indeed the man she passed outside the bookstore. She feels a wave of impatience pass over her, and he sees it, sees as well that she is too polite to speak of it, yet. He has to work fast.

"Pardon me for interrupting once again, but might I ask...are you by any chance a scholar? A historian, perhaps?"

"A scholar?"

it builds, as it does, it is in small incre
that by the time he has finished the bool
is a steady, full rain. Umbrellas are open
outside and the awning drips with irregula
water. Then a flash of purple lightning, its
der. He turns his head to see the source, h.
sumed, his cup dry.

He motions to the waiter for more coffe
lunchtime now and a small queue has formed
the window; Carlo is, for the moment, too b\
him. Ware's eyes pass over the men and women
there, shaking the rain from their shoes, pushi\
hair out of their eyes. Just behind a pair of busin\
he sees the American professor.

Margaret has belted a trench coat tight again
weather, and, while he watches, she loosens it and sl
it open. Against the beige cloth, the sudden flash o\
blue and white print dress is innocently lovely. He wis
he had a better view of her legs.

Margaret, meanwhile, is annoyed with herself for n
wearing more sensible shoes. As the waiter leads her t
her table, she moves carefully, trying not to slip on the
damp tiles as she struggles with the weight of her purse
and suitcase.

Watching her precise steps, Lawrence feels the
absurd, delicious rush of joy that unexpected happy circumstances bring, for Carlo is leading the American lady
to the table on his left. She slips past him to take the seat
against the wall, so that they are sitting beside each other
really, then gives the waiter her coat, accepts the menu.

"Thank you."

She has a shiny voice, with deep pitches and awkward lilts. Lawrence believes he is something of an expert

She is genuinely confused. Not a professor after all.

"You see, the book you have there...the Waddell...well, it made me think that you might be...perhaps a teacher."

"Oh," she says, blushing, feeling foolish. "No, I'm just a reader."

"Never say 'just.' Without readers, there would be no writers. We need you in order to exist."

"So you're a writer, then."

"Why, yes, you're right," he says. "Permit me to introduce myself. I am Lawrence Ware. The writer."

She hesitates, then puts out her right hand.

"Pleased to meet you," she says. "Margaret Terry."

Their handshake is interrupted by another rattle of thunder. Their fingers part, and she lifts up her left hand to check her watch. He sees, for an instant, the flash of a small diamond ring and a wedding band beneath it.

"I wish this waiter would hurry," she says, furrowing her brow.

"I would think it best to sit out this storm," Lawrence says. He is certain now that she does not recognize his name.

"Your husband is waiting for you?"

"No," she says, confused, then remembers her rings. It felt false to wear them now, but Angie had told her a woman traveling alone in Europe would be wise to keep them on. Angie has her own fake wedding and engagement set for her trips to France and Italy. Evidently, men there have different ideas about sex, and about single females. Margaret isn't sure if she believes this, or if it extends to Britain, but she is following her aunt's directions, at least for now. After all, she has only been out of the country once before, and Angie has been everywhere.

"He's at home," she goes on. "America, that is. In Maryland. With the children."

"Maryland…"

"Just outside of Washington, D.C. The East Coast."

"Ah. So you're with friends…"

"No, I'm alone. For a while, anyway. But I have to catch the train to Oxford."

"Ahh," he says, "'that sweet city, with its dreaming spires'?"

He is not sure if she recognizes the allusion or not, for he is distracted, disarmed, really, by the smile that breaks over her face. Suddenly, she goes from being mildly pretty to stunning. She has, he thinks, the best smile he's seen anywhere, on stage or off, in his life. She is suffused—there is no other word for it—with light. The words bubble out of her.

"Yes, I'm really looking forward to it. You see, my aunt—my Aunt Angie, she's just a wonderful lady, so kind to me, all my life—anyway, well, she gave me this trip. As a gift. And I've got lots of wonderful places to go. Stratford. Salisbury. We're going all the way to Cornwall."

There is something charming about her excitement. Like a teenage girl setting off on her first real adventure.

"Well, it sounds like a wonderful journey."

"Yes, I think so. Yes."

She drank a good half-cup of her tea, began to peck at her cake.

"Though I must warn you, Mrs. Terry," Lawrence went on, "you may be a bit disappointed—after London, that is. Oxford has its own charms, and in fact, I do still keep a home there. But I would think that London would have so much more to offer to a modern American lady. I am biased, of course, for this is my true home."

"So you own a house in London *and* in Oxford?"

He had forgotten to account for American direct-ness. What could he say? That writers, serious writers, scarcely make that kind of money? That it had been a choice, the car or the flat? That Claire's remarks about what she called the shag pad had finally begun to rankle?

"Just now, I'm between homes in London," he said. "But I could never give up the city. No, no, no."

❈

THAT EVENING, IN HER ROOM on Walton Street, Margaret washes her hands and face in the little sink by the window, and hangs a small bag of toiletries on the doorknob to carry down the hall to the bathroom— the w.c., she corrects herself—in the morning. She is not accustomed to sharing a bathroom with strangers, but Angie said she would quickly get used to it. It only made sense, for a trip this long, to choose a bed and break-fast over the few, astronomically priced hotels, espe-cially since Angie insisted that, once she joined her, each should have her own room. Privacy, she always said, was necessary for sanity. That was some days off now. And though Margaret tells herself she would have been happy to share a double room with her aunt, she is happy now, as she cranks the odd-shaped window open, that she has a door of her own to close.

She leans on the plaster windowsill, looks out at the little back garden, overrun with many kinds of tangled roses. On her walk from the train station, she'd passed many small, wild plots like this one. In her neighborhood, the men did the gardening, and lately the fashion was for hedges shaped like things—cones and pillars, baskets and animals—with the use of all kinds of lethal-looking, electrically powered trimmers and edgers and blades.

She herself knew nothing about gardening. Growing up in rented apartments, she'd never had the chance to learn. But if she did, she thinks she'd rather be digging in one of these tumbling riots of color that seem to have no real order, or to be creating, willfully, an order of their own, than trying to sculpt a pink azalea bush to look like an Easter basket. It is one more part of her old life that she will not miss.

She hears a clatter of feet, of voices, and then the garden door springs open. Three Finnish girls who are staying on the floor above tumble out into the evening light, chattering their way along the diagonal stone path that leads to the gate. One pauses to light a cigarette, pushing her hair out of her eyes, and in her patched jeans and slightly dirty shirt she is, in that garden, so innocently lovely, so full of all kinds of possibility, that Margaret feels a cramp of envy. Had she ever been that young, that light of purpose?

No. It seemed—it was—impossible. If only she'd had a chance, before her marriage, to have such freedom. The girl in the garden wasn't worried, as Margaret had been at her age, about paying the rent, keeping the gas and lights turned on. She was, Margaret could just tell somehow, unused to hardship. This girl was savvy and sought after, with so many options, in work, in love, in life. No, Margaret had never been anything like that.

And with that thought, the darkness she has sworn to herself to avoid comes tumbling over her like a veil. What good is it to be here, to spend Angie's money and her own time, to take herself away again from her children, not to mention her husband—ex-husband, she reminds herself, almost automatically, soon he will be my ex-husband—to take a girl's trip when she is no longer anything like a girl? She should have been here twenty years ago.

She can foresee the night falling over her like a storm cloud, the sleepless sadness, the walls moving in with their blank malevolent stares. Angie calls this "the blues," and believes that the cure is to do something, anything, so long as it is lively and requires action. But then Angie has never seemed to notice that she is no longer young. And she makes friends everywhere she goes.

Margaret stands at the window and looks at the sky, the evening light. That sad-looking gentleman she'd met, Lawrence Ware, had talked about Oxford's spires. She had felt foolish, not recognizing his name. Mr. Ware carried himself like a famous person, someone used to attention. Of course, he was very handsome, though from his complexion, she guesses that he is a drinker. Angie says Europeans don't take care of themselves like Americans—they don't exercise, they smoke and drink too much. And of course, he must lead a glamorous life—a famous playwright, with an actress girlfriend who had even been in major movies.

And he had been right about the skyline, too. It is beautiful, filled with golden spears and silver spirals that pierce the darkening blue expanse. They look like yearning. They look like nothing else she's seen in this life. Though she had planned to spend her evening writing letters to her children—another rule, like keeping to the itinerary—she knows that if she stays in this room she'll do nothing but brood. And meanwhile, the August sky is all magic.

Margaret looks out into the garden one more time. Something is coming her way, she is suddenly sure of it. Something is waiting for her, perhaps just outside the garden gate, or down the road where the pubs are, or further, by the bridge that crosses the Cherwell and leads east. If she leaves her room, something will happen to her tonight.

She is confused by herself, by her life, but she is not a coward. She has proved that much. She will go out and meet whatever it is that waits.

She goes to the tiny closet and takes out a narrow-cut blue silk dress. She puts on her favorite earrings, dangling silver circles, and fluffs her hair out around them. She outlines her eyes and paints her lashes a soft black. Makeup has always given her courage and as she looks at her new, brighter face in the mirror she can see that, for forty-nine, she looks not at all bad. She is still pretty. She is not old, not yet. And besides, Angie says that Europeans think their youth-worshipping American culture is just silly.

Something glistens, catches her eye—her engagement diamond, her wedding ring. Remembering Angie's words, she decides it is time to ignore them. If she does not yet know herself, she is at least beginning to know what she is not. And she is not, anymore, a wife.

She slides the rings off her fingers, lays them in the top drawer of the bureau. Then, with a map of the city tucked into her handbag, she locks the thin door to her room and heads out into the night.

Meanwhile, Lawrence Ware pulls his Jaguar up to the house on Holywell, shuts off the engine. It chokes a little; it is overdue at the shop. Claire says he should exchange it for something more practical, less costly to maintain, but he is adamant. The car is one of the talismans that keep his hopes fresh; as long as he has it, he is still the man he was when he bought it, flush with success, his hands full of cash and coke and beautiful women. Claire can brag about her solid little German car all she wants. He will keep his sedan.

He remembers how the American woman's eyes widened when she saw it. What a funny creature. In his experience, which had been at one time considerable, American women were much more aggressive flirts than their European counterparts. But Mrs. Terry seemed hardly to know how to flirt at all. Despite his efforts at the restaurant, the lady had treated him rather like a tour guide, writing down the various points of interest he suggested as she nibbled at her cake, then scrambling out at the first break in the rain to hail a cab. It didn't help, of course, that though she'd shown no sign of recognizing his name, she had actually seen Claire in a production of *Twelfth Night* on American television two years ago.

It had taken him a while to realize—as he sat in the restaurant over his cold coffee, grousing to himself about Margaret Terry in particular, women and Americans in general—that the lady had been unable to secure a cab, and was still standing outside, where the sky was rumbling again, her hand less and less hopeful in its signals, looking more and more forlorn in her impractical shoes. He had to admit that they did do something wonderful for her legs. And then he roused himself, went outside, and offered to drive her to Kensington Station.

Hope flickered, then died. Their talk on the way was almost entirely of the car. Americans were always predictably crazy for autos, it was almost depressing. When he'd dropped her off, he felt annoyed, vaguely angry, and restless. A Friday afternoon in London, late summer; could it be that he had not a single friend left here whom he might ring up for drinks, for an afternoon that could, with luck and the right sort of coincidence, unfold into night? He thought of his agent, but George was a busy man, and besides, talk would inevitably turn to new work. He did not want to tell anyone—save for Claire, of course—about his new work just yet. He had cause to believe that it might be a jinx.

He thought of his old flat-mate, Stuart, but then remembered that Stu was in America for two months, working on a TV movie. He thought of Alan and Joe and their old meeting places in Covent Garden, but Alan was in Sydney directing *Edward II* and Joe was in America, too, producing something with an avant-garde theater group in Chicago. No one seemed to want to stay home anymore.

Then, almost to his surprise, he found himself pulling up in front of Jill's little house.

After the drama of their last meeting, he'd promised himself he'd stay away. A little shouting, even a thrown plate or two, could in his experience be a fine prelude to sex, but only behind closed doors; he hated such scenes in public. And of course, a man in his position had reason to be afraid of publicity. Claire had nearly left him over a series of snaps of him nuzzling a young actress that had appeared in a tabloid a few years back. Of course, Claire nearly left him nearly all the time. He saw no reason this could not go on forever.

The good news was that Jill was at home and looking gorgeous and greeted him with a warm kiss. The bad news was that, when she led him through the foyer into the sitting room, someone else was already there. Arthur something. An actor, of course. It seemed that he and Jill had dinner plans. All Lawrence needed, he was sure, was just a moment alone with her, so he could make some suggestive comment, get her thinking of him in that way once again.

"Cut him loose," he'd whisper. "Say you're not feeling well. I'll meet you at the corner, love, show you a time."

But Arthur whoever-he-was never gave them a moment alone. Far too soon, Lawrence was out on the street again, the traffic miserable, the sky a stuffy, irritating gray.

He was too angry to eat, too disgusted with life and the larger forces that brought him there to that corner in that city on that night, to seek any other adventure. So he got into his car and drove back to the house on Holywell, to the life he lives now.

A small pile of mail waits in the box, letters from Claire and Stu, a bill from the garage, a flyer from a small theater he once had something to do with, a note from his banker. He tosses it all in a pile on the front hall steps to be carried upstairs to his study later.

He slings his jacket over the banister, walks without thinking to the sitting room liquor cart, pours a generous shot of scotch into one of his grandmother's crystal tumblers. There used to be ten, but then his father, drunk and raging, had hurled one into the mirror that had hung over the fireplace. He still remembers the glass splintering out into the sitting room and down over the three of them. Somehow, miraculously, they were all untouched. Lawrence had one tiny shard in his hair, that was all. His mother and father, frightened into kindness, spent the rest of the night fussing over him and cleaning up the mess. For days, their hands bore tiny nicks from the glass slivers.

He feels around in his pockets for a pack of cigarettes, realizes he finished them in the car. He rummages in the cutlery drawer, where Claire sometimes stashes hers, and then prowls the whole first floor, looking into pockets and under tabletops, opening this and lifting that, finding nothing. He will have to go out.

He shoots the rest of his drink down in one gulp, then quickly pours another and downs that too. After all, it is Friday night. A man can reward himself with a few drinks after a difficult week. In fact, he thinks that while he is out, he'll stop somewhere, have a couple, maybe something to eat. The refrigerator was woefully empty, as it always was when Claire was gone. Last he'd looked, all it contained was a jar of chutney, some cheese, and a bottle of milk already of questionable age. Yes, he should take himself out for dinner.

The London rain has not followed him to Oxford. The night is blue and clear. In the mirror by the door, he watches himself slip back into his jacket, smooth his hair, and straighten his collar. His eyes have begun to droop a bit, but he still has a thick head of hair; he is grateful for that. He tells himself that what he sees reflected back at him is still a young man, or if not exactly that, at least someone with a promising future.

"You've got years and years, darling," Claire would say to him if she were here. He wants to believe—he almost believes—that she is right.

As Lawrence makes his way down Broad Street toward Cornmarket, Margaret Terry is walking past the Ashmolean Museum, which she has already planned for her first stop tomorrow. Then Carfax Tower, then the

Botanic Gardens. Sunday is Mass at Saint Mary's. She will have to save the shops and bookstores for Monday.

On her right, the Randolph Hotel glitters, the windows of its restaurant full of important-looking people. She read in a guidebook that this is where presidents stay when they visit Oxford; Gandhi. The rooms are wildly expensive—Angie had warned her, she had inquired anyway, Angie had been right—but nonetheless, Margaret plans to take herself there for tea one afternoon quite soon. She looks through the windows at the high, arched walls, the big fireplace, the enormous baskets of wildflowers on the side tables. It seems to her like a castle out of a fairy tale.

She turns onto St. Giles, which turns into Cornmarket. She is beginning to find her way. The clusters of passing students out for the night thicken and pick up speed. She spots the lovely girl from the B&B on the other side of the street with her friends, walking past a small pub while a young man in the doorway tries to persuade them to come inside.

"Just for a pint," he implores. "One can't hurt ya."

The girls laugh and keep walking. The boy, looking up, catches Margaret's eyes and shrugs, as if to say, "I tried," and she laughs, too, at his shaggy beauty, at the night, at her blood in her veins. She is half tempted to cross the street, enter the pub, but she thinks again. Twenty years ago, yes. Now, no.

Then she sees, on the opposite corner, a second-story restaurant with a narrow balcony, tablecloths fluttering, a green-and-white sign that says *La Trattoria*.

It looks like a postcard picture—an Italian restaurant in England. Well, why not? She crosses the street and goes inside.

Meanwhile, Lawrence makes his way up Cornmarket a few blocks behind her, having stopped on the way at the Eagle and Childe to buy a pack of Gitanes and to have one, along with a pint of bitters, standing at the back bar. But he needs to eat and he makes it a rule never to eat dinner in pubs. He is certain that what has thickened the bodies of almost all of his male friends is pub food.

Outside again, he sees the packs of students off to their various pleasures, can see as much as smell the heat in them. So many bodies, so much desire, so much fucking to happen tonight. He thinks again of Jill, then stops himself.

He wants something to happen to him, but he is almost too lost, almost too far gone in his bitterness, to let it. He wants someone or something to shake him out of himself, take him somewhere else, but he does not know how to find that.

"Larry!" a voice calls, and he looks up from his reverie to see no one he knows. He looks around, then stops and looks back down the sidewalk he has just traversed. Someone—he was sure he had heard it, a male voice, deep and lively—had called his name. Turning back, he scans the street before him, his eyes stopping at the sign that reads *La Trattoria*. Not a very good restaurant.

Just above the sign, he sees a pair of ankles that look somehow familiar. It is Mrs. Terry, sitting on the balcony of the restaurant at a tiny wrought-iron table. As he watches, she lifts a glass of white wine to her lips, sips it, and then looks at it, as if not entirely sure. Her puzzlement makes him laugh. He lifts his arm, waves up at her across the busy street.

"Not to your liking, madam? The wine?" he calls up.

She looks around—but not toward him—then back to her book. He tries again.

"Perhaps the *red*, Mrs. Terry. I'd go with the red, myself."

She looks up again, and then follows the other diners' turned heads to where he stands. Lawrence is suddenly aware of making some kind of spectacle of himself—everyone, it seems, is watching the two of them—but he is not embarrassed, not at all. It feels wonderful. And when she sees him and gives him that smile, it feels even better.

Funny, how glad she suddenly is to see him again.

He lays a hand on his chest, makes a little bow to her, and calls out, "May I?" She laughs, a low and nervous but still very sweet sound. "Yes, of course."

She resists the impulse to take out a mirror and look at her face, her hair, her lipstick. She tells her heart it is silly to beat so fast. She, of all women, should know better than to be unnerved by just any handsome man. That is all he is, she tells herself. Just a man.

And then he is by her side. Leaning over, he places a kiss on each cheek—the European way. He smells a little of whiskey, a little of sweat and cigarettes, a little of cologne. She sees the heads around them turn, hears murmurs of "Larry," sees one woman in particular, a bit plump and past her prime but still attractive, who purrs his name. But though he smiles, a round-the-room smile, it is for Margaret that he reserves the bright and frankly hopeful look he flashes now, slipping into the seat across from her, dismissing her wine with a quick gesture to the waiter, calling for the list of bottles, ordering a special antipasto, not on the menu, he tells her, but he knows this place, the owner, they will make it for him, for the two of them.

She can feel the old nature calling to her, feel herself slipping into the ease of his smile, his charm, the show he is putting on now just for her. Not immune, after all.

And when the wine does come, and he tastes it and pronounces it fine—"it will be better after it breathes a bit, but who has time for that?"—and they clink the cheap glasses together and meet each other's eyes, she knows suddenly and certainly that they will be lovers. She begins to think ahead, to worry over particulars, then stops. It is his problem, after all, to avoid detection, to escape whatever domestic entanglements he may have for an afternoon, or a night, or a series of nights, or however long they might hold onto each other. She is a free woman now, in spirit if not yet in name.

Today he was an ordinary man. Tonight he is the emblem of who she might become, while she is for him— what? The question hovers like gold dust and black ash in the air between them.

They raise glasses, clink, sip. And so it begins again, Margaret thinks, and gives in.

PART II

Winter Music,
2005–06

6

December came down hard. Sleet and freezing rain left a gray slush on the streets and sidewalks that hardened, making driving and walking an adventure. And my love life was no easier to navigate than the streets outside. In keeping with Vincent's desire to take it slow, we had a few not entirely satisfactory dates. We went to a concert by some of his Berklee friends at the Kennedy Center's Millennium Stage. We met for lunch at a vegetarian café in Dupont Circle. Our best date was a visit to the Isamu Noguchi show at the Sackler on a cold day that was miraculously clear. We walked the streets of the city afterwards, holding hands, stopping to kiss here and there, and then made out for a little while in his Jeep. But fumbling with coats and scarves over the stick shift soon broke the spell. Oral sex would have worked, but I was shy about mentioning that. After a few minutes, he sat up, straightened his shirt, and said he had to go to band practice.

"He's a tease," Lynda said. "He gets off on having the power to say yes or no."

"He's scared," Nat said. "You're older and more knowledgeable and in every way intimidating."

But neither explanation was comforting, or told me what I might do to change things.

And then there was T.J. Part of me felt absolutely obligated to break it off with him—after all, hadn't I told Vincent that I wasn't involved with anyone else? But then, what right did Vincent have to say who I could and couldn't have sex with? It's one thing to ask for monogamy, I reasoned, and quite another to ask for celibacy while you're taking your sweet time warming up and your partner simmers and stews.

There is some rationalization here, I admit. But when I returned to my place from that failed makeout session and T.J. called, I said, "Come over." And soon we were back on our regular schedule of two or three times a week. If either of them had been less busy, T.J. with his restaurant or Vincent with his music, it might have been harder to hide their existence from each other, but for a little while it worked, and a little while was all I needed.

Meanwhile, T.J. was going through a dangerously slow time at the Landing. Real snow was one thing, he said—a good snowstorm, a day off work, and people would come out to eat and drink. But no one wanted to go out in this weather. He was grouchy about other things, too. Elizabeth wanted him in Chicago for Christmas. His parents wanted him on the Eastern Shore. He wanted to go skiing with some buddies in Colorado, but didn't think he ought to leave the Landing when business was so bad. Lynda had some great ideas for promotions; maybe it was time to introduce live music.

"I should probably stay in D.C. and work," he said, "but then everybody would be mad at me. Shit, the holidays. I wish I could skip them, just this once."

I agreed. Dylan had gotten his way, and we were all flying to Boston for Christmas—Dad, Carrie, Katherine, David, me. It was my first Christmas as a single woman in almost a decade, and I was not looking forward to Dylan's teasing, Carrie's unsubtle questions, David's look of benign concern. Katherine would behave beautifully, I knew, and I could always take refuge in playing with Maggie or discussing interior decoration with Jennifer. But like T.J., I would have preferred to stay home and work.

Any idea that Vincent might present a more appealing alternative was quickly banished when he spotted the holiday lights and wreaths as we were leaving the Kennedy Center concert. He hated everything about Christmas, he said. It wasn't just that he didn't believe in God, much less Jesus Christ—he was a Taoist, after all—but our culture's obsession with the holiday season disgusted him. He hated forced gaiety and forced giving. He hated the importance people attached to the gifts they got and the gifts they gave, to the food they cooked and ate.

"It's all greed and gluttony," he said. "It's depressing."

I was about to make a joke about the Seven Deadly Sins, but stopped myself.

"I guess it is a bit much," I said. "But—"

"I knew you'd get it," he said, giving my hand an approving squeeze. He went on to say that in any case he would be out of town the last week of December, visiting his mother, a sensible atheist, at her home in Santa Barbara. They would eat healthy food—she was a vegetarian, too—and do yoga every morning. And she would never expect him to give her a gift.

"The poor guy," Natalie said. "He must be really wounded."

"Or it's a very convenient way to save a lot of money at Christmas," Lynda said. "I don't know, Lou. You *like* gifts. And this does not bode well for Valentine's Day."

Meanwhile, I had bigger things to worry about. Daniel had been calling from the gallery, saying that Dana wanted to make a studio visit before the holidays. I had some idea of how Dana Reilly thought, and would have preferred a few more months of work before showing the new paintings to anyone. I never share work in progress—I've learned the hard way how the wrong comment at the wrong time can derail me from a piece for weeks, for months, forever. Daniel, however, said that Dana would not be deterred.

"She's heard it all, honey, as far as trying to put off a studio visit. She'll see what you've got before Christmas if she has to shimmy up your drainpipe to do it."

"I'm just not sure—"

"Well, she's sure. So pick a date, OK?"

"All right. I'm sorry to be an idiot."

"You're not an idiot, you're just nervous. Of course. But she's excited about you, Louise. We all are. She'll love your new work. It'll be fun. Like a little cocktail party."

"I'll get some wine."

"For Mrs. R., you might want to lay in some vodka. Something to nibble, too."

"The studio's kind of a mess."

"She's used to that. It's the paintings she wants to see."

I'd finished another painting, this one of Benedict, the young musician in the story about Dove Abbey. I gave him sandy hair and hazel eyes and very fair skin. And I'd sketched and then begun to paint other scenes from that piece of story—the monk and the abbess talking in a room hung with drapes, the girl with her ring of stones.

On the big day, I set up a little bar with vodka, wine, ice, glasses, and a tray of appetizers T.J. had brought me that morning from the Landing. He'd seemed even more nervous about the visit than I was, and kept giving me fumbling good luck kisses and equally fumbling words of encouragement. I hadn't told Vincent about the visit at all, for complicated reasons—I didn't know if he had told anyone, much less Dana, that we were dating, and I did not want to ask; more importantly, I am as superstitious about who I share news about my work with as I am about when and how I share the work itself. I could trust T.J. because he did not really understand what was at stake. Vincent would understand, but his opinions might be less than helpful. I was grateful that he was already in California when Dana made her studio visit.

I had five pieces to show her—the diptych of my mother, Angie, and the other, unnamed woman; the landscape of the mountain; the portrait of the musician; the girl with her ring of stones; and the monk and the abbess in her room. The last two were not quite done, but far enough along, I told myself, for Dana to see. I arranged and rearranged them along two walls. Then I draped them all.

At five o'clock—"happy hour time," Daniel had suggested, "that makes it more festive"—I opened the door to him and Dana. Behind them stood Gerry Heller.

That was the first surprise.

I offered everyone drinks, gestured to the chairs I'd put out. But Dana was in no mood to sit down.

"My god, this neighborhood, Lou-Lou," she complained, pacing. "It's so much, well, shabbier than I thought. I thought you said you'd found a wonderful space."

"I did. Look at how much room I have. And the area is coming back, slowly, slowly. I was smart to get in when I did."

"Well, I suppose. Still, you would not believe how we had to circle and circle for parking. And those people hanging around outside the Lotto sign, so depressing— did you say vodka?"

"Yes. Or white wine."

"Vodka," she said. "Light on the tonic."

"I'll get the drinks, Louise," Gerry said, hastily. "No trouble. You talk to Dana."

She stood in the center of the studio, hands on her hips, surveying everything—my shelves and supplies, the various sketches tacked to the walls—left to right, like an unhappy general. Daniel stood beside her, his notepad out.

"You do have good light here," she said, grudgingly.

Close to her now, I felt her nervous, crackling energy. This is not the mood she should be in to see my new work, I thought. I should have been firm in saying *not yet*.

"I thought I'd undrape them one by one, in the order they were made, and say a little bit about each."

She waved her hand in the air.

"Oh, let's save the dramatics for the show. Undrape everything. Let's see it *all*. Without explanation or explication."

She spun around, almost bumping into Gerry Heller, who stood behind her with our drinks.

"At last."

"And those canapés look delicious," said Daniel. "Why don't I get you a little plate, Mrs. R.?"

"I'd rather have a cigarette."

"Dana."

"Yes, Gerry, dear. I'll be a good girl. Promise."

"I'll just undrape these, then."

It was good to turn my back, however briefly, on the tense group. I remembered Daniel saying something about Dana's "crush" on Heller, but I hadn't known he was even in town anymore. It seemed unlike Dana to bring a lover to a business meeting. The nervousness I'd managed to quell before her arrival suddenly asserted itself in a little ring of sweat along my hairline.

When I turned back, they had settled into chairs and were looking at the paintings. On the wall across from them, I'd placed the vertical canvasses. On the wall to our left, I had placed the two horizontal canvases, one of the monk and the abbess, and the other of the landscape with its strangely sloped hill.

I stood behind their chairs, took a sip of the wine Gerry had handed me, and waited.

Silence. Silence. Each of us, Gerry, Daniel, and I, looked in turn at Dana. She sat, cocktail in one hand, the other hand upraised as if holding her longed-for cigarette. One long leg was crossed over the other, and a black suede high-heeled boot twitched back and forth in the air, impatiently. She looked from left to right at each painting in turn, and then from right to left. Still not a word.

"How interesting—blending archaic subject matter with contemporary techniques," Gerry Heller began.

"And I love the colors, such luscious colors," Daniel put in.

They looked at Dana. Nothing.

"I'm intrigued by the use of symbolism in the landscape," Gerry tried again. "There seems to be something in these stones, in that recurring gray."

"And the dimensions of the canvases. An interesting shape, like Tarot cards."

Still nothing from Dana.

"And you've got a terrific hand, Louise," Gerry said, gaining momentum now. "What a line. The way you've captured that woman's face. Such a sure touch. But light, too."

"And the one of the boy," Daniel went on, "you'd think you could reach out and touch his hair, it looks so real."

"All right, all right!"

Dana set her empty glass loudly on the floor, and pushed herself up out of her chair.

"Enough bullshit," she said. "Of *course* she can draw. Of course she can *ren*der—hair, skin, whatever. But that's scarcely the point, is it?"

We all looked at her.

"I think we can all say that twenty-first-century art has to be more than well rendered."

"But these people," I began, "you see how they recur, in various settings—"

"Which brings me to another point. Who *are* these people, anyway? Warhol had Marilyn. Van Gogh had him*self*, for god's sake. But these people—"

"They're kind of a mix," I said, keeping my voice steady. "Historical, personal, imagined."

"Is there some con*nec*tion between them? Something that makes this a *body* of work?"

"There's a story," I said. "Pieces of a story."

"So they're illustrative, these paintings."

"No, not illustrative. They're not meant to accompany a text. But they are narrative."

"So can you tell me the story?"

"It's not finished yet. I'm finding it as I go."

She shook her head.

"I'm sorry, Louise, but I just don't get it."

She sighed a deep, imperial sigh and pulled out a cigarette. Daniel jumped to his feet with a lighter.

"Dana," Gerry said, admonishing.

"The first one today, for Christ's sake."

"More like the seventh or eighth. And Louise might not want you to smoke in her studio."

Daniel's hand hesitated in the air. Gerry was right, I don't let people smoke in the studio. But a cigarette might soften her mood, make her judge the work less harshly.

"It's fine," I said.

She took a long drag, let it out, took another. Gerry Heller got up and began to sift through the things on my worktable for a likely ashtray, found an old paint lid, and brought it to where Dana was smoking and fuming in the center of the room.

"As the other artist present," he said, "I think I should say you're being rather hard on work in progress, Dana. And on Louise. A thing, an idea, develops over time. There are five pieces here. Let there be five more. Then take another look."

She opened her mouth, but he kept talking.

"And it's a big jump she's made. These are very different from the slides you showed me. It's ambitious work. It needs room to grow."

I'd dismissed him as an urban cowboy, with his bolo ties and turquoise and silver bracelets. Now I wanted to hug him.

"That may be the case, my dear. But there's not a lot of room between now and November, is there? For *growing?*"

"What's going on in November?" I said.

"Neil Larsen just got a big commission in Madrid. He pulled out of his fall show, the arrogant jerk. I thought, maybe—well, maybe—"

"Mrs. R. was thinking you might be ready to step in," Daniel said.

"I think I am. I could be, by then."

"I don't know," said Dana, shaking her head. "I'm just not seeing it. I'm just not seeing the makings of a real *show* here."

Suddenly, her tone shifted. Almost conciliatory now, she came and put her arm around me, and began to lead me from painting to painting.

"I mean, look here, these two," she said softly. "With the crosses."

"A monk and an abbess," I said. "They have their own story."

"I'm sure. How interesting *is* their story, really? And here, this landscape—yes, it's beautifully rendered, I'll give it that. But where is it, what is it, why does it matter?"

"Well, it's their setting. One of them, anyway. I mean—"

"And all these stones Gerry was talking about. Where are we, at Stonehenge or something? Druids? Cycles of the moon? Isn't it all a bit Dungeons and Dragons, my dear? Or like something out of a feminist fantasy novel?"

"As I said, there's a kind of story, a broken narrative I'm following—"

"Yes, but to what *end?* And really, is it even a story worth telling? I say, don't waste any more time on this, darling. Scrap it now. Remember those *Seven Deadly Sins* everyone loved so much? What about something like that, only bigger, brighter, bolder? Now that's the kind of work I can *sell*."

I had no idea what to say or how to feel. Could I have really been that wrong about the new paintings? And who was this purring, insidious woman? This wasn't the Dana Reilly I'd met and so admired.

Daniel was looking at the floor. Gerry Heller had retreated to the far corner of the room, and seemed to be studying a row of sketches I'd pinned up. Clearly, neither one of them was going to dive in now. I was on my own.

And then a strange thing happened. I felt a hand on mine, a woman's hand, with slender fingers, steadying me. Then it pulled, and I was out from under Dana's arm. I walked to the far corner of the studio, where my mother's box rested. I put one hand on it, turned to face them. And as I did it, there it was—my mother's perfume, the scent of it unmistakable in the air around me. Shalimar.

"I can't scrap it now," I said. "I'm just beginning to see where it's leading."

"But why waste any more time—"

"Because I don't think it is a waste of time. I just don't. Maybe I can't explain it yet, but it feels right, it feels like what I ought to be doing. I'm on my way to finding something here, I know it."

Gerry Heller handed me a refilled glass of wine. I took a sip, went on.

"And I can't rush it. I'm sorry if that's a disappointment. I'd like to work faster, myself. But if I'm careful, I can survive for a lot more time on that grant. And I'm going to see where this work goes."

"And good for you, Louise. That's just the attitude you should have."

That was Heller.

"Louise did say, Mrs. R., that she wanted to wait a couple more months—remember?—before your visit."

Dana looked around at all of us, blinking her innocence.

"Oh, lord. Now you've all ganged up on me. I'm the evil witch from hell, I suppose. Just because I want to make all of you famous."

"I don't want to be famous," Daniel said. "But I would like to have dinner sometime soon."

The dark mood broke then. Dana laughed.

"It's just that November—"

"November will solve itself, my dear," Heller said. He used the soothing tone on her that a parent would use with an irritable child. I would have bristled, but somehow it worked on Dana. She became her old self, complimenting me on my hair and shoes, taking half-bites of T.J.'s stuffed mushrooms, downing a last drink.

But as they filed out, she stopped in the doorway, leaned in close to me and said, "Remember, Lou-Lou, you're not at A Woman's Place anymore. You're in a different league now."

I closed the door behind them, leaned back against it, and closed my eyes.

I had had high hopes, perhaps too high. Still, it was hard to imagine how the visit could have been worse. I'd had bad critiques before, been turned down for this

or that—it's a part of the artist's life, to deal with rejec-
tion, to get back up, to keep working, keep fighting.
But this, coming when and how it did, was particularly
painful.

I never talked to my mother about such things while
she was alive. I'd never have thought she would understand. But she had come to me, I was sure of it. It was
my mother—it had to be my mother—who had taken my
hand and led me out from under Dana's arm, who filled
the room with her perfume just so I'd know without a
doubt that she was there, and on my side.

❧

I HAD A FEW BAD days after Dana's visit, drinking too
much, not really working very well or for very long on
anything. I stared out the windows a lot, muttered to
myself, paced. This is the danger of being in the studio all
day. Back when I was at A Woman's Place I would have
had to shower, dress, interact with others, function in the
world outside. As it was, I was free to wallow.

What made it harder was that there was no one I
could tell. Lynda would sympathize, but any discussion
of Dana's visit would touch on her own disappointments
in theater and that was the last thing I wanted to do.
And even if I left out the insulting words about the Place,
I wasn't sure I could tell Natalie, either. The advantages
of being with a gallery like Dana's were obvious, but also
represented everything that we'd stood against in founding A Woman's Place. If it was hard for Tim Gould to see
how I could have wanted to make that jump, how much
harder and more complex it was for Natalie, no matter
what she said about it.

"You traded up, leaving the Place," Lynda had said. "Nat's gotta know that, and it's gotta hurt."

Though I'd resisted the cold terminology, that was indeed what I had been trying to do. The fact that I might have failed in the attempt was not something I wanted to share with Nat. It would be like confiding your problems with your current lover in the lover you left him for. In the old days, we had shared everything, every bump and triumph, artistic, romantic, personal. But the world was different now.

I gave T.J. a radically edited version of what had happened, saying that Dana was interested in the new work, but not totally sold on it yet. That she'd be back in a few months to see where it led. I had to tell him something, after all—he'd been so excited for me. But the only person I told anything like the truth about what had happened between Dana and me was my mother's old lover, Lawrence Ware.

While I'm painting, I never stop to answer the phone, and after Dana's visit I stopped answering it even when I wasn't painting. But one night, when I was brooding and drinking, the phone rang and the caller ID said "Out of area." Could it be Vincent from California? The thought of him stabbed—just what I needed, or not? Of course, I answered.

Instead of Vincent's soft tenor, I head a deep male voice, beautifully accented in the way of a movie actor's in one of those English period films about manor houses and marriage plans.

"May I speak with Miss Terry, please? Miss Louise Terry?"

"You've got her."

"At last. At last. I was beginning to think I might have to fly across the Atlantic to find you."

"Mr. Ware."

"Call me Larry, please."

"Larry. That's right, your message. I'm sorry, I should have called you back by now. You said there was something you wanted to discuss."

"Ah, yes. A small matter. But there is no need for haste, at least, not on this end. You sound...well, you sound so like your mother, my dear. Your voice could be her voice. It is such a pleasure, to hear that sound again."

I didn't know what to say. His own voice was delicious, slow and low. He sounded a little drunk. I looked at the clock. It would be just after ten at night in England. Probably he'd just come in from some pub, and was feeling sentimental.

"You think me a sentimental old fool, don't you? Or a drunk. Well, perhaps."

"If you'd called a bit later, I'd have had a few drinks myself."

"Now, that's more like it. You see, if we were in a pub, we'd have no shortage of conversation. So here's an idea. Why don't you put down the phone and go get yourself a drink of something. Something strong. Then come back and we'll have a chat. Like old friends."

"Your long distance bill will be outrageous."

"Yes, but my sister pays it, you see. The price of my bondage to her wretched house."

"In London?"

"Christ, no. In bloody Oxford. Excuse my language, if you would, my dear. Now, about your drink."

I spent a little over an hour on the phone with Lawrence Ware that night. I drank a bottle of merlot, and began another. He was drinking scotch, which he urged me to develop a taste for. Perhaps because of the hour, or that seductive voice, or the fact that I was aching to confide in someone, anyone, I told him the whole story of my relationship with Dana, up to and including her calamitous studio visit.

To my surprise, he laughed.

"Marvelous," he said. "In its sheer predictability, marvelous."

"I don't understand."

"She's testing you, my dear. Don't you see? You seem to have a reputation for, shall we say, independence? Founding your own arts group, and so on?"

"Cofounding. Yes."

"And I believe it was a feminist organization, this, this—"

"A Woman's Place. It's a riff on the old saying, 'A woman's place is in the home.'"

"I did get it the first time, my dear. In any case, she needs to be sure that your political beliefs don't interfere with the, how shall I put it, marketability of your work?"

"I can't think about that crap," I said. "Not while I'm working. No, it's me, it's my fault, I let her come here too soon. I should have held her off. I was too easy."

"It would not have mattered, Louise. Don't you see? She's been building you up, and now it is time to break you down. And never forget feminine jealousy, my dear. You say she brought her lover. Well, perhaps his enthusiasm dampened her own. In any case, it's her way of keeping you on the leash."

"But she wasn't like that before. She believed, at least I thought she believed, in the work, in me—"

"She believes in money, your lady art dealer. You can trust me on that. They're all alike, whatever the genre."

I heard him take a long sip of his drink.

"It's all in the marketing departments now, my dear. That's where the power is. The age of the enlightened impresario, the discoverer and nurturer of the artist, all that is over. There is no altruism left in the world of art, and no idealism. Just money, money, money."

"It's so depressing."

"It is what it is, my dear. Pretending will not make it less so."

"Well, I'm sorry I babbled at you. What was it you called about, anyway?"

"Oh, there's time. Why don't we fetch another round?"

When I came back to the phone, he said that if I wanted his opinion, what I really needed was a change of scenery.

"Why don't you come to London, my dear? I don't have to tell you about the museums, of course. But there is so much else, as well. And I could show you around, introduce you to some people. People to whom, by the way, your Dana Reilly is very small beer, indeed."

"Well, I might be there in spring. If I get into this show. Which I'm not sure about now, actually."

"Don't say *might*, say *will*. You *will* come in the spring."

"Maybe," I said. "Maybe. I'm trying to stretch my grant, you see."

"So you got a lovely big grant and thought you'd spend all of it in your little hole, painting paintings?"

"For one thing, I do not live in a little hole. And not all of us—well, not all of us are as successful as you are.

I mean, you were a star when you were still just a kid, right? Published at seventeen, or something?"

The flattery softened him, as I knew it would.

"So your mother told you the old story, eh? Well, yes, the first book of poems came out at eighteen, actually. The first play one, no, two years later. And on from there."

"Amazing."

"There was some element of luck involved, my dear. There always is. And one learns, over time, to play the game. Which you did quite well with Madam Reilly."

"I did?"

"You stood by your work—"

"Of course."

"You proved you can't be easily managed or bossed about."

"True."

"And by taking such a strong stand now, you've left yourself plenty of room to make concessions later, if need be."

"Concessions?"

"Don't sound so stricken, my dear. You've made them before, whether you admit it or not."

"But—"

"I remember when I was at RADA—the Royal Academy of Dramatic Art, you know—we had a master class with…"

A long story, and then another followed, peppered with important names, only half of which I got. My mind wandered. I looked at the fresh canvas I'd stretched, envisioning what it might soon hold. Vincent, maybe. Ever since I'd sketched his face, I'd been yearning to paint him properly.

"And when you come, my dear, perhaps you might—bring something with you?"

"Bring something?"

"To London. Something that is mine, of course, but which may have got mixed in with your mother's...possessions?"

"What is it?"

"A statue, my dear. About seven or eight inches tall, of a man of the cloth. A monk in his robe and hood. Made of wood, very roughly carved. It is old, and of no real value beyond the sentimental. But your mother, she had a fondness for it."

"A statue."

"Yes. It has been in my family for who knows how many generations. Margaret kept it in her room for a time. But the thing is not mine to give. It is family property."

"Larry, I'm sorry, but I've never seen anything like that."

"Are you sure? Quite sure? She liked to keep it on her bedside table."

"Not that I can recall."

"If you could make inquiries, my dear. Would it be too difficult? Perhaps you could ring your siblings? And your mother's old...her old..."

"Kenny moved back to North Carolina after Mom died. I could call him, I guess. And I'm going to see everyone else at Christmas."

"If you could. I cannot stress how important this is."

"But I thought you said it wasn't valuable?"

"Not in a monetary sense, no. But my...well, my sister is quite distressed about it. If it were up to me, I would never trouble you, my dear."

"Your sister sounds like a difficult person," I said.

"She is a recalcitrant bitch who lives to torture those unfortunate enough to know her. Or, as in my case, share the same blood. But there it is."

I promised him I would do my best to find his statue, and after a little more talk, we said our goodbyes.

Afterwards, I felt briefly guilty, as if after a one-night stand. Why had I stayed on the phone for so long with my mother's lover, having drinks in our imaginary pub? What were we doing, flattering, teasing each other, flirting? And to what end?

It could not have been to bring my mother closer to us. We had scarcely talked about her.

But I did see now a little of what she had seen in Larry. That voice, for one thing. And his arrogance was, well, sexy. It would be fun to let him show me London, to be escorted around by a famous playwright, meet his successful friends. And it would certainly show Dana something, as he had suggested, if I were to make connections across the ocean.

The day after my phone conversation with Larry, an envelope arrived in the mail from Fellowship House, with a printout of the old floppy disk I had sent to Brother Paul. It is a measure of how deeply I had immersed myself in the box's evolving story that I did not even shake my head at the coincidence.

7

It was laid out like a book manuscript. The first page was a title page, with "The Story of Saint Margaret of Evesham, Mystic and Healer, by Felicity Amble-Pierce," neatly centered. The next had this:

While this account is, strictly speaking, a work of imagination and inspiration, it is based on true and actual events in the life of Saint Margaret of Evesham, a great mystic and teacher. According to tales that have been handed down through generations, Margaret entered the religious life while still a girl, taking the veil in an abbey in Oxford some time in the latter half of the twelfth century. Our Lady made Herself known to Margaret in dreams and visions that began when the girl was perhaps ten years old. Though some say that Margaret, like others who have been given the Gift of Light, shrugged off the weight of this life early, others believe that the young woman, persecuted for her gifts and distrusted by those who might have helped her, fled, perhaps in disguise, and took up her work, as well as another identity, in the west or north.

Though the Church of Rome has not seen fit as yet to canonize Margaret, tales of her goodness and her miracles live on in Evesham and Oxford, and prayers to her do not go unanswered.

She is truly part of that medieval flowering of mystic wisdom that included such women as Christina of Markyate and Hildegard of Bingen. It is to be hoped that this work will shed light on the tasks and triumphs of this noble woman.

Some may say our methods have been unorthodox, if not outright sloppy; our reliance on the oral traditions of literature and history excessive; and our conclusions precipitate. To them we say:

"There are more ways of knowing than there are stars in the sky."

Then came a copyright notice from 1995, Hollow Hills Press, Oxford, England, and a dedication page: "To all the women, Amble and Pierce and otherwise, who undertake the Journey. May She be with You."

Amble and Pierce, it sounded like a nursery rhyme. I turned the page, and began to read.

It is like this: The world we are born into
Is like a sheet of embroidered cloth.
On the surface of the cloth, we see the pattern
Of the world as it seems to be: in which
We eat and sleep and love and hate,
Throughout each ordinary day and night.
For some this is enough. But as for us—
We who feel the knots and twists beneath
The cloth as if they lived beneath our own
Thin skin—we cannot rest until we know
The Hand that worked the pattern, until
We see Her, dazzling, aflame with Holy Light,
Her needle in hand, Her thread one long pure
Thread of Fire that will pierce our hearts,
When we are ready, and make us Hers and Whole.
—from The Revelations of Saint Margaret

Imagine a girl from nowhere, a nobody, poor and small and without parents or protection, cast out into this world alone, onto her fate. Imagine her wracked with things she does not understand. Sometimes the trees shiver and call out to her in tongues of flame. Sometimes the river rises up to sing in words she alone can understand. Imagine that her mother had the power too, and died for it.

She would be frightened. She would be cunning. But she would be true to her gift.

Imagine her now in a house of women, taken in, taken under the wing of the abbess who loves but does not understand her. Imagine how the abbess would see the girl's struggle, and love her for it. And yet. And yet. How Margaret will trust her, how she will come to depend on her. How the girl will be loved and cared for, and then treated with suspicion, and then betrayed.

And wherever women of power are gathered there is always a man, there is always at least one man, hovering, waiting, wanting to strike, to snatch. Imagine there are two. One is still a boy, half in, half out of the church, giving himself wholly only to music, the music he makes. Like the girl, he has a gift of his own to protect. The other is a man and powerful, he is not a bad man, really, he intends to help the girl. But he wants, as well, to be near to the light she carries; he wants to help her to bear and then to speak it. He himself once felt such things, once saw the tongues of fire in the grass blades, heard the voices of the clouds, saw the created world as Whole and Holy.

One day it stopped. He did not know why. Then he began to devote himself to finding and fostering the gifts of others.

So these are our players, plus one more. Every mystic must have a scribe, every true servant of the Light must have one friend whose feet are firmly on this earth. And so Margaret had one faithful friend, assigned to her duties, who would soon perform them out of love: she had Christina, named after the Lord's Son Himself, and given to do good.

* * *

Sometimes she knows when it will come upon her. She feels an echoing in her bones as if she is hollow, as if she is being played, a pipe, and the grass singes her feet and she knows it is coming. Sometimes she does not know, and it creeps up to her, then grabs her, splits her, runs her ragged, runs her aground.

After a time, she comes to know three forms:

One, the eternal singing. This is the music the earth makes, going about its business. The bees, the worms, the light, the wind, the seasons. Sometimes it is as if another ear opens within her and she can hear the whole of it, the many voices woven into one song. A wren might turn and say her name, the moss in the rookery might tremble, speak. At first it frightened her, how it turned her flesh translucent; then she came to love and long for it.

This form had gone on for as long as she could remember.

Two, the Lady's Story. Less common than the first, this form was the most taxing, asked the most of her. A lady, some said the Mother of Our Lord, would come to her and lead her somewhere. In this form the created world fell away, and she entered wholly into the Light, the worlds above, the worlds below. Sometimes it was difficult to return; she thought she might leave bits of her soul in the other world and her sisters feared for her. Sometimes she did not want to return, and she feared for herself.

Three, the revelatory moment. These come like flashes, bursts of sight. A door opens, she sees a bit of what is or is to come and then it closes. Seeing the shadow of a girl following one of her sisters across the garden, she knows it for the spirit of the woman's stillborn child forced out of her body before she came here. When the monk comes from his grand abbey with his bright smile and kind words, she sees the hole in him that the death of his abbot has left. Sometimes she sees who will die, and when, or how the seasons will change early or late, bringing with them frost or flood or fire.

This is what they want to hear, the pilgrims, when they come. Only a few, girls mostly, ask about the Lady's Story. No one listens when she speaks of the glowing sky and the singing grass. They want to know: When will the drought end? Will I have a child? Who stole my horse? Who killed my brother?

And so, like an actor who holds the crowd's attention with his antics while behind the curtain the next scene is prepared, she give them bits of what they want to know, interspersed with the Sacred Truth of Our Lady they do not know they need. She gives them a prayer:

> *Oh, Mother of all mercies. Oh, Lady of Light.*
> *Oh, she who is Queen of hill and forest,*
> *Of river and stream and every living thing,*
> *Be with us in our fear, our need, our terror.*
> *Be with us in this hard and burdened world,*
> *This life that aches with what it cannot be.*
> *See how our souls grow weak and restless*
> *Trapped in these bodies that do not fit or suit us.*
> *Know that we would change them if we could.*
> *Help us, oh most High and Holy Lady, to be*
> *Pure spirit, one hard living flame. Help us to burn*
> *From wick to ash, and not to turn away.*

* * *

And what of the abbess, Elizabeth? Surely she must miss the child Margaret used to be. She has her own fires now, and no longer looks at the older woman with those wide and trusting eyes. The abbess still sees that look on the girl's face from time to time, but now it is reserved for Brother Martin, for his visits, for their private meetings that he no longer invites the abbess even to share.

And she wonders...what does it gain the abbey, precisely, to have this girl and her visions? A pile of parchments? The loss of Christina's steady eye and capable hand at other things. Encouraging words from the monk, Martin, whom Elizabeth has come to like less and less. Words are easy things for him, she thinks. He does not have to live with Margaret's gift day to day, nor cope with the envy of the other girls, nor sacrifice the peace of the many for the talents of the one. It is different in Glastonbury, where they are wealthy and novices are plentiful and they can do what they please. From the way Brother Martin talks, it would seem that he and his brothers spend all their time illuminating manuscripts with precious inks, or carving out of wood or stone more ornaments for their abbey, or acquiring relics, or dining with the titled and the powerful.

Dove Abbey is a different matter. She is the mother here.

She was exceptional in her own way, Elizabeth. She was born to privilege, yes, but with a mind as fine as any. She quickly learned to read and write, both the vernacular and Latin. Her needlework was exquisite. She was handsome rather than pretty, strong, confident, and proud. Perhaps she believed herself, like Margaret, to be destined for important things.

She entered the abbey a widow, with some money of her own. She had grown married sons, who did not need her. She had felt her usefulness sour, her abilities drying on the vine. After a life ordered by men, she saw the lure of a society of women. She saw how a woman like her, educated, accomplished, and of good family, might rise swiftly through the ranks. There was much one could accomplish in a house of God.

But Divine Light throws even the exceptional into shade, and Margaret is blazing. It is one thing to be given in the service of Our Lord, and another thing entirely to have the Word direct. In place of faith, Margaret now has fact. While Elizabeth can only pray, Margaret is carried up, emblazoned by Our Lady, and transformed.

She and the monk each have their reasons for not wanting word of Margaret's gifts to pass the abbey doors. Word, like water, will travel anyway. But how?

* * *

Let us see Benedict, left to himself, singing and playing. He writes one song and then another, and then the beginnings of a third, about the girl in Dove Abbey who sees such wonders. He describes the touch of the Lady's hand, the girl's own fears and longings. He thinks, *these songs will be a gift for Margaret.* When he sees her again, he can sing her story back to her.

Let us follow him on a day after days of rain, the sky rinsed
a clear, pale blue. He and Martin are midway between Dove
Abbey and Glastonbury. They stop by the river to feed the
horses, to eat. Martin goes off on some business, Benedict
thinks it has to do with a boy they passed, but does not say it.
He settles himself under a black elm and sings, along with the
old, some of his new songs.

Soon a small crowd has formed, and they listen, he notices,
with particular interest to the songs about Margaret. In between,
one woman asks questions about the stories in the songs, particularly about the girl. As Benedict answers her, saying that
these songs are based on the life of a real young nun, living not
far from there, he feels a sudden pang, as if he has let a precious
secret slip. But then he comforts himself with the thought that
these people will never see Margaret or hear her name. She cannot travel, and they would never bother to find her.

Because he is not truly a believer himself, despite all of Martin's efforts, because God, when Benedict thinks of Him at all,
is a matter for only a vague, doubtful fear, not faith, the young
man underestimates the will of those who do believe. In any
case, he is back in Glastonbury, where Martin has found him
work with a carpenter, still undecided—should he enter abbey
life, as Martin believes? Should he simply make a life here,
learn his trade, and marry?—and far from Dove Abbey when
the first pilgrims arrive looking for Margaret.

* * *

The good time was so brief. From Easter to Midsummer's Eve
the pilgrims came. The abbess did nothing, indeed, could do
nothing, to stop them. They came from no one place. They were
not organized into any coherent group and they would not be
stopped. It would have been unkind, un-Christian, near impossible to turn them all away.

And Elizabeth was weak. What had been going on for
years—the slow, almost imperceptible dimming of her powers—was now accelerated. At the Easter vigil, she had leaned
on a curved stick, tucked half-hidden in her robe; by the Festival

of Our Lady she had needed two sticks and Christina's sturdy arm around her back. Such support must be of the most sly, or she will shove it off, thrust her helper away. She must seem to do it all on her own. While her body curls downward to the ash, the dust, the earth she will become, she strives to stand ever more straight and proud. She listens less and squabbles more. She grows more angry. She will not, cannot, rest.

And she would be jealous, of course. How not? The monk and his favorite messenger, the dirty-faced boy who is always humming, whistling, singing to himself, would become like thieves to her. They steal her peace. They steal her girl. To have her back again she is willing to be cruel. She is willing to hurt in return for her own hurts.

We all know what jealousy can do. We have all seen the serpent, felt the chill of his tongue along the heart.

Meanwhile, in her cell, or in the chapel, or in the fields behind the abbey, going greener every day, Margaret continues to meet the Lady. *This is what I was born for*, she thinks, *whatever this is. Whatever I am. This light and I were made for each other.*

> *I am alone in a dark corridor of stone. I stand*
> *And do not know which way to go. The passage*
> *Curves on either side off into shadow. My heart*
> *Beats hard. The air is cold. I tell myself*
> *To choose. There is a reason. I close my eyes*
> *And feel the Lady, warm, nearby. I see her Light*
> *Through my closed lids, then feel her. I look,*
> *And there she is.*
>
> *She holds her hand out, looks into my eyes.*
> *To begin is everything, she says. It is never*
> *Too early, nor too late. I say, I do not know*
> *If I am ready. She takes my hand. It is warm,*
> *Like water, water running through me. I follow her.*
>
> *The circle of light she casts around her*
> *Made of glittering gold. Her light so pure.*
> *And I, so thin and empty. The corridor*

Keeps turning, turning down, doubling back,
And ever lower. I had thought Her love
Would take me up, not down.

Just then, a flash of light, and we are outside.
It is early night. I hear the sound of water
Over rock. I see a spring running over stone
Into a round pool, the water clear but stained,
As if with drops of ink, to a soft red. I drink
The water. I drink the water. I drink the water.

I enter the water. The Lady puts one hand
On my forehead. At her touch, I am empty.
At her touch I am full. She says: This is the Holy Light
Of the Father that pours like water. This is the Holy Light
Of His Son that burns like fire. This is the Holy Light
Of the Spirit that turns and turns us, the Light everlasting.
Though all else fades, this will remain.
I am lifted then, as if on wings of air. I rise so high
Above the water. Looking down, I see, in the rippling,
Bright red water, an enormous fish. It glows with light.
It shimmers. The Lady says, He will be with you.
Listen. Follow. Here is where you belong.

* * *

Imagine her. She would have been almost always cold, almost always wet. The rough wool robes would have chafed her skin. The sisters would not have practiced flagellation, but perhaps she called her pain her penance. Perhaps she found a kind of pleasure in denying her body comfort, in not eating, not sleeping. Perhaps it brought the Light a little closer.

She had ways, rituals, habits, that helped her to prepare for the Lady's visits. A ring of stones, a dance, a candle flame to stare into until the eyes brimmed over. Perhaps Christina helped her prepare, and protected her from interruption when the flame was at its height. Christina would have had great faith in the Lord and Lady of Light, and in Margaret as well. They would have felt themselves safe for a time inside the abbey walls.

But where was Margaret, really? One foot in this world, one foot in the other; always divided, and always alone. The love of her abbess a thing of the past, the love of the monk conditional, divided. Had she been a man, she might have had a place of honor, like Saint Benedict, who met the devil in battle and was able to beat him. He had visions and was not challenged; he heard voices and could trust them.

How long would it take her to realize that life would be different, better, richer, if she were a man?

Ah, the mess of it. Benedict wants Margaret, Margaret wishes she could be Benedict. Martin wants Benedict for his abbey and Elizabeth wants Margaret for hers, but Margaret as she was, not as she is. Christina wants only peace, but peace is not available now. Peace ended when the first pilgrims came to the abbey gate.

* * *

If there is no trace of her, perhaps she died young. People lived short lives then, before penicillin, aspirin, and sterile sutures. She might have succumbed to any number of diseases. She might have died from pneumonia, from chicken pox, from the flu; she might have eaten a poisonous mushroom or been trampled by a horse.

> *A maze, a map, a hill, a tree,*
> *A place for all, and all for thee.*
> *A Lady's face, a blaze of Light*
> *You enter through the earth at night.*
> *Follow the Fish as He swims down,*
> *Believe in Her, you will not drown.*
> *Your first best place, this well, this water.*
> *Return and know you are Her Daughter.*

The manuscript ended there.

In some ways it was a continuation of what I'd read before—the same characters, the same names. But how differently these characters were treated. And who was "us," anyway? This piece seemed to be written by a group, though there was just that one name at the top of the manuscript. Felicity Amble-Pierce. Could she be someone my mother befriended in England?

Prayers and visions, a magic fish, a girl who sees things, a nun who loves then hates her. A boy who plays music, a monk who is...what? Good? Bad? He seemed like a good man, a kind man, in the first part, though the writer here described him and the boy, both, as being malevolent. *Ready to strike.*

I remembered a dictionary of saints that I had seen in my mother's box, and got it out. There was no listing for Saint Margaret of Evesham, though there were a lot of other Saint Margarets—Margaret the Barefooted, Margaret of Scotland, Margaret the Penitent. There was also a Margaret of England, who died in 1192. That would fit with the dates on both parts of the story, I thought. The entry said she had gone on a pilgrimage to Jerusalem, Spain, and France. Could my mother's saint be her? Pilgrimage would be the answer to what had happened to her. If she had lived, that is.

I HAD SOME BAD DAYS and then some more, working too hard and in all the wrong ways on sketches that I knew would never be paintings, and trying to finish the girl with her ring of stones, the monk and the abbess in her room. It had been one thing to stand up for myself when Dana challenged me. She'd brought an audience, and more, another painter—how could I back down? But now, alone with the work she'd criticized, I began to feel something very close to despair. "Why does it matter?" she had asked. And what had I said? Something about mystery, about following a process. But artists deceive themselves about these things all the time.

My grant wasn't going to last forever. I needed a body of work to come out of it, not fragments. How I wished my mother was still alive, so I could ask her what it all meant. How I wished she could tell me what she wanted me to do with these pieces of a story, tell me what it was she had imagined when she said, "Give it to the youngest. The artist."

How I wished my mother was still alive.

8

y brother drained the contents of his glass, then swirled the ice, nodding for another round. It was the night before Christmas. Dylan had booked rooms for all of us at the Parker House, where he and I sat at the bar, while in their suite upstairs Dad and Carrie were probably already in pajamas, sitting up in bed watching CNN. Dylan had picked us all up at the airport, and was supposed to be back at his house by now, helping Jennifer with the presents.

"I'm gonna need to decompress first," he had said, guiding me to the bar.

Now, his drink fresh, he sighed a brotherly sigh.

"I gotta tell you, Louie, I'm really worried about Kay-Kay."

It was his childhood nickname for Katherine, who, to Dylan's dismay, had canceled the reservation he'd made for her at the hotel and was staying in a Zen center nearby. And she had come alone, without David.

"I've just got a feeling that things are bad with Mr. Sincere. I mean, what's this shit about not showing up for Christmas?"

"Dyl, they're Buddhists. I don't know why I keep having to remind you. They're not exactly big on the whole Jesus thing."

"Louie, I love you, girl, but sometimes you think too much. Christmas isn't about religion. It's about family."

"I'm sure the nuns at your daughter's school would love to hear you say that."

"Whatever. My point is, David's her guy. He ought to be here with her. Especially, you know, after this last year."

He paused for another sip, then went on.

"I mean, when Film Boy didn't show up for Mom's funeral, I knew his days were numbered. Speaking of which, who's the latest?"

"Nobody. I'm off all that for a while. I'm trying to concentrate on my work."

"Don't give me that. I know my little sister. What about that bartender?"

"What is it you used to say? 'It ain't nothing but a thing.'"

"You so sure he feels that way?"

"He's got a girlfriend. It doesn't matter how he feels."

"Whatever you say. Nobody else?"

"Well, there is somebody I'm kind of seeing—"

"I knew it! You never answer your fucking phone anymore—"

"Like I ever did—"

"And you're avoiding my questions, which means there's something not quite right about what's going on, or you'd be bubbling over—"

"Listen to you, Sherlock—"

"So what's his name?"

"Vincent. And it doesn't matter. He works a lot, I work a lot, our schedules are hard to fit together—"

"What's he do?"

"He's a musician, a guitarist. A really good one."

"Somebody I would have heard of?"

"Probably not."

"Rock 'n' roll?"

"No, he's kind of—avant-garde."

At this, Dylan let out a tragic sigh.

"Louie, I know you don't want to hear it. But I just wish you knew your own worth. I mean, you should be living with some millionaire by now. You know, somebody who can take you on cruises, buy you jewelry."

"I don't need cruises and jewelry. I just need time to work on my work. Which is what I'm doing."

"And you could be doing it in a lot more comfort if there was some guy footing the bill. Look at Jen, for Christ's sake. She's got it made."

"Speaking of Jen, don't you think you ought to be getting home? It *is* Christmas Eve."

He signaled for another round.

"One more, then I'm out of here. You know what I've been thinking, Louie? It's time for me to visit the old stomping grounds again. Come to D.C. Shit, I'd like to stay for a week. Hit Georgetown. Have a night out with you and your pals. Speaking of which—how is Lynda these days? You still hanging out with her?"

"Oh, yeah. She's great. Lynda never changes."

"Still hot?"

"Of course. And you're still a pig, Dyl."

"I prefer *dog*, Louie. If you don't mind. And that doesn't change the fact that your pal Lynda is a hottie."

He paused.

"There is this new kid at the firm, you know? An intern. She looks a little like Lynda. All skinny and slithery. And the funky clothes."

He shook his head.

"She came in the other day in some purple animal print thing and I thought old Follett was going to have a heart attack. He said we should have one of the women partners talk to her. It was like she was wearing a tight, furry sock. Christ."

I looked at him.

"Dyl," I said.

"You and your crowd would like her, too. She's really into art. She's got this tiny little studio apartment, and the walls are just covered with posters and pieces of, I don't know, silk or something, and crazy-assed stuff hanging from the ceiling."

"Dylan."

"And she's got this great laugh—"

I put my hand down, hard, on his arm.

"Dylan Terry," I said, "are you *sleeping* with this girl?"

"Well, I—"

"Of course you are. You've been in her apartment. Why did I even bother to ask?"

"So maybe once or twice things got a little out of hand," he said. "But Lou, I have been a very good boy for a very long time. You have no idea how good I've been. Compared to some guys, I'm a saint."

"Define *saint*."

"I mean, one affair. In ten years."

"I count more like three affairs. There's Gwenn—"

"That's her. The only one. And that's not an affair. I really cared about her."

"And there was that waitress at the wharf, what was her name?"

"That was only a weekend, Lou."

"It still counts. And what about your old girlfriend from the North End, what was her name? Joanne? I seem to remember you running into her at some conference somewhere, and letters, and drama, and you thinking about leaving Jen—"

"Jesus, Lou. You could give a guy a break."

"Look, I'm not being judgmental, really—"

"Oh, sure—"

"But every time it's the same story. You start out all crazy about them. And then you do dumb stuff and then Jen almost finds out and the remorse kicks in and you come to me to confess and get absolution and promise you'll never do it again—"

"Am I that Catholic?"

"Evidently. But what I'm saying is, why put yourself through it, Dyl? And Jen, too? Why not either end your marriage or decide to stop fucking around? Just be honest with yourself, for Christ's sake."

He looked at me.

"You're one to talk. Let's see, I remember that Jason overlapped that sculptor character—what was his name? Ivan?—by quite a few months. And then there's Surfer Boy—"

"Who?"

"The bartender. You know, where Lynda works."

"T.J. He *owns* the bar, Dyl."

"Whatever. I know you two had it going on before you broke up with Jason. I could tell the last time I was down there. And don't give me that 'but I'm not married' crap. You were engaged to Film Boy, for fuck's sake."

"I know, I know. I broke his heart."

"Hearts," Dylan sighed. "Shit."

"Look, Dyl, I'm not here to scold you. I just want you to be careful, OK? An intern. Jesus. You could lose your job *and* your family."

"Don't worry, Lou. I already told her that it was over. And she's gonna be back at Yale next semester, anyway."

"And no letters," I said. "You should know better. Think about your *wife*."

"You know, Lou," he said softly, "sometimes I think we inherited it from Mom."

"Inherited what?"

"We're both so restless. We just can't stick, either one of us, with one person."

"In other words, we're hereditary cheaters."

"I was thinking more like, 'hereditary heartbreakers,' actually. But yeah, I think it's *in* us, somehow. We always jump the fence."

"What about Katherine? She and David have been together for what, fifteen years? More, I think."

"Yeah, but who knows what goes on with those two," he said darkly.

"What do you mean?"

"Well, shit, they used to live in a fucking commune. They were probably mixing and matching all the time."

"Dylan, it was an ashram. I wish you'd get it straight. I'm sure Katherine does too."

"And he always acts so *clean*. You can't say I didn't call it. I never trusted Mr. Sincere. And now he doesn't show up for Christmas. Something is definitely fucked up in California."

✖

As the children of a messy family, Dylan and I both tend to be anxious about the holidays. Katherine, however, never seems anxious about anything. You might attribute this to her many years of meditation practice, but Buddhism gave her, I think, only a form for the beliefs that she was born with. Katherine was mindful when she was ten years old; that's her nature.

What else can I say about my older sister? My parents must have been astonished at their luck with their first born, serene even as an infant, who became both a beauty and a brain. She has our father's long-legged height and his long, calm face; she has our mother's curly hair. She was good at everything in school, president of the Chorus and the National Honor Society, and she went out on dates with her handsome, serious-minded male equivalents, the sort all the parents said were "going somewhere." She never wore makeup and didn't need it. I adored her, as everyone did.

But we were never really close. I was too in awe of her for that.

"Ah, Louise," she said to me on Christmas morning and took my shoulders, kissed me on the cheek. When we pulled apart, I saw that her hair had begun to show a frosting of gray at the roots. One lock just behind her left ear was wound into a braid and woven with varying colors of thread. With no makeup on, wearing a baggy cotton dress and pair of oval, wire-rimmed glasses that were new to me, Katherine was still the most beautiful woman I would probably ever see.

"Hey, girl. You look great. As always."

She gave me a little *namaste* bow, hands pressed together in front of her chest.

"And you. And you."

We were in the foyer of Dylan's house. I could hear Maggie running and squealing with joy, and my father's voice, and Jennifer's. There was music on, too. "Jingle Bells."

"Am I hearing what I think I'm hearing?" I asked, as we walked toward the noise.

"Johnny Mathis, yes," Katherine said. "Dylan is in a sentimental mood this morning."

The little glasses seemed, if anything, to make her eyes even more beautiful.

"How are you, Louise?"

"Good. Busy. Working hard. How about you?"

"I am fine."

Her voice was even. And then we came into the living room and Maggie was running toward me, and my father stood up in the slanted light.

"Hello, dear."

"Aunt Louie! Aunt Louie!"

"Always the last one." That was Dylan now, coming out of the kitchen with a tray of glasses. And then Jen was behind him, and then Carrie, bringing platters of fruit and pastry, coffee and mimosas. Christmas had begun.

We all piled our gifts under the tree and Dylan played Santa Claus as my father used to, handing them out one by one and exclaiming over their size, joking about what they might contain—old socks? dead frogs? Maggie, huge-eyed and giggling, hopped up and down from her place on the couch between her mother and Katherine, clapping her hands. Dad and Carrie were settled into a pair of armchairs that looked a lot like the pair they shared at home in Sarasota.

Between opening the presents and dinner there was that melancholy mid-holiday lull. Dad and Carrie deposited themselves in the family room to watch TV, Jen took Maggie upstairs for her nap, and Dylan refused all offers of help in the kitchen. He had had the meal catered by one of his favorite restaurants, and was going to heat and serve it himself.

I opened a bottle of wine, Katherine made a pot of tea, and she and I sat alone together in the living room in front of the fire and the big, glittering tree.

"Jen is so good at decorating," Katherine said. "Everything looks so lovely."

"She does know how to make perfect bows," I said quietly. "Over and over and over again."

There were thousands of them, all over the tree, along the mantle, and tied to lampshades and candleholders— plaid and striped, tiny and enormous. Red plaid bows hung from the windows, dangling oranges studded with cloves.

"And the oranges make me nervous, frankly. What is the point of torturing an innocent piece of fruit like that? What if one of them falls and imbeds itself in your skull?"

"Oh, Louise, you are terrible."

"Better be careful how long you sit still or she might dash down here and tie one of those bows around you. A big plaid one, even."

"Shush," she said, laughing quietly, pointing to the ceiling. "Jen."

"I know. I promise I'll behave. It's just that Christmas tends to bring out the worst in me."

"Actually, you and Dylan are both wonderful at this kind of thing. I'm the one who feels like a wet blanket. I'm afraid I'm preoccupied with other things these days."

"Like what?"

"Oh, we've got time to talk about that. Tell me all about my successful little sister. I want to hear some good news."

So I told her about my grant, and Dana Reilly's interest in me, leaving out, of course, the part about the studio visit.

"I'm so happy for you, Louise. It's long deserved. I did so wish I could have come to your last show with Natalie. I love the two of you together. But the spring was just…madness. Anyway, let me know what happens next."

"I might be in a group thing in London this spring. I'll know soon."

"London? What's this?"

"A kind of swap between galleries here and in the U.K. It's called Atlantic Exchange. Natalie and I both applied to be in it."

"Natalie," Dylan said, passing through from the kitchen to the bar in the living room. "The big hippie chick? Needs to lose, like, fifty pounds?"

"Natalie," I said. "As in, the sculptor. As in, a beautiful woman."

"Jesus, Lou, you think all your friends are beautiful."

"That's because they are."

"Whatever," he said, tossing ice cubes into a glass, pouring a generous shot of scotch over them. "But that girl is overweight."

"That *woman* is big boned."

"Amazing," Katherine said. "You two never change."

"I am still trying to drum a little twenty-first-century thinking into my nineteenth-century brother's head. And getting nowhere fast."

"And I am still trying to acquaint my idealistic and somewhat fuzzy-headed sister with a few facts of life."

"And neither of you will ever win, and it's just wonderful," said Katherine. "It's better than any medicine I know. Thank you, Dylan, for doing this. It is so good to be here."

We raised our respective drinks to each other.

"So, a show in London, then," Katherine said.

"We'll see. I should know any day."

"That's great," said Dylan. "And do me a favor? When you get into this show, which you will, you always do, double all your prices, OK? I know you."

He disappeared again into the kitchen. Soon the persistent thump of a Bruce Springsteen CD floated out from beneath the door.

"That reminds me," I said. "A funny thing happened. Lawrence Ware called me."

"Mom's old boyfriend?"

"Yes. Anyway, he was asking about a statue. A statue of a monk. Old, wooden, and not very big. He says he lent it to Mom, and it's some kind of family heirloom and he needs it back. Or his sister needs it back. Anyway, I've never seen it."

"But I have. At least, I think so. If I'm right, Mom had it with her when we were in Cornwall."

"Cornwall?"

"Angie's old place. One of them, anyway. It must have been...oh, let's see. It would have been nine or ten years ago. David and I had just left the ashram."

"That was after she and Larry had broken up, right?"

"Oh, yes. Anyway, I remember being full of, oh, all sorts of questions. How David and I were to live, together or apart. If we were to take vows, and if so what kind.

And I…you know how it is. I just needed to talk to my mother."

"I've been feeling like that lately myself," I said.

"So I went to visit her at Angie's little house. She kept that statue on the table next to her bed. She did say it brought her luck. But she told me that Larry had given it to her."

"I wondered. Did it seem valuable? Like something his family might be anxious to get back?"

"All I know is that it's very, very old. Very worn. It's hard to see that it is a statue of anything, if you're not looking closely."

"Did you ever see it anywhere else? At Kenny's house, maybe?"

"No. Now that you mention it, no. Though that's not surprising."

"What do you mean?"

"Kenny was always so…prickly where Mom's former lovers were concerned."

"He sure picked the wrong woman."

"Ah, Louise. Still so angry."

"No, not really. Just confused. Just very, very confused."

I opened my mouth, then closed it.

"What, Lou?"

"What was she like? Mom? When you saw her at Angie's?"

"Well, she and Ware had just broken up. I expected her to be devastated but she wasn't. If anything, she was happier than I'd seen her in a long time."

"Did she say anything? About what had happened with them?"

"Angie said more about it than she did. It really bothered her that Mom had done some work for him—secretarial work, research, that kind of thing—without being paid. She called him 'that man.'"

She set down her tea.

"'That *man*,'" she said, adopting a cracked, dramatic voice and shaking her head back and forth quickly, like our Great-Aunt Angie, "'That *man* drove your mother to the breaking point.'"

"Oh, God, I can hear her."

We were both laughing. I had forgotten how good my sister was at mimicry.

"But what about Mom? What did she say? About him."

"She hardly talked about him at all. When Angie brought it up, Mom would just smile and say something about how she'd gotten more out of her time with Larry than she could have imagined."

"That must have driven Angie nuts."

"Oh, it did. She saw that she was losing her control over Mom. Oxford had given her confidence, you see. A famous man had fallen in love with her. And what's more, he had respected her mind. He had given her work to do."

"So she wasn't brokenhearted?"

"Not really. Mom was always such a survivor."

Katherine looked at me.

"I'm sorry, Louise."

"For what?"

"The look on your face. I just realized that it might be hurtful to you—that Mom shared these things with me, and you didn't know."

"I didn't want to know, remember? I was hardly speaking to her then. And anyway, it's as if—it's as if we knew two different women."

"Yes, that's just it. Sometimes I wish that you could have known her as I knew her. But Mom and I had been around the wheel together so many times."

"Around the wheel."

"And we both knew it. I remember being four or five when I first asked her about it. I said, 'Mom, we knew each other before, didn't we?'"

"And she said?"

"Oh, she was perfect. She said, 'Katherine, we have known each other for always, and we always will.' She just got it instinctively. How time is just one more illusion."

"A priest she knew said she had a gift for the spiritual life. I guess that's where you inherited it, Kay-Kay."

"Thank you, Louise. It is a comfort to believe that. Lately I feel so dry. So dry."

She shook her head. There was such sadness on her face it nearly stopped my heart. I had never seen her look this way.

"Katherine, what is it?"

"Well, there's no reason to keep it a secret. David has moved out."

"Oh, Kay-Kay. I'm so sorry."

"It has been coming for a long time, Louie. Years, really. But it could have gone on. David would like it to go on, in fact. I just lost my patience."

"Patience for what?"

"Well, to put it bluntly, the other women."

I looked at her.

"As in, more than one?"

"Oh, yes. Not simultaneously, but sort of in a series. A series of other lovers. Funny, I think he really didn't know I knew. Because I never said anything. Even though I could see so much."

"That sounds awful."

"For a long time, it wasn't, really. It was, well, not OK, exactly, but a part of him, along with so many other parts. And we were together for oh, six years or so before we committed ourselves to monogamy. We both had reservations, perhaps me even more than him. And we knew each other so well."

"But I don't get it. You said he wants to stay together."

"Yes. Isn't it funny? He actually wants us to get married. An institution he's always despised. He wants to get married and be monogamous, he's absolutely sure he can do it now. He's in therapy. He'd like *us* to be in therapy."

"And you said?"

"Oh, Lou, it's so funny, it's not. For seventeen years he was so dear to me, so dear. We worked together, we studied together, everything. And then something just snapped, and I didn't care anymore."

"Mom's death. A catalyst."

"Maybe. But it's more than that. I loved him deeply and completely and I thought the store of it would never run dry. And then it did. And that was that."

"I take it he knows you're not going to marry him."

"I've told him several times. But he is persistent. He seems to want me terribly now."

"Predictable."

"Perhaps. But I know one thing."

"What?"

"You can unplug every phone, burn every letter. But your partner knows what's going on. I knew when David lied to me. Jennifer knows what's going on with Dylan."

"With Dylan?"

"Oh, Lou, you've always been a terrible liar. It's one of things I love about you. He must have confided in you about his latest girl."

"Did he tell you, too?"

"He didn't have to. I walked in on him in the den this morning, whispering into his cell phone. He looked so guilty, it was almost funny."

"Did Jen hear him?"

"I don't think so. But she knows. Of course, she knows."

I thought about Jason walking in on me with T.J. I thought about T.J. and Elizabeth, wherever they were this day.

"At some point, Jen will get tired of sustaining the illusion. She will realize that she holds it up all by herself. And she will let it fall."

Katherine had drawn her feet up underneath her, lotus fashion, on the couch. In the firelight, her eyes gleamed, but not with tears. She rocked a little, forward and back, as she talked.

"After that, what possibility. What liberation, when the old forms fall. The world is so fresh it almost hurts. Beginner's eyes, again. And to live alone!"

She stretched her arms above her head, then dropped them abruptly.

"By the way, let's not dwell on this at dinner. Dad and Carrie already know. When Dylan asks, I'll tell him, too."

"He already suspects."

"He should use some of his intuitive powers to keep his own house in order," she said, more sharply than I was used to. Seeing my surprised face, she laughed.

"You see? My patience really is at an end."

"I don't know, Kay-Kay, but I'm beginning to think—I think I like you this way."

"Well, hello, ladies. How lovely to see you two together again."

Our father was in the doorway.

"Carrie is watching one of her soap operas. Mind if I join you?"

"Of course not, Father."

"Can I get you a drink, Dad?"

"Whatever you're having, dear. Wine, yes. Just a little. We must save room for the feast."

He stood by the fire, looking into it.

"Anyway, don't let me interrupt you."

"We were talking about Mom," Katherine said. She was the only one of us who could mention her easily to our father.

"Oh, yes. Of course. The first Christmas without...without her."

I had never seen him cry, and he did not cry now. He kept his eyes on the flames.

"It must be very hard for both of you."

"And for you, Father," Katherine said. There was always a tender formality in how she spoke to him.

"She has been on my mind...all day. All day. There are times I can hardly believe it. She had such energy. She was so...so alive."

You are still in love with her, I thought. Though she left you and left you. Though she cheated and lied. No wonder Carrie was always so uneasy at the mention of my mother's name.

"It's funny, when we got here this morning, I was sure...I was sure I could smell a cigarette. One of your mother's. You know how she would close the kitchen doors and smoke, thinking we didn't know."

His voice did not break. He did not take his eyes from the fire.

"I thought, how wonderful, Margaret's already here. She is well enough to travel after all. And then...well, I remembered."

We were silent for a while, the thump of Dylan's music in the floor beneath our feet.

"I know," Katherine said. "Something happens, and I think, oh, Mom would love to hear all about that. And then I pick up the phone to call her, and remember I can't."

It was my turn to say something. And then the phone rang, loudly, in the front hall.

Jennifer's footsteps sounded across the floor above us. From the top of the stairs, she called, "Can somebody get that? I've got my hands full here."

"Dylan will never hear her over his music," Katherine said.

Dad did not move.

"Forget it," I said.

The ringing continued.

"Katherine? Louise?" It was Jennifer's voice again.

"All right, I got it," I said. "Hello."

In the pause that followed, I looked down. The caller ID said, "Pay phone."

"Merry Christmas and hello," I said.

A click and a dial tone. I put the phone back in its cradle. In the living room, I saw Katherine get up, walk over to Dad, put her hand on his shoulder. He put his arm around her waist. I wanted to join them. I was afraid to join them.

The phone rang again. I snatched the receiver up.

"Hello, and Merry Christmas. You've reached the Terry residence."

"May I speak to Mr. Terry, please?"

A young voice, trying to sound older.

"May I tell him who's calling?"

"A colleague. With a question...about a case."

"On Christmas Day."

"It's...it's an emergency."

"An emergency. Look, colleague—you wouldn't by any chance happen to be an intern, would you? From Yale?"

"Excuse me?"

"Or own a purple dress that fits like a sock?"

"I...I..."

"Well, listen up. In case you hadn't noticed, this is Christmas Day. Dylan is spending it with his family, which includes his wife."

"I just need to tell him one thing..."

"Now is emphatically *not* the time. Your time, in fact, is over."

"Who are you?"

"The angel of my brother's better nature."

I slammed the phone down a little harder than I had to, and stood there, waiting to see if anyone had noticed. In the mirror over the hall table, I saw my face, and then Dylan's beside it.

"Just as I thought. I come looking for someone to hold a goddamn strainer and where is Louie? Brooding beside the phone for a call from Surfer Boy."

"Very funny, Dyl. Actually—"

"So tell me—what exactly did he buy you for Christmas?"

"Nothing. But listen—"

"Or the guitarist?"

"He's a Taoist. He doesn't believe—"

"That's what I figured. So let's do this."

He reached around the phone, plucked out the cord, and let it fall.

"Dyl, you've got it all wrong."

"Of course. As always."

He put his hand through my arm.

"Tell me about it all later. Right now, it's dinner time."

DINNER WAS EXTRAVAGANT, WITH A soup course, lots of grand vegetable dishes for Katherine, who eats no meat, and various carefully selected wines. If Jennifer did know what was going on with Dylan and the intern, she gave no sign, but seemed to be having a wonderful time. She smiled and drank the champagne he poured, while his Christmas gift to her, a pair of diamond and sapphire earrings, sparkled in the candlelight.

Everyone behaved beautifully. Dad told a funny story about failing a test for his boating license and offered a thoughtful toast to Dylan for hosting the day. Dyl was on his feet all the time, carrying dishes to and from the kitchen, refilling our glasses, urging more stuffing or squash or wine on us, nearly knocking over the gravy. It became like a comedy routine, and the rest of us, especially Katherine and I, were in stitches.

After dinner, we took our desserts into the living room to eat in front of the fire. Maggie started nodding off on the couch almost right away, and Jennifer and Carrie took her upstairs to put her to bed.

A potentially awkward moment was averted when Carrie went to call a cab and realized that the hall phone was disconnected. But Jen was already upstairs, putting

Maggie to bed, and missed it. Later, over last drinks, I was able to ask Dylan about the statue Lawrence Ware was looking for. Unlike Katherine, he had no memory of it at all. Sloshed and sentimental, he bundled me into my own cab at well after two a.m.

We had done it, as he had wanted. We had had our family Christmas.

※

I FLEW BACK THE EVENING after Christmas, took the Metro from National Airport to Takoma Park, and dragged my wheeled suitcase the three blocks to my apartment. It was a clear night, but very cold, and I was looking forward to red wine and a hot bath. As I came up the walk, rummaging in my bag for the door key, I saw someone standing, lurking, really, on the stairs outside the building. It was Vincent.

"Well," I said, "This is a surprise."

"You've been kind of hard to reach lately. So I thought I'd come by and just, you know, say hi."

"I was in Boston. For Christmas. I did tell you."

He looked down at his feet, and then off into the street behind me. His eyes were puffy, he needed a shave—and probably a bath and a good night's sleep. Like me.

"I thought you were with your mom?"

"Yeah, well, things got—a little weird out there. She's got a new guy, and he's kind of a dick. And I—well, I really missed you, Louise."

"You did?" I was genuinely surprised.

"You—you were on my mind. And I was hoping maybe you'd have a minute. Or three, actually. Really, two minutes and forty-six seconds. Currently, at least."

"What?"

"How much time it takes. For what I want you to hear."

He took his hands out of his pockets.

"Hold this," he said, handing me his iPod. He pushed the scarf that I had tied over my head off onto my shoulders, and slipped the tiny headphones into my ears.

"What are you doing?"

"Shush."

He held a finger to his lips, then mine. Then he pushed *play*, took a step back, and watched me listen.

The music started soft and slow, with a single guitar making high, gentle plucking sounds—like drops of color falling slowly onto a canvas, pale gold, pale silver. The melody thickened, seemed to double, and I realized that there was another guitar now, playing a kind of low-pitched counter to the first. The music quickened, growing in volume, swirling.

Then the music stopped. There was perhaps a full second of hesitation before the original single melody line returned, plaintive now, transposed to a minor key. It swelled, then faded, though at the end there was a kind of echo of the earlier theme, a sort of reprise, before the close.

I opened my eyes.

"Well?" Vincent said. "What do you think, Louise?"

"It's beautiful," I said. "It has so many twists and turns. It keeps surprising me."

"Yeah?"

"Yeah. And that silence—I loved the way it stopped, then started again."

His face was flushed, happy.

"You, of course," I said. "On both guitars."

"Six string and twelve string. I just finished mixing it this afternoon."

"I think it's incredible."

"I'm glad. I mean, it's for you."

"For me?"

"Look. Track three."

He held out the CD case to me, and I lifted it up into the blue-white glow of the streetlight. It was hard to make out the letters, written in silver ink on black paper. Then I saw it.

Track 3. Snowed In. For Louise.

"You're kidding. You wrote that for me?"

"Well, you're the only Louise I know. Yes, of course. For you."

I reached for him then, but the cord connecting the headphones to the CD player got in my way. We laughed at the tangle; then he lifted the headphones off, gently, and stuffed all the gear back into his pockets.

"But I thought you didn't believe in Christmas gifts."

"I don't believe in giving gifts for no reason. But this is different."

We stood there, looking at each other.

"Look," he said, "I know I can be an asshole sometimes. I can be very selfish."

"I never said that."

"You didn't have to. I can tell you're not—not too crazy about the way I live. I'm guessing you'd like a guy who could take you on fancier dates. Buy you champagne."

That might be nice, I thought but did not say. Instead I said, "If I wanted that, I'd go looking for it. But I don't. I just wish—"

"What?"

"That I understood you a little better. Sometimes I feel so close to you, and then sometimes you're so...distant."

He sighed.

"I know. My life is crazy right now, just crazy. Everything's up in the air. And even when it's not, it's just my nature, you know? When I've got music on my mind I just *go there.* Completely. It's hard on other people. I know. I do know that."

He reached out, put his hand to my hair.

"I don't have anything to offer you, Louise. And it's not like I've ever even wanted to get married. But it does matter to me, to be able to see you. To be able to hold you. I mean, I thought that you knew that."

He ran his fingers down my face and under my collar.

"Please," he said. "Don't give up on me. Not yet."

He tilted my chin up toward him, put his lips to mine. His kiss was slow and long and sweet. When I opened my eyes, the sky behind his head had given him a halo of stars.

"I guess you'd better come in," I said.

Hours later, I woke up in the dark with Vincent's body pressed tight against my own. His hair had wrapped itself around my neck and I loosened the strands gently, careful not to wake him. *Well, here we are,* I thought. *This is what I wanted.* I should have been content—he'd thought he was losing me and come looking, he'd written such beautiful music, and for me, and he had said the words that I'd been waiting for, or some approximation of them. And at last, we'd made love. The sex had been sweet and awkward—for such a beautiful man, he seemed shy about his body—and I had every reason to be happy. Yet my stomach was tied in a thick knot, my breath was tight.

I stroked his hair, his shoulder, the curve of his arm. He was far away from me, deep in sleep, and did not stir. I asked myself, *What am I frightened of?* For there was nothing in the sleeping form beside me to induce the panic I was feeling now. And then I remembered my night at Vincent's house and the building I'd seen, crumbling into flames.

I got out of bed and went to the studio. There was a canvas already waiting, an interior, a room with stone walls and a window. I made the window taller, wider, then made another. And beyond those windows, I painted a hint of a dark landscape, a ridge of stone, but all consumed by tongues of alizarin crimson, cadmium yellow. Outside that room, I painted a world on fire.

✵

I THINK I CAN BE forgiven for thinking Vincent brought me good luck. That morning, while he was still asleep in my bed, a thick envelope arrived from London. Three artists from A Woman's Place had been selected for the Atlantic Exchange exhibition at Mina's Gallery. Louise Terry, painting, and Natalie Anderson, sculpture, leaped out at me.

But god, whoever she is, must have a sense of humor. The third selection from our nominees was an installation artist who went by the single name Sahara.

9

don't know, girl. I'm just hoping somebody remembers them as well as I do."

Lynda on the phone, the first Friday of the New Year. She had finally persuaded T.J. to let her book bands at the Landing. Tonight was her first show, and she had gotten a beloved East Coast band, the Hollowbodies, to reunite for it.

"Well, I certainly remember them. I think it was a brilliant idea. And I'll be there."

"I'm so glad. You can keep me from collapsing if there are, like, five people in the room. By the way, T.J. is gunning for you, hard. Thinks you've been avoiding him or something."

"Why would he think that?"

"You can save the innocent act. And don't worry, I haven't told him anything about the beautiful guitarist. Speaking of, how did you get out of taking him along tonight?"

"I didn't. He's got studio time somewhere in Virginia this weekend. Said he'd see me Sunday."

"How's it going, anyway?"

"Good. Different. Good."

"That sounds less than great."

"Well, we're going slow. And it's not like we go out on regular dates…"

"Remind me, again? Why you two stayed home on New Year's Eve watching a David Lean movie?"

"Mike Leigh, actually. But he's got problems with, well, the whole consumer culture we live in. Corrupts our every waking minute. If we let it."

"Right."

"And there's the fact that he doesn't eat meat or fish, or drink any kind of alcohol. So the whole restaurant and bar thing is pretty much out, anyway."

"OK, so other than some perverse desire to never have any fun again, why are you with this guy, exactly?"

"Can I say it's the sex?"

"Except it isn't. I've *known* you when it was."

"Well. You know…you know who he reminds me of, really? Me. I mean, *us*. When we were younger. You and Natalie and me."

"Okay…"

"I mean, all he thinks about is his art, his music. He's so on fire with it. Like we used to be."

"You still are. Nat still is."

"You know what I mean. He's so sure he's going to succeed."

"You mean he hasn't had his butt kicked yet. By the big, brutal world."

"I mean, he's still pure about it, somehow."

"Well, he's rich. He can afford to be."

"Never mind. I can see where this is headed."

"I'm sorry, girl. I don't mean to be a bitch. I love you. If you're happy, I'm happy for you. Maybe I've burned myself out on musicians. Just, well, be careful, OK?"

"I will be. I promise."

"And keep your fingers crossed for tonight. T.J. is already grumbling about how many tables we had to take out to put in risers for the band. I need this to work."

"It will."

I'D BEEN TRYING TO COMFORT Lynda—I really didn't remember the band she was so excited about, or when I might have heard them. But as I walked in the door, and heard the guitar lick to a song I suddenly remembered, "Solar Girl," it all came back. A bar in Arlington, who knew how many years ago. A girls' night out. I had been in a rambunctious mood, Jason out of town on another one of his shoots, and Lynda was between boyfriends. Only Nat behaved well. I remember doing shooters with the opening act on the back deck of the bar, and later on, between sets, getting invited into the dressing room where somebody's brother kept stuffing a pipe with what they said was Thai stick. I remembered Natalie dropping me off as the sun was coming up and waking up the next afternoon, hung over, exhausted, and absurdly pleased with myself for having been able to resist the attentions of whoever it was who was flirting with me that night. Those were, indeed, the days.

Behind the bar now, Lynda and T.J. were moving fast, backlit, shining, in time to the music. I felt my stomach tighten when I saw him—when was I going to tell him about Vincent? When was I going to say that I had a real boyfriend now, and our affair, such as it was, was over? All the tables were full, but there were still a few empty seats at the bar, and I grabbed one at the far end, next to the waiters' service station. I could barely see the band from there, but it was usually Lynda's area.

T.J. got to me first.

"So, Louise is in the house!"

He leaned across the bar for his usual discreet, public kiss. As my lips brushed his cheek, he whispered, "I need to talk to you."

"Well, here I am," I said, brightly. "Happy New Year."

"Happy New Year to you."

He strained a shaker's contents into two shot glasses.

"What's this?"

"Something I invented."

It was pine green, and looked lethal.

"I was thinking of going with a glass of wine, myself."

"What? Afraid you might misbehave?"

"Maybe."

"All the more reason, then. Here's to misbehaving."

I looked at him. Was I imagining the edge in his voice?

"All right. To misbehaving."

We clicked glasses, shot the contents down. It burned my throat, like an apple on fire.

T.J. slammed his glass down hard, let out a whoop. I jumped in my seat.

"That's what I'm talking about! Oh, yeah!"

He pumped his fist in the air.

"Whooee! Damn, I'm good!"

"All right now, cowboy, get back where you belong." Lynda was behind him. "You're starting to scare people."

"But—"

She spun him around, pointed him toward the other end of the bar.

"No buts. Now move."

She put a wineglass down in front of me.

"Hey, Louie. Got a new Australian shiraz for you to try."

"Perfect. Good crowd tonight, girl. And the band sounds great."

"They do."

She leaned in over my glass.

"Teej told you, right?"

"He just said we need to talk. But not about what."

"Well, see that couple at the other end of the bar? Down by the band?"

A big guy with a young face was bopping his head up and down in time to the music, next to a ponytailed blonde who looked even younger.

"Yeah."

"That's Elizabeth's *brother*. And his girlfriend."

"Is Elizabeth here?"

"No, no. She's still in Chicago. But *they're* the reason Teej got going on those disgusting shooters. It's the girlfriend's birthday. They're on their way to meet some people in *Georgetown*, or something."

"Should I even stick around?"

"Oh, please. Don't leave me. They should be gone soon, anyway. They'd be gone by now—this isn't really their *scene*—if he didn't keep giving them shooters. I tried to tell her, 'Look, it's your birthday, you want to make it through in one piece.' But finally, I just said screw it."

She topped off my glass.

"Amateurs," she said. "She'll figure it out soon enough."

T.J. let out another loud whoop. He, the birthday girl, and Elizabeth's brother had downed another round.

"Meanwhile," I said, "T.J. seems to have found his inner frat boy."

"Yeah, well, I wish he'd lose it again. Later, girl."

"Later."

The band went into a fast song I remembered dancing to years ago. There wasn't really a dance floor at the Landing. But soon Elizabeth's brother went from nodding to jumping up and down to the music, and then he grabbed his hapless girlfriend and dragged her in front of the band's risers. There wasn't enough room to do more than hop around a little, but by the end of the first chorus, the space was crowded.

I was moving in my seat, swaying to the music, when a voice said, "Looks like somebody wants to dance."

He stepped between the service bar and me.

"Louise, right?"

"Yes." And then I recognized it—a face I saw every day, on the flyer for Einstein's Pillow that hung on my refrigerator door. Phil Wexler, the bass player.

"And you're Phil. We talked that night at Stillmore, when the concert got canceled."

"You remember."

He waved to Lynda.

"So, you have interesting musical taste. From Einstein's Pillow to the Hollowbodies."

It hit me then. Vincent said he was in the studio tonight, with his band. But his bass player was right here.

"I like lots of different kinds of music."

"Another one, Lou?" Lynda was there.

"May I buy you a drink?" Phil said.

I hesitated. What could I say? *That's OK, I'm having an affair with the owner, so I get to drink for free?*

"Say *thank you* to the nice man," Lynda said, filling my glass. "And for you?"

"Grey Goose martini, dry, straight up, two olives."

He turned back to me.

"If I remember right, that gallery we played in—you were there."

"That's right."

"So you're an artist, a visual artist. What kind?"

"A painter, mostly. I worked in collage for a couple of years almost exclusively. Now back to painting."

Lynda set his drink down in front of him.

"And this," I said, "is my pal, Lynda. The best bar manager in town."

"Hello, there, martini man."

I saw him look at her, then look again. Despite the teased bleached hair and the neon makeup she wears at work, Lynda has the kind of prettiness that creeps up on people. Now he had seen it.

"I'm Phil," he said. "Nice to meet you. So you book the bands?"

"This is my first shot here. I had to persuade the cranky-assed owner to let me give it a try. But I've worked at lots of clubs—the Black Cat, the Hotel Monaco, Perry's. And what do you do?"

"I'm on the other side of the business. I play bass."

"What kind?"

"Various kinds. Jazz, world music. I like to mix it up. Right now, I'm in three ensembles."

He gestured toward me.

"Einstein's Pillow, Vincent Volpe's band, is one."

"So tell me something," she said, leaning on the bar and looking into his eyes. "Is this Vincent character even half as talented as my girl here seems to think he is?"

"Lynda," I began.

"That's an easy one," Phil said. "He's got a huge talent. Enormous. As for what he does with it—well, we'll see. He's certainly disciplined. We were in the studio today for seven straight hours and he's still there now, mixing, remixing, laying down new tracks. He never stops."

I felt my heart unclench a little. Vincent was in the studio. He hadn't lied.

"And as far as, say, women go," she went on. "Would you say he's a trustworthy character? A good guy? Or is he—"

"That's enough, now, Lynda." I said. "Talk about scaring a guy."

"I'm not scared at all."

"Ordering! Ordering!"

The band had taken a break and there were waiters lined up three deep for Lynda.

"I'll be back after this message from our sponsors," she said, winking at Phil.

"Wow. She's something, isn't she?"

"Yes, indeed," I said. "By the way—sorry about the interrogation. Lynda's kind of maternal about her friends."

"I don't mind at all. I think it's cool that she cares so much. She seems—"

He was interrupted by the sound of glasses slamming down on the bar, followed by whoops and hollers. It was Elizabeth's brother again, and T.J. They had gathered a little crowd of drinkers around them.

"Buca! Buca for the birthday girl!"

"Buca! Buca! Buca!"

"What are they saying?" Phil asked.

"Sambuca," I said. "They want shots of it."

"They seem so young."

"That's because they are."

"Speaking of—Louise, may I ask you a question?"

"Sure."

"Your friend, Lynda? Is she, well, seeing anyone?"

"I think she's kind of between boyfriends right now."

"Meaning there's some competition out there. Of course."

"Meaning," I said, "that I think you should get her phone number. Tonight."

He smiled, lifted his glass.

"Thanks, Louise."

"Buca! Buca!"

That was T.J., standing in front of us with three shot glasses of clear, sticky liquid.

"For you and your...friend. On the house. Birthday shooters."

He shoved one shot across the bar to Phil.

"Thanks," Phil said, politely, "but that's OK. I'll stay with this."

"Aw, come on. One shot. Good stuff."

"I'm sure. But no. Thanks."

T.J. looked at me.

"So who's he? Fucking James Bond?"

His voice was loud. Heads turned toward us.

"Maybe he just doesn't want to be in pain tomorrow."

"Oh, really? And when did you get so uptight? Why, I could tell your friend about a night in Rock Creek Park, in the back of my car. Brother, you should have seen—"

More heads looked our way.

"You need to shut up, T.J.," I said. "And now."

"Whatever you say, Louie. That's how it is, huh? Well, just...drink this."

"I've had a lot of wine."

"You can take it. We're old pros, you and I."

"Tell you what—I'll do it, if you promise that this is absolutely your last shot of the night."

"That's a deal."

I felt Phil's eyes on me, speculative, while T.J. and I clicked glasses and downed the sambuca. I waited for him to slam his glass down, but he didn't. He set it down gently.

Then he reached across the bar, grabbed my face, and gave me a rough, fast, tongue-slamming kiss. He pulled away with a loud smack that was even louder because the band, just then, was between songs.

I felt eyes running over me like fingers, and I froze. Beside me, I heard Phil's sharp intake of breath. T.J.'s face across the bar looked dazed, triumphant.

"You hold that thought, now," he said, waving his finger in the air as he backed away. He stumbled on the rubber mat beneath his feet, made a show of regaining his balance.

The band went into a slow, sweet song I remembered from years ago, and friendly applause ran through the house. People turned back to the stage.

"Louise," Phil began.

"If you'll excuse me," I said, and slipped away before he could say more.

I had to walk the length of the bar and past the band to get to the ladies' room. Where Elizabeth's brother and his date had been, there were new people. Maybe they'd left before the kiss.

The line for the stalls was short and I spent a long time in front of the mirror after. T.J. was usually so careful where Elizabeth was concerned. What was wrong with him tonight?

I was touching up my eyeliner when a young woman came in, saw me in the mirror, and stopped. I met her eyes in the glass.

"Louise, right? Louise Terry?"

"Yes?"

"You don't remember me, do you?"

"I'm sorry."

"Jason Felden. I was his PA. On the Mayo."

"Oh, right. Rebecca."

The terminology brought it back. She'd been Jason's production assistant on a film he made about the history of Mayo Beach, a World War II–era Chesapeake Bay resort. Jason complained about working with Rebecca, saying that she had an ordinary mind. "Ordinary" was his most damning word. But he had also told me, more than once, that she had a crush on him. "A thing," as he used to say. "I think she's got a thing for me. You know what I mean, how you can just tell?" But then, he said that about a lot of the women he worked with.

I put away the eyeliner, started touching up the mascara, still looking into the mirror. She moved to the sink beside mine.

"So what brings you here tonight?"

"My friend Lynda...is the bar manager," I said, between swipes with the mascara wand. "And I used to...really love this band."

"They're good."

"Very."

"Jason introduced me to them. To a lot of good music."

"That's nice," I said. My mind returned to the problem outside the door. What a night.

"Look, just so you know—Jason and I are very close, now. Very close. And nothing is going to change that."

"Good for you," I said, not really listening. Then a thought occurred to me, and I put the mascara back in its tube and looked at her.

"Is he *here* tonight? Jason?"

"Not yet. But he said he'd try to meet me here later. He's so busy, you know? Everyone wants to work with him."

My heart was loud in my ears. I hadn't seen Jason since I'd moved the last of my things out of his house. Though I had no idea if T.J. would recognize him from that awful morning we'd gotten caught, I had no doubt that Jason would recognize T.J.

"So he *might* be coming? Or he *is* coming?"

"Why do you want to know?"

"I just don't think he'd be thrilled to see me, that's all."

Up close, I could see she was younger than I had thought, maybe a decade younger than me. She had private-liberal-arts-school-spoiled-rich-girl written all over her. I doubted she'd ever been stood up before. But I knew Jason. Chances were that when the bar closed down, she'd still be there, alone, because he'd gotten so caught up in his footage that he'd forgotten what time it was.

I thought about warning her, then thought, *forget it.* What had Lynda said? This one was an amateur, too.

"Oh, I don't think you have to worry. I'm sure he's gotten over you."

"What good news," I said, fluffing my hair in the mirror. "You have a nice night."

She opened her mouth to say something else, but I was already gone. And Phil was waiting in the hallway.

"Lynda thought you might not be coming back. She sent me to look for you."

"I wouldn't do that to her."

"Louise," he said. "She and I had a talk. We thought—well, if you want to get out of here, I'd be happy to give you a lift home."

"I'm fine. And that's way too much trouble for you."

"Look, I'm not asking any questions. But I don't think you're fine. Things seem kind of dicey here. And if you need an escape hatch, well, I could help. You're probably not safe to drive. After those shooters. And I'm coming back later to pick Lynda up, anyway."

"Make way! Make way! Emergency here!"

It was T.J. He and Elizabeth's brother were heading for the ladies' room, the girlfriend propped between them, one hand clapped over her mouth.

"I'm gonna have to go in with her, man," said the boyfriend, and the two of them disappeared through the door. I heard women's raised voices, and the unmistakable sound of someone retching.

"That'll be fun to clean up," T.J. groaned.

"It's your own fault," I said. "Pouring all that crap down her throat."

"It's not like I twisted anybody's arm. And when did you get all high and mighty?"

He turned to Phil.

"Has she shown you her little tequila trick yet? The one where she pours it all over your dick and sucks it off?"

"Hey, man," Phil began, but I wasn't waiting for anyone else to defend me. I was suddenly very sober. And I knew exactly what I was doing when I swung my right arm as hard as I could and slapped T.J. twice, across his face and back. I had a big costume jewelry ring on, and it scraped him on the return.

He put his hand to his face, felt the cut, then looked at his fingertips. To my surprise, he laughed.

"Well, goddamn. I deserved that, Louie. I did."

"You sure did. You said we needed to talk? Well, you were right."

I turned to Phil.

"If you'll excuse me. My *friend* and I need to have a chat."

"Are you sure?"

"Please. Go save my seat at the bar, OK? Tell Lynda I'll be back. This won't take long."

I gave him my best smile, then turned back to T.J.

"You," I said, pointing to the flight of stairs that led to his basement office. "Down there. Now."

He fumbled with the door key, took his time unlocking it. The room was cramped and damp, with painted brick walls and a linoleum floor partially covered with a cheap, faux Indian rug. But it was private, and I needed that for what I had to say.

"You," I began, "owe me a big fucking apology for all the crap you've said tonight. As well as an explanation. As if there is one."

He leaned back on his desk, unsteadily, waved one finger in the air in front of him. His eyes skittered back and forth, and I realized just how drunk he'd gotten. I'd seen him put away a lot of booze, but I'd never seen him like this.

"OK, so I'm an asshole. But you brought your fucking boyfriend—"

"He is not my fucking boyfriend and I did not bring him. I hardly know the guy."

"Oh, sure."

"Ask Lynda if you don't believe me. I was here *before* he was, remember? When you said you had something to talk to me about? And anyway, it's *Lynda* he's interested in. He's giving her a ride home tonight."

He opened his mouth, then closed it.

"And thank god she told me. About your girlfriend's brother. That's another thing—aren't you worried? About what he'll tell her?"

"Who?"

"Elizabeth. Your girlfriend, for Christ's sake! T.J., look at me—what the fuck is wrong with you tonight?"

"Me? I'm celebrating."

He hiccupped, wiped his hand across his mouth.

"Celebrating? Your girlfriend's brother's girlfriend's birthday? That's a reason to get smashed and act like an asshole?"

"I am celebrating a big step. In my life. In any man's life. Louise. I have something. To tell you."

"All right."

"This is news, Louie. Really big news."

"I'm listening."

"I—your buddy, Thomas James Duvall—am going to be a father. Elizabeth—is pregnant."

The words clanged like nonsense syllables in my ears. Then I got it.

"Oh, my. That is big news."

"Yes, indeed."

"I take it...I take it this wasn't planned."

"She was on the pill for a while. It gave her headaches. We—we were trying to time it. You know. With her cycle."

"Oh, T.J., that never works. You know how many Catholic kids were born that way?"

"Fuck, I don't know. I thought she knew."

"So she wants to have the baby."

"What the fuck? Of course, she wants the baby."

His eyes flashed. Anger seemed to sober him up, a little.

"What else would she do?"

"Well, it's not a given," I said cautiously. "Some women—some women might make a different choice."

"Some women, yeah. Not Elizabeth. There's no way she'd ever have—ever do something like that."

I was angry with him all over again. The frat boy drinking, the hangdog look, and now this inability to even say the word "abortion." *Come on,* I wanted to scold, *you're nearly forty years old. You don't have to be coy with me. We both know how babies get made.*

But I could not say any of those things. If T.J. had been just my friend, I could have offered comfort, advice, or at the very least, a listening ear. But there are no rules of etiquette, or at least none that I'm aware of, that govern what the other woman is supposed to say or do in response to the news that her lover's girlfriend is going to have his child.

"So this is what you want."

"What does that matter? What I want."

"Come on. You don't have to lie to me."

"I mean it. There are—other things, you know? Other things."

His voice was soft, cautious. I moved closer to him, so I could hear.

"I mean, everybody's got…ideas."

"Ideas."

"About what they want. In life. Big fucking ideas, right? What they think they could have. If they tried. But I'm not...I'm not getting any younger."

"None of us are. But—"

I was very close to him then. He looked right into my eyes, and I was jolted by the pain I saw there. Pain and fear. This was a new T.J.

"And I'm not a bad guy, Louie. You know? I've been a fuck-up before. I was an asshole tonight, I know. But never—you've never seen me be a real bad guy, right?"

"T.J., why—why would you think—"

"Just tell me, Louie. Just say it. Have you ever seen me be a real bad guy?"

"No. Not ever."

"So I've got to do the right thing. I want—to do the right thing."

"And that is?"

"To marry the mother of my child. And that...that is what I'm going to do."

He put his arms around me, pulled me tight against him. And as soon as that new T.J. had appeared, he was gone again.

"But I'm not married yet."

He kissed me hard, on my mouth and all over my face, my neck. His touch was sloppy and rough. He stank. I tried to pull back, to slow him down a little. But he pushed me back against the hard wooden lip of his desk. With one hand, he pulled at my tights, trying to yank them down. With the other, he undid his pants.

There was no part of me that wanted to do it. And then I realized that this was the easy way out.

After this, I would never have to tell T.J. about Vincent, never have to hear about Elizabeth or his child again.

This was our goodbye sex, our last fuck. After tonight, he would be so embarrassed about how he'd behaved, he would feel so many different, conflicting kinds of guilt, that he wouldn't even be able to call me to say he was sorry. How simple it had turned out to be, after all.

I let him do what he wanted, and it was over too quickly for him, if far too slowly for me. He was still inside me, shaking with the last of it, when the music above our heads came to a stop. The crowd upstairs whooped and clapped. I almost laughed.

"Louie," he said. "I am...I mean, I..."

Then the intercom buzzed, and Lynda's voice was with us.

"Teej, the band's on the way down, they need their stuff. And you need to pay them."

He pulled himself off of me fast, and moved to the far side of the room, tucking in his pants, rubbing his hands across his face. I righted my skirt, my sweater.

"Got it."

"Art says the dishwasher is fucking up again. Oh, and there's a problem in the ladies' room. Somebody hurled."

"I'll be right up."

"But pay them first."

"All right. Jesus."

He fumbled around in the desk drawer for something, not looking at me.

"You'll stick around, right, Louie?" he said. "I mean, after we close, maybe we...can talk?"

"Sure," I said. "Of course. I'll be with Lynda."

The band hooted and banged at the door, and I was past them quickly and up the stairs.

My knees shook, my skin felt cold all over. From the end of the hallway, I could just make out the back

of Lynda's head and Phil's profile. They must have wondered what was taking me so long.

Behind me was the door to the alley, with its sign,
Emergency Exit/Alarm Will Sound. I knew it was only
activated when the club was closed. Otherwise, Lynda
said, the busboys set it off every time they took out the
trash or went out for a smoke. I pushed the door open and
stepped outside.

The alley behind the restaurant was filthy, with
patches of gray ice on the asphalt and the high, cold beams
of halogen streetlights. I picked my way carefully in my
heels, looking out for rats. Out on the street again, it was
a four-block walk to my car, along sidewalks filled with
the last of the night's revelers. They were all so happy. I
felt ghostly, moving between and past them, as if I was
only half-real. They may be amateurs, I thought, but at
least they're innocent.

At home, I thought I'd just fall into bed, but the
smells—of the club, of booze, of sex, of T.J.—were all over
me. So I ran a hot shower and stood under it for a long
time, soaping and rinsing, soaping and rinsing, until my
skin was pink and tender. Then I wrapped myself in an
old flannel robe and went, not to bed, but to the studio.

By now, T.J. and Lynda would know I had slipped
out. Sometimes he'd call at this hour, after he'd counted
out the bank deposit, to see if he could drop by. I wasn't
expecting that sort of call, not tonight and not ever again,
from him. I was sure of that. But still, my mind was alert,
clear, as if waiting for something.

I don't know how long I sat like that, not drawing, not
even doodling, just still. And then I heard it. What I had
been waiting for. A sound at the door, not a knock but a
kind of scraping or brushing. Someone was out there.

I tiptoed up to it and opened it fast. At first, I really did think I was seeing things—a tall man with short stubby hair like a black scrub brush and deep-set, dark brown eyes.

"Jason? You?"

"Oh, Louise. I didn't mean to wake you up. I just thought it was time—past time—to get this back to you."

He held out a paint-stained canvas tote bag.

"You drove here in the middle of the night? To give this to me?"

"It's what's inside it. You moved out, you know, pretty fast. You left a few things behind."

"Right. Well, thanks."

I took the bag from him.

"You drive safe, now."

"Louise, wait. Can I come in? For just a minute?"

"You *do* know what time it is?"

"Yes, and I'm sorry. But it seems we're both awake. And you didn't have to open the door."

Suddenly, I was too tired to argue with anyone.

"All right," I said. "Come in."

I put my old painting bag on a shelf by my drawing table while Jason stepped into the room cautiously, as if it were a foreign country where he didn't know the language or understand the customs.

"So this is where you live now."

"Yes. And where I work."

"You gave up the studio."

"This room is bigger. And with better light."

"Have you got…a living room? A dining room?"

"This would have been both. Instead, I have a studio, a bedroom, a bathroom, and a kitchen."

He paced along the wall where the most recent paintings were leaning, all turned to the wall, save one, a portrait of Vincent I had just started. Pinned in the upper left corner of it was a photo of him I'd borrowed, a shot from his band's promo kit with him in moody light, his guitar slanted across his lap. He looked at it, opened his mouth to say something, then changed his mind.

"Do you like it here?" he asked, doubtfully.

"I love it."

"It's kind of spare, isn't it? Like a nun's room, or something."

I looked at him. Had he picked up something in the air? I had never known Jason to be intuitive about anyone but himself.

"It's what I can afford. Besides, I live alone. How much space do I need?"

"Well, I guess not much."

He walked over to my mother's box, ran his fingers absentmindedly over it.

"Are you still seeing...you know, that guy?"

"Funny you should ask."

"Funny?"

"We just broke up. About three hours ago."

"Wow. I guess I should say I'm sorry."

"You're not, and neither am I. So let's move on."

"What are you working on these days?"

"I'm working. Besides, I think it's my turn to ask the questions."

"All right."

"Am I right in guessing that your, uh, delivery tonight had something to do with me running into Rebecca?"

He blushed, shrugged.

"Yeah, well, Rebecca's not too happy with me right now. She wanted me to meet her at this club, whatever it's called. Wherever you two ran into each other."

"The Landing. So you never made it."

"I had to work. I did tell her that."

"So she's pissed off."

"About that. And other things."

"So what are you saying? Rebecca moved in and decided to get the last of me out tonight?"

"No way. I mean, it's way too soon for that. I don't plan on living with anyone again for—well, for a long time."

He looked at me as if that statement should move me, somehow. He had picked the wrong night. My sympathy for men and their romantic plights had already been wrung out.

"But Rebecca's been helping me clean out the basement of the condo. There were some clothes in one of the closets, clothes of yours. A couple of dresses, a pair of shoes, a purse. And that big bag. I didn't know what I should do with them. Rebecca said the clothes were good stuff, and the bag is vintage Chanel. Stuff you would definitely want back. Anyway, she folded it all up very carefully in that bag, and said I should mail it to you."

"That was thoughtful of her."

"Except you see, I just...well, you know me. I didn't get around to it. I kept meaning to, but I've been so busy."

"You always are."

"I know, I know. But it didn't mean anything. I wasn't...avoiding closure."

"'Avoiding closure'? She really talks to you that way?"

"She's young."

"That's clear."

"Anyway, she called me when she got home tonight. Pretty angry. She said...she said she had a talk with you. In the ladies' room, I think."

"Yes. She told me how happy you two are. Together."

"Well, I don't know what you said to her but she...she kind of freaked out. Said if I loved her, I had to get your stuff out of there. Tonight."

I shook my head.

"You realize this makes no sense. If she's worried, the last thing she'd do is send you to *my* apartment. In the middle of the night."

"Maybe she trusts me."

"Oh, please. Jason, it's late. And you're a shitty liar, always have been. So why don't you just tell me why you're here?"

He looked at the floor, scratched his head. His bashful act. It had moved me, once, but that was a very long time ago.

"Well, she said she...she got the idea that you still have...a bit of a thing for me. You know what I mean?"

"Jason, really..."

"I mean, she said you just seemed like a mess. Drunk and shaky, having trouble putting on your makeup—"

"*What?* I'd had, like, *two* glasses of wine. Besides—"

"Admit it, Lou—you were having kind of a breakdown when we split up. You were out of control. Drinking too much. Mad at everybody. Screwing that—that guy. Pissing off Natalie, who has always been your best pal."

"Unlike you, Natalie understands a few things. About me. About what it means to lose your mother."

He looked me right in the eyes then. And there he was, the man I had spent five years and seven months trying to love.

"You told me you didn't need me, and I believed you. You said you could handle it."

"What are you talking about?"

"Your mother's funeral. I know I was wrong about that, Louise. I know that now. I should have come back for it, anyway. Though you told me not to."

"I told you you didn't *have* to. Come back, that is."

"Right. Anyway, I know now I should have come back. I know that now. I'm...I'm sorry."

Before I could say anything, he went on.

"Rebecca asked me tonight if I still loved you. And I told her that I...that I didn't know."

"So you came here to find out?"

"Where else would I go?"

I closed my eyes. *Please*, I thought, *somebody wake me up. Somebody tell me the last twelve hours were all a bad dream.*

When I opened them, he was still there.

"Jason, you don't mean...you can't really be thinking that we should get back together."

"Is that so crazy?"

"Well, there's Rebecca."

"Well, yes. I'd have to...do something...about that. But I think she expects it. After tonight, anyway."

"And you should know, I'm seeing someone, too."

"I thought you just broke up?"

"Well, that was one guy. But I've been seeing someone else as well."

I pointed to the photo of Vincent pinned to the canvas where I'd begun to paint him. Jason's face went bright red, as if he'd been slapped. But he kept his voice calm.

"And you gave me shit about Rebecca being young."

"I'd say he's a bit more mature. At least, I can't imagine him cornering you in a bathroom and telling you how happy we are together."

I thought that would sting, but he went on as if he hadn't heard me.

"You never take a break, do you, Louie? Sex is so almighty important to you, there's always got to be somebody else out there before you make a jump."

"Whether or not that's true, I'm not sure it's any of your business."

"Let me just ask you one more thing. For the record, OK? When was the last time you went without sex for more than, say, a month? Two months?"

You asked for it. I thought. *Here goes.*

"Well, Jason, that would have been during the last couple of years I spent with you. And what can I say? I found it unfulfilling."

I closed my eyes, again. When I heard the door slam, I opened them. I could tell Jason's vanity had been wounded by Vincent's beauty. My young lover as a weapon. What a thought.

Jason gone, for the last time, and T.J., too. What was it Katherine had said over Christmas? "What liberation, when the old forms fall." The old forms were falling with a vengeance now, all around me. "The world is so fresh it almost hurts." Katherine was right about that, too. The only constant these days seemed to be my inconstant mother, and now, Vincent. I looked into his eyes, the eyes I had painted, large and calm and confident and cold.

He lives only for the music.

Where had I read that? In my mother's pages.

10

he time I spent with Vincent that winter looks to me now as if I were under a sort of spell, an extended waking dream. I was spending long days at work on my paintings, in that fuzzy trance that usually means you're on the right track, or somewhere close. And when I wanted to come up for air, to see and be seen and touched, there he was.

He never moved in; I never even gave him his own key. But every two or three days there he'd be, at my door, usually around midafternoon. If I was painting, he'd get out his guitar and play. After a couple of weeks, he started leaving his acoustic Martin guitar in my front closet. He also left some books on Zen Buddhism, which he liked to read a page or two of before his daily half-hour meditation.

I was able to finish my portrait of him quickly, and included him as well as a background figure in a painting of the young musician in my mother's manuscript. But even when those were done, it felt easy and natural for us to be together in silence, working. I'd never liked to share studio space with anyone, but Vincent was different. I was astonished to discover, early on, that there was no jinx involved in him seeing my work in progress. He'd play and I'd paint and time would disappear. Then we'd shake it off, maybe order carry-out, and make gentle, almost shy, love.

We had the same kind of regard for each other's work. He never offered an opinion, but he did look carefully at every canvas, and occasionally would ask me how I'd gotten an effect, a layer of color, a texture.

"It's like magic, what you do with all those tubes and pots," he'd say. "Pure magic." For my part, it made me deeply proud to think that his music was my soundtrack, that this genius, as everyone called him, was spending hours in my studio practicing his older pieces and working up new ones. Like him, I did not express opinions unless asked. But he knew I loved everything he made.

And no, we did not go to clubs or fancy dinners. I did not miss them, which at first surprised me. But it was so wonderful to be able to be that deeply in my painting, every single day—no dramas at A Woman's Place to interrupt me—that the old extrovert in me gave way to a kind of quiet interiority. And Vincent, so introverted, so quiet himself, was the perfect partner for that time.

Or perhaps not quite perfect. He was, and remained, a mystery to me in so many ways, and while that was alluring at first, it was also unsettling. There was a big difference between a quiet, contented Vincent and a quiet, angry one. The latter did not want to talk, ever, about what might be upsetting him, but he emanated his bad mood. Sometimes he arrived at my door with a real smile and sometimes he arrived stirred up, grinding his teeth, his shoulders tensed like bow strings.

"Something on your mind?" I tried more than once, in our early days. And he'd say something like, "I guess it's obvious," or, "Just having a bad day," or even, "Jay is off the rails again." But when I said, "Would you like to talk about it? It might make you feel better," the answer was always the same. No. Talking does not help. And then he'd get out his guitar and play for a while, and then we'd get into bed.

There was a sadness inside of him that I could never seem to touch, though he called my apartment his hideout, my company his refuge. He clung to me so hard in the night sometimes it woke me. We had ten good weeks—I know, it's pathetic, but I counted—and then, as my trip to London neared, something shifted. What had been warm now cooled; he came by less often, stayed less often, seemed even more preoccupied. Our lovemaking became more hasty, less tender.

Meanwhile, I became more and more consumed with my trip to England. In addition to the show at Mina's, I had other reasons for going now. A little online searching had been fruitless so far in finding a Hollow Hills Press or a Felicity Amble-Pierce. However, a search for libraries whose collections focused on the Middle Ages showed one in Oxford, the Bodleian. I decided to add Oxford to my itinerary. Besides, I wanted to see where my mother had lived, walk her old streets, visit her old haunts.

There seemed to be a correlation between my growing excitement about the England trip and Vincent's diminished attentions. It occurred to me that he might be sad about me going away without him.

During one of his afternoon visits, I was talking to Nat on the phone about our hotel reservations when he came up behind me and wrapped his arms around me.

After I hung up, I said, "You could come with me, you know."

Silence.

"To London, I mean. The room's already booked. Why not come with me?"

Silence.

"London's a good music town. We'd have fun," I tried again.

More silence. He let go of me, and as I turned to face him I saw that his eyes had gone opaque, just as they had in his father's presence. My heart thudded.

"Well, what do you think? There's still time to get a ticket."

He shook his head, jamming the toe of his boot against the floor, not looking at me.

"No, Louise. I'm sorry, but I just can't. Not—not now."

I decided to take "not now" as a good thing, the promise of something more to come. I decided to be content with whatever it was that Vincent could give me. And I worked, and worked, and worked.

A FEW DAYS BEFORE WE flew out, the D.C. Cultural Alliance held a party for all the local artists who were included in Atlantic Exchange. I resented having to sacrifice a minute of painting for the event. But Natalie felt it was important for us to be there.

"I'm just not seeing how it will help," I told her. "We need to save our schmoozing for London. Here, it's just the same old scene."

"The same old scene is just what got us *there*, remember? Come on, Lou, you know the drill."

"I do?"

"We say thanks to the arts council folks, to the alliance chair, have a drink, make a toast—"

"Jesus, it sounds so tame. What happened to coke in the bathrooms, sex in the stairwells?"

"Lou, you're not really old enough to be sentimental about the eighties."

"I know, I'm sorry. I'm a bitch. But there are some people, Nat—and you for one should certainly understand this—there are some people that I just don't want to see."

"You're not the only one. There are some women at the Place who aren't too fond of me right now, either. But I'm going, anyway."

"You're a better person than I am. I've always known that."

"So do it for me."

The night of the party I put on my most severe new clothes—a black ribbed wool minidress, black patterned tights, black boots—and a lot of black eyeliner, along with the silver and turquoise labyrinth earrings Nat had given me. I had enemies to face. I needed armor. I thought I'd let myself have a drink, just one drink, to get my courage up. I poured myself a shot of scotch, looked at it, and left it on the table.

To my surprise, the party wasn't bad. It took place on two empty floors of an office building near Metro Center, another casualty of the tumbling economy. Paper streamers held the names of all the artists, galleries, and organizations involved in Atlantic Exchange, and people made a game of finding their own. The crowd was big enough that it was easy to lose people who might ask uncomfortable questions, and Nat and I stayed mostly together, shaking hands and making our thank yous, talking in the brightest terms about our new work, England, and the future of A Woman's Place. Mercifully, Sahara wasn't there. And the *Post* had sent a young woman we'd never met to cover the party.

"At least Tim Gould isn't here," I said quietly to Nat.

"Oh, don't you know?"

"Know what?"

"Tim left the *Post*. He's still got his blog, of course. But he's going to start a gallery."

"What? Where?"

"I don't think he knows yet. But he says he's got a couple of investors. He dropped by the Place last week. And he sent out a press release. You should check your email."

"My, my. Tim Gould. Who would have known? I'm impressed. Really."

She laughed.

"You're terrible. He's always liked your work, you know."

"Do you remember his last review? 'Combining the influences of Robert Rauschenberg and Rembrandt? Not always successfully?'"

"But they are two of your favorite artists.'

"But, Nat—"

"Never mind. Anyway, I'm happy for him. Now, come on. We need to go shake some hands. And then, London."

Nat and i left the party a little after ten—still early, though I could not persuade her to join me for a nightcap at one of the lively bars along Ninth Street. Her flight left the day before mine and she still had packing to do. I walked her to the Metro, watched her dark hair disappear down the escalator and into the caverns below, and stood there for a while, watching the people come and go, feeling wound up, not wanting the night to end. There was a tapas bar on the corner, and behind the front windows I saw warm candlelight, people moving back and forth; the door swung open and two chattering couples tumbled out into the street. I heard laughter, and talk, and the low throb of music.

Inside, the restaurant was packed and warm. I was scanning the bar for an empty seat when a voice called out to me from one of the low leather couches that were at a premium on a night like this.

"Louise! Louise Terry!"

Dr. Volpe was out of his seat and coming toward me, his hand out.

"What a lovely coincidence. Who are you with? Alone? Do join us!"

My coat was whisked away and I was ushered onto a banquette next to a scented cloud of blue-gray silk, blonde hair, and pearls.

"Sherry and I were at the theater tonight, and we always stop here. Louise, this is my wife. Sherry Ives Volpe."

I put my hand out.

"And this is Louise Terry. She's one of Dana's discoveries."

"Oh, how lovely!"

She eyed me up and down. Her eyes were blue, enormous, slightly uptilted. Pearls swung from her earlobes, nestled against her collarbone, ringed her wrists. She must be fifteen or twenty years younger than he is, I thought. She must be, well, about my age.

"First, we must get you a drink. Do you like champagne, Louise?"

"Very much."

"Oh, good! Then you'll love this cava. Connie, get her a glass?"

My glass appeared, was filled by Dr. Volpe from a tall green bottle. We settled back, Dr. Volpe with his scotch on the rocks, Sherry and I with our flutes.

"Cheers."

"Now," Sherry said, "just how did you two meet?"

"We were on the Mayor's awards committee last year," I said.

"And then we met again at Dana's gallery," Dr. Volpe said. "The night you missed, my dear. When Vincent's outfit played. Excuse me, gigged."

He raised his eyebrows.

"After all these years, I am beginning to know the lingo. Gigs. Blending."

"*Mixing*, dear," she said, then turned her bright, beguiling face on me.

"So how was the boy genius?"

"Vincent? He was very, very good. And it was…surprising. Not the usual background music you hear at openings."

"Oh, Connie's son is full of surprises. I will give him that."

"Yes, he is. But that's part of his charm, isn't it?"

"So you know Vincent?"

"Oh, yes," I said, then stopped.

She looked at me. I went on, a little stupidly, "He gave me one of his CDs. We stay…in touch…"

Dr. Volpe saved me.

"Vincent mentioned that you had come to see him play. I would be so glad, Louise, if the two of you became friendly. I feel that Vincent needs the influence of, well, someone a little older, someone who has made a life in the arts, who knows how hard it is—"

"Darling, we are not going to linger on this again tonight, are we?" Sherry broke in.

Older, I thought. A good influence, of all things.

"If you ask me," she went on, "Vincent's only problem is that he's spoiled. And if he would deign to speak to his stepmother about anything important, which he doesn't, I could tell him all he needs to know about how hard life is in the performing arts."

She changed gears.

"There goes our waiter now, darling. Get us another bottle, would you? Go get him, sweetie, otherwise it will take forever."

He trotted off. His wife turned to me, all curled-cat interest.

"You must tell me. How did Dana discover you?"

"She found me in the paper. A write-up in the *Post*. And then she came to visit me at a women's collective I cofounded. A Woman's Place. She liked my paintings."

"A collective! That sounds marvelously bohemian. And when do you have your next show?"

"I leave for England on Friday," I said. "I'm in a show in London."

"Oh, how exciting! I adore London, especially the theater. That was my first career, you know, though that was another life, now..."

She went on to tell me a long, unconnected story about her early years in the theater, peppered with famous names. Gesturing, stretching, showing herself, she looked like a fashion spread, her blue-gray silk dress glowing against the dark red leather of the couch. She was tall, probably as tall as I was, but oh so thin, just a hint of breasts and hips, a tiny waist, and the soft French manicure, the black suede kitten-heel pumps, the soft, silvery-pink lipstick. Her skirt came to just above her narrow knees.

I saw myself next to her—black clad, big hair, red lips, big, rattling jewelry—and felt ungovernably large and clumsy. The low slant of the couch pitched my knees up, my short skirt exposing far too much no matter how I shifted in my seat, while my heavy black eyeliner, almost a uniform at arts parties, seemed a relic from another, rougher time. I tucked my feet sideways, trying not to scrape the couch with the sharp heels of my boots. I didn't know whether I should worship this woman as some kind of ideal female, or try to kill her quietly for the good of all women everywhere. I shifted, and shifted again, trying to get comfortable.

She was interrupted by Dr. Volpe, returning with menus.

"More cava is on its way. And, I don't know about you two, but I say order freely. Shakespeare always makes me hungry."

"It wasn't Shakespeare, dear, it was Marlowe. *Tamburlaine*. Not the most exciting night in the theater, I'm afraid," she added, turning to me. "But we subscribe. And I'm on the board, of course. It is *so* important to support the arts. I mean, when Connie first *dragged* me here—"

"Don't listen to her, Louise. She was dying to get out of Manhattan."

"Hah! Anyway, the theater here has improved *so* much. So many more options. And I love the summer Fringe Festival, don't you? Though my dear husband is *always* ready for Maine by then, which—"

"Which you love. Every year it's the same, Louise. She complains about going to the sticks, as she calls it, and by the third day she's thanking me profusely for getting her out of the rat race."

"Liar," she said, leaning over to kiss him on the cheek.

A champagne cork popped. The waiter was there, pouring.

"To new friends," Dr. Volpe said.

We sipped. Sherry clasped my arm again.

"The Spanish are so good at wine, aren't they?"

Beside her, Dr. Volpe was talking quietly to the waiter, asking for a seemingly endless list of dishes.

"I usually just let him order. It's always too much and it's always fantastic. But if there's something in particular you'd like, Louise—"

"I'm not really hungry, thanks."

"Oh, you must eat. I insist. Our treat. Now, Connie, Louise was telling me all about—"

"Oh, my god, Sherry Ives! I cannot believe it!"

There was squealing behind us, answered by squealing from Sherry, who was out of her seat and embracing a brunette version of herself.

"If you'll excuse us for just a moment, darling...an old friend."

I saw my chance.

"Dr. Volpe—"

"Connie, please."

"This has been a lovely surprise, thank you so much, but I really should be heading home."

"Nonsense! We've just begun!"

"No, really, I—"

"Just one more, then. For the road, as the old song goes."

He refilled my glass, then shifted closer in his seat. When he spoke, his voice was soft and hesitant.

"If you don't mind, Louise—Sherry is tired of hearing about this, but now that we have a few moments, I'd like...I'd like to ask you. Just what do you think of Vincent's new plan?"

"Plan?"

"Oh, I know he would hate to think we're talking about him. So private, my son. So..."

"Sensitive."

"Yes, exactly. He interprets every sign of concern as some kind of...indictment. And yet, I can't help but worry about this new endeavor. I mean, tell me, Louise—and be frank, really, I want to know if I'm off the mark—what do you make of this Portland thing? Do you think it's a step in the right direction, do you think it's progress? Because it seems quite foolish to me. Here he is, a new band, a new record about to come out, and all of a sudden he wants to take off and start all over? On the other side of the country? I just do not understand it."

You can hear a thing and still not grasp its meaning. Words clanged in my head—*Portland, foolish, start all over*—but made no sense.

"Well," I said, slowly, "I don't know. I thought his primary goal these days was to get the new CD out. To see how it's received, if it gets any press."

"Oh, I know he *says* that. But how can he promote it without his band? Jay is furious, and I can't say I blame him. They've been friends since they were five years old, and Vincent has always been the leader, always. Jay would follow him off a bridge, as my mother used to say. And now my son repays him for his loyalty by throwing the whole project to the winds. To move to Oregon, of all places!"

Oregon. Moving.

"Well, he and Jay do have their problems."

"Of course, of course. And no one is saying that Vincent has to be tied to him forever. But it's the suddenness of it all. One day it's all Einstein's Closet—"

"Einstein's Pillow."

"Yes. Right. And the next it's all West Coast, West Coast, that's where he has to be, and right this minute. The East Coast is dead and done, as far as he's concerned. A waste."

I was on firmer ground here.

"Oh, lots of artists, of all kinds, complain about the East Coast. It's sort of a conversational habit. But mostly we just want peace and privacy to work. And Vincent has that lovely house, his studio—"

"Ah, a pragmatist. I knew I could talk to you, Louise. This is exactly what I tried to tell him."

The waiter arrived, one-arming a tray burdened with platters. I took a drink, tried to steady myself.

"Remind me," I said, as the waiter set dish after dish before us, "just when is Vincent planning to take off?"

"The end of the month. That's what he said this afternoon. There's some festival he wants to be there for the last week of March. And then, as I understand it, the plan is he'll just stay on."

I would be in England then.

"Just a moment, young man. I specifically asked for this salad without beets, and now here it is—"

"If you'll excuse me," I said.

I gathered up my purse in a showy fashion, to indicate I was going to the ladies' room. Dr. Volpe, busy correcting the waiter, didn't see me slip my jacket from the back of the banquette. But when I was halfway across the floor, Sherry saw me, and rushed over.

"Louise, you *aren't* leaving? I was *just* coming back. All that lovely food—"

I knew of only one infallible excuse. I told Sherry that my period had just started, early, bringing with it some wrenching cramps. She offered sympathy and ibuprofen. And then I was outside, feeling around inside myself for a broken place, a sore place, wherever it was that the news of Vincent's departure had just landed.

I remembered asking him, after Nat and I got the news, if he'd like to come with me to Atlantic Exchange. I remembered the look on his face—guilty, furtive—when he said he had too much work to do here. I'd dismissed it as my own paranoia and suspicion; work was what he lived for. But now I saw it again, and what I had missed.

He hadn't told me. He was never going to tell me. He was simply going to disappear.

※

FELLOWSHIP HOUSE WAS DARK AS I drove up, only a few security lights on around the main house. The dormitory buildings were all dark as well. I parked and walked up to the front door, but could not bring myself to knock on it. There was no noise inside, none at all. But Brother Paul was, like me, a night person. He'd said so.

I remembered the day I'd visited him in his office, the path we'd taken through the house. That way, I thought, looking to the right, and started walking, slowly and lightly as I could in my tall boots, along the flagstone path that dipped down as it circled the building. The moon was just past full, and helped me see my way. Paul's office had been near the back, on the side that faced toward the hill. But if he was still awake, he wasn't in his office. The entire floor was dark.

At the back of the house, I stood on the little patio, edged with the statues Paul had cleaned the day of our hike. A light came on in one of the second-story windows. The blinds were half-raised, and I could see someone moving around inside the room. Then that someone came to the window, and pushed it open. For a moment, I had a glimpse of Brother Paul, backlit, his arms raised to push up the sill, to let in the cool night air. I was about to say his name when he turned away again and disappeared. Then the light went out.

I looked around. There might be a ladder somewhere, but I certainly wasn't dressed to climb one. A stone bench on the far edge of the patio might have been useful, if it hadn't been too heavy to move. As it was, there was nothing to stand on, no way to get to my monk. I felt the eyes of the little statues all looking at me, a ring of saints waiting to see what I would do.

I looked down. The flagstone path was old, crumbling along the edges. I picked up a chunk of it and winged it at Paul's window. It tapped the brickwork just below. I picked up another, bigger chunk and threw it, harder, at the window. This time I missed it by a wider mark. I had to get higher.

I climbed up onto the stone bench. I had a real rock in my hand, the flagstone proving too soft. Aiming for Paul's window, I overthrew my target. The rock bounced off a chimney pipe with a loud clang, and then clanged again on the metal gutter before hitting the drainpipe, where it bounced loudly down to the ground.

"Shit!"

The light in Paul's window came on, as did the ones on either side, and two more on the floor below. I jumped off the bench, twisting my heel, and half scrambled, half crawled behind a woodpile. I heard voices, the sound of windows being raised. A light went on outside the house, illuminating the patio and the bench where I had just stood.

I tried to stay still, though something sharp was pressing into my back. Slowly, far too slowly, the voices quieted, the lights went out, and I was left alone in the dark, my arms and legs scraped by prickly azalea bushes, wondering what to do next.

The back door opened. Someone stepped out onto the patio.

"Louise?" Paul said softly. "Are you there?"

I stood up, my ankle tender and shaky. Then he was next to me, his hand on my arm.

"Steady, now. Anything hurt or broken?"

"No. Nothing. Except my pride."

"I take it you'd like to talk to me?"

"Yes," I said. "I have come to an enormous realization."

"Yes?"

"I've been a fool. A total, complete fool."

"Why would you think that?"

The light above the back door went on and off, on and off. A soft voice, Sister Kathy's voice, said, "If you want to talk, my dears, I suggest the dormitory. Or the guesthouse. Others are trying to sleep."

"I woke her up?"

"She heard your car pull in. Saw you walk around the back."

We were both whispering, now. I had a sudden picture of myself as she must have seen me, tiptoeing, wobbly-ankled and drunk around her house, throwing stones at her windows.

"I'd better go. I feel like an idiot."

"Oh, please. You've done wonders for my reputation. Most of my brothers consider me, well, a little dull. Or at least not someone at whose window a beautiful woman would be throwing rocks after midnight."

He looked me up and down, assessing.

"But Kathy is right. The guesthouse. Can you walk?"

"How far?"

"Not very. Here. This way."

No hike this time, just a slow walk into the woods, Paul's arm tight around mine, his other directing the flashlight. And then we were at the door of a house so small it was nearly hidden by the trees.

"We think this might have been a gardener's cottage, back in the 1700s," he said. "We used it as shed, until Tom had it restored. He thought that we needed a real hermitage."

"A what?"

"A place for solitary prayer and meditation. To balance out our emphasis on service. And for retreatants."

Inside, the overhead light showed one small, neat room. On one side, a bed, a dresser, a desk, a chair; on the other, a sink, a two-burner stove, a tiny refrigerator, a small square table, and a propane heater.

"The toilet's behind that wall. Only one chair, you see, and it's not comfortable."

He gestured to the bed.

"So why don't you sit there, and tell me all about it."

As long as I was standing, I had been fine. But as soon as I sat down, I felt something give inside. Only a little while ago, I'd had a thousand things to say—so much to mourn, to pick apart and cry over. Now I could barely open my mouth.

"I don't know what's wrong with me," I said. "I'm just suddenly so...so..."

"Tired? I'm not surprised. It sounds like you've had a hard time. Why don't you rest?"

"Rest?"

"Sleep here. There's a nightshirt in the dresser, a robe and slippers. It's quiet here. You can sleep as long as you like. And then, when you get up in the morning, we'll talk."

"I can't...I mean, I shouldn't..."

"Why?"

I had no answer. Paul went to the sink, poured me a glass of water, and brought it to me.

"Drink this, then sleep. We'll talk in the morning, yes?"

He leaned over and kissed me on the forehead, as he had so many months ago.

"God bless you, Louise Terry."

He let himself out, and I fell back on the bed, suddenly too tired to even take off my boots. I drank the last of my water, turned out the light. My sleep was peaceful, dreamless, broken only by the gentle knock of Brother Paul at the door, bringing me coffee, the green-gold light of morning at his back.

INTERLUDE 2

Glastonbury, 1996

She opens her eyes and she is running, running. Someone ahead of her. Another behind. The first one stumbles. She grabs him by the shoulder and rights him. A smell of burning. If they aren't quick enough, they will be dead. They can be sure of that.

He pushes the rock away that hides the entrance to the tunnel, a hole in the ground that they fall into, one after another. A brief rest, then. They pass a skin of wine between them—are there three? Four?—and wipe the sweat from their faces. Someone says, "We have done it!" Her heart thumps. No time to celebrate now.

And then they are running again, the clay walls sweating around them, narrow then wide, then narrow again. It is hard to breathe. She gulps at the air, holding onto it. As they come up out of the tunnel they are still running, running full out, so when the ground beneath their feet slopes sharply down, they tumble head over heels down the northwest slope of the Tor, knocked breathless by the running, the falling, by their own deeds.

The wind carries the smell of smoke, then black flakes, cinders. She can see now that there are only two others. One of them fumbles at the folds of his robe, as though trying to free himself from something. The other is weeping.

She drops to her knees. She gives thanks to the Goddess for her life, wherever it will take her, now.

✻

THE AMERICAN WOMAN OPENS HER eyes to see the teacher's face, sideways above her own. The hand on her forehead is warm and seems to hold her in place where she lies. She feels the texture of a short, tough rug beneath her, rising to meet her skin as if through a layer of dirt and grass.

"Margaret. It is time to come back, my dear. This journey is over."

"Where...am I, exactly?"

She hears a disapproving sniff. One of the others, one of the two or three others who had looked at her with unmasked disapproval when she arrived. Just a beginner, she told them. Here at Eve's invitation. Still, some of them had looked at her as if she could not possibly belong.

Sitting up, she remembers finding the address on Benedict Street. Going alone because Lawrence had said, at the last minute, that he and Eve's husband had business to discuss. Geoffrey wanted advice; he and Eve were thinking of publishing books themselves. Eve had seemed relieved to hear that they'd gone off together, but it bothered Margaret. They were probably in a pub right now, while a few streets away, a High Priestess of the

Old Religion was guiding a handful of people through the folds between worlds.

Lawrence had brought her this far. Lawrence should be here now.

"Oh, yes. Yes, I remember."

Lying down for the meditation, their feet made the center of a wheel, their bodies the spokes. Eve had walked around them counterclockwise, banishing the world of daily forms, making invocations to the spirits of the four directions: south, east, north, west. So light on her feet, and so precise.

Eyes closed, they had all followed her instructions. "Imagine a place you love," she'd said, and Margaret had recalled a grassy park, near her old home, in June. Buds bursting, birds hovering. "Don't just visualize it. Use all your senses." Margaret, listening, heard the creek running, adding its background music, the snap and whisper of water on stone. Margaret felt the grass and dirt beneath her skin, sun warming her body. Eve chanted:

> *You the child in her palm,*
> *Find refuge in the Lady's calm.*
> *She will lead you where She will—*
> *Under water, over hill,*
> *On moon-dark night or blaze of dawn,*
> *Following the Lady's song,*
> *Your first best tune. Learn it by heart.*
> *Step through the veil and make your start.*

"Looking around, you see an entrance into another element," Eve went on. "Perhaps a hole in a tree or a hedge. Perhaps a body of water, or a tunnel." Margaret looked, and saw a tree she did not recognize from home. A redwood, its trunk was burned open, just like some she'd seen in California. It had made a kind of doorway into the huge tree.

"Enter it," Eve said. "The hole, the niche, the tunnel, the water. Whatever it is. Enter it." And so Margaret stood, and approached the tree, which seemed to invite her with the lifting of its branches. And then she was falling, falling into that other world.

AFTER EVE HAS GROUNDED AND opened the circle, after the others have left, Margaret sits in her kitchen, sipping sweet milky tea, trying to sort out her next steps.

"I think you are moving along quite well," Eve says. "For most, that was a simple exercise in guided meditation. But you...you did cross over."

"Yes. I felt that. I wish—I wish I had found this years ago."

Eve's silver-blue eyes are cool, steady.

"You came to the Old Religion when you came. There is no right or wrong to it."

"But Lawrence—"

"It depends on you. Not him."

"But he wants—he has started to write about this, you know. The male characters, they interest him more. The monk. The boy. But Margaret—"

"You seem so sure she has your name."

"Not just my name. She is—me, somehow."

"A past life, perhaps," Eve says. "That is certainly possible. Still...it is best not to become...too attached."

"You sound like my eldest. Katherine, the Buddhist," Margaret chuckles.

Eve looks at her, unsmiling.

"This has nothing to do with Buddhism. You must not have designs on the Goddess. On what she might choose to show to you, or not."

"But the girl—that girl, with her vision, her stones—I feel her. I saw her in Oxford, remember? And now she has followed me—"

"No. You have followed her. You are not in charge. Never think that it is your own agency. You are the vehicle, not the source. Always."

Eve stands, takes their cups to the sink. Margaret knows it is time to go.

At the door, Eve embraces her.

"You might tell Geoffrey, when you see him, that I have dinner ready here."

"I hoped you and he might join us—"

"Ah, I am tired. But thank you, my dear. Blessed be."

"Blessed be."

Inside the King Arthur Pub, she finds the two men at a small corner table, pints in front of them, the ashtray between them filled with the butts of cigarettes that have added weight to the already thick air around them. Larry kisses her on the cheek and heads for the bar to get her a white wine. As she settles into the chair across from him, Geoffrey's eyes linger on her bosom. He is a good-looking man, Eve's husband, with thick-muscled arms, and a head of hair not unlike her own, dark auburn, disorderly natural curls. A goat, she thinks; that is what he looks like. But there is something about Geoff Darrow that has always made her uncomfortable, a kind of crackling sexual energy that strikes her as dangerous. She prefers Larry's cool charm, his civilized accent. Still new to English class distinctions, she does not know that Eve has married down.

Geoff leans across the table, lights her Marlboro, holding onto her hand a little longer than he needs to. Larry, returning with her drink, notices with pride. He likes it—within reason, of course—when other men find her attractive. She is his prize, his woman.

He pulls his chair up close to hers, puts a proprietary arm across her shoulders.

"So how was your first real circle, my love? Did it live up to your expectations?"

"Oh, yes. It was amazing. A whole other world, again. And I saw—I was with my girl—"

"How many of you?" Geoff interrupts.

"Let's see. Eleven—and Eve makes twelve."

"You see what I mean, Larry? She could have had eleven paying customers. But not my wife, oh no—"

"But Eve says one never takes money for magic," Margaret replies. "It is not done for hire."

"Ha! Tell that to the Farrars. Or to Maxine Sanders."

"But we all made offerings."

"And I provided Margaret with quite a substantial one," Larry says coolly.

"Oh, no, no, I don't mean you two. Of course not." Geoff flushes at the rebuke but keeps going.

"But I doubt the rest of them gave much at all, eh? And sometimes instead of money they bring paintings they have made, or poems they've written."

"Eve says any offering made with a clear heart is equal in the eyes of the Goddess."

"Yes, well, perhaps. But the Goddess doesn't have a roof to put over her head, or a larder to fill."

Shocked at the blasphemy, Margaret exhales sharply. Under the table, Larry squeezes her knee in warning.

"You must forgive our Geoff," he says. "While you were occupied with the other world, my dear, we were talking the business of this one. Which reminds me, Geoffrey—what are you and Eve doing for dinner?"

"Nothing in particular."

"Eve said she's too tired," Margaret puts in. "And that she's made dinner for you both at home. The circle was exhausting for her, I'm afraid. She had to work so hard, with so many different people."

Geoff sighs in disappointment.

"I suppose I should be off, then. Can't tell you how good that was, Larry. What it means to have a real professional on board for our Hollow Hills Press. Eve will be so pleased."

He shakes Larry's hand, kisses Margaret on both cheeks, and is off.

"So," Larry says, turning to her, and running one finger along her chin, "how is my favorite witch?"

❧

LATER, AFTER DINNER AND COGNAC and a particularly energetic session of lovemaking, Margaret lies on her side, awake while Larry falls into a satisfied sleep beside her. Tomorrow they drive back to Oxford. In two weeks they will be in London again, with a full schedule of plays and parties and dinners with Larry's friends. The film version of his play, *The Fallacy of Pleasure*, has been cast with Jeremy Irons and a Scottish actress Margaret has never heard of, Tilda Swinton. Larry is flush and happy and Margaret is proud of him, so proud. Even Aunt Angie who thought the affair had gone too far, too fast, that Margaret needed more time to be on her own, free of husband and children, is cautiously approving of this new love.

"Well, he's certainly successful," she'd said, over tea with her infatuated niece. "And being with him broadens your horizons. Still..."

Still, Margaret had thought, but did not say, you'd rather be the one to do that yourself. On your own terms. But if I am to be free, it must be even from you.

Knowing sleep will not come, she gives up, gets up, slips into the blue silk robe Larry bought her—an elegant, kimono-style thing with deep sleeves and patterns in pink and white of lotus blossoms. So different from the plain flannel gowns she'd worn for years at home. But that home is off limits to her now. She knows she can never go back. Leave your house and your children once and people may well excuse you, write it off to the midlife crisis of a girl married young and not quite ready to be fully grown up. Leave twice and you are persona non grata. And though the wounded husband she left behind has nursed his grief in silence, and her two older children, Katherine and Dylan, have coped in their various ways, it is her youngest, Louise, who is the mirror of her guilt, whose spiked rage, delivered over the phone when Margaret had dared to call her, is the embodiment of all her mother's demons. Dylan says he will talk to her, work with her, persuade her to come with her siblings when they make their planned visit. But Louise is stubborn, and right now very angry. Margaret doubts Dylan will be able to soften her, despite his famous charm.

She misses them in a place so deep the ache is physical. It bends her over, twists her guts with its heat. It is only at this hour, in the darkest part of night, with Larry asleep, that she allows herself to feel it. Otherwise, she would be incapacitated, lost.

In an effort to shake it off, she uncorks the bottle of cognac Larry brought with them, pours two fingers' full into the cheap, scratched hotel glass. She remembers the afternoon's events, the circle, Eve Darrow, her vision of the girl Margaret. Had she stayed in Maryland, she would never have had all this. And though England was Angie's idea, everything else about her new life is due to Larry. Larry, who had chatted her up at the café in London during the rain, who had found her again in Oxford and encouraged her to talk about herself, her feelings, her longings, her own deep discontents.

And it was Larry who had told her that much of what she already thought and felt was pagan in its origin. Of course, he said, a vibrant woman like her had had to shuck off her Catholicism! An ossifying religion, he had said, with all its hatred of the body, of need, of sex. She'd known instinctively that sex was holy, with its own rules and presumptions. Divine blessing. Gift of the gods.

He had told her about Maxine and Alex Sanders, who had run a coven in London in the 1960s and '70s. They were like rock stars, he said, both so beautiful, and people flocked to them. He had been in his teens and twenties then, in love with the vibrant city, and fell in with their group long enough to recognize the pagan in himself, as he had in Margaret. It had been Larry's idea to introduce her to Eve and Geoffrey. She had missed so much, he said, in her life as wife and mother. She was fifty-one, after all, though they all said she did not look it. It was time she started living by her own desires. In this, he and Angie were in complete accord.

She moves to the window, parts the curtains, and sips her cognac as she looks out into the velvet of the Glastonbury night. Whatever else she is, she is not a coward. She will swim in this new element, this world of passionate magic that Larry and Eve have given her. She will give herself to that, and to this new life, entirely, whether it lasts for a year or the rest of her time on this earth. Guilt stricken, frightened, in love, on fire—she has never felt so alive as she does now.

PART III

An Atlantic Exchange,
2006

11

I remembered Heathrow Airport as an awful place, buzzing with too many people and almost impossible to navigate, but either it or I or both of us had changed. At every turn, there were helpful-looking employees in efficient vests who offered directions, advice, and connecting information. A blond boy barely out of his teens recommended the bus instead of the tube; the friendly ticket lady explained the fares. Soon I was bound for Bloomsbury, watching the sun coming up over London.

Again, surprise. What I remembered of London from a couple of brief visits was gray weather, dirty air, and chilly people. But the busman at the Russell Hotel greeted me with a smile and a compliment on my new boots. The lobby was full, a cluster of people checking in and out. A young man who looked like he could have come from the musical *Oliver!*, with calculatedly mussed hair and a mischievous smile, said my room would not be ready for an hour or two yet. As I was trying to decide what to do, I heard Nat's voice behind me.

"Louise! You're here!"

"Nat!"

I spun around to hug her, then stopped. Beside her was Sahara. She and I mumbled greetings, Sahara averting her eyes, as if she could barely stand to look at me. The feeling was mutual, of course.

"We're going to Mina's," Nat said. "To look at the show. Why don't you come with us?"

"I don't know, girl. I can't check in yet. And my bags—"

"Oh, come on. They'll keep your bags for you here. Aren't you dying to see the show? And it's only a few blocks away."

Sahara's presence made the walk to Mina's long. She began with an impassioned speech about the lack of vegan options in the hotel restaurant, then moved onto how shockingly expensive everything about the hotel was. Most of her friends, she said, were staying in small, women-run B&Bs where they bunked two and three to a room.

"Well, maybe you should switch over to one of those," I said. "I mean, if you're so unhappy."

Natalie shot me a warning look, but Sahara, unfazed, said, "Oh, I couldn't. Not with my allergies. They've all got dogs and cats, and I need hypoallergenic bedding. My goal is to get through this whole trip without an asthma attack."

"My goal is to see as much art as I possibly can," Natalie said, conciliatory.

"And my goal," I put in, "is to have sex with a British man as soon as possible. Actually, I just want to be naked while somebody talks to me with that accent."

Sahara let out a puff of disapproval, Nat elbowed me, and we walked the rest of the way in silence.

The scene at Mina's was not reassuring. We were a little more than twenty-four hours from opening and half of the work hadn't been installed. Mina, a worn, papery-skinned brunette with a smoker's voice, was overseeing a team of three very tired-looking women. They had had, she told us, every kind of problem.

Customs had held up two crates of what looked like skinned rabbits, intended for a piece on animal rights that employed realistic-looking latex and rubber versions of the atrocities being protested. Several sculptures had arrived in pieces. Three paintings hadn't arrived at all. Two of the gallery's three DVD players weren't working, there was a problem with the electricity in the main room, and the bathroom pipes had backed up. Sahara's installation, whatever it was, had yet to be unpacked. Natalie's sculptures were uncrated but still in their bubble wrap, leaning against a wall. They looked like a row of tiny mummies, which added to the grimness of the place.

"And mine?" I said. "Paintings. *The Seven Deadly Sins.*"

"Oh, yes," Mina said, waving her hand dismissively. "Those were easy. The more traditional ones, we did those first. Over here, then."

They were crammed too closely together, in two stacked rows, three on top, four on the bottom, wedged between a Burne-Jones parody and an enormous, hideously colored reworking of Georgia O'Keefe's poppy. I should have said something, I guess, but the relief of seeing that my work was safe translated immediately into fatigue. The morning's high had disappeared.

Natalie and Sahara stayed to help. I walked back to the hotel alone, careful to look right, then left as I crossed the busy streets, little spots of light dancing and popping in front of my eyes. I felt rubbery, stretched, as if my joints had been loosened by the flight and the lack of sleep. As if to add a final insult, it began to rain when I was a few blocks from the hotel.

My room was narrow and overlooked the square. Too tired to even undress, I kicked off my shoes and lay down on the bed, reviewing the chaos at Mina's gallery. What if the show was a full-fledged disaster? What if we'd come all this way for nothing, or less than nothing?

I drifted of into a few hours of fitful sleep. When I woke, it was early evening. The room was stuffy, and the window sighed when I pushed it open, slivers of paint falling to the sill. Outside, the wet sidewalks were filling, people leaving work, heading for the tube and the train, and cabs were thick in the streets. The rain had stopped, and the clearing let angles of light through the trees in the square—silver-green light, with smudges of umber and gray, gently rubbing the damp stone buildings. The effect was beautiful and a little eerie, the undulating light of dreams.

My eyes stopped at a woman who was by far the brightest thing in all those silvered, muted colors. Her hair was red-brown, a little wild. She wore a blue and white dress with a full skirt, not quite in fashion, that swung like a bell from side to side as she walked. She disappeared, then reappeared in the crowd of people moving across the intersection at the far side of the square. By a fountain, she stopped and looked around, then lifted her right hand and smoothed her hair. It was the gesture that did it, that provided the final kick.

It was my mother who stood across the square from me, nervous, obviously waiting for someone, touching her beautiful hair.

I had my shoes on and was out the door before I knew what I was doing.

Outside, I lost track of her again in the moving bodies, then saw her cross the street. I cut across the square, followed her as quickly as I could, but the sidewalks were full. In front of the British Museum, I lost sight of her, then saw her again. At the edge of Bloomsbury Square, she stepped into the street, was almost hit by a passing car. I opened my mouth to cry out, then saw her safe on the other side. I looked once, twice, then darted across to follow her, a taxi bleating its warning as I ran.

She was only a few yards away now, stopped in front of a bookstore window. She was looking a little away from the books, into her own reflection in the glass. Then she did it again—lifted her hand to smooth her hair. I watched my mother looking at herself and in her reflection, for a moment, she saw me.

I am sure she saw me.

Then a group of laughing teenagers, five or six of them, pushed between us.

"Sorry," said one.

I had to look down to keep from tripping over the curbstones. When I looked back up again, she was gone. I made my way to the place where she had stood, slowly, cautiously, as though I was tracking a wild animal. If I was quiet enough, maybe she would reappear.

But even the bookstore was gone, and in its place, a smoothie shop with pictures of unnaturally colored fruits in the windows. I put my hand to the glass. Inside, a teenaged girl with a pierced nose and ink-black hair stirred her smoothie with a fat straw, looked at me, and smiled.

The world as it was had returned. Whatever doorway had opened, allowing me to see my mother, had closed

again. It seemed to take an eternity to walk back to my
hotel.

Inside the lobby, a man looked up from his paper as
I came in, and then looked twice. I had only an impression—silvery hair, a dark jacket—and was about to turn
toward the elevators when he spoke.

"Excuse me, but you are, perhaps, Louise? Louise
Terry, am I right?"

His eyes were cerulean blue, his shirt blue-white, his
jacket charcoal gray cashmere. He stood up, tossing the
paper aside.

"That's me," I said.

"Well, it is really no great surprise that you don't recognize me. It has been, oh, let us not say how long. I'm
Lawrence Ware."

"Mr. Ware," I said.

He took me by the shoulders and kissed me once on
each cheek.

"Larry, please," he said. "Thought I might pop around,
see how you were settling in. Everything going well?"

He had a deep voice, with a little tremolo, like a cello.
I hadn't realized, years ago, how tall he was. He looked at
me closely, with those sharp, bright eyes.

"No," I said. "Not really. Things are really actually a
little bit rough right now."

"Well, then," he said, "consider me the one who
smooths the path before you. A good thing I'm here, don't
you think?"

THAT NIGHT, I SAT ACROSS from my mother's old lover
at dinner in a candlelit restaurant while waiters clicked
and fussed in a little ballet around us. He knew the

owners, got us a prominent window table. People kept coming over to say hello, and it began to sink in that I was with a celebrity. He introduced me with wild generosity—"One of the best young artists in America," he told them. "Here on a very prestigious grant. You'll be hearing about her." His voice was not loud, but it carried. He was the sort of man people turn to look at, who they can tell must *be* somebody, and his charm soothed me. I smoothed the skirt of my blue silk dress—"Ah, lovely," Larry had said, when I came down the stairs to the lobby. "You shine like a sapphire, my dear"—and tossed my hair a little to one side and basked in the cool sparkle he gave off. He asked intelligent questions about my work, and made me feel, with his interest, like just the artist he'd described—important, brilliant, doing great things.

It wasn't until they were clearing away our entrees that he mentioned the statue. I told him what little I'd learned from Katherine.

"And your sister has no idea what happened to it after that?"

"I'm afraid not. My brother has never seen it. And Aunt Angie—"

"Ah yes. The dragon at the gate."

"Well, she's dead, too. She passed away a few years before Mom."

"I don't suppose it would be worth...well, her estate, her heirs might have, perhaps..."

"She had no children. Mom was her only heir. My mother's parents both died young, you know. Angie really raised her."

"There was a man, wasn't there?"

"Oh, you mean Kenny. I—I haven't seen him since the funeral. And besides, we all—my sister and brother and I—were at the house a lot when Mom was sick. We would have seen the statue there if she still had it."

Larry turned to look out the window. A chattering wave of people had just exited the theater across the street.

"Ah, look at them," he said. "I remember when your mother, your lovely, lovely mother, saw her first West End play. She was like a girl, so thrilled, so thrilled. I thought she would float right up off the ground."

When he turned back to me, he had tears in his eyes.

"I still cannot believe that someone so alive, so brimming with life, could be...oh, I cannot even say it."

He put one hand to his eyes, closing them, and stretched the other across the table blindly, nearly knocking over the flickering candle. I covered it with mine. It was suddenly hard to swallow.

"It may be just an old man's foolishness, my dear," he said. He opened his eyes, and took my hand in both of his. "But I cannot help but think that if I had...if I had that statue back...I would have a part of her to keep. Surely, someone must know what became of it. Her husband, perhaps?"

His voice cracked. His eyes searched mine. Something knocked at the back of my mind, some kind of warning.

"Well, I don't know Kenny very well," I said. "It wouldn't feel right to me to call him. But my brother, Dylan—well, he gets along with everybody. Maybe—maybe he could call Kenny, I could ask him, anyway."

"If you would, my dear...I do hate to ask, but I cannot tell you...I..." He lifted my hand to his mouth and kissed it, all the while keeping his eyes on mine. I felt it like a jolt, his handsomeness, his silvery charm.

Oh, Mom, I thought.

"I'll call him tomorrow," I said. "I promise. I'll work on it."

As we left, Larry took my hand again and drew it through his arm. A party of four waved to him from a few tables away. I could tell, from the way their eyes traveled over me, that they thought Larry and I were lovers. I shook off a twinge of almost-guilt. Who cared what strangers thought? I was out on the town with a handsome man in a city I was suddenly starting to enjoy. I smiled back at them, leaning into my mother's lover's arm.

The walk back to the hotel was beautiful. Rain was falling very softly and Larry held an umbrella over us and we took our time. The streets were shining with reflected lights, and the sound of the rain was like good jazz music, rising and falling, varied and unified at once. On the hotel steps, he gave me a kiss on each cheek, said he'd see me at the opening at Mina's.

It was much later, after I'd washed my face and fallen, exhausted, into bed, that I knew what it was that had bothered me, before. When Larry called me about the statue, he had said his sister wanted it back, was being a "recalcitrant bitch" about it. But tonight, his plea had been for himself, to bring Mom nearer. Both were convincing, in their different ways. But which was true?

I woke late the next morning, dry-mouthed from all the wine, and it hit me, suddenly: My first show in London opened tonight. I dialed Nat's room.

"Girl, I'm starting to feel it. Pre-opening nerves. What kind of state are you—"

"Hold on a second, would you, Louie?"

I heard a voice behind her, female, high-pitched, and knew right away who it was.

"Sorry, Lou. Sahara and I were just getting ready to go to the Tate Modern. Want to come along?"

"So you two are attached at the hip now?"

There was a silence. I started over.

"Look, I'm sorry. I just need—I mean, I wanted to talk about our plans for tonight."

Again, she asked me to hold on. Again, I heard a whining voice that set my teeth on edge. When Nat got back on the line, she and I decided to meet at the hotel bar that evening, before the opening, and walk to it together.

After some truly awful coffee, I found the hotel business center, a tiny, windowless room with two computers and no ventilation, and sent Dylan an email, asking him to get in touch with Kenny about the mysterious statue.

Outside, the sky was clearing, the last of the night's rain drying on the pavement, and I took my sketchbook to a bench in Russell Square and drew what I saw. It had been a long time since I'd sketched like that, purely and simply, for the sake of the seeing, the feel of the charcoal pencil in my hand. I spent a lot of time on one sketch in particular, of three young women eating wrapped sandwiches. After a while I packed up, and took my sketchbook back to my room and spent the afternoon simply wandering with no direction and no goal. Though the sky began to fill again, the rain miraculously held off. And it felt so good to be alone, in a foreign city, with no one to please but myself. Mom might have felt that way as well, when she first came here. Something else, perhaps, that she and I had in common.

❋

Nat is never late for anything. It's one of the reasons we work so well together—we both believe in punctuality. But that night, I was on my second drink in the hotel's mahogany bar, where I'd staked out for us a pair of armchairs by the fire, when the bellman came to me with a wireless house phone.

It was Nat. She and Sahara had gotten back to the hotel that afternoon to find a message from Mina begging for further help. The latex bunnies still had not arrived. The multiple DVD players had blown two fuses, then frozen the electrical system. One of the gallery volunteers had backed into a plinth and knocked over a large ceramic sculpture, and the artist was threatening to sue. Nat was at the gallery now and expected to be there until the doors opened.

"But after the show," she said, "we'll have a nice long talk. Everyone's supposed to go out for Indian food somewhere, and we'll sit in a corner and get all caught up. I'm so sorry, Lou, but I've got to run now."

"But, Nat, why should you—"

"And by the way, I made them move your series. I thought it was a shame to tuck it away like that, and so close together. I think you'll be a lot happier when you see it."

I realized, as soon as I hung up, that I should have offered to come and help. But then, Sahara was probably with her, anyway. *Shit.*

I checked my watch. I had planned to arrive at Mina's with Nat, who would have insisted on us having something to eat first. A good meal was always part of her opening night plan. I have a nervous stomach, and left on my own, I have a tendency, on big nights, to skip food. Suddenly horribly nervous at the idea of walking into

Mina's by myself, I ordered another drink. The place had looked like a nightmare, anyway. It was typical of Nat to want to help, but what good could she do? Mina was clearly in way over her head. My first show in London would be a disaster.

I had a brief, cowardly thought of not showing up at all. The Russell Hotel bar was so comforting—big enough for a dozen little groups of loveseats and chairs around low, carved coffee tables, but still cozy, too, softly lit, music discreetly piped in, waiters with elegant manners who called me "madam," which I loved, and made brief, friendly chat when they brought my drinks. I wondered why there were no bars like this at home. I saw a pair of men at the bar—tall, in suit jackets with longish, swept-back hair—and when they made eye contact, one, then the other, I began to think about other possible ways the night could go. But I had less appetite for the old game than I had for dinner.

I signed for my drinks and pushed myself out into the night. About a block from the hotel, I realized that I had also counted on Nat to lead me to Mina's; the day before, I'd been too tired, and too irritated by Sahara, to notice the way. I was scowling at the tiny print on the Atlantic Exchange brochure, searching for Mina's address, when I heard a newly familiar voice.

"Surely you're not going to the gallery now?"

Larry was in front of me, his smile sharp and white.

"I'm trying to. If I could figure out where it is. The reception is going to start in about two minutes."

"You Americans. Tell me, my dear, do people arrive at the stated hour for…for gatherings of this sort…in Washington?"

"In D.C., people arrive on time and leave early. At least, these days they do."

"How sad. A nation of rebels, and look what you've become."

"I could really do without the America bashing tonight," I said. "I'm nervous enough as it is."

He tilted his head and made a half bow of apology. He moved elegantly, a tall man who knew and liked his body. Like Vincent.

"I do apologize, my dear. Believe me, my intention is not to criticize, but to assist. Allow me?"

He led me to a small, dimly lit, exorbitantly priced wine bar. Larry seemed to know just about everyone there, and we left without being handed a check, but with a handsome forty-something couple, the Clarks, who, the woman whispered to me, were just mad about Larry's work. A few blocks later, we stopped again at a hotel bar where a friend of Larry's, a gray-haired actor whose face was familiar to me from BBC costume dramas, joined us, and again at a place called the Poet's Café, where a pretty blonde—somebody's niece, who was studying film at Goldsmiths—already knew about Atlantic Exchange and decided to come along.

By the time we got to Mina's, the crowd was spilling out onto the sidewalk. The group of us, chattering, high, made quite an entrance, Larry and I in the lead, his arm through mine, his face raised as if for flashbulbs. I realized that he'd given me an entourage.

Nat had made a difference, indeed. My *Seven Deadly Sins* now had a big wall to themselves, well lit, in the front room of the gallery. Larry and his friends crowded around them. People knew he was someone; by extension, it seemed, I might be someone too. I found myself talking to one and then another young journalist. I tried to work my way over to Nat, but kept getting stuck. While I answered questions, Larry worked the room, and I could hear his introduction—"Tremendously talented young American, highly original style, you'll be hearing about her"—as he moved through the crowd.

I was just beginning to relax, to believe that the show might be a success, when he slipped up to me on those noiseless feet and said, "Good job. We've got a few more spots to hit. Shall we go?"

"I have to come back here later," I said. "All the artists are supposed to go out for curry."

"My dear," he said, "why waste your time? You have got all the good you can get out of this."

"But I said I would go."

"This is your opening night, Louise. In London. There are hundreds of people you might meet, who might go home tonight having heard your name. The Clarks are already interested in buying the whole series."

"What?"

"You see? Now, listen to me. The next time you show your work in London, you want it to be at a bigger, better place than Mina's, am I right?"

"Yes, but—"

"Then let's go."

Of those five days in London, what I remember best is the feel of Larry's hand, on my shoulder or the small of my back, as he guided me into one event after another. Opening night, he got us into a private party at the Tate Modern. I chatted with Andy Goldsworthy and Sean Scully while Larry made approving noises at my elbow and judiciously gave out the new business cards I'd had made up. Dana would have loved it all, especially the way he'd whisked them out of my grasp earlier.

"It's ever so much easier to sell someone else, my dear. And besides, I was born for this. You run along, have a good time. Please, do not talk money. I'll do the rest."

He took my career and the job of promoting me with flattering seriousness. The Clarks, he said, were going back to Mina's to take another look at the series; he was almost positive they'd buy all *Seven Deadly Sins*. A friend of his at BBC-4 interviewed me for a radio program on Atlantic Exchange; another spent an evening asking me questions and taking notes for an essay on contemporary women painters.

Once or twice I said something to Larry about how I must be keeping him from his own work, but he shrugged it off. He never said much, specifically, about what his work actually consisted of right then. There was talk of a film deal that might take him to Toronto, and of a play that might be produced in Sydney. Meanwhile, he was "between places" in London—there was something about a down payment on a condominium, construction delays, arguments with a builder—staying with friends somewhere in a flat on the South Bank.

"You do me a favor, my dear," he'd say, "distracting me from the uncertainties of my future."

The list of must-see shows that Natalie had put together was tossed aside in a few moments over lunch.

"But this is so dull, dear, don't you think?" he chuckled. "I mean, 'an installation depicting the cycle of poverty, east and west'? A 'performance piece'—what a term!—that 'explores the artist's history of sexual abuse and eating disorders'? Rather grim, don't you think?"

"Of course, it's grim," I said. "Grim is the point. These people are making political statements."

"As they have every right to do. And we have every right not to attend."

I began to confide in him. He got the Vincent story out of me in one late night over a bottle of single-malt scotch, turning and polishing it into the tale of an impossible but passionate love, with me as the glamorous, slightly world-weary heroine. This led to other revelations. In every case, he took a story from my life and made it smoother, richer, better. Seen in the mirror he held up to me, I found I liked myself more and more.

He could be testy, too. Natalie's name made him grumble—he referred to her as my "Sapphic friend"—as did references to certain playwrights, particularly Harold Pinter and Tom Stoppard. He seemed to carry innumerable small grudges, against theater directors and actors and critics, against certain drama schools and against academia in general.

And it was hard to get any actual information out of him about my mother. I tried, over and over, to ask him about the manuscripts, about the nun's story, about Felicity Amble-Pierce, but he always managed to deflect my queries. His voice would tremble and he'd say something about my mother—her beauty, her enthusiasm, her innocence. Then he'd shade his eyes with his hands, as if to save me the sight of his tears, shake his head, and change the subject.

✳

HE'D BOOKED A SPECIAL PLACE for dinner for my last night in London—hoping, he said, to be able to celebrate the sale of my *Seven Deadly Sins* to the Clarks. I had managed to schedule a lunch with Natalie, mercifully without Sahara, as well.

As I repacked for Oxford that morning, I came across my mother's old Chanel purse, the one Jason had brought me in the middle of that awful night. I'd brought it with me because it was so beautiful, with its ornate braided gold and leather straps, its quilted surface. And she had taken good care of it, as she did of all her purses, storing them in separate cloth bags, stuffing them with tissue when not in use. She had been meticulous about such small things, and so reckless, so reckless about the big ones.

The inside of the bag was spotless, the black silk lining cool to the touch. Just a hint of Shalimar lingered, the after-image of a scent. Oh, Mom. There were a number of inner pockets, and a zippered compartment. I unzipped it, slid my fingers inside it, felt more silk, then something else, a string, a ribbon. I pulled it out into the light.

It was a printed silk bag, tied off with red ribbon, and stuffed with something soft—a handmade sachet, I thought, the kind she used to moisten with perfume and keep in her clothing drawers. It, too, was almost scentless. I was about to throw it away when something stopped me—call it sentimentality or intuition. Turning it over in my hands, I decided to keep the little bag.

NAT WAS NERVOUS WHEN WE met up—I could tell from the way she twisted her pendant, a little goddess statue, between her fingers as we ordered. Though we agreed on a half carafe of house white, she poured herself little more than a taste. We made small talk, like strangers.

Finally, watching her push her salad around on her plate, I could take it no more.

"Nat, what's on your mind?"

"I've got something to tell you, Louise. It feels funny to even talk about it. I mean, it's a very new decision. But I feel quite strongly that it's the right one."

"Well, come on. Don't keep me guessing."

"I've been offered, and I've accepted, a six-month fellowship in Taos. The Mabel Dodge Luhan House. You remember it."

"Nat, that's fantastic! You deserve it, you'll love it, it's perfect!"

I sloshed some more wine into her glass, tapped mine to it.

"Here's to you, girl!"

We drank.

"So, are you renting a condo? And I guess you'll need to pick somebody to run the Place. While you take your leave of absence, I mean. A word of advice, girl—do not make it Angela. That's a weak link, there."

Nat's silence grew.

"What else do you want to tell me, Nat?"

"I'm not taking a leave of absence, Louie. Because I'm not coming back."

"What?"

"I'm not planning on coming back. I'm moving to Taos."

She looked me steadily in the eye for the first time since we'd sat down.

"There's a great arts community out there, a lot of women artists in particular, doing exciting things. But then, you know that. We used to talk about it."

We did. We had made a pilgrimage to New Mexico as undergraduates. We both loved Georgia O'Keefe, and the Native pottery, especially the Maria Martinez work, black on black that was so subtle and hard to imitate. We'd sat on the ground beside Frieda Lawrence's grave and talked about getting a place somewhere near Taos or Santa Fe together. I laid flowers on D.H.'s shrine.

"Yes, we did. But, but I..."

"What, Lou?"

"Well, I can't believe you'd...you'd really leave the Place."

"Why not? You did."

She looked at me.

"You're not the only one, you know, Louise, who can walk away from something. If what you're walking toward looks good enough."

"I see. So I take it you've found a place to live?"

"The fellowship gives me a room and a studio in the old ranch house. It'll give me time to look around, get to know the town. And Sahara might—well, she might want to go in with me. Own a little house, maybe. We'll see."

"So you two are a couple. Why didn't you just tell me?"

"I didn't have a chance. I thought we'd talk that night, at the opening, and then you disappeared. And it's all happened so fast, how it came together. You know me, Louie, I'm careful. I take my time. But this, this just fell into place. All at once."

She looked at me.

"I'm not pulling a Pollyanna on you here, Louie. And I know you and Sahara aren't exactly each other's type. But please don't say that it's impossible for me to love you both, in different ways, at the same time? And for you both to get along?"

I took a long sip of my wine. What could I do but laugh?

"You always know best, girl. And I am happy for you. Before you take off, I'll treat you both to dinner somewhere spectacular. Back in D.C., OK? I'll find— I'll find the best hypoallergenic vegan food in town. I promise."

"You don't have to do that, Louie. Just—just be nice to her, OK? She's scared of you. She thinks—she thinks you've been avoiding me because of her."

"I have not been avoiding you, Nat. I just got swept up in—other stuff."

"The writer, you mean."

"Yes, Larry. I was hoping—I was hoping he'd be able to tell me things. About my mother, I mean. But he's been, well, cranky about her. He knows I'm going to Oxford next, and I'm guessing she must have some friends still alive there who I could meet. But he's been critical of the whole idea."

"I'll bet he has."

Nat's voice was cool.

"What do you mean?"

"He just wants to keep you here in London with him."

"Well, he's being fatherly, really. He wants me to meet people, make contacts, that kind of thing. He might be able to sell the whole *Seven Deadly Sins* to one collector."

"Well, that would be wonderful. But fatherly? You've got to be kidding, Lou."

"The man has never hit on me, Nat. Not once."

"Not yet."

"Oh, come on. That would be too creepy. After Mom, I mean."

"He is kind of creepy, I think, Lou. I mean, I saw how he was with you, opening night. Like you belonged to him, or something."

"Nat, that's crazy."

"And Mina knows him. She says he's a real bastard with women."

"I've never even seen him with a date."

"And she says he doesn't even really write anymore. That he's still coasting on some big hit he had twenty years ago."

"*The Fallacy of Pleasure*. But he's written, like, another ten plays since then. He's hardly a failure, Nat."

"Yes, but Mina says that he's really bad news."

"So what's Mina, the fucking Delphic oracle?"

I realized I had raised my voice.

"You're the one who had to rescue her," I went on more quietly, "opening night of the show. And has she sold anything yet?"

"She's working on it. The show isn't exactly about selling. Though I am happy for you, Louie. I think it's awesome that you'll be able to keep the series together."

"Maybe. I may be able to keep the series together. And that was Larry, all Larry."

"It was you, Louie. You made them."

Natalie really is the nicest person I've ever known. I felt like a bitch, snapping at her.

"Thank you, girl," I said. "And look, Nat, I know what you mean. The guy's not exactly squeaky clean. But who is? He has never been anything less than a perfect gentleman with me. And I want…there are things I want to know. About my mom. And he can tell me. There might be things that only he can tell me."

Nat reached across the table and took my hand.

"Oh, Louie, I know. I know how important that is. And I'm sorry. I probably shouldn't have said anything. It's just…just be careful, that's all."

"I am. I will."

I lifted up my glass.

"Here's to you, girl," I said. "To you and Sahara. I think Taos is just a perfect fit. I'm happy for you, I really, really am. And I'll be nicer to Sahara. I promise."

LATER, I WOULD WONDER IF it was London that made life flow like this, in huge ups and downs. All I know was that it seemed like some kind of carousel ride was spinning me faster and faster. And I was still struggling to regain my balance from the swerve of Natalie's news when a new blow came.

Back at the hotel, I spent a little time in the business center checking my email. Still no word from Dylan. I checked the *Post*, but if they had sent a stringer to cover Atlantic Exchange, the story hadn't run yet. Then, knowing it was a stupid, high school girl thing to do, I tossed Vincent Volpe's name into a search engine. There was nothing new—a couple of write-ups on Einstein's Pillow, a couple more on his old band, Tea for Five, and some Berklee School of Music alumni pages. Silly girl, I thought, and was ready to close it all down when I saw mention of Constantine Volpe, Vincent's father. I clicked on it, and it linked me to a story in the *Post* Metro section. The headline read, "Local Doctor to Be Charged with Insider Trading." There was a picture of him and Sherry at an opera gala. I skimmed the story, then went back again.

Wealthy plastic surgeon...with a taste for the good life. May have gone too far...federal court will charge that Volpe, on the board of Plexico, the drug company whose patent on...shared this information with others who stood to benefit, including his fourth wife, Sherry Ives Volpe...and his long-time friend, gallery owner Dana Reilly. All will most likely face charges.

My heart was thumping. Dana, in federal court? She seemed too smart, too savvy for such a screw-up. I kept reading.

None of the alleged conspirators would return calls...Reilly Gallery was closed last week for what was said to be a water main break...Volpe to issue statement in the next few days.

I went to the Reilly Gallery website. Indeed, there was a chipper little notice from Daniel about being closed for repairs. But I saw that Daniel's gallery blog, which he updated daily, had not been added to in more than a week. And when I clicked on "Now Showing," I got an error message. Not good. Not good at all.

Back in my room, I placed a call to Reilly Gallery. It was after business hours at home, but I thought I'd leave a message for Daniel. However, there was no cheery voice encouraging you to leave a message, or visit during gallery hours, or go to the website. Instead the phone rang and rang, as I sat holding it, not quite believing that what I'd seen as my future, or one very important part of it, anyway, had suddenly disappeared.

12

I was putting on makeup for my last London dinner with Larry when the phone rang. On the other end, someone was holding the phone up to a stereo speaker. I heard thumping guitar, then Joe Strummer's voice, mingled with my brother's, singing "London Calling."

"Hello, Dyl."

"You like that, huh? The Clash. God-*damn*. Brings back memories. How is my baby sister? And how is London?"

What could I say? Dylan was the one person who might actually be able to explain to me just what it was Dana had gotten herself into. But he was clearly not in the mood to talk about things like that.

"All good, Dyl," I said. "All good."

"And the show?"

"Seems like a success. They say there's a big review coming out in the *Guardian* tomorrow."

"I'll check online. Sell anything?"

"There's a couple who might want to buy the whole series. Friends of Larry's."

"Congratulations, girl! That's awesome. And who's this Larry? The latest conquest?"

"Mom's old boyfriend, Dyl. Remember? I emailed you about him. About his statue."

"Oh, right. Yeah, I'm sorry, girl, I've been up to my ears in shit, lately. And fucking Kenny has been at, like, the *bottom* of my list. Ah, shit. Remember this one, Louie?"

In the background, I could hear Prince's "Little Red Corvette."

"That's what I need, baby. A little red Corvette. God-damn. Remember when I took you to see him, Louie?"

"For my high school graduation. It was awesome."

"My boy is a freak, no question, but a genius. A musical fucking genius. *But it was Saturday night, I guess that makes it all right/And you say, What have I got to lose?*"

He stopped singing and let out a whoop.

"Speaking of, what is my little sister doing on Saturday night in London-town?"

"Oh, just dinner with Larry. I've got to get up early and—"

"Larry? What's that old sleazebag sniffing around for? He wants more than some statue, I guarantee. You be careful, Louie."

"Dyl, he likes my work. He wants to help me sell it here, to get another, better show in London. What's wrong with that?"

"Louie, I love you, but I don't get it. How can you be so naïve?"

"Dylan, this may come as a shock to you, but your little sister can tell when a guy is hot for her. Trust me. Call it a skill that I've developed."

"Well, excuse me—"

"And Lawrence Ware does not want to sleep with me. At the most—"

"Here it comes—"

"He enjoys being seen with me, OK? A younger woman, an artist—"

"And hot, Louie. You *are* hot. And he *is* a man."

"OK. But that's still harmless, you know? He's a classy man, Dyl. And a very well-respected writer. People know who he is. Besides, there's...some stuff I want to ask him. About Mom. About that book she was maybe writing. Speaking of which, I've got to run, or I'll be late for dinner."

"He better be picking up the tab."

"He is. And tomorrow I'm off to Oxford, and no more Lawrence Ware. But call Kenny, OK? How many ways do I have to ask you? I call, I email..."

"I promise, I'll call him. But you, you've got to promise me something. That you'll check in, OK? I worry about my baby sister wandering around alone over there. You think because some guy has a fancy accent and has writ- ten a couple of plays, he's like, above it all. Doesn't think with his dick, or something."

"Like I said, it doesn't matter, anyway. I'm *leaving* tomorrow. Now let me go put my makeup on, OK? And don't worry. I'll call you from Oxford. And call Kenny."

"I will."

"Tonight. It's still early enough. Promise me."

"Geez, I promise. Love you, too, girl."

"Love you."

WHEN I ARRIVED AT THE restaurant, Larry was at a little table in the bar, an empty glass in front of him.

"What are you drinking, my dear? The usual *vin rouge*?"

He summoned the waiter, ordered my wine and another drink for himself.

"Now, my dear, do an old man a favor. I have had a trying day, very trying—"

So have I, I wanted to say.

"—and I need some good news. Have you found my little statue?"

"My brother hasn't been able to reach Kenny yet. There's the time difference, you know. But if I hear from him in Oxford, I'll let you know right away."

"Speaking of which, my dear—I do believe you will have to change your travel plans. I spoke with Celia—"

"Who?"

"Celia Clark, my dear. You do remember her? And her husband David? Your new patrons?"

"Oh, right. Are they still interested? In the series?"

"Yes, yes. But they're off to Edinburgh for a few days. Something at the university, who knows what. But they do want to have lunch with you. Just as soon as they get back. And they're going to bring their checkbook."

"Larry, that's wonderful! Thanks so much. When do you think they'll be back in town?"

"I'm not sure. Perhaps the middle of next week. But it is worth waiting for, obviously."

"I don't know. That hotel I'm in isn't cheap—"

"Nothing is—"

"And Oxford is so close. Why don't you just call me there when they're ready? I gave you the name of the hotel, right? And I can just hop on the train—"

"The train to bloody Oxford. When you could be in London, meeting people, seeing things…"

He drained his glass.

"Christ. Where's that waiter?"

He was loud. People turned to look at us.

"He's on his way," I said. "Anyway, Larry, listen. I've only got ten more days before my flight home and there's a lot more I need to see. I want to go to Oxford, and to Cornwall, too, if I can. I want to see...see where Mom lived. What streets she walked down. Where she shopped."

The waiter was setting down our drinks.

"Retracing your mother's footsteps? Ah, Louise. I would have thought you'd be more original than that."

I took a deep breath. I did not want to lose my temper, not when he held the possibility of selling *The Seven Deadly Sins* in his hands, and not when there was so much I still wanted to ask him about my mother.

"About Mom," I went on. "I remember her saying that she loved Oxford. The old buildings, the gardens..."

"Oh, nonsense. Putting a good face on it, that's all. We met in London, we came here as often as we could. The Oxford interlude was...temporary. A family home we had the use of for a time. But your mother adored it here. Why, I remember when I took her to her first West End play..."

His eyes misted over, as they had before. But I was not to be deterred this time.

"Larry, I need to ask you something. Did my mother ever talk to you about...about a book she was writing?"

He looked up from his drink and at me, cold light in his pale eyes.

"Who might have told you that?"

"A monk who knew her."

"A monk."

"It's complicated. He worked with a priest my mother went to, when she became a Catholic again—"

"Convenient, that. Like Augustine. 'Lord, make me free of sin, but not yet.' As if god, if he actually did exist, would be so easy to fool."

"Larry, listen."

"I am listening, my dear. Indeed, I am all ears."

"Evidently, Mom was working on some kind of book— some kind of scholarly book—when she died."

"Scholarly? Your mother? You must be joking."

It was almost what I had said to Brother Paul at our first meeting. But it made me angry to hear it now.

"Your mother was a charming woman in many ways. But surely even her daughter will admit that when it came to intellect, she was, shall we say, somewhat limited?"

"Her opportunities were limited."

"Ah yes. The Dragon's line, again."

"The Dragon?"

"Your mother's duenna, protector, whatever you might call her. The famous Aunt Angela. It must be wonderful—it must have been wonderful for your mother—to have someone in your life who is utterly convinced of your undiscovered gifts, your hidden talents. Who thinks that if only you had just the right setting or knew just the right people or read just the right books, you'd produce something, manifest some kind of genius. It must be fantastic—"

"I don't know what you're talking about."

"Waiter! Another round, please. Before we perish of thirst here."

Above the quiet chattering of the bar, his voice rang out. Faces turned toward us.

"Larry, keep your voice down. The guy is busy."

"That is the problem with you Americans, isn't it? Excuses for everything. That man isn't busy, Louise, he's slow and stupid. Your mother wasn't a latent genius, despite what your aunt may have thought. Margaret was, when I met her, a very pretty middle-aged woman, possessed of a finer than average body and an overactive imagination. With, perhaps, delusions of grandeur, fed by the great Aunt Angela, who had plenty of delusions herself."

"Delusions of grandeur? My mother?"

"Of course, this cannot be news to you."

"But if anything—if anything it was the other way round. She didn't have *enough* confidence—that's why she let Angie push her around."

"Excuses, again. Ah, yes, our drinks. At the rate we're going, waiter, we'll order another round now."

"Larry, I don't—"

"And bring us some nuts, or crisps, or whatever is in those little bowls that seem to be on every table save our own."

He turned back to me.

"Let us change the subject, my dear. As I said, I have had a trying day. Very trying, indeed."

"Do you want to talk about it?"

"Ah, you are kind. But you—you are too young to know what it is like. The constant struggle to be understood. The endless battles against stupidity, against the facile, the crass, the obvious."

"Of course I know. We're both—"

"The sheer absurdity of being judged by one's inferiors. Of being told, after a career built brick by brick, word by word, that one is old school, out of touch, adrift. Ha!

And meanwhile the bright new boys, the shiny children of tomorrow, bray their way into the public consciousness. If it can be called consciousness at all. When the corpse is rotting. A putrid, rotting corpse."

"Larry, what happened?"

"'Like flies to wanton boys are we to the gods.' Oh yes. Oh, yes. But now the boys have taken over. And the gods are dead."

"Larry?"

He drained his glass.

"The film is off."

"The Canada film."

"Yes. The director has decided it's not the film he wants to make after all. He's off to Madrid now. To work on something else. A script based on a cartoon."

"But the producers—"

"Are no longer interested in producing. Without him. A boy-man who'd rather blow things up and swing his actors from strings than tell a story. A serious story."

"Can't you look for someone else? Or call your—"

"Do us both a favor, my dear, and do not try to be helpful. It was a favorite strategy of your mother's, as well, and it was most emphatically unhelpful."

"Well, I'm sure she only wanted to do her best to—"

"How would you know, my dear? You and your mother were scarcely close. And it was your choice, wasn't it? Not to know her?"

"What do you mean?"

"She told me. How angry you were. How you were the only one of her three children who would not accept her new life."

"She told you this?"

"Some of it. Some of it I simply observed. Your brother and sister were always writing, calling. Never even a postcard from you. And that one visit you made with your siblings—well, I hardly like to mention it, but—"

"You took us all out to dinner," I said, "and it was *fine.*"

"It was. And then the next day your mother came sobbing to me about some awful lunch you'd had and how you'd sworn you'd never forgive her, never speak to her again—"

I suddenly saw it. The pub I'd insisted we meet at, knowing it wasn't her sort of place. Still, we'd been all right together, if a little awkward, until she asked about Dad. I don't remember everything I said, but I know I was horrible to her.

"It wasn't—it wasn't quite like that," I began. "I mean, I was upset, yes—"

"Let me come to the point."

"Which is?"

"That not so long ago, Louise Terry hated her mother, had washed her hands of her, in fact. Which makes me wonder why you're so concerned about her now. Now that she's gone."

I tried to swallow my anger. I had things I needed to know, and though I wanted to walk out the door, leave him stewing, I couldn't. Not without another try.

"Because she left me something," I said. "A piece of a story. She left it to me, not Katherine or Dylan. To me. She must have had her reasons for that."

He shrugged.

"And I think you could help me figure it out. Larry, when Mom was here—did she ever talk to you about a saint she was interested in? A nun, a mystic—I think she was from near here. The twelfth century, it would have been. Did she ever talk to you about a Saint Margaret?"

At the sound of the name, he drew back.

"Oh, no. Not you too, Louise. Not you too."

He wagged his head theatrically back and forth.

"I would have thought it was too early, but then, who knows?"

"Too early for what?"

"I would have thought you far too young to have your mother's, well, what we might call a kind of female malady. A certain menopausal hysteria."

"Now, wait a minute—"

"What else would you call it? When a perfectly ordinary woman, faced with the end of her reproductive powers, suddenly decides that she is being visited by divine messengers? That God or Old Dorothy—now *there's* a combination!—are speaking directly to her?"

"Dorothy? What are you talking about?"

"A wholly imaginary character who was nonetheless worshipped by a rather dubious pair of charlatans your mother misguidedly befriended in Oxford."

"A pair? Who were they? Do you still know them?"

"Why would I? It was bad enough they encouraged your mother in her delusions. Why, do you know that for a time she actually thought herself a seer—"

"A seer?"

"A prophetess. She believed she could see the future—and the past. Oh, you have no idea what I had to put up with."

"And this had something to do with Saint Margaret?"

"Oh, my dear, don't be ridiculous. There *was* no Saint Margaret. She made her up!"

"So Mom was…writing fiction?"

"My god. If you had ever read her letters you would know that she could not have been said to have mastered the English language."

But I thought you loved her, I wanted to say.

"OK, let's back up," I said instead. "You said she was having visions. And that priest she knew—he said she had a gift for the religious life."

"Your mother had a gift for one thing, my dear."

He took a long sip from his drink, tossed it back, scowled, and turned a cold, malicious smile on me.

"She was very, very good at pleasing men. And at getting what she wanted from them in return."

It took everything I had not to throw the rest of my *vin rouge* in his face.

"You know, Larry, I think we'd better call it a night."

I drained my drink, tossed some pounds on the table, stood and reached for my jacket.

"I realize that you're pissed off about your film deal, but that doesn't give you the right to insult my mother."

Larry began to sniff, then to giggle—a nasty sound.

"Ah, Louise, you are so funny. You fancy yourself a rebel, with your tight blouses and big hair, and your faux medieval, slightly sexy paintings that never quite get off the ground—"

"You've seen one work."

"No, I've seen seven. All your deadly sins, indeed. Oh, my dear. You have no idea. Why, you're green! You're a green girl."

"Oh, bullshit. You don't know me—"

"That's where you're wrong. You and your mother do have something in common after all. Beneath the sexy clothes and rather ordinary promiscuity there's a good little Catholic girl—can't you see her? In her white veil

and her shiny shoes?—on her knees in some grim mod-
ernist church, longing to hear the word of God, or should
I say, the Goddess, straight from the source. But there is
no source. There is only—"

I walked away before I could hear any more.

Outside, I felt shaky in my knees and in my fingers.
I should have slapped him, I thought, hands bundled
into fists inside my pockets, as I made my way, eyes
on the ground, through the churning sidewalk crowds.
I should have made him tell me who her friends were.
I should have asked him about Felicity Amble-Pierce. I
should have told him that he was all wrong about my
work, that he didn't get it, he was too unreconstructed,
too sexist, too blind. One talent, indeed. Oh, Mom.

He had been angry when I got there, then more angry
when I asked about Saint Margaret. And he lied. That's
why he couldn't look at me. Maybe they worked on Saint
Margaret's story together? Perhaps that was the work
that Angie said she should have been paid for? Lawrence
Ware was known for his plays and stories about the present day. But he could have written about the twelfth
century, maybe a story published somewhere obscure, or
never put out at all. If only I could find out who those
two "friends" Larry had mentioned might be. I had an
old address of Mom's from her time in Oxford—what
Larry had called a family house. But skulking around
her old neighborhood might not be the best way to find
her friends.

Exhausted, angry, lonely, I slid into bed, setting the
alarm clock for early morning. I was suddenly ready in
every way to get out of London.

✹

MAYBE IT HAS TO DO with how the sun fell that day, which was in fact an accident of timing. My first sight of Oxford was in the high slanted light of late morning, when the spires of the medieval colleges glisten gold and silver. I got off the bus at High Street and Queen's Lane, less than a block from my hotel. I stashed my suitcase at the check-in desk there, then crossed the street to a coffee shop, and snagged, by some miracle, the last tiny window table. I had a cup of tea and an apple tart and felt the tension of the past week fall away from me, dissolved in the warm light, the good food, the waitress's smile. I decided to put my trip to the medieval library off until the following morning. So I went for a walk, and fell in love with Oxford.

I had spent my life in the cocoon of the new. I lived in buildings not much older than I was; I drove down wide asphalt streets designed for wide American cars. My favorite music was modern jazz. Even the restaurants I favored described the cuisine as new—nouvelle French, nouvelle Italian. Only in my work, where I was drawn to representation, expressionism, symbolism, could I be said to look back. Now, in Oxford, there was no need to hunt for the old forms that inspired my new paintings. Except for the occasional anachronism—the Internet café on High Street, the Marks & Spencer department store— it may as well have been three or five or seven hundred years ago. The past was all around me, written on the buildings, present in the cobblestones whose ancient dust clung to my boots as I walked, mirrored in the meander- ing thread of the river. If London had seemed to demand from me a kind of polished vigilance, the projection of a public, successful self, Oxford asked for something else. Call it a sense of history, of one's proper place in the larger stream of time. Call it a humbling, a correction, a bringing down to size. It was all right to relax, to stop striving so hard, to simply be.

The streets themselves encouraged it. There were no straight lines here, no simple paths from A to B, and any given street might change its name twice in as many blocks, going, say, from Market Street to Brasenose Lane, or from St. Aldate's to Cornmarket. Parts of Cornmarket and Broad were closed entirely to cars, and there pedestrians shared the space with bicyclists and buskers. Cafés with open fronts disgorged coffee, ice cream, sandwiches wrapped in white paper. Clusters of young people laughed and argued and held hands; purposeful middle-aged women in sensible shoes pulled two-wheeled shopping carts behind them; balding men in corduroy trousers walked swiftly, important-looking books tucked under their arms. From open pub windows, music floated. There was a carnival feel to it, and a continuity, a sense that life had gone on in this way here for a long, long time.

I got to Debenham's just before it closed, bought some hand lotion, eye shadow, and, on impulse, a bottle of my mother's perfume. "A classic," the saleslady said, spraying a little on my wrist. "You can't go wrong with Shalimar." She was maybe in her fifties, with piled red hair and tired, kindly eyes. I imagined her saying that to my mother, who would have shopped here. She would have walked down these same streets, with Larry, or alone, or with friends I'd never met.

Back at my hotel, I unpacked, laid out my things for the morning's trip to the library. My room was small but very bright, with one whole wall of windows, and overlooked the university's Examination Building, which was built around a grassy courtyard, with wrought-iron gates trimmed with surprising pink metal flowers. Beneath them, two young men huddled, smoking. One of them had shaggy dark hair and long legs; when he turned his head, I saw a slim, pale face and dark brows. His fingers on the cigarette were long, elegant. I remembered the last time that Vincent had made love to me, tense, preoccupied, and already, as I now realized, planning to leave. I remembered the awful last time with T.J. Sex had gone from being a source of joy and release for me to an anxious, potentially hurtful act. Next time, I promised myself, whoever I was with, it would be different.

✖

THE NEXT MORNING, I DRESSED carefully, as if for a job interview. I had had to get a letter of introduction to use the Bodleian Library, and wanted to make a good impression. But the library itself was a struggle. I'd expected rows of computers for looking up books, and to be able to browse the stacks at my leisure. Instead, I found that many of the library's holdings were still listed on index cards taped into tall, thick leather-bound books, heavy to lift and slow to read. The stacks, wherever they were, were off limits to the public; you had to write out your book requests on slips of paper, then wait for them to be brought. The reading room they were kept in was enormous, gorgeous, intimidating, with ceilings three stories high, built again of that faintly warm-colored stone—an amber-gray so old it could not help but remind you of the generations of scholars who had come here to study, to pursue with great gravity the life of the mind. I felt intimidated, overwhelmed by history, and wholly inadequate to my task.

The librarian I consulted seemed to agree with that assessment. After some wait for books to be brought to me, some paging and scribbling and confusion, and some more requests, it seemed that there was "no such saint," the librarian informed me, "historically tied to Oxford."

She was a large woman whose flared nostrils and labored sighs clearly communicated her scholarly disdain. Yes, Margaret and its variations was a common enough name among religious women—there was a French legend that featured a Saint Marguerite, and a legend of a woman from Evesham named Margery who had the power to heal sickness in animals and people. But as for the woman in my mother's box, nothing.

No Dove Abbey. No abbess named Elizabeth. No Margaret.

"In what is now Oxford, there was, at that time, St. Frideswide's Priory, Osney Abbey, and Godstow Priory," she read off for me.

"If you're looking in the twelfth century, my dear, I'm afraid your Dove Abbey simply doesn't exist."

Then she turned to a young man clutching a stash of search requests, a Greek textbook tucked under his arm.

I felt my face go hot with embarrassment. Back at the big leather books, I turned a few pages listlessly, not even sure what I was looking for. I was discouraged beyond belief. But how could I give up so soon?

Glancing back to the information desk, I saw that the terrifying librarian had disappeared on some mission, replaced by a short, slight, older man whose thick glasses magnified his eyes. He looked gentler, somehow. I decided to start over, from a different angle. I told him I was looking for a book on the Middle Ages by an author named Felicity Amble-Pierce.

"Are you sure that's the name, madam?" he said.

"Well, it's the name I have," I said. "Here, I'll show you."

I pulled the manuscript out of my bag and showed it to him.

"'The Life of Saint Margaret, by Felicity Amble-Pierce,'" he read. "If you don't mind, madam—where did this come from?"

"It was my mother's," I said. "It came to me after—after she died."

"I see." He scanned the top page quickly.

"So you are sure this work has been published?"

"No, I'm not," I said. "That's what I'm trying to find out."

"Oh, it's a *story*," he said, still reading. "They say right here, a work of fiction, not history."

"Yes, but keep reading. It says a real and historical person. My mother—my mother thought she was real."

"Did she? Hmm…well, there may be one or two other things to try. Miss Amble-Pierce—you've been able to find nothing by her, you say?"

"Nothing. I looked her up online from home and—no, nothing."

He flipped a page or two ahead, reading quickly.

"I want to find the author. So I can find the end of the story, if there is one. And I have another manuscript, too—about the same woman, I think—but it's, well, different. Very different. And there's no name on it at all."

"Hmm, a mystery." He looked genuinely intrigued. Behind those ugly glasses, his dark eyes sparkled.

"Well, Miss Amble-Pierce may never have published her work in book form. Or Hollow Hills Press might be a private concern. She might have had her work printed up, for a few friends, perhaps."

"In which case, how would we find her?"

"Well, there are various directions we might explore."

Someone coughed. I realized that a small impatient line had formed behind me.

"Here's what I suggest," my new friend said. "I need a little time. Write down for me the names and dates you're interested in—and not just this Margaret, but anyone else connected to her, any name you have. Come back tomorrow, about midday, if you will, and we'll see what I've found."

"Of course. Thank you so much."

I gave the list to my librarian—Bob Middleton was his name—and walked outside. It was a beautiful day, cool and half-cloudy, half-clear, and the light slanting down the stones of the medieval buildings had a weight, an identity of its own. I wanted to catch it in my hands, to sketch it now in a way that would help me to paint it later. But there was something else I wanted to do, or rather, to see, first.

After checking the map, I decided it was doable, on foot. And in a little while I stood in front of a small house in a series of small houses on Hollywell Road, looking at my mother's old home in Oxford.

There was a tiny driveway with a very old Jaguar in it. Dylan would have been able to tell me the year, the model. All I knew was that it needed a good waxing. The house, as with all the ones around it, was set on a tiny plot of land, at least by American standards. There was a very green garden out front, with a stone birdbath and boxwood hedges. So this must be Lawrence Ware's family home, the place he brought my mother after she'd moved out of her

B&B, abandoning Angie's itinerary for her new lover. Had it seemed small to Mom, after our sprawling suburban house? Or was the difference liberating? I could almost hear her saying it would be a lot less bother to clean.

The windows were small and deeply curtained. It was impossible to see inside from where I stood on the little sidewalk. I thought about simply walking up the path and knocking on the front door—*Hello, so sorry to bother you, but my mother used to live here and I just wondered, if you wouldn't mind*—when I heard voices coming from behind the house. A female voice, high and crisp, and then a man's.

The front garden had a wall of poplars on the left, and I ducked quickly around the corner and behind them, inching my way along the grass behind the trees, hoping there was no one home in the house next door. When I was about midway across, I began to make out words. The woman was in midsentence.

"...a bit unfair, don't you think? After all, this is a difficult time—"

"For all of us, yes."

"But you must admit that his particular field is more precarious than most."

"Perhaps. In any case, he chose his particular field. And you must admit, my dear, that Lawrence rather attracts difficulties. I'm sure that would be the case no matter what his work."

"Perhaps. More tea?"

"I'd prefer some more of that Hendricks, if you don't mind."

"Isn't it a bit early?"

"If I have to endure yet another conversation about your poor, misunderstood brother, I shall need it."

"Now, Simon, that's scarcely fair..."

I heard pouring, the clinking of glass and china. So this was Larry's sister. He'd described her as a recalcitrant bitch. The reality seemed more complex.

"You must at least admit that there are fewer and fewer people who can afford to see a play these days?"

"Oh, I don't know. What was that…spectacle that Eleanor took us to some time back? She said it had been sold out for months, though who knows why. I barely understood a thing."

"*Sweeney Todd*, my dear. By Stephen Sondheim."

"Worst night at the theater in my life. I mean, the ridiculous plot—"

"Simon, please. I am trying to talk to you. I am seriously concerned."

"Forgive me, my dear. But you have been seriously concerned, as you say, about your reprobate brother a thousand times. And every time, somehow, he winds up in the pink. It's not him I'm worried about, my love. It's you."

"But I'm fine."

"No, you're not. You've worked yourself into a knot. Now put down that tea—you drink far too much of it, you know—and let me make you a proper drink. And then, well, then let us sit and enjoy the garden. It is lovely right now, Victoria. You are an absolute magician."

"Well, thank you, Si. Perhaps you're right. Let's just sit and look, shall we?"

The sudden warmth in their voices embarrassed me, as if I'd caught them making love. This was the second time in as many months that I'd been sneaking around outside someone else's home. Time to go.

As I slunk along behind the trees toward the sidewalk, my eyes on the damp ground, trying not to make a sound, a woman's voice interrupted me.

"Pardon me. What is it you're doing there?"

"I...I'm, uh..."

"Speak up."

She stood on the sidewalk across the street from the house, her hands on the bars of a sturdy-looking bike. She had short, efficient black hair over a pale smart face with rose-pink lips. She wore an old-fashioned-looking black suit, a cropped jacket above a wide skirt that fell just below her knees.

"Oh, I was just looking for someone," I said, lightly, quietly, as I made my way from grass to sidewalk. "A friend. But I have the wrong address."

"It is customary, in this country, to go to the front door and knock."

Her voice was stern but her eyes sparkled, amused. She reminded me of Mary Poppins, or rather, Julie Andrews as Mary Poppins. How old was she, anyway?

"I understand," I said. "I'll try that next time."

She opened her mouth to say something else, but I waved, quick and half-smiling—like a parody of a movie star avoiding the paparazzi—before walking off briskly in the other direction.

Back at my hotel bar, I fell into a conversation with three young men, all students, who were wearing black tie, having just come from some event at one of the colleges. They flattered and flirted with me, and it felt good to be sure of my attractiveness again, even if just for a few hours. They bought me champagne, and were trying very hard to persuade me to go to a club with them when the bartender gave last call—last orders, he called it—and I extricated myself from their laughing company. The one I liked best—the smartest of the three, though he didn't know it—gave me a farewell kiss that was more than friendly, then held me a little away from him, looking to see if I might ask him upstairs. But it was enough to have him look at me that way, and to know that I could have spent the night with him if I'd wanted to.

The next morning, I woke with a fierce headache, remembered that I'd skipped dinner the night before. And then all those drinks. It was early afternoon when I got to the library, my eyes still puffed from the night's excesses, my stomach raw.

Bob Middleton told me that he'd met with the same dead end on Felicity Amble-Pierce that I had. But he had looked up the other places and names I'd listed for him. There had, he said, been an annual horse fair in medieval Oxford, on Horsemonger's Lane, just as there had been in the anonymous manuscript, when Benedict arrived in town.

"You cross that street on your way here from your hotel," Bob said. "It's Broad now."

It was also possible, he said, that Dove Abbey was a stand-in for one of the abbeys the other librarian had mentioned.

"My guess would be St. Frideswide's, where Christ Church is now. It would fit the location. And that abbess might be based on someone real. There were some very strong women religious in those days. And that monk—"

"Brother Martin."

"Yes. The name of his abbot,Robert? That could well be Robert of Winchester, who was abbot in Glastonbury, from, let's see, 1171 to 1188."

"I don't suppose there would be any information about Martin anywhere. If *he* existed, that is."

"None that would have survived. There was a fire at Glastonbury Abbey in 1184. A great tragedy. So many of the great abbeys burned in the Middle Ages. And with them, so many great libraries."

He paused.

"However, there is something. Do you know *Viator*?"

"Excuse me?"

"*Viator*. A journal of medieval scholarship. I thought you might have consulted it before. It's available online, you see. In any case, I took a brief look at the journal's index, and did find one article that mentions a Saint Margaret. I took the liberty of having it copied for you. Ordinarily you're supposed to pay, of course, but with things so topsy-turvy here—I mean, really, the construction of the new wing has us all betwixt and between— well, I went ahead and did it myself. It's a fairly lengthy article, but I thought it might be helpful. And there are quite a few sources in the notes."

I took the stapled sheets from him, thanked him for his help.

Outside, the clouds were gathering behind the golden dome of the Bodleian. I was just a block or two from my hotel when the rain started. Beneath a sign that said "The Old Bank," a restaurant, glass-walled, beckoned. I took a corner table on the bar side, tossed my bag onto the narrow banquette, ordered a ginger ale for my hangover. Then I pulled out the article my librarian had found for me.

It was slow going. The title, "Uncovering Virginity: As Fact, as Trope, as Composite," did little to direct me through the mire of historical data and theorizing that the coauthors had constructed. Just when I'd think I was getting somewhere, I'd read a sentence such as,

"Twelfth-century hagiography is shot through with gene-alogical systems and traditions, often weightier and more complex in the vernacular than in Latin, but signifying in each case and to varying degrees a kind of inheritance of enclosure, through which interpolated versions may be consumed or subsumed into a single system." Six pages in, I still hadn't gotten to Saint Margaret.

I sighed, gave into temptation, and ordered a glass of wine. I was underlining a sentence that seemed to be important, when a woman's voice said, "Excuse me, is anyone sitting here?"

I saw a hand gesturing to the table next to mine, a pair of legs in tights.

"No, no. Feel free."

I pulled my bag closer to me so that she could slide onto the banquette, and went back to the article. It wasn't until the waiter returned with my merlot that I looked up long enough to see her. Black hair, merry blue eyes, pink lips. Mary Poppins.

"Is that good?" she said, gesturing to my glass.

I took a sip.

"Very good."

"That's what I'll have then." She smiled up at the waiter, and a blush spread over his pale, pretty face. She watched him walk back to the bar, then turned to me.

"Dishy, isn't he? Too bad he's so young."

I looked at her. Despite the resemblance to the young Julie Andrews, she was, I saw, probably in her early forties. I could see the little networks of fine lines around her eyes, and the place beneath her chin where, despite her slimness, the skin had gone a little slack. But she was still head-turningly lovely.

"Oh, I don't know," I said, flipping the pages closed. "The bartender is more my type."

She turned and took a long look at him.

"Ah, he looks Italian," she said. "I had an Italian lover once. He was marvelous."

Her wine arrived.

"Cheers," she said, lifting her glass. We clinked, drank. Then she leaned in over the low table, smiling like a schoolgirl with a secret.

"I just want to say, I'm glad to see you looking so much better. He simply isn't worth it, you know. Despite all that charm."

"Who?"

"Oh, you don't have to be embarrassed in front of me, my dear. I know all about making a fool of oneself for love. And he does have a reputation—though it has been slipping lately, I must say—for breaking hearts."

"I'm sorry, but who—"

"Old Larry, of course! Larry Ware, darling."

Dropping her voice an octave, she did a sharp imitation of him, tremolo and all.

"'It is so good to see you, my dear. You make this old, jaded fraud of a man young again.'"

I had to laugh.

"That's very good. How do you know him, anyway?"

"A friend of mine was entangled with him some years ago. I had a chance to observe his technique. It's surprisingly effective."

"You've got it wrong. I'm not entangled with Lawrence Ware."

"Of course not. You were just creeping around outside last night because, well, you have a particular passion for

English poplars. And wanted to see them up close, as it were."

"Very funny."

"Anyway, no need to try again. I hear he lives in London, now."

"No, really," I said. "It was my mother who is—who was—involved with Larry. She died last year."

"Oh, I am sorry."

"Thank you. I know it must have looked funny, but I—I wanted to see where she lived."

She cocked her head at me.

"So your mum lived here? When was that?"

"Well, she came to England in '96, in the fall. And by January, anyway, she was living in that house."

"I wouldn't have met her, then. I was in London. Oh, by the way, I'm Jessica Payne."

"And I'm Louise Terry."

Over the wine, we got to know each other. Jessica had lived in London with her husband and twins, a boy and a girl, until the previous autumn, when the children went off to college and he asked for a divorce. She came to Oxford, a town she'd always liked, and was staying with her aunt while she looked for a place of her own. "A fresh start," she called it. She was a solicitor—a lawyer—and had a job at a firm in Oxford to start in a week. And though she hadn't wanted her marriage to end, she didn't seem bitter or sad at all. In fact, she was full of enthusiasm, for Oxford, for her new life, and evidently, for men.

In return, I told her a little bit about A Woman's Place, and about the Atlantic Exchange exhibit. I told her how helpful Larry had been to me in London, but left out our fight, as well as Dana Reilly and the crisis at her gallery. And though I said I was in Oxford in part to see where my mother had lived, I left out the box, and the story of Saint Margaret, as well. It was too complicated, and I was frankly tired of thinking about it. When she asked about men, I hesitated.

"Come now," she teased. "As lovely as you are, there must be someone."

"There was," I said. "But he…well, he was…"

I was going to say complicated or tormented or confused.

I said, "To be honest, he was kind of a selfish jerk."

"Oh, there's a bit of that about, isn't there?" She leaned in close, looked at me. "I hope you won't mind, Louise, if I give you a piece of advice. Probably not necessary, but I am a bit older than you are, and so perhaps just a bit wiser, as well. No good can come from studying one's heartbreak. Believe me."

"But what if it's your own fault? Your own bad choices?"

"My dear, we all make bad choices. But you are pretty and smart and talented, and there are many men in the world. Many sorts of men."

"More fish in the sea?"

"Yes. But you won't meet them sitting by yourself in a bar, reading—what is that you're reading?"

"Well, the title of this article is, "Uncovering Virginity: As Fact, as Trope, as Composite.""

Her laughter rose in bubbles.

"Good lord, darling, I hope it's not as bad as all that! Virginity, indeed."

"It's for some research I'm doing. At the Bodleian."

"Of course. Now, let's see. You are here through the weekend, yes? In Oxford?"

"That's my plan."

"Good. Some friends and I are meeting at the King's Arms tomorrow night for drinks, a sort of end of the week thing. Why don't you join us? And Saturday, if you'd like, we could do a bit of shopping. You can't spend all your time in the library, you know."

13

I spent the next day wandering the city, sketching what I found—the dome of the Bodleian, the Bridge of Sighs with its diamond windows, the spires of Christ Church—until rain drove me inside. At home, so much rain would have depressed me, but here it had a contextual beauty—it made the buildings shimmer, sparkled the old-fashioned windowpanes, and most of all, created the extraordinary shades of green that were all around me. I'd never been much for gardens, but the Oxford Botanic Garden, with its sleek glass houses and mazelike paved walks, edged with every green one could name and some more seemingly of their own devising, snagged my imagination. I bought a new sketchbook at Blackwell Books, and promised myself that, when the rain stopped, I'd fill it with views of the garden.

Maybe, I thought, this will lead me somewhere new. Maybe Dana's gallery closing will leave a space for something else to open up.

I was about to set off for the pub when the front desk called. A lady was there to see me. I thought Jessica might have surprised me by coming to lead me to the King's Arms. But the woman waiting for me in the lobby looked nothing like Jessica. A thin, forbidding-looking woman, her hair tied in a knot so tight it seemed to pull her eyes back in her head, she greeted me with, "You are, I suppose, Louise Terry?"

I put my hand out to shake. She kept hers in her pocket.

"And you are?"

"Victoria Greenham. Victoria Ware Greenham. I am here on behalf of my brother. Lawrence Ware."

I remembered her voice from the garden that afternoon when Jessica caught me snooping.

"He would have preferred to come himself, of course, but there has been a bit of an accident. He is immobilized at present. But he would like to see you."

"Isn't he in London?"

"He came to me yesterday, to our home in north Oxford. It's not far."

"But I'm supposed to meet a friend."

"This won't take long. He was quite insistent. He tells me you two are close. The car is outside."

She was implacable, an iceberg.

Outside, the sidewalks were filling with people just off from work, with that tingling weekend energy about them. I was supposed to be setting off for a girl's night out with my new friend. Instead, I felt like a teenager whose plans had been interrupted by an interfering and hostile parent.

As we settled into the old Jaguar, Victoria said, "Ordinarily I would have taken the bus, but he tells me you are not used to such things. So I took this ridiculous car, which he absolutely refuses to sell."

"It is kind of a classic, right?

The car snorted into life.

"Precisely the kind of foolish sentimentality that has got my brother into so much trouble. I am going to be plain with you, Miss Terry. My brother is a great writer, a very great writer. But he lacks judgment, always has." She sniffed, jerked at the gear shift. "In any case, I consider his insistence on your visit to be the capricious act of a frightened and helpless man."

"Helpless? Larry?"

"Your Larry," she said, drawling the name in a nasty imitation of my accent, "was hit by a bus yesterday afternoon in London."

"What? Is he hurt?"

"What do you expect? His right ankle is broken in two places. There are various large bruises on his head and body, and most likely some internal bruising as well. He spent the night under observation in hospital, then we brought him here."

"I'm surprised he wanted to leave London."

"He didn't. But he cannot be on his own. And none of his London friends are the sort who could take on such a responsibility."

"But he will be OK, right?"

"It will take some time."

"By the way," I said. "Just so you know. He's not *my* Larry. I mean, we are not dating, or anything."

"It is no concern of mine. Frankly, I'd rather not know with whom my brother is currently involved."

"Well, he's not involved with me. He was involved, years ago, with my mother."

Another sniff.

"Oh, yes, I know. I do remember her. One of Lawrence's more impulsive decisions."

"He said they fell deeply in love."

Another sniff.

"Look, if you're angry about the statue, all I can say is I'm sorry."

"Pardon?"

"Larry told me that you're anxious to have it back, and I'm trying, I really am. But I keep hitting dead ends."

"Indeed?"

"And look, I know my mom. She was no thief. If she had it, it must have been a gift, or she must have thought it was a gift, from Larry. Otherwise she would never have taken it with her. I'm sure of that."

"Miss Terry, I have absolutely no idea what it is you're talking about. Though my brother has a habit of being absurdly generous, particularly to his female friends."

We rode the rest of the way in silence. As we pulled into the driveway, the front door swung open. A man who was definitely not Lawrence said, "My god, Vicky. I can't believe you actually did it."

"What else was I to do, Simon? Given the circumstances?"

He looked at me.

"You'd best come in, then. Here, let me take your coat. And you must be Miss Terry."

"Yes."

"Would you like a drink, my dear?"

"Simon—"

"If she must be put through this, we can at least offer her a nice G and T."

"G and T?" I asked.

"Gin and tonic."

"Actually, that sounds wonderful. Thank you so much, Mr...."

"Louise? Louise, is that you?"

There was no mistaking the voice that came from behind the closed door on my left. Victoria and her husband looked at each other, a weighted glance I could not interpret.

"You two go ahead," he said. "Best get this over with."

Victoria opened the door. The room was dark, curtains drawn against the night, and the air full of smoke. There were a few candles burning on a low table beside an overflowing ashtray. Propped in a tall armchair next to it, half in the dark, was Larry.

His right ankle was up on a footstool, wrapped in a cast. His left hand was bandaged, his right eye ringed with a purple-black bruise.

"And so we meet again, Louise."

He lifted a glass to me with his right hand. I saw a tremor there I hadn't seen before. It wasn't only the bruises and bandages that had changed him; he looked as if he had aged ten years in the few days since I'd last seen him. His cheeks were sunken, lips narrowed and folded in on themselves. A blue vein pulsed above his brow.

"Larry! What's happened to you?"

"That, my dear, is precisely what I want to discuss with you."

Victoria's husband appeared in the doorway, holding a tray with glasses, gin, and ice.

"I'll just leave this, you can serve yourselves. Victoria, will you come upstairs?"

"Not just yet. Lawrence may need me. And I should at least open a window. He might set himself on fire."

Again they exchanged that load-bearing look. But Larry interrupted it.

"Run along now, Vicky. I will be fine."

The door closed behind them.

"Well, my dear, do tell me—how are you enjoying your time in Oxford? By the way, do help yourself. Simon has good taste in spirits, I will give him that."

His right hand dipped over the winged arm of the chair, and emerged holding a crystal decanter.

"Unless you'd prefer some Macallan, of course. This is not a wine-drinking household, I'm afraid, but then, my visit was somewhat unexpected."

He poured himself a generous amount.

"I think I'll stick with the gin," I said. Mixing a drink gave me time to compose myself. I was still angry at him, yes, but his appearance frightened me. Shrunk in that high-backed chair, he looked like a ruined king giving a last look at his crumbling domain. And just a few days before, he had been so vital, so fierce.

"Come close, if you would, my dear. I would like to look at you."

I looked around for a chair to pull up, but didn't see one. He gestured, a weak wave of his good hand.

"There is an ottoman."

I pulled the little stool up on his left, so as not to dislodge his cast, and settled myself, a bit awkwardly. In the candlelight, his face flickered. His voice was a low croak, with little catches all along the way.

"I cannot tell you how I regret our last encounter. It was horrible of me to speak that way. The disappointments of the past few years have taken their toll, you see. But I should not have punished you for that. Nor disturbed the memory of your bright, beautiful mother, for whom I cared so deeply, so deeply. Can you forgive me, Louise?"

"Larry, I just—I just need to know—about her—"

"I will answer whatever questions you have, Louise. I promise you that. But first, can you, will you forgive this foolish old man?"

His chin shook, his eyes were wet, his breathing labored, loud.

"Yes," I said. "Yes, I can."

"Say it. Say, Larry, I forgive you."

"Larry, I forgive you."

He let out a long sigh.

"Good, good. Thank you, my dear."

"Larry, what happened to you? Your sister said you were hit by a bus?"

"Yes, yes. In Russell Square, in fact, not far from your hotel. There is time to talk of that. But first, Louise...how do you find Oxford?"

"It's incredible. Everywhere I look, there's something beautiful—the buildings, the skyline, the streets. It's like—it's like a setting for a fairy tale. I've been drawing like crazy."

"And how long do you plan to be here?"

"I don't know. I was thinking of going to Cornwall, but now I'd like to stay here for a while. And I've made a new friend."

His eyebrows shot up.

"A gentleman friend?"

"No, no. A woman. I'm supposed to meet up with her tonight, in fact. At a pub."

"Which one?"

"The King's Arms."

"Ah, yes. You'll find a lively crowd there, no doubt. If only…if only I were well, Louise. I'd show you Oxford as…as your mother and I saw it."

"I thought you said you both preferred being in London."

"One has to reject the land of one's boyhood if one is to become an adult."

"But they're just a short train ride apart."

"To my parents, my mother especially, they might have well been two different worlds. When I went off to RADA, she wept as though I were going off to war. She thought the contemporary stage a very seedy occupation, indeed. Anything after Shakespeare was suspect, in her eyes. In any case, I did not bring you here to talk about that."

"What did you bring me here for, then? To forgive you?"

"In part," he said, pouring himself another scotch. "In part. Oh, and do serve yourself, my dear. And while you're up, fetch me that cigarette case, if you would? On the shelf, there? Vicky keeps moving it out of my reach. As if I cannot see what she is about."

I made myself another drink, brought him his case and a pack of matches.

"If you'd light one for me…and help yourself, by all means."

"No, thanks. Here."

I had to kneel to reach him. In the brief flame, his eyes held mine. So blue, so beautiful, still, even with the bruises. He took a long drag on the cigarette, and exhaled, blowing out the flame, his eyes never leaving my face. He leaned in closer.

"You are so like her, I sometimes think she has come back to me. She sent you, surely. But I wonder why." His fingertips grazed my cheek, the hand still holding the burning cigarette. "I think you might know. I think you might know, indeed."

For a wild moment I thought he was going to try to kiss me. Then he sank back in his chair again, and closed his eyes.

"What stays is not of a piece," he said slowly, softly. "It is all bright flashes, single pictures. I can see your mother in that blue and white dress she wore the day we met. I see her walking into that bookshop, me holding the door for her, and turning, turning to see. That wonderful hair. Those lovely legs."

His voice grew quieter and quieter. I had to lean in to hear him.

"I remember thinking, 'Lawrence, Lawrence—what bright, unsuspecting angel is this now? Stop, fool. Stop.' But there was no stopping it."

"So it was...love at first sight?"

He opened his eyes and looked at me.

"You put it so simply, my dear. Love is such a...puny word for it. Plato was right. It is a kind of madness. Though I had...other entanglements...I moved her into this house. Within a fortnight we had established...a life together."

"What was it like? What did you do, in that new life?"

"Well, I was hard at work at the time. My greatest fear was that this new...passion would disrupt my writing. But quite the contrary. Your mother, you see, had the gift of...inspiring a man. When I met her I was struggling, struggling with the project at hand. But with her here...well, the words flowed like water. We'd spend a few days here, working, and then off to London we'd go, for theater, for parties, for sheer fun."

"And Mom was happy?"

"She had a tremendous capacity for...happiness. It astonished me. I was accustomed to a...tougher sort of woman. But your mother...well, a good meal out would send her into ecstasies. A quite adequate production of a play would have her in tears by the interval. She...loved...everything."

"She could be like that. I remember how she was, when she was like that."

Pictures. Flashes. Mom at somebody's backyard cookout, her tanned shoulders, a white sundress with flowers, laughter. She's pouring a drink from a pitcher, Dylan beside her. Mom at Christmas time, looping boughs of greenery around the front hall banister, or handing string after string of lights up to Dad on a ladder outside. Mom on the phone with one of her girlfriends, bubbling with gossip, twirling a curl of hair between her fingers. Mom on the beach, giggling as the cold waves hit her, then plunging in.

"Yes, yes. She had a smile that would put many a professional beauty to shame. You have her smile, you know, Louise. You have her eyes."

So lost in the past I was, I hardly heard him.

"You sit now where she sat. Many an evening we would spend in this very room, with drinks and candlelight. She liked me to read to her, from my day's work."

"How long were you two together, Larry?"

"Three seasons. Autumn, winter, spring. It might have gone on if it were not for some...ridiculous friends she made. They turned her head, turned her in the wrong direction. Oh, it was very sad."

"You said—you said she thought she was a seer. She was having visions. Is that what those friends—"

"They encouraged her delusions. They were fools. And she, she listened to them, when she should have known better, when anyone could have told her—"

"Who were those friends, Larry? Where are they now?"

"How should I know?" His voice was rising, the color back in his cheeks.

"They were truly ridiculous people, the pair of them. A couple, you see. Skilled in chicanery, passing themselves off as mystics. Oh, they made a fool of her. Of us."

His good hand rummaged around on the little table between the candles. He picked something up, rolled it between his fingers, put it down.

"What were their names, Larry? These people?"

"What does it matter? They were liars, dilettantes, meddling in something they did not understand."

"But I'm here to find her, to find out what I can. And I need your help, I—"

"If you'll excuse me, my dear, I have to visit the loo. What goes in must come out. If you'll hand me those crutches. And I'll need your help of course, in getting to my feet."

I stood. He put his good hand out, and I took hold of it, pulled him up.

We were face to face, his breath on my skin, his mouth so close to mine.

"I called for you and you came, Louise. Right away. Without protest. You dress in your mother's favorite color, you wear her perfume. I think you know the spell, don't you? I think you know so much more, so much more, than you have told me."

He ran one hand down the side of my face, lifted a lock of my hair.

"We consecrated it with sex, you know. Your mother and I. Our spell. So tell me, how do we break it, Louise?"

"Larry, what are you talking about? What spell?"

"Your mother, your mother and I, and the spell we cast. And now everyone who was there is dead, save for the Priestess, the High Priestess, who hates my guts, who will never free me, never. And me. I am still alive."

He shivered, and gripped the back of my neck in his big hand.

"And now you are here, blood of her blood. Young, still. Though not for long. Perhaps you are here to free me, Louise? Is this how it works?"

He put his mouth on mine, dry lips pressing mine apart. The room spun. I pulled back fast, and he lost his balance, crashing to the floor. As if she'd been listening, the door flew open, and there was Victoria.

"My god. What is going on in here?"

"I tried to help him up and I—I slipped, he slipped—"

She had him on his feet, crutches under his arms, in no time. As she steered him toward the door, she said, "Clearly time for you to go, Miss Terry. My husband will ring you a taxi."

Over his shoulder, Larry said, "And we were just getting started! Do think about what I said, my dear. I believe you will find it to be true."

Alone in the little room, I reached for my purse, hands shaking, blood pounding in my ears. In the smoky dark, I saw what Larry had been fumbling with on the little table. It was sachet, like the one I'd found in my mother's purse, a little bundle of blue silk.

I picked it up, shoved it deep into my bag. And then I got the hell out of there.

Back outside, the rain had started up again. I pulled my coat up over my head and walked toward the lights of Banbury Road. There was a little Italian restaurant on the corner, and the maitre d' was a gray-haired man with courtly manners who brought me a towel for my hair and poured me a sambuca to sip while I waited for the cab he'd summoned. One taste and I remembered Jessica. Shit.

I looked at my watch. It was after nine o'clock. I doubted she and her friends would still be at the pub. In the cab back to the hotel, watching the rain streak the windows with light, I shivered, remembering the evening. I did not want Larry. I had never wanted Larry, not in that way. He was handsome, of course, and he was very charming, but that was not what I had wanted. I liked the way I felt when I was with him, worldly, interesting, even mysterious; I liked, more than liked, the fact that he wanted to sell my work. I had hoped he might open a door for me, one that would lead me to a greater understanding of who my mother was, why she had come here, loved it here, decided to stay, and what all this material about her and Saint Margaret really meant.

But I had never flirted with him. I had never led him on. And yet. And yet. A spell, he said. A spell cast by sex.

I lay down on the bed, still in my clothes, and I must have slept for several hours, though it felt like only moments before the phone rang. Morning light was slipping through the curtains. It was Jessica, concerned about my non-appearance at the pub. Her voice called me back to this world with a start. I found myself agreeing to a shopping adventure. Less than an hour later, she was in the hotel lobby waiting for me, bright-eyed and crisp as she had been before.

I doubted that she could distract me from my brooding, but she did. It was impossible to be unhappy for long around Jessica—she was lighthearted without being silly, pragmatic without being boring. And she had wonderful taste, taking me to little shops where I found things I'd never be able to get at home. At a boutique in Jericho, I bought a turquoise lace and silk dress that looked like it belonged at a garden party; in the covered market, I found a shawl to go with it, crocheted of cobweb-fine silver and white yarns; at a shop on Broad Street, I found necklaces for Nat and Lynda. The sun was bright, the air was cool, it was a beautiful day in a very beautiful town. Jessica settled on just one thing, a red and white patterned dress, very low cut, that showed off what turned out to be a lot of bosom.

"A date dress," she laughed. "Definitely not a work dress."

We decided to drop our bags at my hotel and find a spot for dinner. Back in my room there was a huge, almost funereal-looking bouquet on the little table. The card was from Larry, who was, again, all apologies.

"Well, it seems you have an admirer," Jessica said.

"Want some flowers?"

"Not really. It is a bit…extravagant, that arrangement."

"You could say that. Or inflated, like the ego of the man who sent it. You know him. Lawrence Ware."

"Oh, I see. Your mother's old beau."

"Such a gentle word for such an asshole."

"So he's done something dreadful."

"You could say that."

"Would you like to talk about it?"

"I—I think so, yes. If you're up for hearing it."

"Over dinner, then."

As we walked to Jessica's restaurant of choice, she looped her arm through mine. I started my story that way, arm in arm with her, as we wove our way down High Street to Beaumont to Woodstock. At a lovely old restaurant, the Parsonage, I continued it over our dinner. In the bar, after, I finished it. I told her everything. About my mother and the box she'd left me, and what I'd found inside, and about Lawrence Ware and his statue. I even told her about the visions I'd had at home, and what Larry had said and done the night before. Jessica listened to every word.

"My goodness," she said. "You certainly have been through quite a lot."

"You probably think I'm nuts," I said. "Creeping around his place. Seeing things."

"Oh, no. I'm sure that when my mother passes, she will continue to visit me in whatever way she can. As I will visit my children, however I can. It makes complete sense."

"I hadn't thought of it that way."

"And Oxford...well, you've certainly come to the right place. For metaphysical experiences, that is. Home of J.R.R. Tolkien, among many others, who see the enchanted side of things."

"I can see why," I said. "It looks enchanted here. The old buildings. The stones. The way the little river runs through it, like a story-book town."

She drained the last of her wine, poured more for both of us.

"So, what do you intend to do, Louise? With this mystery on your hands?"

"Well, I'm stuck. I need to find this couple Larry keeps talking about. The ones who taught Mom about witchcraft. The ones who believed in the visions she was having."

"And he won't tell you anything."

"No. He gets furious if I even ask."

"But at the same time, he wants something from you. He wants—"

"Me to fuck him."

"Surely, Louise, that could not have been a surprise."

"He was my mother's boyfriend!"

"Yes, and still a man. One with a reputation you surely must have heard of."

"Well, sure, but—"

"Darling, I am not criticizing. It's just that you might have seen it coming. In any case, he also wants that statue. So we need to figure out a way to trade what he wants for what you want. To create a mutually beneficial relationship."

"I have no idea how to do that."

"I might."

Jessica's smile was clever, mischievous.

"I've got an idea, Louise, about how we might be able to get Lawrence Ware to tell you what you need to know."

"Christ. The last thing I want is to be alone with that creep again."

"But you won't be alone. My idea is that you respond to those flowers by asking him to meet you someplace wonderful. Not too loud, not too modern. Let's say, the bar at the Randolph Hotel. Early evening. Say, six thirty."

She flashed the smile again.

"All right," I said. "And then what?

"I'll tell you. But first, I want you to tell *me* one more time everything you've heard about this matter of the statue—who saw it, when, and so on. And don't leave anything out."

THE DOORMAN AT THE RANDOLPH smiled me inside and led me to the small Morse Bar, named after a TV mystery series I'd never heard of. Larry was already there, at a table by the fireplace, in animated conversation with the waiter, who knew all of Larry's plays. The waiter's presence eased what would have been an awkward reunion. As it was, Larry was able to make his quick apologies, blaming his "quite foolish" words on the painkillers he'd taken for his ankle, while the young man brought our drinks. By then, a pair of women had recognized Larry as well, and he was puffed up with all the attention. This was the Larry I had liked—effortlessly charming, full of funny anecdotes about famous or near-famous people, wearing his man of the world airs with ease.

We were only halfway through our first round when Jessica arrived.

"Louise! My goodness, what a surprise. I just left a message for you at your hotel. And this must be—why, the great Lawrence Ware. You probably don't remember me, but we met through an old friend of mine, Jill Bloom. I am Jessica Payne."

"Well, it is lovely to meet you, Miss Payne."

"Oh, Jessica, please, Mr. Ware."

"And Larry, of course."

No, he didn't seem to recognize her, at first. But when she shrugged out of her coat, revealing the dress she'd bought the day before, his eyes lit on her cleavage. Amused by the change from the prim Jessica I'd first met,

I watched her work her magic, introducing herself as a friend of my brother's, someone who had worked with him briefly in the States. Dylan had asked her, she said, to look after me in Oxford. They gossiped a bit about mutual friends, Jessica laughing, beguiling. And then she fired.

"I am sorry to bring this up, but well, with both of you here...Louise, I've got some rather troubling news from your lovely brother."

She turned to Larry, all serious now.

"I'm afraid, Larry, that you may have unwittingly upset a hornets' nest. And Louise and her siblings may well get stung."

"Why, my dear, what can you be talking about? Louise, I—"

"Louise knows nothing about this. I just found out today myself. When Dylan called me."

"Jessica, what's happened?" I played my part.

"As I understand it, Larry, you made a request recently, through Louise, that Dylan make inquiries regarding the disappearance of an item that you claimed to be, in fact, your property."

"Why, you sound like a solicitor."

"I am. That is why Mr. Terry rang me. You see, he followed up on your request and contacted his late mother's widower, who, as you know, found nothing."

"Yes, yes."

"But the inquiry aroused his suspicions. His line of thinking seems to be, what else might be missing from his late wife's estate? And whose property was this missing statue?"

"Mine! I told Louise, it was mine, mine."

"Family property, I believe you said. And yet, according to Louise, your sister knows nothing about it."

"You've spoken with Victoria?"

He turned large wounded eyes on me.

"The night she picked me up, Larry. In the car. She was so frosty, I thought she was mad at me about the statue. So I tried to explain to her that I'd tried, really tried to get it back. And she didn't seem to know what I was talking about."

"So now you've hired this woman to, to investigate me?"

Jessica was smooth.

"Please, Larry. No one has hired anyone. When the trouble arose, Louise's brother asked me to look into it. Simply as a friend. He only wants to protect his family. And he feels that Louise has been through enough, what with the loss of her mother, and should not have to bear the burden of pursuing this matter any further."

"Well, he and I are certainly in agreement there."

Mollified, Larry took a long sip, assumed an avuncular face, all benign concern.

"Now, if you can answer just a few questions, perhaps we can solve your problem and Mr. Terry's. First, I need to know when you bought the statue, and what its value is."

"I would prefer," he said, "To discuss this without the lady's daughter present."

It took me a moment to understand what he meant.

"But, but—" I began. But Jessica jumped in.

"Please understand, Larry, that whatever you tell me I will feel obligated to pass on to Mr. Terry. That is, if it will enable him to defend his mother's estate against this new potential problem."

"I see. Still, does Louise absolutely need to know as well?"

"Well, as I said, her brother would prefer that she be...unburdened by this matter. Still..."

As she trailed off, Larry sighed, then polished off the rest of his drink. I met her eyes. She tossed me a quick wink, tilted her head slightly toward the door. I decided to trust her.

"All right," I said. "I'm sick of the whole thing, anyway. I think I'll get myself some dinner."

"Why don't you, my dear?" Jessica said. "I'm just going to settle one or two points with my new friend Larry. And then," she added, touching his arm lightly with her pale-pink fingernails, "I'm going to ask him to tell me, once and for all, just what the last lines of *The Fallacy of Pleasure* really mean."

She turned to him, her eyes sparkling.

"My ex-husband and I used to sit up ever so late debating the matter. If you could resolve it for me, it might be quite a triumph."

"And do you and your current husband have such discussions?"

"He has yet to be selected."

INSTEAD OF HEADING BACK TO the hotel, I turned left, where the uneven sidewalk was crowded with bodies. I saw a pub sign for The Eagle and Child, and remembered it from the guidebook. I had to duck to enter the doorway, the little steps descending unevenly into a skinny hallway with dark, cozy rooms on either side. The hall opened up into a bigger room, with a high bar for placing food and drink orders. It was crowded with men of various ages, all tall, all loud, and I was about to back away and find someplace quiet.

"Miss Terry! I thought that was you."

I turned and looked into the eyes of my librarian, Bob Middleton.

"My wife and I are up front, by the fireplace, with some friends. Won't you join us?"

Before I knew it, I was settled on a wooden bench near a small fire, a menu in front of me. The room was small enough that Bob and his party took up half of it. There was his wife, Dorothy, another couple, Fran and George, and their son, Lewis. Dot was short like Bob, but very round, with disorderly, bleached hair that had gone orange in places, and a motherly smile. Despite the mild weather, Fran wore a nunlike ensemble of heavy wool jumper dress over a long-sleeved, high-necked blouse, as well as thick tights, well-worn boots of indistinct color and shape, a wool hat, and at least three layers of clashing sweaters. This look was becoming familiar; it seemed to be one way that English women dressed themselves. George and Lewis were both tall, and mostly silent. It was the women, along with Bob, who did most of the talking.

I'm not sure how it happened—I was intent on a burger, a glass of wine, and then to bed. But Bob and Dot were shocked that I'd been in England for so long without trying what they called real ale, not to mention fish and chips. Soon I had both in front of me, and both were delicious. Another pint, and they decided that what I needed, really needed, was "a bit of a pub crawl." So we left the Eagle and Child for the Bear, an even smaller place whose walls were covered with school ties, where we sat outside at picnic benches. Then it was on to the Turf Pub, Oxford's oldest, the sign said, which was down a little alley off of Queen

Street. I would never have found it on my own. It was my favorite of the night.

The talk ranged everywhere—politics, sports, music, Oxford gossip, the economy, and like a refrain, the varieties and qualities of various ales. Lewis finally opened up a little, about his economics studies at Exeter College, his desire to work in the Ivory Coast, his girlfriend, who was in art school in London. She'd be up the next weekend for a party—would I like to come? Fran and George knew a painter they thought I should meet—maybe one night next week? And Bob and Dot suggested all sorts of plans. They just took me in, as Jessica had, with friendly openness, an assumption of similarities, and a presumption of good will. Just so easily, I thought, a life could grow up around you. I'd been in Oxford less than a week and already it seemed I had a social life if I wanted one. Dot even mentioned a flat for rent, somewhere on Merton Street, and I began to fantasize a life there, walking everywhere, painting my paintings, living under those spires and that sky.

Walking back, alone, I thought about my mother. She'd walked these particular streets, had her own afternoons of pints in the pubs, her own forays into the library, into imagining another time. Saint Margaret—whoever she might have been, or whatever sliver of another story she might have been based on, or whatever my mother may have conceived her to be—may have walked here, too. Did they allow her to stray from the convent walls? While the monk and the musician were out on the streets and in the world, was she locked up with other women, with her visions?

On the steps of the Sheldonian Theatre, people were gathering for a concert. I cut across the crowds into the square outside the Bodleian Library. In the softness of the streetlamps it looked less intimidating, the stones shimmering a softly inviting light, the dome generous, almost maternal, in its curve. It had opened in 1602, Bob had said, and was named after its founder, Thomas Bodley, more than four centuries after Saint Margaret and Martin and Benedict would have been here. If they had been here. What would this place have been like then?

The River Cherwell, at least, would have been somewhat the same. I turned down High Street then, moving toward it, and the air around me began to thicken with waves of rising mist. It had been a warm day—"you have got lucky," Dot had told me, "with our weather"—but now the sky was cooling fast and I could feel the moisture penetrating my thin jacket. Air that damp reminds you just how much water you are made of; it becomes hard to tell where your body leaves off and the world around you takes over. I felt fluid, almost permeable.

The moon was beginning its slant across the river, and I followed it, passing the hotel. From the map, I'd expected Magdalene Bridge to be something grand, but it was a simple arc over a narrow finger of river. I stopped midway across, looking out at the long triangle of grass stroked by mist, bordered by water. All around me, people were on their way somewhere—to home, to dinner, to pick up the children, to meet a date, to buy a dress, a roast, a book. But I was alone.

Mother, I came all this way to see you. Now I am here. The moon was higher now, and smudged with the beginnings of clouds. *Now I am here.*

She would not have been accustomed to being alone. Our house had been a lively place, with things going on—Dylan and his friends banging on drums and guitars in the basement or shooting hoops outside, Katherine in the den holding meetings with the glee club or the drama club or whatever school group had adoringly voted her its president, Dad whistling his way around the house starting projects, repainting the kitchen, redoing the ceiling of the family room. I spent as much time as I could with him, avoiding her for fear of her moods, her frightening silences, her unpredictable tears. I'd refused to listen to her for so long. What had I expected, that she would appear, materialize on a bridge in Oxford to set her story straight?

Now I am here.

The clouds were gathering, I could smell the rain coming. I was suddenly sober. It was time, in every way, to go back to the hotel. But I stayed there, leaning on the low stone wall, looking across the long grass at the trees now turning their leaves over to drink the coming water. Bodies hurried past me, pulling up hoods, reaching for umbrellas. In the dark, the world was all anticipation.

Now I am here.

Then it was there—suddenly, almost dizzyingly, the smell of Shalimar and cigarettes. My mother's smell. I leaned into it, and closed my eyes. And as the first light drops of rain fell on my face, I felt my mother's hand on my forearm, patting it twice, then squeezing it, the rounded tips of her nails pressed into my skin just as they used to when I was a child, when I'd been scared or discouraged or tired and she'd needed to comfort me.

Now here you are.

I opened my eyes slowly, as if afraid I might shake her off. When I looked, there was no one there. But the weight of her hand remained.

I walked back to the hotel slowly, letting the rain come down on me in all its cool forgiveness.

BACK IN MY ROOM, I fell into dreamless sleep. At some point, the phone woke me: Dylan, sounding irritable, a little drunk. He'd reached Kenny, who, he said, knew nothing about any statue. And by the way, when was I coming home? I tried to tell him about what Jessica and I were doing, but he got furious when I got to the part that involved him. How could I throw his name around like that? What if Larry called his firm? There was a thing called professional ethics, and I had violated it. Annoyed, half asleep, I told him I'd call him tomorrow, and hung up.

But I never had time to make the call. Jessica was at my hotel first thing the next morning, with a name and an address. A little before noon, we said goodbye and I boarded a train that would take me to another train that would take me, I hoped, to the woman who had introduced my mother to witchcraft. Her name was Eve Darrow, and she lived in Glastonbury.

14

The first thing that happened in Glastonbury was
that I got sick.

It started on the train out of Oxford, cough-
ing at first, then sneezing. By the time I switched
trains in Reading, my throat was sore. By the time I got
to Castle Cary, congestion packed my sinuses, and my
eyes had puffed up, red at the rims. I was miserable.

During the long, expensive cab ride to Glastonbury,
the driver offered me cough drops and tissues, and apolo-
gized for the weather. His name was Brian. He was a little older than me, with blue eyes and red-gray hair and a
round belly. He also had a terrific bad-boy smile, despite
the lack of a few important teeth.

"By the way, miss, that hotel you mentioned?"

"Yes?"

"There's better just around the corner. A place called
Hawthorns. Better pub, better food, better everything."

"Let me guess. You know the owner."

"Close, close," he chuckled. "I know the fellow who
runs the pub."

"And it's more expensive, right?"

"That's where you'd be wrong. Sometimes better is cheaper—despite what you Americans think."

He tossed me a wink over his shoulder.

"And there's music some nights. I'll bet you like music, right?"

"Doesn't everybody?"

"My kids don't. My daughters, you know what they listen to? A band called Garbage. Now I ask you, what kind of people call themselves that? And you should see the get-ups."

"Oh, I have."

"Please don't tell me you like them, too."

"No, not me. But I know some people who think they're quite profound."

"Are they teenagers?"

"No."

"Then I'd say there's no hope for them, then."

He was right about the hotel—clean, quiet, off the main street, and with a pub whose chef made delicious-smelling curries and a bartender who mixed me a hot toddy. The bar held half a dozen regulars, who all knew Brian, of course. The music he'd used as a selling point would start up again the next night. They were friendly, the room was warm, and I wanted nothing more than to order another hot drink and relax into their chatter. But Eve's address was burning a hole in my pocket. The bar-man lent me an umbrella and I made my way, through variable rain, to 13 Benedict Street.

The diamond panes of the small front windows were curtained shut. I rang again, and was about to turn away when I heard the sound of quick footsteps, a woman's voice muttering. The door opened just a few inches. A face, or rather, a sliver of a face, peered up and out at me—half a nose, one big dark eye, a fall of dark hair.

"Yes, what is it?"

"Hello. I'm looking for someone, a friend of my mother's, who I think might live here. A lady. Eve Darrow?"

"And who are you?"

"Louise Terry. My mother's Margaret Terry. She and Mrs. Darrow—"

"The Lady no longer lives in town." She stepped back to close the door.

'You mean, Mrs. Darrow is not in Glastonbury anymore?"

"I mean that the Lady—or Mrs. Darrow, as you say— has retired from public life. She does not *see* people. If your mother truly *is* her friend, she would have told you."

"My mother's dead. That's why—"

"I am sorry. Nonetheless, I cannot help you."

"Does she live near here, then? Can you at least tell me that?"

"I cannot. No."

"Can you give her a message, maybe? Tell her Margaret Terry's daughter is in town?"

"I am not a messenger. And you are not the only one who has tried to see the Lady since she retired. My advice to you is to find another teacher. Good day, Miss Terry."

I opened my mouth to say I wasn't looking for a teacher, but she had already shut the door.

The next morning, I fortified myself with three different kinds of cold and flu medicine, and then set out into the little town.

I'd felt at home in Oxford right away; Glastonbury, though smaller, was more intimidating. Perhaps the smallness was part of it—people noticed strangers, and looked at them, unabashed, assessing.

And then, of course, there was the fact that the town was full of witches.

I had had no idea that a place like Glastonbury existed. Nearly every shop, bookstore, or café catered to those who worshipped the old gods and goddesses, attended rituals, cast spells. Stores called the Magick Box or the Green Man advertised Tarot readings and past life regressions, full moon celebrations and other Wiccan festivals. The people who staffed and frequented those shops dressed the part, adorned with significant jewelry—pentacles, spirals, blades, and moons made of silver, pewter, brass, hung on chains or strips of leather, the clothes faintly medieval, velvet and leather and lacings and soft boots. Most were much more welcoming than the woman I'd met the day before, but there was still that pervasive sense of otherness, as if they were all in on a secret I'd yet to discover.

In the Magick Box, I bought two introductory books on Wicca, as well as a silver bracelet, a round disk or full moon in the center of it, crescent moons on either side. The moons had sharp points; I'd have to be careful when I wore it.

"Interesting," I said to the woman behind the counter. "I used to draw this shape, the circle and two crescents, when I was a little girl. I had no idea what it meant. I just liked it."

"Oh, I know," she said. "I used to draw the double spiral myself. Like your earrings."

Her smile encouraged me. She had a lovely, long face, like a Renaissance Madonna. I asked her if she might happen to know a friend of my mother's, Eve Darrow.

"I've met her once or twice, but I don't really know her. She stopped teaching, I believe, three or four years ago. So your mum knows her?"

"Knew her. My mother died last year."

"Oh, I am so sorry," she said, patting my hand. "Eve's niece lives in her old house, on Benedict. She might be able to help you."

"Her niece? Short woman, dark hair?"

"That's her."

"I already tried her. She seemed annoyed that I'd even asked."

"Oh, Gwen," she laughed. "She can be like that. Shy, really. And very protective of her auntie."

I was about to ask more, but a gaggle of customers came into the shop.

"If you'll excuse me," she said. "By the way, my name's Emma."

"Thanks, Emma. I'm Louise."

"Good to meet you, Louise. Do come back. Enjoy your bracelet. And good luck finding the Lady."

The encounter with Emma cheered me up. The rain had cleared and the sky was almost sunny. I decided to explore Glastonbury Abbey grounds.

The entrance to the abbey was just off of High Street, on Magdalene. I paid my entrance fee, made my way through the indoor displays, models and drawings of the abbey in centuries past. A quick reading of the sign revealed that none of what I was seeing was what might have been there in Saint Margaret's time. Brother Martin's Glastonbury had disappeared in the fire of 1184. The reconstructions I saw were of the rebuilt abbey.

Its ruins were smaller than I had expected. Walking the grassy expanse between the crumbling walls, I had trouble imagining what it might have been like in its glory. Not much was left—the deep stone foundation and part of three walls of the main church, or what was called the Lady Chapel; one small chapel of Saint Patrick, still intact from 1512; and a round stone building, formerly the abbey's kitchen.

I sat on a low stone wall that had been part of the main church and opened one of the books I'd bought from Emma, *The Wiccan Way: An Introduction.* I read that there were various kinds of Wicca, mostly based on geography and whatever pantheon of goddesses and gods made up the local lore. But there seemed to be one central principle and two big rules. The central principle was that the divine was immanent—in everything, everywhere. The rocks, the seas, the trees were all holy, all held that sacred spark that unites us all. And then there were the two rules. First was "An ye harm none, do what ye will," simple words for a hard task. To think, every time one wanted to act, will no one be harmed? In the past year, I'd broken that one rule so many times.

And the second was even more stark. "The three fold rule: whatever you send out will come back to you, times three." Perhaps that was what was happening to me. After all the destruction I'd caused, for Jason, for Natalie, even for T.J., I was getting paid back now.

I closed the book and opened the second one, which was more specifically about various sacred sites in England, including Glastonbury. It revealed that the abbey was one of three famous spiritual sites here; the other two were the Chalice Well, and the hill, or Glastonbury Tor. From the looks of the map inside, the Tor required a strenuous hike; the Well I could easily walk to.

I read that the Chalice Well went back to the Romans; later the Druids, nature-worshipping pagan monks, had had a school nearby and used the Well for their rituals. There were stories that the Holy Grail was buried nearby. It was all such a jumble of Christian and pagan, of folklore and history, that it was hard for me to sort out what was real and what was imagined or conjectured.

But the place itself was beautiful. The well was surrounded by a small wild garden, and fed into a tiered fountain shaped of two overlapping circles. The lid of the well had the same interlocking circle design. The intersection of the circles formed a fish shape.

The *vescia piscis*, my book said. Symbol of the two worlds, and of their intersection.

I sat for a while on a bench at the top, listening to the air as it came through the good green things around me. Oh, Mom, you must have loved this place. It was like her somehow, the disorderly green against the neatly carved stones. After a while, I climbed down to the wellhead, where the water poured from the mouth of a carved lion. His nose was broad, his eyes were sightless, the water fell in a gentle stream to the steps below it. Though all the stone was a soft gray-brown, where the water fell had been dyed a deep crimson, as if the stone itself was bleeding.

I suddenly knew just what to do. Kneeling, I scooped up a little water and lifted it to my forehead. Another scoop and I tasted it—cold and not bitter, and very clean. Then I took my bracelet off and rinsed it, blessed it, in the water. I closed my eyes, as words from my mother's manuscripts came back to me.

*There are more ways of knowing than there are stars
in the sky.*

May the Lady bless and help me.

Safe in her arms. Making sanctuary. A ring of stones.

I heard a rustle and opened my eyes, just a little. A
man, no, two men, were crouched at the other side of the
wellhead. They washed their faces, ran the water over
their arms and necks. One had blond hair, the other a
mousy stubble. I could hear them talk.

"This is foolish," the blond said. "It is not a matter of
if we are caught, but when."

"We will not be caught," the other said. "Not if you
still your tongue."

"I can keep my own counsel."

"It is not what you say, but what you sing, that wor-
ries me."

"You have not forgiven me."

"Yes. No. Yes."

The stones beneath me seemed to shake, then spin.
I felt a bright light whirling above my head, inside it. I
blinked, and air around me began to vibrate, humming,
making its own kind of music. It was like before, with
Vincent, with my mother on the streets of London. One
minute they were there, the two of them, so near we
might have touched. The next I blinked again, and they
were gone.

The blond must have been Benedict, but who was the
other man? He was far too small, too young, to be Brother
Martin. Eve Darrow would know, must know, what all
this meant. I had to find her, even if it meant going back
to her niece's door.

BACK AT THE HOTEL, I took more cold medicine, a couple of spoonfuls of cough syrup. In the pub, the music had started up, a five-piece band in one corner with a drummer, two guitarist-singers, a bassist, and a fiddle player. I sat at the bar as near to them as I could get, planning to order some dinner and then find an Internet café where I could look up some facts about Eve Darrow. But before I was fully settled in, the bartender poured me a shot of Macallan.

"This is on the gentleman over there," he said, pointing to a corner booth. I looked and there, with another man, was my cabdriver, Brian. He smiled and waved me over.

"I thought maybe a nice scotch might get a smile out of you," he said. "You look so down in the mouth, my dear."

"Oh, it's just this cold. I can't seem to shake it."

"Ah, you're in luck then. Music and whiskey. The best remedies."

He patted the seat next to him and I slid in.

"This is Tom. That's his brother's band up there. Tom, this is Louise Terry."

"Hello. Are you a musician, too, Tom?"

"That depends. Do you like musicians, Miss Terry?"

Tom's eyes were beautiful, green with glints of gold in them, like the glints in his waving dark blond hair. It fell to just a little past the shoulders of his black sweater. A crystal earring dangled from one ear.

"I used to," I said. "But not anymore."

"Good thing I'm a carpenter, then," he laughed, tapping his pint against my shot glass.

The band went into a song everyone seemed to recognize. Tom banged his palm on the table. People sang along. I sipped and coughed.

"Are you taking something for that?"

"Oh, plenty. But nothing seems to help. And I can't waste my time here being sick. I've got a mission."

"A mission? That sounds exciting. Care to tell me about it?"

"Well, I came here to find somebody. A woman. She was an old friend, a teacher, of my mother's. Mom died last year, you see."

"I'm sorry to hear that."

"Thanks. Anyway, it took a long time to find this lady's name and where she lives. And when I went there today her niece was, well, not very helpful."

"That's too bad."

"She said her aunt no longer sees people. I guess she's become some kind of hermit."

"Has she, then? I wonder who—"

Just then, the song ended. Beneath the clapping, Tom turned back to us.

"What did I miss?"

"Nothing," I said, suddenly embarrassed. "I'm just boring this nice man." I gestured to Brian.

"Nice, eh? You can see I've got her fooled," he said to Tom. Then, turning back to me, "Let's back up a minute. You say you're looking for a particular lady?"

"Yes. I came to Glastonbury to find her. Eve Darrow."

Brian and Tom looked at each other.

"What? What is it? Do you know her?"

"Well, she's got a bit of fame around here, anyway," Brian began, but Tom broke in.

"Now what would a pretty lady like you want with an old witch like that?"

"I take it you mean witch in the Wiccan sense of the word," I said.

"Listen. I grew up here. I know about the old ways, and I know they were probably better. And I've dated a couple of witches. But this lady you mention? There's something funny about that one. She's got the coldest eyes I've ever seen."

"Now, now, Thomas, you don't really know the lady."

"I know her type," he said. "She hates men. Really truly loathes and detests them. She blames all of us for the fact that most of the world isn't worshipping a goddess instead of the guy on the cross. She hates us, *personally*, for that."

"Now, Thomas, have some respect," Brian said. "The girl's late mother was her friend. And besides, you don't know any of this. You're just making it up."

"All right, all right. It's my turn anyway."

He stood to get us another round, then turned back.

"All I'll say, Louise, is be careful of that Eve Darrow. Be very, very careful."

He picked up a salt shaker from the table, shook a little over his left shoulder, and set it down hard before heading off for the bar.

"In my experience," I said quietly to Brian, "men who talk like that usually don't like women much, either."

"Ah, Tom's not a bad lot. His problem with women, if you ask me, is that they like him too much. They seem to think he's handsome. Can't see it, myself."

We laughed. It really did help, talking to him.

"In any case, Louise, this lady you mentioned. I've heard the same as you. That she's a hermit, I mean. I've heard...that she lives in a little house up on Weary All Hill."

"Well, that narrows it down, at least."

"Not much. There are fifty or sixty houses up there."

"Well then, I'll just go door to door—"

"You would, wouldn't you?" he laughed.

"What else can I do?"

"Do me a favor. Give me a day or so to ask about. Cabbies meet everybody, one way or another, and there aren't that many of us. Even a hermit has to leave the house sometime, right?"

"I suppose you're right. It's just…"

"What, then?"

"Well, I'm sick and I'm tired and I'm just not sure how many days I can keep doing this. I want to go home."

I heard the childlike tone in my voice and was mortified. But Brian only laughed again.

"Of course you do. It's awful to be sick away from your own bed and pillow. Just give me a day or so. And then, if I can't find your Eve Darrow, well, you can start knocking on those doors. Just don't ask Tom there to help you."

The rest of the night is a bit blurry. I remember another round or maybe two at the pub, and the band and a couple of girlfriends joining us after their last set. I remember Brian going home for the night. I remember the rest of us making our way out into the damp, soft night, and down an alley to a basement pub where a kind of after-hours party was in full swing. I remember Tom asking the bartender for a special bottle he kept there and telling me it was his uncle's famous homemade elderflower liqueur, and that it had healing powers. I remember him urging it on me, and how sweet and bitter it was, and how he ordered me a half-pint and then another to wash it down.

And then somehow I was back at the door of my hotel and Tom was saying goodnight.

"Can I see you to your room, then?"

My eyes could barely focus.

"That would not—that would not be a good idea."

"Why?"

"Because you'd expect me to invite you in."

"No, I wouldn't. You think I'd be that cheeky? Just meeting you?"

"Why not?"

"Well, I'm not like that. You see, I'm really a very romantic fellow. And all I want from you, tonight anyway, is just a kiss."

"One kiss."

"Yes. You see, a long time ago, a wise old woman read my palm and told me that one day a beautiful American lady'd kiss me and it would change my life."

I was suddenly so dizzy that it was hard to see him.

"Really?"

"Yes. But you see, it's important for me not to be greedy. It has to be just one kiss. At the beginning, anyway."

"And you expect me to believe this?"

I wasn't really going to say yes. I was just teasing him. But my body decided for me.

"Thomas, I think...I think..."

I stepped away from him, one hand to my mouth. And then I vomited, quickly and almost neatly, onto his shoes.

THE NEXT DAY ARRIVED WITH the worst headache I'd had in years and a stomach so tender that even a glass of water made it lurch. I tried to tell myself it was a stomach flu, on top of the cold I'd caught, but I knew the truth: It was a hangover, notable only for its intensity. So intense, in fact, that it blocked, for a moment, the memory of all my struggles—my inability to find Eve Darrow, Dana's pending indictment and Reilly Gallery's demise. Then it all came back with a thud, and another round of vomiting.

I was beginning to believe the worst was over when the phone rang.

"Miss Terry? It's Brian here. How are you today?"

"Frankly, I'd have to feel better to die."

"Well, don't die yet. Because I've got some news for you, my dear. I know where you can find the lady you're looking for."

"No way."

"Yes, way. But you'll have to get moving. She'll be up by the Holy Thorn, or the remains of the Holy Thorn, at half past four this afternoon."

That was a little more than two hours away.

"Gee, I don't know. I'm in awful shape. Are you sure she'll be there?"

"Sure as can be."

"Today. Not tomorrow."

"That's what I'm told. Come now. Pull yourself together. It's a bit of a walk, not too bad, and it might help sweat the booze out of you."

"It's not just the booze. I'm frigging sick, Brian. I told you."

"Yes, and you also told me you had to meet this lady. Well, now you can."

"Thanks to you."

"That's not what I meant, girl."

"I know. But it's true. And it is what I came here for."

"There's the spirit."

"I'm very grateful to you, Brian. Thank you so much for doing this."

"Ah, it was nothing, girl. But just a piece of advice, if I may."

"Of course."

"The lady is nowhere near the monster Tom makes her out to be. But she can be, well, rather intimidating. A bit tough. No nonsense, if you know what I mean. She does not suffer fools."

"Well, then I'll try not to be one. A fool, I mean."

Propped up in bed, I spread my mother's manuscripts out, along with the article Bob Middleton xeroxed for me. In my sketchbook, I wrote two columns of what I knew, one for Margaret, one for my mother. In Margaret's, I listed the arrival at Dove Abbey, the relationship with Mother Elizabeth, the visions, Benedict, Christina, and Martin. On my mother's side, I wrote Aunt Angie across from Mother Elizabeth—for surely they were both double-edged mentors, each in her own way—then Paul's Father Thomas across from Margaret's Martin.

I took up the xeroxed article on virginity again, scanning it for Margaret's name. There was a bit of what I'd already learned—possibly apocryphal, a healer perhaps, from Oxford, bits of visions that survived. Following the footnotes, I came across this one:

> *Stories of this Margaret also often involved the trope of cross-dressing. In this, Margaret is one of a lineage of women mystics, including Julian of Norwich and Saint Natalia, said to have passed as men. This would enable them to travel unencumbered, as well as to penetrate the men's abbeys. The difficulty of this does of course suggest apocrypha again, to be read as symbol, rather than as fact.*

Cross-dressing. Of course. Perhaps that is why my mother's saint seemed to disappear midstory. Perhaps she had decided to live as a man. And if she had, it must have been here—here in Glastonbury, in the abbey where her mentor, Martin, lived—that she took up that life. If Margaret had passed as a man, it would have been right here.

That must have been her and Benedict I saw at the Chalice Well.

15

I found Eve Darrow just where Brian had said I would, sitting alone on a bench by the Holy Thorn. The tree itself was a surprise. Someone had clearly hacked away at it, its branches sliced, not pruned. There was, mercifully, a break in the rain that afternoon, though it was still chilly outside, with intermittent, nasty guts of wind. My throat ached, I could not breathe through my nose, and my stomach burned. I stood back, shifting my heavy bag, with all my mother's manuscripts and my sketchbook inside.

She was dressed in layers and shades of white—eggshell skirt and tights, bulky cream-colored cape, a yellow-white scarf wrapped over her head and around her neck. Inside it the face was small, wrinkled, intelligent. She gazed unblinking at the wounded tree, its branches stripped. There was a green wire fence around it, to which offerings had been affixed—pieces of cloth, ribbons, tiny shapes made of paper or corn-husks or clay, depicting animals and angels and people. And tiny packets, like sachets, like the ones I had in my bag.

Not sachets, then. Some kind of magic. I walked toward them, my hand out.

"Be careful," said a dry voice behind me. "Careful of what you touch. And why."

"So these are for making magic, then?"

"If you call it that."

"I'm new to the language of all this."

She rose and came toward me. Though she was barely five feet tall, there was a kind of force field around her, a clear bubble of energy that made her seem much taller. And her gray eyes were, if not cold, exactly, distant— designed to conceal rather than express the emotions of their owner.

"So. You must be the young lady who has been making inquiries about me."

"I'm Louise Terry."

"And as you so clearly know, I am Eve Darrow."

I put my hand out to shake. She didn't take it. Instead, she leaned in, and turned her head to the side so that her left ear was toward me. It was as though she was listening to my body.

"How long have you had that sinus infection?"

That was not the sort of question I had expected.

"I don't know," I said. "Two or three days, I guess."

"You must stop taking that nonsense you purchased. It only dehydrates and does no good."

"But—"

"Nor does your love of spirits and dairy products."

"But how—"

"Nor will Thomas Lawson's flower liquor, or whatever he calls it, help you."

"How do you—"

"And I do hope you haven't succumbed to his latest approach, whatever it is, so far as kissing is concerned. The last I heard, it was something about having seen the lady previously in a dream."

"Well, now it involves a fortune teller. And no, I did not succumb."

But I blushed, and Eve saw it.

Eager to change the subject, I gestured to the thorn and said, "Who would do this?"

"Who can say? We all have our guesses, our theories. An attack on the Old Religion. An attack on the man who technically owns these grounds. An attack on Christianity."

"I don't understand. I would think it could only be one or the other. Between Christianity and Wicca, I mean. And Glastonbury is a Wiccan town, right?"

"Is it, Miss Terry? I would say that it is an old town, a very old town, with many histories. Many different kinds of pilgrims have come here, looking for their various goddesses and gods. And they all seem to find what they seek."

She looked at me.

"So. What is it you are seeking, Miss Terry?"

"My mother, Margaret Terry—you must remember her—left me a box full of papers, bits and pieces of stories. About a girl and her visions, and a monk who befriended her, and a boy, a musician. I wanted to see you because I think—I think you might be able to tell me the rest."

"But you did not get my name through reading your mother's papers."

"No."

"Tell me. How is the *writer* these days?"

The chill in her voice ran down my back.

"You mean Lawrence Ware? Well, I'd say he's a mess."

"That is scarcely news."

"Is that because you and my mother put a curse on him?"

Eve looked at me sharply. For a moment those cool eyes blazed.

"No. It is because he always was and always will be a *mess*, as you put it, though he has been offered ample opportunity for change. And as for this notion of a curse— well, again I would advise you to be careful, Miss Terry. You do not know what you are saying."

"I'm only telling you what he told me. Which is that you and my mother cast some kind of curse, or, I don't know, a spell on him, and that since they broke up his life has fallen apart. He can't get his work produced, his agent dropped him, he's basically living off his sister and the kindness of his friends. Oh, and he's...well, impotent."

"He *told* you this?"

"Well, not all of it. But a woman friend of mine, a lawyer, was able to get things out of him that he wouldn't tell me. Like the part about...not being able to get it up. For, like, years. And she's the one who got your name and address, your old address, anyway, out of him."

At that, she let out a low chuckle, not at all mirthful.

"Well. We may have things to talk about, after all. Come. Walk with me."

The ridge of Weary All Hill was windy, the mud beneath our feet sucked at our boots, and the sun settling down behind us was too weak to pull the damp away. Still, as I had learned, the English love to walk, whatever the weather. We passed many clusters of folks going toward town, dog walkers, and tourists with large cameras exclaiming over the views. Eve's pace was not quick, but it was steady. How old was she? Sixty? Sixty-five?

"Mrs. Darrow, if I may ask—how did you meet my mother?"

"It was when I was still teaching. An old friend of mine invited my former husband and me to give a kind of lecture to a few interested folk at her home in Oxford. Your mother attended, with the writer. He had told her a bit about the Old Religion."

"What?"

"Oh, yes. It was he, not I, who awakened her interest. Not that he knew much about it. You must remember, Miss Terry, that witchcraft was at one time quite fashionable. No doubt he thought it lent him a certain mystique, to say he kept company with witches. But he was never serious. Your mother, however, was very serious indeed. Full of questions, intelligent questions. Afterwards, we spoke for a while, and I invited her to one of our introductory sessions here in Glastonbury."

"Introductory sessions?"

"We held them at every equinox. An introductory circle for beginners. Most of the attendees came and went. Very rarely we found someone appropriate for initiation. Your mother was one of those. Very gifted."

I thought back to my afternoon's reading.

"To be initiated—one would need to choose a particular tradition, am I right?"

"Well, choose is one word. Ideally, you would have some family tradition, however buried or suppressed, to follow."

"Which was my mother studying?"

"I taught the wisdom that women in my family have known and taught for years upon years. The tradition is now called Gardnerian Witchcraft, or Wicca, if you will, after Gerald Gardner. But that is a misnomer. The woman who taught him was my mother's mother's sister. Her name was Dorothy Clutterbuck. Some people call her Old Dorothy."

"Lawrence believes she didn't exist."

"The man is an idiot," Eve snapped. "And he hates women. Really truly loathes and detests us. And is terrified of us, of course, at the same time. No, Miss Terry. Old Dorothy did exist. She was the last of her kind. The contemporary imagination has no place for her."

"And in your tradition—what does initiation consist of?"

"There are various stages to it. Beyond that, I cannot tell you."

She stopped and turned back to look at the Tor. Though it was a misty afternoon, I could see the shape—one side steeply sloped, the other more gradual. The shadow of the tower on top of it delineated what looked like terraces ringing the Tor's sides.

"You say this is a Wiccan town, Miss Terry. A town of the Old Religion. So why is that tower allowed to stand?"

Eve's tone suggested that she held me accountable, personally, for the presence of the tower. I recalled what I had read.

"I don't know. It's from the fourteenth century, right? Two earlier ones fell down. Some people think it was the old gods and goddesses knocking it down. Or Mother Earth, maybe, shrugging it off. Some archaeologists think there used to be a circle, like at Stonehenge, up there."

"But, Miss Terry, it is called *Saint* Michael's Tower. And it was built by Christians."

"I don't know. Maybe it's as you said. All the different pilgrims bring their own desires to it. So now it—it belongs to everyone?"

"Everyone!" Eve made a snorting sound, then turned and headed up the hill again.

After a silence, she said, "Remind, me, Miss Terry, why it was you wanted to see me?"

"I want to find out how the story ends. I want to know what happened to my mother's saint. Did she sneak into Glastonbury? Did she pass as a monk? Did she—"

"You seem to think that your mother owned this story, Miss Terry. You would be wrong. This Margaret, as you call her, has served as a guide to many of us. Hers is one strand, one part, of a complex mystery going back hundreds of years. Matters people have devoted their lives to understanding."

"So other people have had visions of her, too?"

"She is one of several presences who have made themselves known from time to time. Your mother took a particular interest in her. Perhaps too much interest."

"What does that mean?"

"One can become enamored with certain phenomena. Visions, as you call them, are only one part of the witch's practice. And not necessarily the most important."

"I should tell you, Mrs. Darrow. I've been having visions, too."

Again the unpleasant chuckle.

"Of course you have. I knew as soon as I saw you. If I had a pound, Miss Terry, for everyone who comes to me with tales of their newfound visions, believing that this makes them in some way special, that they can leap right over the hard work of learning the Craft, and go straight to spells and visions and astral projections, well, I would own the whole of Weary All Hill. Your mother, at least, had the wisdom to begin serious study. It was unfortunate that it had to be broken off."

"What if I want to take up serious study, as well? What if I'm here to learn the Craft?"

The words were out of my mouth before I had thought them.

"Miss Terry, please—"

"I mean it," I said. "What if Mom left me a box full of threads that she knew would pull me here? To you?"

"That seems a rather fanciful interpretation."

I barely heard her. It was as if fireworks were going off in my mind, illuminating all the dark places in flashes and pops. I stopped walking, the better to see them.

"And that would make sense of why she left it to me, not Dylan or Katherine. My sister, she already has a spiritual path. She's been a Buddhist forever. And my brother—well, Dylan would never do this. Come here. Knock on stranger's doors. He'd have looked for anything important, which for him means anything to do with money, and then he'd put the box on a shelf and forget about it. Whereas she knew, she must have known, that I was her one child who would be imaginative enough and stubborn enough and crazy enough to see it through. 'My youngest,' she said. 'The artist.' It all makes so much sense now."

We stood there looking at each other.

"But even if that is truly what she intended," Eve said, "your mother's wish alone cannot make you suited for practicing the Craft. It is a demanding path."

"Can you teach me?"

"What, in a day or a week? Such study takes years, Miss Terry. And you have only just now decided that this is what you must do. And I no longer teach. You live on the other side of the ocean. Oh, there are all sorts of reasons that this is ridiculous."

"But everyone starts somewhere," I said. "I saw all sorts of postings in town, signs for introductory workshops, Wicca 101, that kind of thing."

"You would pick your teacher from a shop's bulletin board?"

"Or you could recommend someone."

"You are nowhere near ready to take up study with anyone I could recommend. You have spent, I would estimate, perhaps three or four hours at most actually researching the things your mother left you. You are ready to hop on a plane and fly across the ocean, but it had not occurred to you to read up about the various traditions, as you call them, until you came here. You know literally nothing of what you claim to want to study."

"That's not true," I said. "I have spent most of my waking hours with this material. It's all I work with, day and night."

"I suppose you refer to your own visions."

"In part. But I'm a painter, Mrs. Darrow. An artist. And I have been painting scenes from my mother's stories. And of her, and her life with the writer. And other things, too. Things from my own life. That's part of how I study. How I process information, you could say. I draw it. I paint it."

I reached into my bag.

"Here, look at my sketchbook. There are studies in there for some of the paintings. I have been living with these characters for months and months, Mrs. Darrow.

And I have seen them myself. I saw Margaret and Benedict both by the Chalice Well. Just yesterday."

With a grunt, Eve took the sketchbook out of my hand, flipped it open. I helped her balance it as she turned the pages. She saw the drawing of the girl with her ring of stones, and one of Benedict, and one of Mom and Lawrence. Though she was silent, I could feel her changing, softening, in front of me.

"As someone," I began, "once said, 'There are more ways of knowing—'"

"'Than there are stars in the sky.'" We finished together.

How long did we stand there, silent, Eve's eyes on mine, the wind tugging at our clothes? At last she sighed.

"Very well, Miss Terry. I will provide your introductory lesson, however unwise it may prove. Now, here is what you must do to prepare."

I SPENT THE NEXT THREE days following Eve's instructions for how to purify myself for my first lesson. I could drink no alcohol, eat no animal flesh, and no cheese, though a certain amount of yogurt was allowed. Instead of coffee, mornings started with a prescribed herbal tea concoction that smelled like peat and tasted like tree bark. Each day, I was to walk at least five miles—Eve was big on walking as a way of opening the mind—until I found a place conducive to meditating. She gave me a symbol to meditate on every day: first the triple moon, then the spiral, then the pentacle. She told me which oils to buy to put in the bath I would take each day. "Not a shower, but a hot bath, Miss Terry," she said. "You need to soak. And the steam will help those sinuses." Sex and any kind of sexual contact, including kissing, were off limits, too.

I thought the hardest stricture would be no alcohol, but though that was tough, the biggest challenge was the complicated kind of secrecy Eve asked for. I was not to tell anyone, not even Brian, who had brought us together, what I was doing. However, because a witch's word is her bond, I could not tell lies. So when Emma at the Magick Box asked if I had had any luck in finding Eve Darrow, I mumbled something about being on a new path and got out of there fast. When Brian offered to buy me a round in the pub, I had to turn him down and not say why. And when Tom Lawson turned up, with his beautiful eyes sparkling, smelling of some cinnamon-sweet cologne, and asked if he could take me out for a proper date—to make up, he said, for getting me sick that crazy night—I had to fight every impulse and turn him down.

"I'm sorry," I said. "I'd love to. I just…can't."

"I hope it's not because of what happened last time. No harm done. See?"

He pointed down at his obviously brand-new shoes. I had to laugh.

"You're very kind. But no, it's not that."

"So there's somebody else, then. Back at home, I expect."

"No there isn't. There used to be, but it ended badly."

"So you're taking a break from the lot of us, eh?"

"Something like that," I said. "I just have a few things to figure out first."

"Well, that's too bad, that is. But do me a favor, Louise—when you do get things all figured out, as you say, will you let me know?"

I agreed that I would.

Meanwhile, Jessica and Dylan were both calling and leaving messages. Jessica wanted to know if I had found

Eve Darrow. I called her back when I knew she would be at work, and left a vague message about interesting people I was meeting in Glastonbury and how much I was learning. Dylan was tougher. He was determined simply to get me home and used very piece of emotional baggage he could; Katherine was having trouble adjusting to single life, it would be good if I could get her out to D.C. for a few days of play and cheer her up. He would come, too—he and Jen were having a tough time, it would be good to get away, he needed to talk to his baby sister. Worst of all, Dad had been having chest pains. The doctor had scheduled a stress test for next week—would I be home? We might all have to go to Florida if surgery was involved. They all thought I'd be home by now. What was going on? Was I all right? And how could I afford this long stay, anyway?

The last question particularly nagged. Indeed, I could not admit it to her, but my first thought when Eve said three days was simply *how can I afford it?* I thought ruefully of the pounds I'd spent on hotels and wine and food, thinking I'd have a show in the fall and sell some work. I'd believed, as well, that Larry's friends would buy *The Seven Deadly Sins*. Meanwhile, I'd spent myself into a hole.

It was a relief to leave behind thoughts like that and concentrate on Eve's meditation assignments. Starting was always hardest, as it involved calming and clearing the mind. I would sit with my knees crossed and breathe in and out, slowly, regularly, until the current of my thoughts had stilled. Like my mother's empty altar. Like a still pond at midnight. Then I would draw a circle around me in the air with my mind, and imagine it stretching up and down, so that I was encased in a cone of light. Within this sacred space, I was safe. Then it was time to call up the day's symbol, which I would draw and redraw in my mind until I was in a kind of altered state, where images might come, or words, or insights.

I had thought it would be hard to do this in public. But that first day, when I decided to walk to the Tor, it seemed that everyone there was involved in some kind of spiritual practice. Here and there, young people in ragged or medieval-looking clothes stood or sat in circles. About halfway up the south side, a gray-haired woman was dancing. She wore loose fringed clothes that swooped and made designs in the air as she moved. Three sheep eyed her, bending to graze and then looking back at her, thoughtfully, as they chewed.

The tall, narrow chapel at the top was crowded with people. Two girls sat facing each other on the stones, eyes closed, meditating; tucked in one corner, a boy swung a pendulum, while in another, a ponytailed man moved through a sequence of tai chi poses. Around and through them, various visitors made their careful way. Everyone was respectful, quiet, and patient.

Outside, I found a spot on the terraced side, about halfway down the Tor, and sat on the grass to meditate. It felt good there, on the southwest side, and in those three days it became my spot. By the last, people would greet me, perhaps with a bow, perhaps with their hands pressed together, but without words. I had never seen such a place. Was I on holy ground?

For the decision to study Wicca had come upon me; in that sense, it was not a decision at all. And yet now it seemed to me to be inevitable. The walking became a pleasure; my body loved it, as it also loved the absence of wine and scotch and meat. I ate mostly fruit, which I had never been a fan of, but found that it gave me energy without the caffeine buzz I thought I'd miss so much. I never did come to enjoy Eve's special tea, but it or something else was definitely improving my sinuses, and it was a pleasure to throw away the pills and powders I had used to no avail.

After meditating, I would often have little flashes of insight. They came in words, as if written on some kind of chalkboard in my mind. *Do not fear yourself. Never be ashamed of where you came from. Don't close, open. Be still and know that you are suffering. You cannot save your brother's life. You cannot save your mother's life.*

I was surprised that Eve had not assigned me books to read, after her scolding about how little research I had done. When I asked about it, she said that would come later, if at all. Desire was not enough; she would discover if I was suited to this path. And she reminded me that she had offered only one lesson.

"I want you to understand," she said, "that this is a very special circumstance. Not at all how things are usually done."

"In your coven?" I asked.

"In any coven worth the name. This is not typical. I am accelerating the process."

"I am very grateful."

"You may not always feel that way."

✳

ON THE EVENING OF THE third day, I arrived at Eve's for our lesson. I came to her back door as she had requested, taking the path up Weary All Hill that we had walked together and entering her back garden through an iron gate. It was a cool night with just a little breeze that lifted my hair as I went. I tried to quell my nervousness by imagining my mother walking this same path. *Very gifted*, Eve had said. I was about to learn just what that might mean.

A stone path curved this way and that, obscured by overgrown foliage that snagged at my hair. I had gone only a few steps when I heard Eve's voice.

"Louise Terry."

"Yes?"

"Do you come before the Goddess of your own volition?"

"Yes, I have come here of my own volition."

"In perfect love and perfect trust?"

"In perfect love and perfect trust."

"Come in. Come in. Come in."

She stepped out from behind a thorny tree, took my hand, and led me into the circle for the first time.

The sun was already fading behind the ring of trees that Eve had so artfully placed to conceal her ritual space from outsiders. Inside, gray stones etched out a pentacle on the ground between patches of deep green grass. Eve handed me a sort of long poncho, purple-blue with a silver belt. She wore a similar gown, in white, with a gold belt.

"I would prefer that we work sky clad, but it is chilly tonight, and damp. Wear this."

I realized that, like her, I was to be naked beneath it.

As I slipped out of my clothes, Eve walked around the perimeter of the circle, going counterclockwise, gently waving some kind of burning stick in her right hand. As she passed me, I sniffed the air.

"Sage, for cleansing."

She made three trips around, ending where she had started, at the pentacle's top point, before a stone altar that backed up into the trees. Between its many candles, various objects appeared as she lit the wicks one by one: a long, double-edged knife with a chunky handle; a carved stick of some sort, with one wide and one sharp end; a clay and metal cup, chalice shaped, with no handles; another pentacle, this one made of stained glass.

Eve gestured me to the center of the circle, then turned to face me, the altar flaming at her back. Taking up the long knife, she called out invocations to the spirits of every direction, west, south, east, and north. I could see the circle as she conjured it, a glowing circle of yellow-white light that warmed my skin. I felt the presence of those spirits as she beckoned, her power in calling them to enter the space. Eve glowed with fierce intent, splendid in her robe, her long hair white and silver on her shoulders. I shivered inside the moment.

"Why have you come here, Louise Terry?"

"Because my mother sent me."

"What do you want?"

"To know what she knew. To see what she saw."

"Very well."

Her hands on my shoulders, Eve spun me around, none too gently. A blindfold was around my head and tied tight in a flash. Then her hands again, pushing me down onto my knees, then onto my back. A piece of folded silk was put over my eyes. I felt a kiss on my forehead, another on my feet. She was chanting something I could not quite make out. And then I could.

A maze, a map, a hill, a tree,
A place for all, and all for thee.

The Lady's face, the blaze of Light
You enter through the sky at night.
Follow the Bird as She flies up,
Trust in Her, drink from her Cup.
Your first best drink, Her well and water.
Step through the veil. You are Her Daughter.

And then I was gone, up and out of my body and into another world.

※

I OPEN MY EYES TO the sound of drumming. No, running. Feet in front of me. Feet behind. A field of slanting sun to cross before the trees will hide us. I stumble, and someone grabs me by the shoulder and rights me. A smell of burning. If we don't run fast, we're dead. I'm sure of that.

A hole opens up in the ground and we fall into it, one after another. How many of us are there? I can't tell. I am falling for a long time, so long that I can see the light below as it comes toward me, growing, growing, as I fall into it. A room under the ground, filled with light. There are others there, women and men, and they are arguing about something. They do not know that I am there. Someone says, "It must all come down. We must sweep clean." They look up and see me. The moment freezes, and spins.

And now we are running again, stumbling out of a tunnel and into a gray afternoon, gray sky about to open. The ground beneath my feet slopes sharply down and I tumble, and come to rest. There are three of us, two men and me, the same ones I was running with before. The wind carries the smell of smoke, then flakes of cinders. There is something between my legs, a small pillow, a knob of cloth. I am trying to work it free when the other two begin to argue. One of them is crying. One of them falls to his knees and prays.

❈

I OPENED MY EYES IN a room that was softly lit, lamps in the corners. Eve stood over me, watching as I drank a cup of tea.

"Well, Louise. You have had quite a night."

I looked at her.

"Did you see—what I saw?"

"Some of it, yes. Some I have seen before."

"What—I mean, who—"

"There, there. You are very tired. Ritual takes a great deal of energy. Drink that."

The tea was sweet and milky, nothing at all like what she'd given me before. She was right, I was tired down to my bones. But there was still so much I needed to understand.

"But those people—they are—was she…"

"I have decided to tell you what I can."

She moved away from me, toward a window. She wore a plain white skirt and blouse. I was back in the clothes I'd arrived in. The room, I saw now, was a kitchen, the table I sat at round and plain. There was nothing around me to suggest what had happened, where I'd been.

"I had always believed in lineage," Eve spoke slowly, looking out at the night sky. "I did not think that one could practice the Craft without some true bloodline, some root source. And I knew right away that he was all front. I made it hard for her. But she took it. She was stronger than she looked."

"You mean Lawrence. And my mother."

"Yes, yes. But Geoffrey, my husband, did not see it. He wanted both as students. I agreed. For the basest of reasons. Because I thought that, with a partner, she would be less of a problem for me."

"Problem?"

"I thought she wanted to take what was mine. My husband. My Oxford coven. Have you ever noticed, Louise, what an ugly, whingeing sort of word that is? *My. Mine.* Like a spoiled child lamenting having to share her favorite toy."

"Mrs. Darrow, wait—you mean my mother tried to—"

She turned around. She seemed to have aged since the ritual ended, all her priestess power drained away. Now she was simply a sad, frail lady.

"I think I need some of that tea, myself."

Eve told me that after the introductory session in Oxford, Larry and my mother had continued to meet with Eve and Geoffrey, at first with a small group of witches in Oxford. It was there that my mother had had her first vision of the girl mystic, Margaret. It was also there that she and Eve had cast the spell Lawrence had talked about.

"It was not a curse. Just a simple binding spell. The writer wanted to turn Margaret's story into a novel. But she was a presence many of us had known and seen. And we were worried that he might divulge secrets, coven mysteries that were not his to tell. So we cast a binding spell, tying him and your mother together in the matter. They vowed to serve and protect Margaret's story, and to tell it in a form that would do no harm."

Eve reached into a pocket, then, and pulled out a little bundle of blue silk tied with threads.

"What is in that?"

"A few herbs, a stone, some salt. Your mother had one, as well, and her writer. A spell bag. It is—what did you call it?—Witchcraft 101. A beginner's skill. Nothing that could cause such disasters as you say have befallen the man. It is his own guilt and his own fear that he feels now."

"So then what happened?"

After the spell was cast, Eve invited Larry and Mom to Glastonbury for various rituals and festivals. Members of the coven there had also had contact with Margaret, and began to use automatic writing and other means of divination, such as the journey Eve had taken me on that night, to try to complete her story. Geoffrey, buoyed by an inheritance, decided they would start a press devoted to the Old Religion. They would call it Hollow Hills. The story of Margaret would be their first book. Felicity Amble-Pierce had been a pen name Eve and Mom had come up with, to signify work that had been done by various members of the coven. But it was Mom who first believed that Margaret had cross-dressed, passed as a man to get into the abbey.

"I did not believe her, at first. I was tired. My seeing was not what it had been. I thought she was embellishing, perhaps for her writer. It would have been no easy thing. Imagine what it would take, what it would have taken, then to convince everyone around you that you are a man and not a woman."

"You might take the chance. If you were as unhappy as she—as Margaret might have been."

"Or if your motive, from the start, was to burn it to the ground."

"You mean *she* started the fire?"

"I have come to believe that she did, yes. Your mother thought she acted with one or two friends. The boy, Benedict, and someone else. I am not sure. I do not believe, quite, in that boy. He seems to me like a French importation, if you will. Like Lancelot in the Arthurian legends."

"But—but why would she burn it down?"

"To reclaim this land, this holy land, for the Old Religion."

"But didn't she start out in a convent?"

"And how near are any of us to where we started?"

Eve went on to tell me how the coven had argued over the new information my mother's visions brought. The story of a nun converting to the Old Religion, passing as a man, and setting the famous fire—some saw a meal ticket, a path to fame like other famous writing Wiccans, like Starhawk or the Farrars. Some said it was ridiculous, a fantasy.

And then one day Eve came home from an afternoon with Guinevere to find a farewell note on her kitchen table. Geoffrey had moved out.

"I assumed that he had run off with your mother. He had had his infatuations before. I had ignored them. I believed that our bond was of the Goddess. But your mother had power, too. Undisciplined, which made it all the more appealing."

"But Mom didn't go off with him, right?"

"You are right. Oh, he had tried. She admitted that, when I pressed her. But I had wronged her. She, Goddess bless her, had turned him down."

She shook her head.

"Funny. When we married, he said it was like marrying a Queen. Royalty of the Old Religion. Old Dorothy's blood. I was the Goddess, manifest on earth, for him. And in the end he ran off with a slip of a girl who chews her nails and writes abysmal songs about the Return of the Goddess. I hear they are running some sort of spiritual healing center in Exmoor. I do not know. I do not want to know."

"Then what happened? To you? To Mom?"

Mom and Larry had one last fight about something or other and she left him. She showed up on Eve's doorstep in Glastonbury, a little fragile, but all right. They stayed up late, talking about the future. Mom said they should start the press, anyway. She said she'd work with Eve on it, they could do it together. They made a plan, the two of them, for life without the men who had treated them so badly. The coven was in a shambles, but could be restarted. Mom left to take Aunt Angie to Cornwall, promising she'd be back.

While they were in Cornwall, Angie had a heart attack. Mom, devoted to her and wanting to do the right thing, called Eve to say she had to go back to the States with Angie, make sure she got safely on the plane and safely home.

"I did not believe her. I thought that aunt had used her money to lure her home. It was clear the woman did not approve of me. I was alone, distraught. I wrote an awful letter."

Eve wrote to Mom and told her not to bother to return. She, Eve, was moving on. No more Margaret, no more Felicity Amble-Pierce. A new coven had assembled, with help from her niece, Guinevere, who was proving to be very gifted herself. And she told my mother never to say her name, and never to contact her again.

I was suddenly cold all over.

"Did you—cast a spell on her?"

"On your mother? No. But I hurt her, very deeply. And I hurt myself. Things were never the same after Margaret."

"My mother? Or the girl of her visions?"

"Both. Both."

"You must have been very jealous of her."

"I was, I was. But I loved her, as well. I do not think she knew that. I wish that...were not so."

"Mrs. Darrow—"

"Oh, I think you can call me Eve, now."

"Eve. Did you ever hear from my mother again?"

"No. I thought about trying to reach her, to say I was wrong. To say, perhaps she might come back after all."

"But you didn't."

"No. I didn't. And then, a few years ago, the writer got in touch with me. With his talk of spells and what we had done to him. I said, this is nonsense. If you cannot get work, that is your affair to sort out, not mine."

"Did he ask you about a statue?"

"Yes, But he was wrong about that, as well. That statue meant nothing. It was a trinket, something your mother became attached to. I believe he gave it to her, though I am not sure. She thought—well, it was said to be from Margaret's time. The late twelfth century. But why he thinks it is related to his misfortunes, I do not know."

She pointed to the little spell bag on the table.

"If you care to, you may give him that. He should have one of his own. Your mother had one, as well, but two should do."

"I have—I have them both now."

"Well then, you can do it for him. Release the spell. Though as I said, he is wrong about what it meant. But this is easy. You untie the bundles, mix up some salt water. I can write it down for you."

"But you never told Lawrence that."

"He should have known it. If he had been a true student, and not in it for his own personal gain, he would have remembered how to conduct a simple saltwater purification. We did one tonight."

"I don't remember it."

"You will. By tomorrow, I expect you will remember everything. The question is, what will you do with what you know?"

"I—I'm not even sure what it is I know yet."

"You know you have your mother's gift. Her way of slipping between the worlds. You moved so quickly."

"So, it's not always like that."

"No. Oh, no, indeed. Tell me, Louise, have you had other experiences like this?"

I told her about the fire, and the various times my mother had come to me, and seeing the boy who I thought was Benedict outside of my apartment that night.

"But before," she said. "In the rest of your life?"

"Well, I'm not sure if this is what you mean. But it is like—well, it's like—"

"Yes?"

"Like painting. When it's going really well and I'm *in* the canvas. When there's no separation, I guess you could say, between what I'm making and what I am. If that makes sense. It feels like entering another world."

"Anything else?"

"Well, like making love. Not all the time but sometimes. But in those moments when you're all there and he's all there and it's like flying. You know you were made to do this. Painting. Fucking. And now this."

"And now, this."

Eve got up from the table.

"I do not take students anymore, Louise. My niece runs the coven now. But if, after tonight, you are still firm in your desire, then I would make myself available to you. In order to begin the process of your initiation."

"But I don't live here."

"Yes, well, of course you would have to alter that. Temporarily, at least."

"How long would this take?"

"It depends on how far you would go. There are stages. Like the Catholic sacraments. Another form they took from us."

"Let's say, for the first two stages. Maybe three."

"Perhaps six months, perhaps nine. You would not have to live right here in Glastonbury. Though of course that would be preferable."

"Well," I said, to my surprise, "That might be something I could do. I'd need space to paint, of course."

"Of course. That could be arranged."

"But—well, I—"

"Yes?"

"Well, no offense, but I kind of like Oxford a bit better. As a place to live, that is. More user-friendly that is. Easier."

Eve shook her head, but she was smiling.

"You are on pilgrimage, Louise," she said. "Why on earth would you expect it to be easy?"

EPILOGUE

The Secret Women, 2006

The Washington Post, November 5, 2006

A Gallery With a Difference: Process Art Opens
Tonight With One-Woman Show by Local Favorite

By Tricia Maleski, Staff Writer

When Tim Gould made the jump from art critic to gallery director, he faced a steep learning curve. But one
decision, at least, was a no-brainer: the artist he'd
pick for his inaugural show.

"I knew Louise Terry was the artist I wanted to lead
with," says Gould, 35, whose new Woodley Park gallery, Process Art, opens this week with a one-woman
show by the respected local painter, entitled "The
Secret Women." "Of all the artists I've written about,
she's the one whose new work I looked forward to the
most."

But if the decision was an easy one, tracking down
the artist was tough. Terry, who cofounded the feminist cooperative gallery A Woman's Place, parted
ways with the group last year. When she went to England in April as part of Atlantic Exchange, a U.K./U.S.

arts festival, the 37-year-old found inspiration there for a new series of paintings. She decided not to come home.

"I fell in love with the place," says Terry. "The quality of the light, the history that's built right into a walk down the street. I knew I had to figure out a way to paint there."

Help came when a wealthy couple decided to purchase the entire series Terry showed at Atlantic Exchange, a sequence depicting each of the seven deadly sins. Terry returned to D.C., put her furniture in storage, and went right back to England. Since then, she has lived in the towns of Oxford and Glastonbury, working on the paintings that became "The Secret Women." Gould managed to catch her on that brief trip home.

"I couldn't reach her by phone or email, and was about to give up, when I heard through a mutual friend that Louise would be back for a few days. So I kind of staked out her apartment." He adds that he thought the artist had already signed to another local art dealer, the high-end, recently defunct Reilly Gallery.

"Turns out, she needed a gallery and I needed an artist. Perfect timing, perfect fit."

Terry was less optimistic, at least about the "fit" part.

"I think of Tim as more post-modern in his sensibility than I am. For years, I was doing a lot of mixed media work that drew on more modern sources, but with this series, I was going for pure painting. The subject matter is narrative, romantic, realistic. With a bit of magic thrown in, of course."

Magic moments are what these pictures are all about. In 17 paintings, Terry tells the story of a 12th century woman mystic who, constrained by the convent, decides to pass as a man in order to be free to follow her visions. Along the way, she forsakes Christianity for the Old Religion, or Wicca, as it is more widely known today. Contemporary characters appear from time to time, including the artist herself, as well as her late mother. Some of the paintings involving those two are less successful than the rest, complicating the narrative to the point of confusion. But Gould was right: Terry is a breath-taking painter, wielding her oils with a skill seldom seen in contemporary gallery shows. And she has another gift Gould was looking for: the ability to articulate her vision in discussion with non-artists. For though Process Art is a for-profit endeavor, the gallery director also has a pedagogical agenda.

"So often, you go into a gallery and all you've got to guide you is a press release and maybe an artist's statement that most folks don't even read," Gould says. "I wanted to aim for more. I wanted to help people get inside the art they were looking at."

So behind the main gallery room at Process Art is another, smaller room called the Studio, where attendees can see the work behind the work displayed. In the case of Terry's exhibit, this means you can look at the artist's preliminary sketches for her paintings, as well as a couple of manuscripts on which the narrative of "The Secret Women" is based. There's even a bit of juvenilia—a painted box, Madonna-blue with various symbolic flowers, that the artist made as an adolescent for the mother featured in the paintings. Throughout the run, Gould has scheduled a variety of talks, demonstrations and panels, some of which will feature Terry herself. The idea of getting behind the art was one his financial backers fully supported.

"They loved the idea of breaking down the wall between process and product, and were with me all the way in finding a space big enough for both," he says. And that is all he'll reveal about his funding sources, save for the fact that there are three individuals involved, and that they've given him free rein to show what he wants.

"We live in tough times for the arts," he says. "People don't get this stuff in school like they used to. I'm trying to do my part to fill that gap."

✖

A GALLERY BEFORE AN OPENING is like a theater before the patrons file in. The art on the walls won't come to life until it is looked at, seen, digested, and this looking will change the art itself. For now, the paintings linger for the last time as their private selves, known only to the artist who made them, the gallery director who said *this one, and that one, but not that*. In the dark they seem to speak to each other, some nervous as a teenager on prom night, some proudly confident, some calm and cool. In a few minutes, they will be something else entirely.

Louise is thinking of her paintings now, caressing each one in her mind. She will miss the intimacy of having them all to herself. In her little borrowed room, she lights a stick of sage, waving it gently so the smoke will curl around her. The ritual is second nature to her now, as are her daily meditations, her following of the cycles of the moon. She thinks of her teacher, wishes that Eve Darrow had been able to make the trip to see the show.

She thinks of the others from England who are coming, and smiles to herself. She is not nervous, exactly, but strung taut and humming with anticipation.

A silver pentacle inset with onyx, rose quartz, and lapis dangles from a silver chain around her neck. She smooths down the skirt of her long, slim-fitting black dress with its swirl of color down the front, fastens the buckles on her ankle-strap high heels, shakes out her thick auburn curls, now streaked here and there, with Lynda's help, in inky black. Downstairs she can hear Lynda clattering the dinner dishes in the sink, Phil opening the back door to let Chloe, the golden retriever, inside. The little house in Cabin John is perfect for them, near Phil's musician friends and a three-block walk from the bar where Lynda now presides. Though so much in her life has changed, Lynda has not—she is still the same generous, blunt, kind friend, and Louise, who misses Natalie, relies on Lynda more and more for support and advice. In another week, the two women will stand side by side when Phil slips the ring onto Lynda's finger. Then the newlyweds will go off on a month-long honeymoon, leaving Louise to mind the house, participate in the various gallery events that Tim Gould has arranged, and attend to sweet-natured Chloe.

By the time they return, Louise hopes she will have decided something, at least, about what she will do next, and where she will do it. Options—Tim tells her she will have many options, if all goes well tonight.

As Louise and Lynda climb into Phil's four-wheel, Tim unlocks the gallery doors. He is nervous, definitely, but the little crowd that has already formed outside eases his mind. His two new gallery assistants, Caitlin and Jack, are smoothly making conversation, guiding the guests to the food and drink table, talking knowledgeably about Louise Terry's biography, history, and work. Local fine arts students, he picked them for internships based on their willingness to work long hours and wear many hats. And they both adore Louise, who was her best, most charming self to them while the show was being hung, springing for pizza and beer and showing an unfeigned interest in their own work.

At first, Tim hadn't been sure if he could trust the gentler, less volatile Louise who came back from England. She still has her opinions, yes, but she does not batter people with them. Hanging the show had been a true collaboration between the two of them, and he had lost track of the number of times she thanked him for this or that, or complimented him on his ideas for arranging the paintings. He thinks this new softness may have something to do with her newfound spiritual path, but has been reluctant to ask her about it. Whatever has happened to her, he believes *The Secret Women* paintings are Louise's best work yet. He smiles at his favorite, of a girl with a sober, intelligent face sitting in the middle of a ring of stones.

Louise had been insistent on only one point: she did not plan to be there, waiting, with Tim, when the first guests arrived. She'd be there soon, but not yet. Let them wait a little, she told him. Let some drama build.

Another wave of people come through the door, and Tim spots the *Post*'s new, young art critic, another from the *City Paper*, and a couple of popular bloggers. He shakes off his reverie, and goes into salesman mode.

Daniel Orton, formerly of Reilly Gallery, moves slowly from painting to painting, remembering a long-ago gallery visit. His former boss, Dana, is in the Betty Ford Center now, for alcohol and prescription pills; her lawyer says this will win her some sympathy from the judge when she is due in court. Daniel is beset by contrary feelings: He grieves for the Dana, the Mrs. R. he so admired; he is angry at himself for not having seen her plight, not being able to intervene; he regrets that she would never have allowed that, anyway. To Daniel's surprise, Gerry Heller has remained loyal through it all. He is here tonight, flirting gently with Caitlin, making modest replies to inquiries about his own work, and diplomatically dodging queries about his lady love.

Natalie Anderson, in town with her girlfriend Sahara for the opening and Lynda's wedding, thinks she spots Louise in the studio room. But the woman who turns to greet her is Katherine, Louise's older sister. They embrace; though they don't know each other well, they have always felt an affinity for each other. Each, in her way, knows how to act as ballast for Louise's shifting moods. The lean, ponytailed man at Katherine's side introduces himself as Thai Mali. Katherine's new and clearly besotted beau, he goes off in search of non-alcoholic drinks for the three women.

At the drinks table, he runs into Dylan Terry, getting sparkling cider for his daughter Maggie, and wine for himself and his wife. Though Dylan thinks the other man's name is beyond pretentious, he has a certain niggling respect for how his sister's new boyfriend has managed to wiggle his way under Katherine's considerable defenses. And the guy's therapy practice must be lucrative: over the summer, he took her to Paris and Venice, staying in fine hotels instead of her customary Buddhist hostels, and his house, on a hillside in Sausalito, sounds expensive. So far, Dylan has found no satisfactory nickname for him, Thai Stick being too obvious.

The room is packed now, voices muffling the soft strains of harp music on the speaker system. Tim cannot yet afford live music. A squeal from Maggie alerts them all to Louise's arrival. Flanked by Lynda and Phil, she enters the gallery to a wave of spontaneous applause and is immediately surrounded by well-wishers. Caitlin slides up to her with a glass of wine. Louise has grown fond of this young woman, seeing something of herself in Caitlin's earnest integrity, her passion for her art, her strong work ethic. Caitlin guides her toward the *Post* reporter. The party swells.

The English contingent arrives in a cluster, led by Jessica Payne and Lawrence Ware, who have the unmistakable glow of recent and very satisfactory lovemaking. Free of his curse, Lawrence is on a roll again. A festival of his plays is being produced in Edinburgh this winter; James McEvoy has signed onto a film version of *The Fallacy of Pleasure*, to start shooting next spring; and best of all, he has new work coming out, a novel about a young male painter with a complicated love life. He believes that what has released him from his curse is the sale of Louise's *Seven Deadly Sins*. Running into Jessica last night in the hotel bar was the icing on the cake. She is a woman of real substance, he thinks. And what exquisite breasts.

Behind them, Bob Middleton helps Dot out of her coat, goes off to fetch her a drink. At Louise's suggestion, they dined last night with Brian Welch and Tom Lawson. It is obvious to Bob and Dot that Tom's interest in Louise is more than artistic in nature; in bed last night, they discussed the matter. They have both come to feel a bit protective of Louise, this motherless woman who popped up so unexpectedly in their lives. They like Tom well enough, but are not sure of him yet. They are keeping a special eye on him, for Louise's sake.

Louise spots them now and hurries over, hugging each one in turn. She thinks again of Eve Darrow. Brian had tried to persuade Eve to come along, but though she has given the show her blessing, the Lady does not want to draw attention to herself. Her public life is over. She is, however, delighted with the painting Louise has done of her, with a chapel-less Glastonbury Tor behind her. A setting to rights, a settling of old scores, that she deeply appreciates. Margaret Terry's daughter has turned out to be a blessing after all.

Vincent Volpe, too, is represented only by a painting, a diptych with him on one side and Benedict, his counterpart, on the other. Disappointed in Portland, he has moved on to Vancouver, where he has found another older girlfriend and is putting together yet another band. Louise has heard all this, gently filtered through Lynda and Phil, with only a little pain. Vincent and her passion for him seem like part of another life, now. T.J. Duvall is absent as well, of course, though he sent, through Lynda, his congratulations. Relocated with his wife Elizabeth in Chicago, he manages one in an upscale chain of seafood restaurants, an employee now rather than an owner. His baby daughter is a source of continual joy for him, and the deep, fierce love he feels for her is a physical thing, surprising in its single-minded intensity. Now he knows what it means to say you would give your life for someone else. But he finds the weather in Chicago depressing. He misses the East Coast, the Rehobeth and Bethany beaches; he misses owning his own business; and he misses Louise, with whom, he has come to realize, he was in love.

Louise's father, John, is represented by the huge bouquet that stands on a corner plinth in the main room. After years of fussing over his health, it was his wife Carrie who had bypass surgery just a few weeks ago. He is taking good and tender care of her recovery, and has at last persuaded his children to come to Sarasota for Christmas. He is perhaps not entirely sorry to miss these paintings of his late first wife, his first great love. Mortality is already too much on his mind these days.

Mortality is what Sister Kathy is thinking about as well, as she stands before the painting of the abbess and the monk. It reminds her of herself and Brother Paul, who is right now planting a gentle kiss on Louise Terry's forehead. Sister Kathy had hoped to keep him at Fellowship House for another year, at least. But he has decided to go back to Brazil, having cooled perhaps too much in rural Maryland. He needs his liberation theology brothers. He needs to reclaim his real calling.

When he told Louise of his decision, she hung up the phone and wept. In long letters from England, he has become her confidant; she was surprised by how much she missed him, his gentle voice, his smile, his eyes. What was it Lynda had said? About Catholic girls getting crushes on priests? In her dreams, sometimes, Louise and Paul make love. But then, her dreams these days are full of sex, unlike her waking life. It has been nearly a year since she's had even a kiss. Not that there weren't chances. But she was surprised by the surplus of energy produced by her celibate life, which she channeled into her paintings. And it had been a relief to get out of the game for a while. It had given time for some part of her she hadn't even known was broken to mend, to heal.

The room is buzzing now. Tim Gould proudly affixes a red dot, then another, then another to the walls. He can scarcely believe it—seven sold so far, none for under three thousand dollars, and this is just the first night. Looking for Louise to give her the happy news, he finds her in the studio room, deep in conversation with one of the Englishmen. Whatever the man is saying has made her blush; she looks away, clearly embarrassed, and spots Tim with relief. When he tells her the news, she throws her arms around him, plants a big kiss on his cheek. Now it is his turn to redden. The other man, who introduces himself as Tom, is clearly sizing Tim up, assessing possible competition. A momentary tension is broken by Dylan, who has been counting the dots as well, and comes whooping up to his sister.

"Damn, baby! That's what I'm talking about. Jen and I are gonna buy one, too, we're just trying to decide which one."

"Well, you'd better decide fast," Tim says. "At this rate, we'll be sold out before midnight."

"A salesman at last!" Dylan says, and slaps Tim on the back so hard he almost drops his drink. "Any chance for a family discount?"

"Well…"

"Just kidding! Let's go talk to the wife. She's got her eye on the fiery one, but I was thinking…"

As Dylan leads him away, Tom steps closer to Louise. She smells that cinnamon-sweet cologne he uses, and sees all over again how handsome he is. Chiseled straight nose, high cheekbones, a dimple in his chin.

"I was wondering," he says, "if later on perhaps you might be interested in a bit of supper? Maybe a drink?"

"That would be lovely," Louise says, feeling shy and out of practice at this sort of thing. "I'm...very hungry."

"At the hotel they were telling me about this neighborhood over the bridge with lots of restaurants—"

"Adams Morgan."

"Yes, that's right. Sound good?"

They are interrupted again, this time by a good-looking man wearing a backpack and a short, plump lady who could be his mother. Louise looks at this man so lovingly that Tom is worried all over again, then relieved when Louise introduces them as Brother Paul and Sister Kathy. A monk, then. Good.

"If you'll excuse us, dear," the woman is saying, "we have a long drive ahead. And a big day tomorrow."

"Will I see you? Before you go, I mean?" Louise asks.

"Of course. Why don't you come out for a hike?"

They laugh as if at an old joke.

"It's a beautiful show," Paul says. "I wish I could afford one of your paintings."

"I'll give you one to take to Brazil," Louise says. "That way, you'll never be able to forget your old friends here."

"As if I could."

They look at each other in silence. It is Kathy who breaks the spell.

"Paul, the statue."

"Oh, I almost forgot," he says. He slips the backpack off, unzips it.

"I was cleaning out the storage room in the retreat house and I found this. In a box with some of Father Thomas's old things. I wondered if it might be what you were looking for last year."

He hands her a small wooden statue, maybe eight inches high, very roughly carved. You have to look close to see that it is the figure of a monk, robed and hooded, with just the barest trace of a cross hanging from his neck.

Lawrence Ware, who has come looking for Louise with Jessica on his arm, stops in his tracks, stunned.

"My god," he says. "There it is."

"My mother's statue," Louise says. "The one you were looking for."

"I thought so," Paul says. "There are initials on the bottom."

Louise turns it over.

"C.T. I wonder—'"

"Christopher Turner," Tom says. They all turn to look at him.

"The fellow who taught me carpentry. He just passed away last year. There was nothing that old Chris didn't know about wood. He made a series of these figures, all to look as if they're much older than they really are. He used to sell those in the shops in Glastonbury."

Louise turns it this way and that, stroking the wood in a way that reminds Lawrence, again, of her mother Margaret.

"That is where we bought it," he says. At the memory, tears come to his eyes.

"Then you know the secret," Tom says to him.

"Of course."

"What secret?" Louise says.

"Watch this."

Tom takes it from her, and feels along the hem of the monk's robe until he finds what he is looking for.

"No offense, now, Sister, Brother. But it's meant to show the Old Religion beneath the new."

With a clicking sound, the little statue seems to split itself in half down the front. Each side slides back.

Beneath it is another figure, as carefully carved as the other is rough. It is a woman, naked save for the long hair that waves down over her shoulders, and an intricately chiseled necklace of pentacles.

"Lovely, isn't she," says Tom. "The priestess in all her natural glory. Before the Christians decided that it was sinful to be naked. Again, no offense."

"None taken," says Paul. "My, my. Another mystery solved."

"Well, Larry, now we have got your statue back, just as we promised," Jessica says.

"No, no. I wouldn't dream of taking it back now. Louise should have it. I bought it for Margaret because the priestess reminded me of her. That hair. Her smile."

He turns to Louise.

"You do look so like your mother."

Silent, Louise stares into the carved eyes of the little statue. And for a moment, she could almost swear that the wooden priestess closes one eye in a friendly, intimate wink, as if at a secret meant to be kept between just the two of them.

Acknowledgments

THANKS ARE DUE TO THE following people and institutions:

Joanna Biggar, who read and commented on multiple drafts, while also providing wine, food, and loving friendship; my A-team of anachronism finders, Patty Hankins, Alex McRae, Monica Payne, and Sarah Pleydell; the Collage Goddesses, Sandra Bracken and Katherine Williams; the dedicated members of the ASP Consortium, particularly Andrew Gifford and Wendy Cervantes of Santa Fe Writers Project, Chris and Ginger Andrews of Chris Andrews Publications Ltd, and Linda Watanabe McFerrin and Lowry McFerrin of Left Coast Writers; Nita Congress, who raises copy editing to an art of its own and became my *sorella nelle lettere*; Randy Stanard, who so beautifully brought Louise's art to life; Steve Waxman, who makes book-dreams come true; and Grace Cavalieri, Meinrad Craighead, Lisa Shelle Davis, Doug Hale, Vaughn Howland, Bill Lawrence, Ebby Malmgren, Cynthia Matsakis, John Patterson, Richard Peabody, Rita Ricketts, Alan Sonneman, Betty and Joe Tate, Hank Thomas, and Priscilla Tolkien for the blessing of their support, friendship, and example.

For invaluable help with my research into medieval England, I am indebted to the librarians of the Bodleian Library in Oxford; the staffs, tour guides, and shopkeepers of the Chalice Well Trust and Glastonbury Abbey in Glastonbury, Somerset; and the cabdrivers of England, who provided history and geography lessons, philosophical insights, and sympathy.

And finally, a very special thanks to James J. Patterson and Verlyn Flieger. Verlyn restored my equilibrium early on after a devastating blow, and later, provided three magic words that, pinned over my desk, guided me through the last revisions. And there are no words to accurately describe what James has meant to *A Secret Woman*. From my first research trip to England to the last line of the last page, he has been my mainstay, my support system, and the best possible companion. I can only hope to be worthy of all his faith in me.